MW01286008

WEST, ALEX

Olivia R. Bellep

WEST, ALEX

Vanguard Press

VANGUARD PAPERBACK

© Copyright 2025
Olivia R. Bellep

The right of Olivia R. Bellep to be identified as author of
this work has been asserted by her in accordance with the
Copyright, Designs and Patents Act 1988.

All Rights Reserved

No reproduction, copy or transmission of this publication
may be made without written permission.
No paragraph of this publication may be reproduced,
copied or transmitted save with the written permission of the publisher, or in
accordance with the provisions
of the Copyright Act 1956 (as amended).

Any person who commits any unauthorised act in relation to this publication may
be liable to criminal prosecution and civil claims for damages.

A CIP catalogue record for this title is available from the British Library.

ISBN 978-1-83794-325-8

This is a work of fiction. Names, characters, businesses, places, events and
incidents are either the products of the author's imagination or used in a fictitious
manner. Any resemblance to actual persons, living or dead, or actual events is
purely coincidental.

Vanguard Press is an imprint of
Pegasus Elliot Mackenzie Publishers Ltd.
www.pegasuspublishers.com

First Published in 2025

Vanguard Press
Sheraton House Castle Park
Cambridge England

Printed & Bound in Great Britain

Dedication

J—For being my support, my partner, my strength.
My once in a lifetime person.

My name is Alex West. I have five brothers. We're a dysfunctional but loving family. I work for West Enterprises Incorporated, the company my father founded, which now my two eldest brothers manage as the family business. My role is unique; I'm the only one in my line of work. But what I do, it's better to be alone. This isn't a story about my life. Rather, it's a story about death, family, forgiveness and redemption. Someone I meet is going to change everything and make me question it all.

ALEXANDRA E. WEST

Employer: West Enterprises, Inc.

Role: Agent

Status: Active

Specialty: Terminations

PART I

Alexandra West

Mission Location: Philadelphia, Pennsylvania

Walking on Broad Street towards City Hall on a late spring day, some guy standing in line at a food truck whistles at me while making a snide comment about my long, fire-red hair. I roll my eyes; too bad it's just a wig. I nod briefly behind my too-large-for-my-face sunglasses, the hem of my red dress and nondescript beige coat billowing in the sewer breeze while I flash a quick smile, taking the win for its face value. My client meeting starts in thirty minutes and I always make sure that I have plenty of time to spare; you never know when life is going to throw you a curveball. Always be prepared was one of my father's famous mottos.

As I climb up the stairs to the set of doors, which lead to the administrative entrance, I take a quick inventory of my surroundings. I walk into the entryway of Philadelphia's City Hall, a small, outdated and unimpressive building in the midst of miniature skyscrapers. I approach the so-called security guards at the visitor's desk, noting two mounted cameras pointing at the building's entrance. I keep my sunglasses firmly on the bridge of my nose and brusquely address the two men in front of me. Although their job titles are security guards, they remind me of rent-a-cops with their eyes glazed over and the waistband of their pants battling with their bulging stomachs. I instantly know that I can take them both out in a matter of seconds, immediately recognizing the one guard's weak knees as he stands to greet me, and the other guard's wince as he rolls his shoulders. Satisfied with my quick and probably accurate assessment, I flash my photo identification and a fake smile at the guards who barely glance at the ID card, their attention instead is trained on my bustline. They don't inspect my identification thoroughly, so of course, they wouldn't figure out that it was a counterfeit. That I wasn't really the person my identification is claiming that I am; that Erica Balogh doesn't really exist. Ugh, amateur security, they give the rest of us professionals a bad name. But thankfully their lack of professionalism makes my life easier and I intend to fully take advantage of their inexperience and lack of qualifications. The so-called guards don't even log my entrance into their computer system, which is kismet, that'll just make my exit strategy even easier since I, or Erica Balogh, never officially stepped foot in this place.

The Philadelphian mayor is under the assumption that he's meeting with a Ms. Erica Balogh to discuss various educational grants for the city's public educational system, gifted by a generous but anonymous donor who has a vested interest in the Philadelphia school system. He is also under the assumption that Erica Balogh works for a legal consulting firm based in the Delaware County suburbs and that I'm representing a private donor on behalf of their preferred firm. My meeting is being held under the guise of needing to discuss the legalities of the donation and to ensure the donation will be kept private, so the potential donor doesn't get inundated with future requests from additional charities and non-profit organizations. Funny how life will be full of surprises for the mayor and this wretched city.

One of the security guards absentmindedly motions me over to a row of metal detectors as a cursory, precautionary measure. I remove my jewelry and shoes, placing my belongings in the provided bin and I saunter through the electronic archway. The guard openly smiles as I walk over to my bin, no doubt appreciating the view of the lower neckline of my dress previously hidden under my coat. I grab my necklace, bracelet and ring before I grab my purse. I swing my hips, purposefully distracting the guards as I walk toward the elevator bay, just for fun and for diversionary purposes as well. Men, how predictable, typical and easy. And it all will benefit my purposes in the end.

I take the elevator up to the sixteenth floor and approach the receptionist's desk located to the immediate right of the elevator bay. The receptionist, who introduces herself as Michelle Klay, offers me a selection of either coffee, tea or water as she escorts me into the mayor's outer office suite. I look around at Ms. Klay's workspace, which is swathed in various tones of yellow to ascertain who the woman is as she takes her seat behind the desk. The only personal effect I can see is a framed picture of her with one of her friends, another young woman who is of Asian descent. Korean, I think, off the top of my head, based upon her companion's bone structure. Ms. Klay is finely dressed in tailored, high-quality clothes, which is contrary to what I know to be her current salary grade, her authentic gemstone jewelry glitters in the natural sunlight, creating prisms of light on the immediate surfaces. On the Amtrak train ride down, I reviewed her compiled dossier as I was going over logistics of the operation. I briefly wonder where she is getting this additional stream of income, but I dismiss the thoughts so I can stay focused on the endgame, the mission. Michelle politely offers to take my coat, gloves and hat. As I decline, I smile at the receptionist and remove my glove to properly shake her hand. She grimaces just slightly at the sharp pain of the needle enters her skin, her eyes opening in mild shock before glancing down at our joined hands or more specifically, my ruby and emerald encrusted ring, now twisted around to allow the hidden needle to pierce the skin of her palm. Her lids slowly droop until they close, her posture beginning to sag as the toxin begins to take an immediate effect. After twisting my ring around and replacing my glove, I toss her arm over my shoulder and drag her limp form to the restroom. After I lock the overly elaborate restroom door behind me, I take a moment to readjust my temporary red hair before I head back to the receptionist area, avoiding all camera line of sights, just as I did with Ms. Klay's prone body moments ago. I know the cameras won't catch me as I have memorized the blueprints in advance and I know the exact placement of the security cameras throughout the building. There are a lot of blind spots in this old building and having a signal jammer as a backup also helps. Michelle's memory will be fuzzy, she won't remember specific details about me, courtesy of one of my signature cocktail paralytic drugs with its infamous memory-loss side effects. Trial and error for drug dosage amounts and prior years of… experience have made me an expert of biological weapons on a one-to-one, intimate level, not as a terrorist.

As I patiently sit in a chair outside of the mayor's office in his plush suite, I keep an ear out for the telling sounds of the mayor's approaching footsteps. All the while, I'm deftly replacing the contents in my ring, switching out the toxins and quickly injecting in a different liquid than the paralytic I had reserved just for Ms. Klay, this time it's something a little more, well, and fatal. I hear the elevator announce the arrival of my intended target just as I'm putting away my supplies in my purse. I put the small vial back in my bag as I slip my ring back on before covering my hand with my glove, stretching the worn material over the back of my hand. As he walks in, the Philadelphia mayor welcomes me by saying, "Hello, Ms. Balogh. Thank you for taking the time to meet with me about the city's educational grants. Did Michelle offer you anything to drink?" At the mention of her name, the mayor looks around for his assistant, his brow slightly furrowed with annoyance and concern. Schooling my features, I wonder about the nature of their relationship ever so briefly and if he's the source that's financing her expensive wardrobe.

"Oh yes, thank you," I politely respond, specifically taking a vague and detached tone as I walk into his office, redirecting his attention back on to me. "I'm fine," I turn to say to him with a saccharine smile as the mayor comes to stand behind me. "I am not anticipating this conversation stretching out too long for me to require anything further. I do have a train to catch."

"Oh? Is now a bad time? We can always reschedule if needed," he genially offers as his facial expression changes to confusion and worry of a loss of funds as he closes the door behind us in his office.

"No, that won't be necessary," I respond as I walk toward him and give him a warm smile. I remove my glove and offer my hand while saying, "We haven't formally met."

The mayor goes to shake my hand with an unsuspecting smile on his face. I grip his hand firmly as suddenly the smile drops from the mayor's face, his gaze, like Michelle's, quickly lowering to my hand. I can see the exact moment, he realizes that he's in mortal danger, the arrogant confidence wiped off his face, fear and apprehension flickering in his eyes. I see the effects of the toxin quickly taking hold of his central nervous system as I smile a cruel, sardonic smile that I know doesn't quite meet my eyes. He reaches for his chest, his now frantic eyes full of disbelief as he stares at me, slowly backing away from me, as if distance will be the key to saving his now shortened life. He reaches beyond me for the emergency alert button I know to be located on the right underside of his desk. Knowing his intention before he even decided to desperately reach for help, I firmly push him into his black leather chair and wheel him over to the window—far away from his salvation.

I center myself in front of him, making sure he focuses his last moments on me and my message. "Ms. Akers says goodbye," I state emotionlessly, the previous smile wiped from my face, focusing my attention back to finishing the job. His eyes widen with recognition briefly before glazing over, the poison's purpose almost complete.

I twist my ring around with the toxic jewels positioned right on top of my finger before I move the chair and the body of the now former Philadelphian mayor back in front of his desk. I finish staging the scene, with the appropriate paperwork and furniture suggesting he was alone at the time of his cardiac arrest. I have a friend in the Philadelphia coroner's office who, I know, will make sure the pinprick from my ring gets conveniently overlooked during autopsy. I log onto his computer with my gloves on, sheathing my fingerprints, already knowing the man's passwords from previous reconnaissance. I browse around his calendar, emails and back-up copies located on various servers and drives. I also log in remotely to Michelle's computer to delete all records of my, or Erica Balogh's visit. I have some previous hacking experience and I thoroughly enjoy getting my proverbial hands dirty now and again in the world of hacking. Once I confirm I am the ghost I thrive on being, I wipe all logs and walk away with a satisfied smile. I shoot off a text to one of my hacker friends to review my work as a second set of eyes on my wipe job. Tech and hacking have never been one of my strongest skill sets, even though I dabble in them from time to time. I'd be stupid and suicidal not to admit that and not to ask for additional assistance to cover my tracks. I'm great a leveraging people whose talents complement my own areas of opportunities.

I walk to the elevator bay with a contented smile upon my face. I am now ten million dollars richer, not that I need the funds in my bank account, but the thrill and adrenaline of the risks of my job are still thrumming through my veins. I know the medical examiner won't find anything when they run a toxicology report, even if the puncture wound is officially documented. My toxins are legendarily anonymous and untraceable, the envy of many others in my line of business. For the mayor of Philadelphia, I specifically designed this particular toxin to mimic a natural cause of death, given his family and personal health history of heart issues and diabetes. I fully anticipate this little town to be up in arms about their beloved mayor's untimely death. But my job is done. The contract money had already been transferred into my account by the time my feet hit the pavement outside of City Hall. I exit the building, bypassing the now empty security desk and walk outside, heading toward my hotel.

Once inside my room, I gather my pre-packed bag and leave my key on the room's desk, making sure there is no trace of me including DNA, hair, fingerprints and any other biological or identifying markers that could be forensically found after my departure. My room is booked for another week and my hacker friends will ensure there's a digital trail of me playing tourist to avoid any potential suspicion that may arise in response to my abrupt departure. As I walk to 30th Street Station to purchase my ticket with cash and board the train, I pull out one of my many burner phones from my bag, turning it back on. After I find a seat and settle in for the approximate two-hour train ride back home, I turn my attention to my phone, the numerous amounts of notifications alert me of the breaking news headline. "City of Philadelphia Mayor Found Dead, Foul Play or Natural Causes?" immediately catches my eye. I peruse the article and smile as the train departs from Philadelphia, thinking about how fast word has spread with the advantage of social media and the age of immediate communications. What a silly little city and now its governmental head has been proverbially chopped off. Too bad the people of this city won't ever know just how corrupt their precious mayor truly was or how he cut corners to further pad his own pockets. Oh well, I'm sure a summarized albeit watered down report will come out later. I relax, lean back and adjust my sunglasses to cover my face, the contract fulfilled and the job done. I artfully arrange my fake red hair to cover my face as naturally as possible so I can take a light nap as I am pulled to the city that never sleeps. The city I lovingly call home: New York City, New York.

New York, New York

Waking up with a surprised jolt, I realize that I'm almost back home. I calculate the train is about five minutes from Penn Station based on the landmarks and signage that passes me by. I stretch my arms and gather my few belongings, pleasantly surprised that I slept as long and as soundly as I did. I take the time to quickly self-reflect. People I meet for work often call me inhumane, cruel or a bitch. I always shrug it off. I'm there to kill them; of course they're going to lash out, it's only natural. I never take their words personally. I can understand and sympathize with the majority of my targets on a superficial level. My brothers have mixed opinions about my occupation, but they all heartily believe that I don't have a great grasp on my emotions or at least, their ideas of whatever the correct emotions are. There have been many discussions around the dining room table about what constitutes a "correct" emotion. I've always wondered what their versions of correct emotions are defined as. Giddiness? Naivety? I have emotions. I have pride, which is an emotion as well as one of the biblical seven deadly sins.

But nevertheless, I can't disagree with them, even if I would be remiss to admit that to them out loud. One of my brothers actually bought me a book on Emotional Intelligence for the holidays. I never read it, I think I either donated it or left it as a snide joke at one of my target's offices. What I do doesn't come naturally to the average human being. So, I had to change at a very young age, altering my perspective, my approach to life and how I was going to navigate through this world. I would ascertain that my current state of emotions is a direct result of the changes I had to make and the course of profession I chose to take.

Another one of my brothers, Luke, often jokes that I have the ability to turn off my emotions and that my proverbial emotional switch has been turned off for so long, even I don't know where the on button is any more. He thinks his comment is funny but I'm usually annoyed, which is yet again another emotion, but I don't fight with him. I'm constantly being told to get in touch with my inner positive feelings, which of course I don't have, so I disregard their suggestions and focus on what I can control. I am phenomenal at my job and am content with how my life is; I'm satisfied, fulfilled and fiscally comfortable. I know my craft, inside and out, backwards and forwards. I have more money than my family's company could make in ten years. And those in my similar line of work know that I have set the highest standards which all of us assets, or assassins as we're labeled by the media, adhere to worldwide. My industry knows how talented I am, with unrivaled success and varied interests, which gives me a competitive, professional edge. My lifestyle is all I have known for a long time and it works for me. I am the best at what I do. The best of the best in my line of work and am respected on an international level. So why would I ever realize the need to change? Why would I even entertain the thought? That's what my brothers don't, or won't, understand.

Upon the train arriving at Penn Station, I quickly exit, knowing that the station's security cameras will be vigilantly sifting through all the footage of the passengers arriving to New York from Philadelphia, along with all forms of transportation in and out of the city from within a certain timeframe. I breeze into the nearest restroom, closing the stall door and quickly changing my clothing from loud, red tones to more neutral tones of grays and black. My naturally long and straight jet-black hair flows freely down my back and I replace my sunglasses for a baseball hat and an oversized scarf. My hoodie further adds to my intended college student look along with my gray Converses and exaggeratedly slumped shoulders. I've become a master of blending in, of disappearing in crowds, choosing colors and styles that will make me invisible to observers. I pack my Philadelphia outfit and accessories in my stored book bag, leave the stall and check the reflection in the mirror. All traces of Erica Balogh gone, dead, just like all of my other aliases. I hate loose ends, constantly going through identities as often as a person changes their clothes.

Satisfied with my natural look, I exit the restroom and make my way toward the terminal entrance while strategically dodging the camera line of sights. I hop on a regional train from Penn Station, heading to Long Island. After I arrive at my final destination, I hail a cab and tell the driver the address for West Enterprises Incorporated, avoiding the profiles, names or pictures required for the popular rideshare apps. The ride to my destination should take about twenty minutes, so I check my messages and emails. I see that I received a secured email file with a contract number in the subject line while I was traveling back from Philadelphia. I go to click open the email just as the car pulls up to my destination. I sigh and lock my phone, deciding to review the contract once I get settled in the house. I gather my personal items and pay the cab driver in cash, tipping generously before I swiftly grab my bag and walk up the driveway.

West Enterprises Incorporated is housed in my former childhood home along the Atlantic shoreline of Long Beach, New York. An imposing, 6,000-square-foot manor looms into view, with an open, brick-paved driveway, which leads to the garage bay off to the left. The two-story home's front of house is painted a classic white with black accent shutters, with port hole windows sparingly placed throughout the stairwells. The landscaping is timeless, the trees brimming with late-May blossoms, the warm summer air beginning to pervade the flower's scent into the sunshine-filled air. Crepe myrtle bushes tastefully line the first-floor window bays with bursts of red and pink while white lilies and light pink geraniums provide underbrush coverage. I've always found the front of house to be in direct juxtaposition to the back of the house. West Enterprises, or my family's home, backs up to the Atlantic shoreline. The back of house foliage is characterized with sea grape and sand dune grasses that propagate along the dune ridges before opening to the blue sapphire expanse of the ocean. Wooden board pathways, reminiscent of New Jersey's iconic boardwalk, lead around the house to go directly to the backyard and beaches while a stone paved path leads directly to the home's front and side entrances. The two remaining Japanese maple trees I used to climb during my childhood frame out the driveway's gated entrance before leading to a ten-foot bricked perimeter wall. An assortment of dogwoods, silver maples and magnolia trees provide coverage and privacy so outsiders can't peer over the walls.

Being one of six children and the only girl, my parents were concerned with providing us with a large house where my brothers and I could each have our own space to form into the individuals we are today. As we all have opposite and sometimes extreme personalities, we have plenty of room to relax with the entire family. After my mom passed away and each of us kids got older, my dad decided to convert our home into the headquarters of West Enterprises, Inc., his newly formed company. Gone were the family's movie, vinyl record and music collections stored in the media center. Away went our heavily laden bookshelves which also displayed our knickknacks and treasures from family trips and vacations. Our dad converted the first-floor common rooms to look clinically professional where meetings, formal events and functions could be held as well as adding a safe room in the basement to ensure all precautions were being considered. Our father went to great measures to protect his family and his company's assets, which my brothers and I eventually became over time through our employment and careers with the family business. But the price for our success was sanitizing our home of any personality, the memories of our family's happier times were wiped clean. My dad basically did a hard drive reset to our lives, boxing all those smiles and fond memories and storing them in the basement or attic, destined to collect cobwebs and fade from memory.

The entire house is equipped with a state-of-the-art security system, including motion sensors with cameras constantly recording the action of the entrances, hallways and common areas. There are fingerprint and biometric locks as well as manual and electronic locks for an added level of security. The cameras are programmed to instantly identify all visitors, family members and West employees, and compare facial recognition scans to known threats versus previously approved individuals. My brothers and I all stood our ground to keep the second floor, where our respective bedrooms are located, private and camera-free. Thankfully our father relented. So, the second floor is the area that's most private for the family with the least invasive technological security. It's the only place where we as the West family can truly be in a state of full repose, something that as we've all gotten older, has become more fleeting, although it is very much needed.

After entering my personal series of security codes and facing the cameras for the biometric scan, the driveway's massive iron gates swing open. I easily clear the driveway, heading toward the breezeway that connects the garage to the main house. I enter the secondary level codes and enter through the side door, which automatically snaps open with a slight click. I yell out a hello in search of anyone in the house, dropping my bag on the mudroom bench and pocketing my phone as I shrug off my baseball hat and hoodie. I hear a series of grunts, mumbled hellos and a "We're in here" coming from the back of the house. I casually walk deeper into the house, heading toward the kitchen and back deck in search of my family. I read a text from my contact saying that all camera stills of me have been successfully wiped in Philadelphia, as well as any traces of my presence in the offices of the city's mayor. I shoot a quick text off to my coroner friend, reminding her of the favor she owes me regarding the pinprick from my poison ring. She immediately texts back and confirms I have nothing to worry about, that she'll send the coroner's report as soon as it's available for confirmation purposes. My coroner contact adds that the police questioned a Michelle Klay in connection with the mayor's movements this morning. Ms. Klay's statement had no mention of a red-haired woman and I feel a small jump of glee at the success of my neurological toxin.

Satisfied, I flick over to the encrypted file before I'm about to cross the threshold into the open-plan kitchen area. Deciding that the file can wait a little longer, I lock my phone and repocket it into my jeans. It's in the kitchen where I finally end up finding all five of my brothers, each doing their own thing, all for the benefit of our namesake employer. Will, the oldest and self-appointed arrogant patriarch who primarily manages West Enterprises, Inc. from behind the scenes, is engrossed on his laptop. Considering we have never got along, I am not surprised he hasn't looked up to acknowledge me. I also know he won't unless pressured by one of my other brothers to do so.

William West or Will stands at 6'4" with a muscular build and confident gait. As the oldest of the group, he likes to pretend that his thirty-five years of life is enough experience to hold over all our heads as leverage and superior knowledge and wisdom. His light brown hair and hazel eyes offset his often shrewd and distrusting facial expressions. He is well-known in hacking circles and is the technology genius of the family. Out of all the West siblings, he's the most argumentative, always seeming to need to competitively prove that he is right, to whom though we collectively never know. He and I don't get along, we never really have. I can't even say that there was or is mutual respect between us anymore. He's my big brother, so of course I have always looked up to him. But in true big brother fashion, he has always seemed to see me as the annoying little sister, the extra tag along who annoyed him when we were kids. This has created a tension that has continued and intensified into our adult lives. Now as professionals, Will opposes what I do for a living as it diametrically competes with his own chosen profession of saving people, although we all function within the same company. He also thinks that what I do as an assassin opens our father's company up to be vulnerable against unnecessary risks. West Enterprises primarily accepts contracts to protect people; to act as security consultants and protection agents. I do the exact opposite; I eliminate people based upon specific contracts. But it's part of the security business, just not Will's personal values or definition of what's ideal. Consequently, we often get in a lot of heated arguments, meaning the rest of my brothers usually need to step in to break us apart and try to mediate peace.

Kevin, the second oldest and the executive face of West Enterprises, looks up from his smartphone and smiles at me. His eyes are green like Will's, but Kev's hair is dark brown. He often stands by Will's side in arguments, even if he doesn't always agree because he, out of all of us, understands Will on a deeper level the best. Kevin West, who goes by Kev much to Will's chagrin, is the much-needed foil to Will's short-tempered and somewhat explosive nature. He stands a little over six feet tall and is extremely intelligent. Kev is calculated and constantly analyzes his surroundings for threats and opportunities, an expert in situational awareness. He's the mixed martial arts fighter of the family; strong, lethal, precise and quick. Many people underestimate him due to his calmer personality, but I've seen him throw down with guys bigger than Will and win without question. He can be absolutely ruthless in the ring, or for any adversary that tries to attack the West family or its company assets. Kev and Will are the closest within our family, other than Dave and me. But that doesn't mean Kev is condescending, rude or dismissive to the rest of us like Will tends to be. Kev is in tune with what we are all doing and considers his family's safety to be one of his top priorities, if not his foremost precedence. Kev, along with Sean, place a high value in the concept of emotional intelligence and active listening, people skills as he's fond of calling them. Kev's phone loudly notifies the room of an incoming message and back he goes down the rabbit-hole of company e-communications and e-commerce.

Sean West is the quietest of the six West children. In the loud and boisterous West family, he will be the one sitting in the background, watching the scene unfold, calculating and chronicling every moment. With brown hair and a smaller, leaner frame, Sean is 5'10", the smallest of the males in the West family. His uniquely gray eyes, however, see all the interactions in the household, which sometimes can be unnerving, since he seems to notice everything while being a silent, unobtrusive fixture. He has wisdom beyond his years and when he speaks, which isn't often, everyone tends to listen. He is the youngest of the family, only a year younger than Dave and me. Dave and I are the closest with him because we're so close in age, but Sean has always held himself back a little, by his own choice. Sean is the one who sees things others don't normally notice, which comes in handy when you're making plans and need a detail-oriented perspective and someone who can anticipate threats based upon previous scrutiny. On a family level, his keen eye for observation and matured wisdom can be frustrating and infuriating, especially given how accurate his assessments always are. Sean also is the most protective of keeping the family relationships harmonious and I know it takes a toll on him whenever any of us fight, especially in the arguments between Will and me. Sean comes over to greet me, giving me a smile and lightly brushing a kiss on my cheek, knowing to limit his physical connection with me due to the fact that I don't enjoy being touched. He assesses my outfit, notices my tired eyes and takes in my slightly hunched shoulders. As per usual, he notices the fine details but says nothing to which I'm generally grateful for. I reflexively look away to avert my eyes so I don't show anything else Sean hasn't already intuitively picked up on. Sean uses his well-honed skills to understand my nonverbal communication, my need for distance and desire for space. He nods with compassionate understanding and heads back over to the windows, standing in the beam of the afternoon sun.

While Sean probably is the wisest of us all, Luke is the comedian that is a direct juxtaposition to our intense, alpha aggressive family. Lucas or Luke West is the charmer of the group. He likes to brag that he's the handsomest brother in the West family. He's a bit shorter than Will, standing at 6'2", but his almost black dark hair and golden-brown eyes often capture a lot of attention wherever he goes. His personality is that of a golden retriever, fun-loving, playful and optimistic. But don't let that easy-going and carefree exterior fool you. If you really piss him off or threaten those he loves, he instantly becomes mercurial, dark and intense. His larger build is all muscle and you'd be a fool to think he would be an easy adversary to take on. But overall, Luke is a thirty-one-year-old jokester, always pulling pranks around the house or watching some comedian on whatever streaming platform has caught his fancy. He then takes those jokes he hears and tries to retell them, usually resulting in his cracking up before he can finish the joke, leaving us all without the punchline and rolling our eyes with mild frustration. He's loyal to a fault and his heart is always in the right place with everything he does.

When he sees me, Luke grabs me and pulls me up in a bear hug, ignoring my protestations as he easily lifts me off the ground. I kick my feet, connecting my toes with his shin in what I can only describe as a sisterly way. Luke good naturedly laughs and responds, "All right, all right. I'm putting you down now. Geez, Sissy, relax!"

I grit my teeth at Luke's nickname, but truth be told, he's one of only a few that can get away with calling me "Sissy" without me horrifically maiming them. To me, having a nickname means that you have to let people into your inner circle and that they're close enough to get to know you. For you to feel comfortable enough to drop formalities and make an unspoken agreement to be called something other than your legal name. I don't let that many people in, let alone do people rarely get close enough to broach a nickname conversation with me. Be it as that Luke is my brother and is the one with whom I was close to while growing up, he has the nickname honor bestowed upon him. But other than my twin, no one else in my family has a nickname for me that they've successfully called me. I internally sigh as Luke takes his time bringing me back down to earth. Once my feet are planted, I look up at Luke who gives me a wry smile, which I reluctantly return as I shake my head with mock admonishment. As soon as my feet touch the ground, I lightly punch Luke's arm to try to reproach him for picking me up. His smile only grows bigger as I feel the presence of someone coming to stand directly behind me.

Instinctively smiling, I turn around to face my twin. David West, who goes by Dave, is my twenty-nine-year-old twin. He likes to brag that he's the older twin, even though his definition of older is one minute and forty-two seconds. He's my best friend and only confidant. When he was deployed with the military, I felt as if I had lost a piece of myself, since it was the first time we were separated by continents for more than a week. For months, I sat around the house and just moped. I refused to take any contracts. I lost weight and became a hermit. Finally, Kev, Luke, Sean and Will staged an intervention with Dave who joined us via video chat while he was deployed in the Middle East. From what I heard afterward, a couple of them had to cash in favors in order to locate Dave and get a secured video chat line connected. Dave and I had a tough talk, a heart-to-heart conversation, where I recognized that Dave and I were on our way to a different style of work, protection versus elimination. This would be our future and it would be prudent to face the fact that this will be Dave and my new normal. It was then that I had to redefine myself as an individual, not a part of the pair and safety net that I had known all my life.

Growing up, Dave and I were always inseparable. When we were kids in school, we'd always be off, doing our own thing together; even the teachers couldn't distract us away from each other. To not have my twin at my side was such a foreign concept, I ended up in a bout of depression with separation anxiety on the side, which thankfully changed once my family intervened. When he got home, Dave confessed to me that he had the same experience and we made a pact we'd do everything in our power to see each other on a regular basis, whether that's in-person or virtually. Now as adults, not much of our dynamic has changed. Although we're in opposite professions, we still are very close. We communicate every day and see each other every weekend, at the bare minimum. He is the only one of my five brothers who has permanent space allocated in my apartment and has stayed over more times than I can count. Sometimes, it feels as if we are smothering each other with our closeness, but I wouldn't have it any other way. He's my partner in crime and sticks by my side, regardless of the situation. My twin has always had my back and he's the first person who I call when I need advice or help.

Coming back to the present, I meet Dave's eyes as I walk deeper into the kitchen toward him. He looks me over and communicates his concern with his eyes at my tired appearance and casual clothes. Normally when I come to West Enterprises, I'm either in combat attire or professionally dressed for meetings. My twin's raised eyebrow signals to me that he's telepathically asking if I had anything recently to eat. I nod my head and gesture my head to the protein bars I have stored in my go bag that's sitting just inside the breezeway's door. Our brothers commonly refer to Dave and my ability to communicate non-verbally at an almost psychic level as "Twin Power" and much to their disdain, we use it often to our advantage. He cocks his head to the side, I slightly raise my right eyebrow in silent response. I let him know without words that I am fine. My twin smiles and walks over to Luke who just asked him a question about some new weapon that just showed up on the market. I take in my five brothers as they all go about their day and although there always seems to be some sort of conflict, this all still feels like my closest definition of home.

After telling you all about my brothers, I guess I should take the time to tell you a little more about myself. I go by many names. I wear many costumes, hats or wigs. I have many faces, can change my personality at the drop of a dime and I have a closet full of disguises to mask my true form. Professionally, I'm known as Alex West, strictly for the male name misdirect, allowing me to gain an advantage for those who don't know anything about me which is shockingly more often than not. I like to use the bias and assumptions people make about to me to my own advantage. But my brothers and close friends have a wide range of names for me. My brothers tend to call me Lex, so as to concisely shorten my name. Dave is the only one who calls me Lexi. Sissy is reserved for Luke. Internally in the company, I'm known as either Alexis or sometimes A-West, an old nickname back when the West family all worked together with minimal conflict. I occasionally use some of these names in my aliases and usually outwardly cringe at the sound of them, but inwardly I know they are usually said with good intentions. Although my full name is Alexandra Elyse West, all my legal documents are in the name of Elyse West to protect my identity as well as my family's integrity and West Enterprises.

In regards to my physical features, I'm the smallest in stature of all the West children. My long, natural jet-black hair and chocolate brown eyes are mirrored in Dave's features, but where Dave is a little under six feet, I stand at 5'4", which makes things interesting when I'm going toe-to-toe with Will in a common heated discussion or argument. My smaller size allows me to have the agility my significantly larger brothers don't necessarily possess, especially in any hand-to-hand combat situations. I'm an expert marksman and have always been a bit of a tomboy, even when I was younger. As a woman in an alpha-male dominated industry, I have had to fight and earn my way to the top, shattering glass ceilings and conquering sticky floors. I personally see these types of obstacles as challenges to accept head-on. Even if my brothers don't agree with my professional choices, they still are proud of my accomplishments and as an indirect result, me. My pride and self-confidence are some of my largest strengths. However, I have always hated being the center of attention and I prefer minimal physical contact and interactions, even with my family members. Unfortunately, my brothers know this about me and will still purposefully continue to show their affection in what they say is a healthy and normal manner, then again, there are also times when they use that knowledge against me as well. But for the most part, they don't weaponize my preferences against me. This means that there are usually hugs that I mentally have to prepare for when I see Luke, the most offending brother. Will would never be caught dead hugging me. Kev thankfully respects my boundaries. And Sean and Dave will hug me, and then immediately give me space, but not before they give me a parting, knowing grin. And I usually get at least one lecture a month about the right emotions. But again, I ask my brothers to define what is a healthy emotion. What is a normal emotion? Healthy and normal aren't terms usually found in our chosen professions, only disagreements and fights, and those words are also highly subjective and interpreted based upon the perspective. But conflicts and misunderstandings are a given normal in all family dynamics, right? At least, that's how the West family has always functioned. This is how our father raised us. It's all we, as the West family children, have ever known.

I walk deeper into the kitchen, dropping onto one of the kitchen stools quite unceremoniously. "How did it go?" Kev asks, knowingly referring to my day's previous activities without giving too much away.

"Fine. It's done," I respond monosyllabically while opening my email app on my burner phone. I start the process of uploading information from my burner to my main cell phone, something that I know will take only a couple of minutes.

Turning my attention to the group while I wait, I ask the group, "What's up? What's with the impromptu family meeting?"

"Sissy, you should really—" Luke begins to suggest something as I whip around and face him, my senses already on immediate alert, defenses instantly engaging.

"What. Is. Going. On?" I firmly ask my brothers, looking them each in the eye, waiting for one of them to break.

While they all look guilty, Dave is finally the one who has the courage to step forward and take my hands in his own grasp. "Lexi, Sissy," he begins. Dave is the only other person who can call me Sissy and get away without incurring permanent bodily harm. He also is the only one who is allowed to call me Lexi. But I also know if he calls me Sissy, there is a serious issue that needs to be discussed.

"Lexi, a contract has been issued. But there's a small problem," Dave says before hesitating.

"Who is the target?" I automatically ask, the problem-solving gears in my mind already beginning to turn as I effortlessly slip into my professional persona.

Finally, Will acknowledges my presence by looking up and curtly answering, "We'll get to that once we have reviewed the files."

Okay, so there's nothing to do but wait for either more data or for my brothers to stop being annoyingly ambiguous. Therefore, I know exactly what I'm going to do. I start to walk toward the false door that leads to the safe room hidden in the basement that houses a fully insulated gun range when Sean quietly asks, "Lex, where are you going?"

I turn around to face my brothers. Five men, who are ruthless, intelligent and observant are all apprehensively watching me. Their unease and uncertainty clearly displayed in their eyes and held in their stances. I know something is going on, and I know whatever it is, that it will be something I'm not going to like. I won't be able to focus on any of my missed messages or emails, not until I get this pent-up energy out of my system. From my perspective at the top of the basement stairs, I see that the five boys I grew up with have all turned into men, stifling their sister with overprotective kid gloves, failing to, or not willing, to admit that she herself has also grown up alongside them and has come into her own.

"To the range," I answer automatically and tonelessly. Dave starts to follow me, but I shake my head. Dave takes a step back, a flash of pain crossing his face before he quickly schools his expression into a more neutral, unaffected and detached appearance. I just need to empty a clip and get whatever emotions that are trying to surface out of my system before I make the mistake of showing any of those pesky and reckless human emotions to my brothers who are insistent upon seeing my weaknesses.

Once I'm downstairs and in the range's armory, I select my favorite 9mm handgun, a Ruger SR9c from the gun racks, and grab some ammunition before I head to range. I rapidly fire off a couple magazines into the paper target hung farther down my stall. Finally feeling more relaxed, I review my targets and am satisfied that all my shots are in the kill zone. All from one hundred and seventy-five yards with my concentration not fully on target practice. Not bad, considering that it was just a cursory exercise, even when I'm not putting a lot of effort, or my heart, into it. I'm the weapon that I was trained to be, even when I'm absentmindedly disassociating. Dad would be so proud. The corners of my mouth slightly twitch upward with a flash of pleasure and pride. I trash the targets before I refill and replace the magazines and store the gun back in the secured gun cage.

Taking a deep, calming and centering breath, I take the stairs back up to the house's main living area to the sound of the regional news playing over the house-wide sound system. I hear the reports of the Philadelphia mayor's passing due to natural causes which his previous health conditions had contributed to, as ruled by the city's medical examiner. I smile discreetly, but Sean still catches my eye. He knows. Which means all of my brothers know. Great. This is going to be an epic discussion and messy confrontation.

"Alexandra," Will sharply bellows, "weren't you in Philadelphia earlier today?"

Rolling my eyes and sarcastically answering, "Why, yes, Brother William, I was! How could you have possibly ever guessed?"

Getting in my face and trying to intimidate me by using his height and weight class to his advantage, Will sardonically responds, "Gee, by the dead body in City Hall. That's what you do, isn't it? Leave dead bodies in your wake? This is not what West Enterprises does!"

Sighing, I robotically recite my repeated mantra without vocal inflections, emotions or varied facial expressions, "Yes, West Enterprises does these sort of things. Just because you do not personally carry out these contracts, or even morally agree with them, does not mean that the company ignores these types of opportunities. It's an incredibly lucrative business and it has served the company well financially over the years, especially during times of economic recessions. Our stakeholders and investors would also agree with my assessment, judging by their hefty bank accounts and comfortably lined pockets. You and the rest of our darling brothers save people, rescue them. All admirable actions that deserve public accolades, rewards and medals, which you all receive ad nauseam. You need the proverbial foil to all that goodness and light all five of you do. I'm that foil, the darkness so your light can properly shine that much brighter. I get the job done and move on while padding each of our own respective pockets so that we can live comfortably and accept contracts we actually believe in. This is NOT a new concept, Will, neither is this conversation. So just drop it, for the good of everyone and our sanity."

During my speech, I subtly tracked how Kev, Luke, Dave and Sean had all stood up and edged closer to where Will and I are standing, facing off against each other as usual. They are all aware that Will and I often butt heads, sometimes resulting in minor scrapes and bruises. Ever the protectors, they stand at the ready to interrupt and head off a potentially heated and volatile argument. Dave and Luke stand near me while Kev moves toward Will as Sean positions himself off to the side, between both parties, the typical standing alliances in our family. Will continues to stare me down, vitriol flashing in his eyes while I return his gaze, already bored and mentally disengaged, knowing my facial expressions are showing my disinterest. Will abruptly turns on his heel and storms off, heading out of the kitchen, muttering unintelligible words under his breath. Kev takes one look at me, making sure that I'm fine before following after Will's retreating form. I see both Dave and Luke physically relax as evident by their shoulders dropping while Sean silently observes me to an unnerving, uncomfortable level.

"Sean, knock it off, you're giving me the creeps," I say a little too curtly. Sean, completely unaffected with a slight smile on his face and a quick wink, turns away and sits on the couch, not the least bit offended by my annoyed outburst.

I stalk through the double French doors that lead to the deck as I hear Dave telling Luke not to follow, that he's got this conversation. It always bothers me that my brothers act like I am some breakable, fragile doll who can't handle her own life. Considering that I'm one of the top assassins in the world, if not the best, and that I have never failed a contract, I have no clue as to why they are under the impression that I am weak or delicate. Must be a brother thing. I'm hoping that sentiment will eventually fade over time.

I hear Dave close the double doors behind me and sense him as he comes to stand next to me. I'm looking out across the water at the soon-to-be, blossoming full moon, a faint whisper barely visible as the sun has started its descent to the horizon. In my mind's eye, I picture the way the light will make the dark ocean look like a vibrant, living organism. It's one of my favorite images, the moonlight shining on the sea's surface to give the illusion that the water is covered in glittering diamonds, a phenomenon that occurs once the moon reaches its apex in the black as ink sky which will be in just a few hours. Any time I can be on the water, or at least close to it, it always seems to have a calming effect on me, allowing me to become centered, assuaging my raging nerves after an argument with any of my brothers or after a particularly long day. I faintly hear the waves crashing upon the shoreline below and I deeply inhale the salty air that is the staple of so many cities that line the Eastern seaboard.

Once Dave senses that my nerves have calmed, he softly says, "Wow. That was pretty intense. Philadelphia assassinations, you and Will arguing and ending the night in a screaming match—just like old times."

"I haven't changed, Dave," I exasperatedly say, blowing off his futile attempt at levity. "I'm still the same person I've always been. I've been doing the same thing that I've always done, since I've been in my teens. This isn't new. All five of you do the opposite of me. You all protect people from assassins and threats, you all save your targets from people like me. The people I target are the people you defend. I'm the balance to it all, and I'm damn good at my job. Dad didn't want me to change my angle or adjust my focus, so I haven't, even after all these years. Nothing's changed, but with every argument, it seems like that's what all of you are trying to push me toward. You, of all people, should not be surprised."

"Oh, I'm not Lexi," Dave begins, attempting to mitigate my tirade before I blow a gasket, "but Dad's been gone for a while now. Maybe he wouldn't want this life for you anymore."

"Dave—" I start, thinking of how I need to defend my position.

Dave hastily continues, "I know, I know. I'm not starting that conversation, that's too much to unpack after such a long day. But I know Will's still investigating the events which led to Dad's death. I'm just not so sure there's anything left to go over. I know some of the guys have been starting to move on. Maybe we should try it too."

After a moment of silence, I ask, "You know if I ever find out who did it, they will be living on borrowed time, right?"

"Yeah, I figured," Dave responds sheepishly. "I actually think the rest of our brothers wouldn't be opposed to that happening, even if they would never admit it out loud. They might even offer to help you."

"Even the upstanding, perfect, moral, above reproach William West?" I question in mock astonishment tinged with slight condescension. "He's so against what I do and who I am as a human being, for that matter. Why would he want me to avenge Dad's death?" I ask, turning to Dave, truly interested in his opinionated response.

"Because he's family, and so was Dad. It's what the West family does. And maybe Will has a darker side that he doesn't want to come to light, a dark side that rivals even yours," my twin suggests with wisdom well beyond our years.

Dave is right; this would be the only time Will would give me his blessing to take a life rather than save one. And maybe Dave's theory of Will's dark side does have some merit. I've seen flashes of it pass through his eyes sometimes, especially in the heat of an argument. As cliché as it sounds, it does take one to know one. What an interesting dichotomy: Will constantly insisting that I be ethical, yet murdering my father's killer would directly clash with that upright and stringent moral compass.

I look at Dave, who returns my look with an understanding smile. Regardless of Dave's opinions on what I choose to do for a living, I know he will always support me and have my back, just as I have and will continue to do the same for him. That's what we do. I nod and turn toward the door, understanding Dave needs a minute to himself.

***

After crossing inside the house's threshold, I head directly to the fridge, grabbing a beer and popping the cap off, taking a long pull of the crisp German lager. I plop down next to Sean on the couch and join him as he watches a London Derby between our team, Arsenal Football Club, and the despised Tottenham Hot Spurs. I barely tune in to the match as I think about my next contract, remembering that I received an offer I haven't reviewed or accepted yet. I dig out my phone from my pocket and open the secured email I earlier closed upon my arrival at West Enterprises to review the contract specifications.

Name: Cole Harris

Age: 30 Years Old

Height: 6'2"

Weight: 192 lbs.

Physical Characteristics: Blue Eyes, Brown Hair, Average Build

I read his profile and short biography. Seems like a non-descript, boring individual; this is going to be an easy assignment. The file says he's a low-level employee at a tech firm, an introvert who leads a quiet life. I briefly wonder why he's being targeted but as quickly as that thought arises, it dissipates as I start thinking about my attack strategy. He lives in Manhattan, near the Financial District. Interestingly, he must have a job in that area; FiDi tends to close down at happy hour. I continue scrolling, oh yes, my suspicions are confirmed. He works as a technical associate for a *Fortune 500* company. Easily replaceable and quickly forgotten. Perfect candidate for my special set of skills. He frequents the local watering holes on Friday nights for happy hour with some of his co-workers. But based on his dossier, he isn't dating anyone nor does he have a roommate who would immediately notice a prolonged absence.

Continuing my perusal of the contract specs, Mr. Cole Harris' parents live in the ritzy part of an upscale West Coast community. I note his father's company and file that away for another day. Cole doesn't seem to have established a large friend network in his three years of living here in the Big Apple. This contract couldn't get any better: non-descript, unnoticeable and isolated.

That is, until I hear Kev ask, "Hey, Dave, do you have the Harris file for the new contract?"

Well shit, this is bad. Now I understand why everyone was freaking out when I first arrived. Judging by all of my brothers' suddenly frozen body language, I see each of them change from reposed postures to defensive stances the minute they realize Kev's blundered announcement and that I have been sitting with Sean reading about Cole Harris this entire time. I have a knowing, prickling sensation running down my spine.

"You wouldn't be talking about Cole Harris, would you, by any chance?" I casually ask, schooling my tone and features, already knowing the answer.

"Yeah, how did you know that?" Luke nervously asks, pretending to play dumb, the vein in his throat bulging ever so slightly, one of his tells that shows me his elevated stress level.

"Because she has the same damn contract," Will angrily minces out, all the while closely watching me for my response. I know Dave sensed my emotions as he quickly comes back into the house, pausing between the couch in the living area and the kitchen where Luke, Kev and Will have been working on their laptops. Four pairs of eyes swivel to me, looking for confirmation of Will's assessment. At my lack of verbal response, all eyes open a bit wider and look toward each other, uncertainty settling over our entire family.

We're all speechless really, in a slight state of shock. In all of our years working as West agents and our company's history, we have never had competing contracts for the same target at the same time. Which is surprising really, given how many contracts we each have had and that there are six of us, we're working with a higher statistical probability here. It was bound to happen though, really it was only a matter of time, it just seems like no one decided to prepare for this momentous occasion when it eventually came but me. Here comes even more fuel to the turbulent inferno that is the West family dynamics.

My brothers are smart enough though to not add their own personal pleas in trying to convince me not to take the Harris contract. They know that they'll only lose, just as I know not to tell them to stand down. No one will win, it's the ultimate of standoffs within my family. I meet the eyes of all five brothers, seeing the stubborn determination in their eyes, knowing the same resolve is reflected in my own eyes. I know that this is my cue to leave West Enterprises' headquarters and head to my place on the island. I nod goodnight to all five brothers without saying a word. I casually grab my bag off the mudroom bench, after intentionally taking a languid pace through the house as I head to the breezeway, which connects the kitchen to the garage where one of my personal vehicles is stashed.

"Wait," Dave says while jogging after me, "I still love you. You know that, right? I know you're going to do what you have to do. I'm here and we'll figure this out. Family first."

"Always," I reply with more certainty than I feel. I give Dave a swift hug, hoping it won't be forever until I see my twin again as I gracefully but quietly take my leave. I open the garage, dump my bag in the backseat and climb into one of the SUVs I normally keep at the house. I rev the engine in a moment of impishness before I head toward the city. As I'm pulling out of the driveway, I say out loud, just to myself as I look over my shoulder at the elegantly lit house that once was my childhood home, now the headquarters to the family business, "May the best West win."

***

I cross over into Manhattan after the elongated rush hour has just concluded and the cars have thankfully thinned out. I head south toward the Financial District. While it's only Thursday, I want to proactively start scouting the locations where I can organically meet Cole Harris by "accident," to make it seem even more practical and realistic, to set the proverbial stage. Even though my brothers will be trying to save his life, I still have to do my job, this isn't personal, even though this situation hits closer to home than any other previous contract that's come before. I park my vehicle near the New York Stock Exchange and walk toward Chase Plaza that's located right off Pine Street. Surveillance photos have shown Mr. Harris frequenting a local pub right off the plaza, The Bailey, on nights before the weekend. So I pull out my headphones and sync them with my phone, pretending that I am listening to music while taking in the setting sun on the Plaza. I position myself with a direct view of The Bailey's entrance while I sit on one of the benches off the main Plaza, waiting for my target's potential exit and noting the normal traffic patterns of those coming and going.

Shortly after my arrival, when dusk is closely upon the concrete and steel jungle of Manhattan, I catch my first, live glimpse of him. Cole Harris exits The Bailey with a couple of his friends in tow. He claps his companions on the back as his group exits the bar and walks past the Plaza heading north. I know his apartment is close by, so I keep an eye on him while remaining seated as he walks right past me, not even glancing at or noticing me. I thought his file said that he was anti-social, a loner and an introvert. I wonder about that discrepancy, but I set that aside to stay focused on my reconnaissance job. After Mr. Harris is out of my view, I walk into The Bailey and plaster a large smile on my face, feigning that I am a stereotypical drunk post-college student who took happy hour too seriously. I walk up to the hostess stand and ask her if Cole is still in the building, faking that I forgot to give him my number. The hostess, tightly smiling with little patience, informs me that Mr. Cole Harris had just left. I act upset and she is quick to assure me that he will be back tomorrow after five p.m. Apparently, there is a retirement party scheduled for one of his colleagues and he'll be back to celebrate during the going-away party. Yahtzee. I thank her while a throw in a giggle for show and pretend to stumble out onto the street. The minute I pass all of the restaurant's windows, I straighten my posture, slip my Alex West mask back on and internally smile with my good fortune. I walk back to my vehicle, a plan already formulating in my mind for tomorrow. I decide to head back uptown to my place, having enough of today and knowing there's nothing else I can do until tomorrow. Feeling like I accomplished a lot today, I head home to my apartment building located in the Upper East Side to decompress and relax.

Once I get to my street, I turn into my building's underground garage, enter my resident security code and park in one of my designated parking spots. I walk toward the resident's underground elevator and am greeted by one of the company's doormen. He briefly nods at me, immediately recognizing me and keys my floor number in on the elevator console on my behalf. I briefly nod my head in gratitude and enter the elevator, enjoying the wordless exchange. My favorite interactions are those where I do not have to verbally communicate with others, and where I can keep moving forward in the direction that I need to go without a pause or a stop. When I reach my floor, I step out of the elevator and I'm let out in the ornate lobby. I haven't had the chance to redecorate since the previous tenants. Grateful to be home, I sigh at the productive day I have had while reminiscing about the other elevator bay I was in almost one hundred miles away, earlier this morning. I turn my key into the door in the lobby of my apartment and enter my series of codes on the security panel, resulting in the door opening with a whoosh as I step into my private, inner sanctum.

My apartment spans the entire length and width of the building on the top floors, otherwise known as the penthouse suite. As the door behind me closes, I faintly smell lavender as I move throughout the modern open floor plan. I drop my bag by the stairs to the right and head toward the kitchen off to the left of the entryway. I pop open a bottle of white wine and grab a wineglass as I cross from the kitchen, through the open dining area into the recessed sitting area near the expansive windows. I switch on the sound system as Debussy's Clair de Lune softly plays throughout the apartment, the calm but moving musical piece matching my mercurial mood. The surround sound system was my single and only guilty pleasure that I splurged on when I was designing the floorplan, ensuring that I could listen to my music in every room and all levels of my personal retreat. I delegated the majority of the interior design to a professional, giving general color schemes and generic patterns but allowing them to design my inner sanctum. It was a necessary concession, as I would not allow any designer to use photographs of the 4,000-square-foot prime real estate for their portfolios or websites. My lawyers had drafted multiple non-disclosure agreements to ensure my safety and security, let alone my sanity of having the privacy I require to decompress from my job.

With my wine glass in one hand and the wine bottle in the other, I walk over to the attention-grabbing floor-to-ceiling windows. I look over the Manhattan skyline, watching as the moonlight plays upon my city, my home. I look down at the sidewalks, already enshrouded in shadows and darkness. The streetlights and store signs are already lit up, trying to appeal and attract the teaming masses that populate and visit New York City every year to turn them into a sale. I turn my attention back to the darkened sky. At my vantage point from the building's height, the moon's beams are gracing the building tops, dancing over roofs and infiltrating through the skyscraper's utmost floors, illuminating the empty rooms by liquid silver beams as they further highlight the beauty of my city. I have always loved to study how the light and shadows play on the city, the dichotomy a direct intersection of balance and allure. I briefly hope that there's enough light in my life to offset my dark history.

Since the sun has set and the skyline is wrapped in the dark blues and purples of the night, I decide to use that metaphor to relax and slow down my mind. I pick up my most recent reading, a book by one of my favorite authors, V. E. Schwab, as I sink lower into my gray leather sectional. I quickly pull out a remote and press the button to activate the fireplace as I face the darkened sky through the windows of my private, safe haven. I turn my attention to my book and sip my wine, getting lost in the world within the words and paragraphs crafted by an artist. Between the wine and the fire, I warm up quickly and start to nod off, the travel and events of the day finally triumphing over my tired body and tranquil mind.

***

I wake up to hear the morning's rush hour traffic consuming the streets, the sounds lifting upward to reach the top of the New York City skyscrapers. I open my eyes to my fireplace still roaring, which I immediately reach to switch off, feeling the heat immediately cool from my face once the flames die down. My empty wineglass and a half empty bottle of white wine still sit on the glass coffee table from last night. I slowly get to my feet and make my way over to the kitchen with empty glass and bottle in hand, yawning and stretching my muscles as I go. After corking the wine and placing it in the wine fridge, I open the main fridge and find some orange juice which I pour into my former wine glass. I stretch and roll my shoulders as I walk back toward the sunlight windows. Although my windows are floor to ceiling, they have been tinted for privacy, shade and ultraviolet light protection, along with being as bulletproof as technologically possible. I enjoy watching the signs of life below from my invisible and impenetrable tower.

As my brain wakes up, the gears start turning as I begin to resume mapping out my game plan for the day. Mr. Cole Harris finishes work at five o'clock and from his office, it will take about fifteen minutes for him to walk over and arrive at The Bailey for the retirement party. My plan is to get to the restaurant in the late afternoon, sometime right before five and stake out a table near where the retirement party will be set up and held.

Satisfied with my plan, with orange juice still in hand, I climb the stairs to the second floor, passing three bedrooms and three guest bathrooms. I had one bedroom converted into a home office with a futon in the corner. The second room, previously the guest bedroom, had been claimed by Dave and hence, been redecorated to his preferences. While the majority of the décor in my condo is white walls and gray or black furniture with accents of gold and red, Dave thought it would be amusing to spice up his designated area, as a way to stick it to me, I guess. He decorated his room with dark blue hues and light browns. At first, I thought it was too much, but it was a small splash of color in an overarching neutral environment. Furthermore, whenever I get sick of it, I simply just shut the door. He is my brother after all, my only twin, and it's his personal space where I gave him full carte blanche on how he wanted to utilize his room. The last room is my mini armory, always kept under various locks and controls known only to me. Even Dave isn't aware of the vast contents in that room.

I walk to the end of the second floor hallway and enter the spacious master suite. My eyes scan pass over the furthest door that leads to the master bathroom as I stroll further into the master bedroom. A custom four-poster California king bed is centered in the room with a delicate sheer white canopy that provides texture and just a small touch of femininity. A gray oak dresser and nightstand compliment the lighter tones of the room, grounding the space in the accented darker tones. The spacious sitting area that overlooks lower Manhattan has corresponding built-in gray oak bookcases that are filled with mostly thriller and murder mystery books, Agatha Christie being one of my all-time favorite authors. I bypass my bed and enter a walk-in closet that would be the envy of any woman. My shoe collection of heels in various heights, flats, boots, sneakers and wedges outlines the perimeter shelving. The closet contains all different styles of clothing for New York's four seasons are displayed in their respective categories around the room, ranging from professional to casual clothing. My vanity contains my makeup and sunglasses for all occasions and looks, as well as custom drawers containing my extensive, multi-colored wig collection. Lastly, my jewelry chest is mounted in the wall, which contains items ranging from expensive gems to inexpensive costume jewelry, ensuring that I am prepared for all events, easily able to blend in, assume a different identity and effectively shed that identity whenever appropriate and when the contract is complete. The big-ticket and expensive items are hidden in a deeper wall safe, obstructed from obvious view and inconspicuous with its surroundings.

Thinking of the upcoming retirement party that I'm going to crash, I carefully choose my clothes, just in case the hostess from last night is there and could remember me by sight. The biggest part of my job is to blend in, to be non-descript, it's one of the best ways to survive in my business. So, I choose a blue dress, beige cardigan and nude low heels. I pull my hair into a loose bun to add to my inconspicuous, office clerk character. I keep my large sunglasses on top of the dresser, and I select a beige pair that will complement the colors of my outfit. My subtle jewelry and makeup will mimic a fellow, young co-worker who left the same office as Mr. Harris, but whom he has yet to meet. Checking the clock, it's already past nine thirty a.m., and I haven't even properly gotten ready for the day. Deciding to maximize the day, I choose to go for a quick run through upper Manhattan before I begin to get ready with my prepared and planned disguise that will be ready for later tonight.

After showering when I get back from my run, I meander around my bedroom, leisurely taking my time while getting ready. My phone reminds me of a text which had come in from my twin while I was in the shower. Dave is telling me the entire family should meet again tonight, given the delicacy of our conflicting contracts. I toss my phone away, already irrationally annoyed at the peacekeeping attempts. I know Will or Kev encouraged Dave to send me that text, the former two wouldn't dare ask or imply for me to back down from a contract, they don't have the guts. Needless to say, I decide that I'll text Dave a response later tonight after I get back from the job, that way the conflict will be resolved one way or the other. I carefully apply my makeup and slowly put on each article of clothing that will make me into a forgettable employee in a city of over eight million souls. Lastly, I pin my black hair back and secure my light brown hair wig in place, making sure I cover my wig cap and hair pins skillfully, my quick and efficient movements a testament to having been wearing wigs for years now. I walk to the subway's entrance near my building, exiting through the side door from the underground garage to further blend into the crowd. I scan my metro card and board the one train which is heading to the Financial District. I arrive at the Wall Street station and hustle with the masses onto the streets in the fading sunlight to Chase Plaza.

I make my way to the restaurant while dodging cameras and checking to make sure that I haven't been tailed or followed. I arrive fifteen minutes earlier than I planned to, right before the retirement party is scheduled to start at five p.m. at The Bailey. I also know that I'll have extra time from when the party is scheduled to start and when people will start to arrive, since the party's attendees are coming over directly from the office. I smile in satisfaction of being early, but that smile quickly turns into a deep frown upon seeing five familiar, looming figures right outside The Bailey's front door. My brothers, forming a barrier to the door, look like a small army willing to take on a crowd, but instead I know that they're here just for me. Even with all their training with being inconspicuous and covert, they stick out like a neon blinking sign to people like us, instantly drawing in my attention. I have to fight my instinctual urge to hug the shadows as I roll my eyes at their obvious play. I can only hope that they didn't attract the attention of those nine-to-fivers who are making their way to either happy hours or to their apartments.

But I know why my brothers here. What I don't know is how they knew the exact time I'd be here. I speculate how much they know about my final plan, wondering if Will hacked into my phones and tracked my location. I approach them with a fake smile plastered to my face, feigning glee while

I know they were planning on being here at the exact same time as me. Will and Kev change their stances, going from an at-attention posture to a more aggressive position the moment they spot me. Dave takes a step forward to peacefully intervene. Luke and Sean seem to be disconcerted by my sunny, albeit fake, demeanor, as it is out of my usual character and they both take a tentative, small step backward.

I'm used to keeping my targets off their toes, not my own brothers. But right now, it's about survival and getting the job done, and they're in the way of my end target. Familial ties can be mended at a later date, if needed, after the contract is done. "Hello, brothers," I greet them cheerfully.

Dave, coming closer so that only I can hear him, whispers, "Hey, I texted you."

Meeting my twin's eyes, I state, "I'm aware. I was prepping for this."

"Nice wig, Sissy" Luke interjects. I feign a slight curtsy with a smirk on my face.

Will finally bursts out in a low, menacing growl, "You can't do this, Alexandra."

I was wondering when his opposition and anger toward me would finally word vomit its way out of his mouth. Silently cringing at my full name, I shoot Will a scathing look as I spit out, "Why, William? It's a free country! I am entitled to meet my contract obligations just as you are. This is the country of opportunity! Just because this is the first contract which would pit us against each other, why is this any different from our usual business?"

Kev calmly approaches me like I'm a lioness about to attack. Putting a hand on my shoulder, my second eldest brother says softly, "No one is saying this is easy. And we're not here to argue with you. We merely want to compromise so we're not hurting each other and damaging this family beyond irreparable means."

"Kevin," I start, "we have two very different mindsets and agendas when accepting contracts. We're in opposite businesses. There isn't a

45

compromise here. It's either life or death, there isn't a purgatory, meeting in the middle option here."

"What if we found out more about Cole Harris and why he's being targeted," Sean diplomatically begins, "maybe the reasons why you have a contract are wrong. Conversely, maybe our contract is wrong. But we should at least figure out what the truth is before deciding which contract we should move forward with. Have you ever considered that you've killed an innocent person before?"

"No," I flatly state, "I haven't. Because there is no such thing as an innocent person. Have you ever considered you saved an immoral waste of space?"

I know my temper is flaring and my eyes are beginning to flash like a New Year's Eve fireworks display, but I do NOT feel like having this conversation at the intersection of Pine and William Streets where people who are passing by may easily overhear us. "Let's go inside and civilly discuss this," I discreetly and calmly suggest in a low voice.

My brothers all seem to suddenly realize that we are in a very public location and there are a lot of people around us, too many people to be comfortable with while having a conversation about potentially killing someone. The guys immediately nod in agreement, as they reluctantly follow me into The Bailey. We all file in, silent and pensive, each of us lost in our own thoughts. I briefly converse with the hostess and we are seated at a table by the front door on the second floor, an ideal location that I specifically requested for reconnaissance purposes. The decorations for Mr. Harris' retiring associate have been set up near the back of the second floor, within clear eyesight of my five brothers and me.

"Lex," Luke calls out to me, grabbing my attention, "let's just talk to him and see why there are two competing contracts that just happened to be issued at the same time."

"And say to him what exactly? 'Hey, I'm here to kill you and my brothers are here to protect you, but we want to know why before we decide which side is going to win.' Not exactly a brilliant method of gaining his trust and getting any useful information out of him," I sardonically answer, the sarcasm dripping from my voice.

Kev suppresses a chuckle while Will rolls his eyes. Sean leans in with a grin and Luke doesn't hide the twinkle of amusement in his eyes. Dave smirks as I look over to him and give him a knowing glance. I know, however light the conversation is right now, neither side will budge from its position. And neither side will easily come to a compromise either.

Realizing that we're at an impasse, I offer a suggestion. "Why don't I get to know our Mr. Harris, lure him away from everyone and we get him back to the house? Maybe even slip some barbiturates in the mix just for some spicy fun. That way we can keep him in a confined area, safe from other contracts like my own until we figure out what we're going to do. It's not a compromise so much as putting a pause on all of our actions," I strategically state.

I look around at all my brothers, meeting their eyes and reading their expressions. Luke and Dave are nodding in agreement, Kev and Sean are busy contemplating my proposal until they realize it's the closest thing to the best of both worlds. I can see the exact moment when Sean and Kev realize that this is the best and only true way to move forward for everyone, the gears in their heads clicking into place.

Lastly, I zero my gaze onto Will's. He's staring me down, just like he always does. He is searching me for any signs of deceit which is always a compliment, especially coming from a family member. I see the moment my eldest brother realizes that I'm serious and Will internally battles with what I have suggested. We both know that if he and I don't agree, we inadvertently will cause a scene which will undoubtedly draw undue attention to us.

Eventually I sense my oldest brother's agreement before he ever so slightly nods his head, much to his chagrin, and says, "No barbiturates though. Well, only if we have to."

I smile at the small win, glad that he didn't outright ban the hidden stash of barbiturates I have in my bag. As the only woman in our little group, I have an in and advantage for this situation, and all my brothers, albeit some begrudgingly, know it. I'm the only one who could be the one to get close enough to gain Cole Harris' attention and trust to set him up for our containment trap. I'll be bait with my brothers acting as back-up or protection, however, you want to label it. This is by no means a concession; I'm not saying that I need their assistance. The protection perspective is really so my brothers can protect Cole from me. The five of them will provide additional support after Cole is under my spell and they'll handle the transfer under West Enterprises' protection, including transportation and questioning. While I continue to keep an eye on Will, I overhear my other four brothers discussing how they will strategically position themselves throughout the restaurant to provide additional eyes and ears while maintaining their inconspicuous covers and appearances. However, I know they are also sticking around to make sure that I keep up my end of the bargain. They're hoping to prevent me from eviscerating Cole Harris in some back alley like the monster they think I am. What they haven't recognized yet is that what I do takes artistry and skill. If I was a butcher, people would notice. I like my anonymity too much to be a savage; it's just not my style.

Will shoves his hand toward me in an unprecedented attempt of diplomacy and civility. I shove my much smaller hand into Will's larger one and firmly hold on. I hide my surprise as he holds onto my hand, realizing this is our first handshake ever, and our first point of compromise. This has to be symbolic in some sort of way and when this is all over, maybe I'll reflect upon that. My brothers seem to also sense the gravitas of the moment, although I can't put my finger on why it is so paramount in this specific moment in time. Will and I finally break our handshake. We all nod and go to our respective areas throughout the restaurant and wait for our target to arrive.

***

Finally, it's five o'clock and The Bailey is starting to get a consistent stream of patrons finishing up after a long day at work and ready to start to drink the weekend away. I am nonchalantly standing at the bar with Dave. We are casually chatting all the while keenly watching the door and windows for Mr. Cole Harris' imminent arrival. I spot Mr. Harris approaching the front door, coming down Williams Street and I signal to Luke and Kev who are standing closest to the door at one of the high-top tables, slowly sipping on beers, of Mr. Harris' impending arrival. Dave walks over to the other side of the bar where Sean and Will are staked out as I take my place in the area designated for the retirement party. I immediately slump my posture, drop my eyes and smile an open smile.

I'm greeted by a lot of employees as I read their facial expressions as they quickly try to place me in their minds. Easing their discomfort and wanting not to show my amusement, I delve into my pseudonym and cheerfully announce, "Hi! I'm Alexis! I'm new in the finance department. I just started this week! They told me they had great drinks here and that there was a retirement party slash happy hour where I'd be welcome to join!"

Instantly, my fellow employees' faces relax and we strike up a casual conversation. It always amazes me at how easy civilians are fooled, how trusting they are, even with the opaquest bits of information, just because I said that I received an invitation from someone in the finance department. My "coworkers" inform me that the party is for Robert, retiring from the IT department. Robert apparently has been with the company for over thirty years and is a beloved colleague, mentor and friend to many. I nod and soak in all the information being passed around me, acting like I know Robert— of course, he's my BFF at work and he definitely helped me set up my workstation on my first day this past Monday morning. We all fall into an easy discussion, transitioning from work to what everyone's plans are for the rest of the weekend.

I sense Mr. Cole Harris' approach before I see him, instantly feeling my muscles tighten and coil as an automatic and biological response, a natural instinct and side effect of my profession. Old habits die hard, even with your brothers' watchful and judgment-filled eyes upon you, I suppose. The woman closest to me, Ashley Bridges from the risk management team, slightly swoons as her pupils dilate when Mr. Harris comes within her line of sight. Wow, can you be any more obvious Ashley? I internally shake my head, silently judging her, all the while continuing to studiously and intentionally ignore Mr. Harris, making a strategic decision to further gain his attention with a game of cat and mouse. Ashley, ever the social butterfly, takes the opportunity to move toward Mr. Harris and places her hand possessively on his chest, drawing the attention of all the people in our little cluster with a pithy attempt to blatantly mark what she wants to be her territory.

Ashley Bridges finally finds her voice and speaks so loudly, I'm sure the people in Yonkers heard her, "Hey, Cole! So glad you could make it! Have you met Alexis? She's new to the finance department! Do you know if Robert is coming soon? I have to catch the train home soon!" All of us, including Mr. Harris, take in her rapid fire, one-sided soliloquy in stride.

Mr. Cole Harris catches my eye and turns all of his attention to me, much to Ashley's dismayed expression. "Hello, I don't believe we've met. I'm Cole Harris. Please, call me Cole," he politely and smoothly says, ignoring Ashley's bloviations and disregarding all of her questions. The deepness of his voice catches me slightly off guard. The hint of dissonance resurfaces as I think about the file I received and the man that stands in front of me, but I'll do more research when we get back to West Enterprises headquarters.

"Alexis, nice to meet you," I promptly respond, not trying to further the conversation by breaking eye contact, turning my body away from him and focusing on the person and their riveting conversation across from me. Cole Harris is different from what I thought he'd be and I'm trying to not hyperfocus on that. He seems comfortable with his height of 6'2", with a build showing his strength and dedication to fitness. Judging by his physical physique, I can take a guess that he probably works out at the gym at least four times a week. Cole's clear blue eyes were full of questions, inquiry and excitement. Even with his casual, Friday attire of khakis, a blue dress shirt which accents his eyes and his sleeves rolled up to his elbows, I could see he fills out his clothing well and he knows how to look and dress presentably. I was expecting him to be quiet and mousy, but he has undeniable confidence and charm.

In my gut, I immediately know something is off, I don't need to research this to confirm my suspicions. I trust my gut, and my gut says this man needs to be taken to a place where he's safe while my family and I figure out what the hell is going on. My intel file said he was aloof and a loner, an overall easy, forgettable target. The vibes radiating off him right now are not consistent with that assessment. I briefly glance at my twin, who immediately identifies and understands my concern. Dave gives me a subtle nod, indicating that my twin and our brothers have my back and that he'll inform the rest of the family of the details we shared through our Twin Power.

Sensing Cole wants to say more to me, I intentionally detach myself from present conversation and move on to find another group of my "colleagues," initiating my game of cat and mouse, one of my favorites to play. I hear Cole attempting to follow me through the crowds, but my smaller frame fluidly moves around the crowds with the ease of practice comparative to Cole's larger and bulkier frame. Cole mutters a slew of "excuse me" and "sorry" exclamations as he attempts to quickly follow me in my wake. Knowing he is interested, that I successfully baited and trapped him, I head towards the bar to order a drink, abandoning benign conversations. No one else from the party is at the bar counter which I chose on purpose, singling him out and drawing him away from the work crowd. Allowing him to finally catch up to me, I feel him come to stand beside me while I keep my gaze trained on getting the bartender's attention.

"Alexis," Cole begins only slightly out of breath at which I am mildly surprised and impressed at. "Hey. So, you're in the finance department? I didn't know, otherwise I would've had a reason to visit your group this week."

My natural instinct is to gag at his lame icebreaker. How basic and standard of a pick-up line. Maybe my intel was right. But that eye-rolling is something Alex would do, not Alexis from the finance department. I lazily tear my gaze from studying the back of the bar and smile sensually at my target.

"Oh, it's all right, Cole, I just started," I coyly reason as the bartender finally takes notice of us and walks toward us. "I wouldn't expect you to be the head of the welcoming committee anyway!" I continue in a bombastic manner, unusual for me but necessary for my character.

Cole chuckles and also notices the bartender walking our way. He motions for her to come over and places his drink order, a Manhattan. He turns to me and asks what I'd like to which I simply reply to the bartender, "A Long Island, please."

Cole turns to look at me, impressed, his eyebrows slightly raised. I return his gaze, pretending to shyly reply, "You ordered a Manhattan. I only thought it was fitting to match your drink's origination in this city with mine!"

Cole smirks and turns his attention to our delivered drinks and pays the bill, much to my protest. I negotiate and we settle that I'll leave the tip. We end up grabbing a table by the window in a more private area and start chatting, forgetting about the party going on around us, its attendees and any socially constructed norms that we should, in theory, be following. Cole regales me with stories of his department, work and career. Every now and then, someone from the office comes over to chat with us, which Cole seems to delight in. Cole has this magnetism about him that in very different circumstances, I as Alexandra would consider being attracted to. He makes sure to introduce and include me to everyone who comes our way as I graciously embrace my "Alexis from the Finance Department" persona. I catch Ashley Bridges staring daggers at me throughout the night, her competitive prowess on high alert as I poached her prey right from under her manicured acrylic clutches. What a bitch. Scorn isn't a good look for her, it definitely will leave long-lasting mars and wrinkles on her made-up, Botox-filled face. I'm momentarily amused with her trying to maintain her perilously tenuous grasp on the little power she possesses. It's quite comical, comically pathetic. Eventually, the fellow partygoers take the hint and leave Cole and me alone to talk and get to know each other better.

Cole then delves into regaling me about his personal life when the alcohol lifts some of his inhibitions. The night moves on, and I find that I'm enjoying Cole letting his guard down, showing me that he's beginning to trust me. I almost forget that I'm on a job, I'm enjoying the conversation and getting to know Cole so much. People like me don't have relationships other than family. Especially in the business of assassinations and terminations, a lot of us lead lonely lives by default. My time with Cole is making me almost consider changing my lifestyle, to consider more for myself. Almost.

David West

Ever since I walked over to Sean and Will, I can't take my eyes off Lexi. I trust her implicitly; I know that she would never kill a target in such a public place in front of our family. But I don't know, nor do I trust this Cole Harris. What if this guy is on to our plan and takes her as a hostage to leverage and ensure his safe departure? What if this guy hurts her right here, in front of me, and for some reason, I can't get to her in time? What if someone else tries to kill him who is less skilled than my sister, misses their shot and accidently hits her? I know I'm playing with fire, playing the "what if" game on an endless, torturing loop. Choosing not to continue catastrophizing, I turn my attention to the Jack and Coke drink that I've been nursing, hoping that I look like I'm casually leaning against the bar counter so I can keep a clear line of sight on Lexi and Cole Harris.

Sean gently nudges my shoulder and I turn to him, annoyed that I have to take my eyes off my twin for a brief moment. "Yeah?" I gruffly ask, not in the mood to entertain any small talk, even if it's from one of my brothers.

"Dude, I think Cole Harris is catching onto you. He keeps looking over here, staring directly at you. Stop being so conspicuous, you're not exactly hiding your gaze on her," Sean confidently states while he simultaneously admonishes me.

I look over again at my sister, only to stare directly into Cole Harris' eyes. I begrudgingly realize that Sean's right and I turn to face my brothers, noticing that Will is also watching me with a wary and guarded expression. I shrug off Will's look and try to focus on the conversation at the table and hope that Lexi's safe when I eventually turn back around to check on her.

William West

"Of course, she's here," I hiss out and seethe, barely able to contain my vitriol, my veins are humming with pent-up rage.

Sean looks over at me with an amused look and sardonically asks, "Are you really all that surprised, Will?"

I grunt without giving Sean the satisfaction of a response. Instead, I sip on my soda, knowing Sean's right but I would never admit that out loud, least of all to my youngest brother. In the end, I begrudgingly shake my head and take a quick peak at my little sister with Cole Harris. Sean and Kevin both did warn me about this before we left the house to come to the city, about the probability of her already scoping out the area when we initially started talking about our plan for tonight. For some reason, I just didn't think she'd act this fast. I really wasn't surprised to see her, but I am still annoyed that we're now competing for conflicting contracts, all under the same roof at the exact same time.

This has put a damper on all of the plans us brothers made at the house last night. And now she's running point and controlling the show without knowing the mission, without me knowing her angle. She's making decisions on behalf of West Enterprises without considering any other perspectives, other than her own agenda. She has always been a brat, even when we were younger, but this is pushing the limits and putting the company's reputation and integrity on the line. That is something that I cannot let happen. And if my father were still alive, he would never stand for that either.

Sean West

I look over at Will who is silently, but not inconspicuously, boiling over with nefarious emotions. I turn my gaze to Dave who is intently but now discreetly watching the interaction between Cole Harris and our sister. Dave is overly concerned and Will is oversensitive. It's a consistent theme within the West household that I've tried but mainly failed to maintain and manage for years.

I look over at Lex and she seems like she has the situation under control, just as I suspected that she would. And I'm not just saying that because she's my big sister and that I have admired her for as long as I can remember. She is naturally showcasing all the actions of a woman flirting with someone she is genuinely attracted to. There's a brief moment of pain I see flash through her dark eyes and it makes me wonder. My instinct says that she's actually enjoying herself, not just as a job or Alex, but as Alexandra. I know she would never admit that to anyone, so I file that information away for a much later date.

Refocusing my priorities, I know, however, that part of this flirting façade is all an act, an image she wants Cole Harris and those around her to see. Lex is an expert mirror, showing her audience what they want to see, but never giving away a piece of herself in the process. Right now, I don't think she's truly into Cole, probably the opposite; she's most likely bored and going through the motions in order to get out of here. She's trying to display what we, her brothers, keep telling her are appropriate and socially acceptable behaviors, qualities and traits that we advise her to hone and develop, since we keep telling her she doesn't possess the right set of emotions. But we never do define the terms "appropriate" and "socially acceptable" which only frustrates her even more and ultimately discourages her long-term growth. She's been wearing the same mask for years, going through the motions, displaying the appropriate emotions on her face but not truly feeling them, not since Dad died. She's still hurting, grieving and mourning on the inside, and I don't know how to reach out and help her. But I know someone has to get through to her before she eventually self-destructs. That it's only a matter of time. Maybe that brief flash of pain is a tell that she's getting closer to wanting to open up to someone.

Kevin West

I can see Lex over Luke's shoulders. She's doing great. I'm not worried about the op. Secretly, I was never worried in the first place. But as I look over to Will, he looks like he's about to explode with rage. I fight the impulse to go over and try to calm my eldest sibling down. That's always been my job, calming Will down. I'm the only family member Will has ever let into his inner circle, where I can see a glimpse of the emotions that circulate through his head and heart. It's exhausting, like constantly playing translator for two sides who don't have any interest in effectively communicating with each other on their own.

Turning my attention back to the mission, I observe the interesting situation that we're in. In my routine perusal of the room, I've noticed there are other men who have focused their attention onto my sister, regardless of her speaking exclusively to Cole Harris in a semi-private area. I'm not surprised. Even with her disguise and hunched shoulders, her natural beauty shines through, it always has. I doubt that anyone will approach her, but I still keep an eye on those interested parties throughout the night, tracking their movements throughout the restaurant. I don't want any complications or added distractions tonight. We're in a very public location with innocent civilians surrounding us, let alone a lot of internal tension running through the West family itself. I'm waiting for the pre-discussed signal from her telling us that we need to go. My sister will tug her left ear with her right hand with a flirtatious smile on her face. I just want to get this night over with so we can all get back to the house and sort this entire situation out. But until then, we all have to stay put and wait for Lex's signal to move in and neutralize the situation.

Lucas West

Kev ordered some appetizers for the table, which is a good thing because I'm starving. I totally forgot to grab a snack before we headed out from West Enterprises. From our vantage point, we can see Lex and Cole Harris, as well as Will, Dave and Sean off to the side. She doesn't look bad with the lighter brown hair, even though I've seen her with hair all the different shades of the rainbow. But I've always been partial to her natural jet-black hair color. She always jokes her black hair matches her black soul, but I know my Sissy better to know that she has a big heart, she just hasn't let anyone in close enough to see it since our dad died. The server interrupts my train of thought as our food arrives and Kev and I immediately start to devour the food.

Every now and then, I cast a subtle glance at Lex in between bites. She's doing fine, just like I knew she would. Everyone else was so worried, but I have never understood that. She knows how to handle herself; she's proven that many times with us and within her world of assassin ninjas. None of us have ever seen her in action live and in person, but I'd bet it is truly impressive. No wonder she's so successful, she's a true professional. She's reading Cole Harris like an open book and playing him like a fiddle. It's comical how easily she can slip in and out of the various personalities that her job requires, but it's also a little sad. I wonder which of those identities she resembles the closest to now, considering all the changes she's been through over the past years. I'm not sure we, as her brothers, would recognize the woman she is now under the layers of disguises, aliases and characters that she's accumulated.

Nevertheless, I'm so proud of her. She's kicking ass just like we always thought she would. My only wish is she would find her own identity and not get lost in all the personas that she pretends to be. I hope that she can be the amazing person that she, as just Alexandra West, truly is. But Kev keeps telling me that it will eventually happen in time, to give her space to find that version of herself. I'm just not that patient. I never have been, especially when it comes to Sissy.

Cole Harris

Man, this girl is gorgeous! I haven't seen her around the office, otherwise I know I would have remembered her if I did. Maybe I missed her in passing, though didn't someone say she just started this week? Did she say that? My memory is getting fuzzy. I realize that I've had a good amount of alcoholic drinks tonight and things aren't as clear to me anymore. But I feel good, really good! I feel confident. I feel like I've talked a lot about myself, but I haven't learned much about her. Every time I ask her a question about herself, I end up talking about me. That makes me feel like a terrible, selfish and self-centered person, which I'd like to believe is out of character for me. But the drinks are so good and I figure I can learn more about her later. Maybe I'll ask around to see where she's located in the office, be a friendly face at work. I could even see myself dating her after getting to know each other, taking her to meet my family back home in California. Alexis would not be a one-night stand. She's someone unique, something valuable and special.

Alexis is definitely feeling me and is sending the right non-verbal vibes to tell me that she's picking up what I'm putting down. She's flirting back with me, matching me stride for stride and we've been talking for a while, almost the entire night. But there's this guy by the bar who keeps staring at her. The guys he is standing with have also looked over at her a couple times too. There are a couple of other men who have been watching her throughout the night. I wonder if she knows them or if she needs my help. Even though I don't know much about Alexis, I'd protect her. I'd make sure she was safe. I'd be her hero if she needed me to be one.

Alexandra West

After another round of drinks, although I have subtly switched to water earlier, Cole's pupils are dilated and he is smiling to the point where I wonder if his smile will permanently crack and break his handsome face. *What a maudlin mess*, I mentally say to myself as I try my damn hardest not to roll my eyes. The barbiturate I slipped in his fifth drink has taken hold, his inhibitions are lower and he's lost all track of time. So naturally, I'm getting bored now. I've already gained his trust and loyalty. He's shown his hand, that he's attracted to me. The fun of the game is all over for me now. When Cole is finally ready to go, and when I'm almost at the limits that test even a saint's patience, I look over at Kev and Luke and send the signal that it's time to leave.

I turn my attention back to Cole and whisper in his ear seductively, "Hey. Want to go back to my place?" His sloppy lopsided grin is all the answer I need and I help him put on his jacket as we start to leave.

"Wait," Cole interrupts my thoughts and movement by suddenly grabbing my wrist and stopping me in my tracks, "you're really sweet; I want to get to know you better. I don't want this to only be just one night and that's it."

I mentally roll my eyes and refrain from saying something bitingly sarcastic, like some unrealistic expectation about how I want our relationship to last forever too. I've been called many things in my lifetime but sweet, or any other related synonym, has never been one of them.

Instead, I smile at him just as Alexis would and say, "Oh no, neither do I. Let's just see how tonight goes. Besides," I add with flirtatious flair as I arch my eyebrow, "I know where you work!" I playfully poke Cole in the chest as I watch Will and Sean leave the bar with Luke following behind them.

I grab Cole's arm and steer him toward the door, aware that Kev and Dave are behind me as we all make our way to the exit. I direct Cole's steps to turn right on Pine Street and start walking down the hill, away from the hustle and bustle of people and the brightly illuminated Chase Plaza. I do my best work in the shadows, and even though Cole will live to see another day, I always prefer to be away from the lights. I check to make sure Kev and Dave are ready and I swiftly inject a tranquilizer into Cole's arm. In a flash, Kev, Luke, Dave and Sean have surrounded us as to not draw additional attention to the state of Cole's sudden lack of consciousness and motionless form. Wow, I'm impressed; my brothers really do know what they're doing.

"You just had to use drugs, didn't you?" Kev says with a knowing smile on his face.

"She dropped something into his drink a couple drinks in, too," Sean offers with a knowing smirk on his face.

I look at my sometimes too observant little brother with scorn in my eyes as I bite out, "Tattle."

My brothers all chuckle as Will rolls his eyes and grunts out a non-committal response before he rushes off to get the vehicle the boys arrived in. The rest of us step deeper into the shadows of the closest alleyway before Will pulls up to the curb and we carefully load Cole's limp but surprisingly heavy form to the SUV, all of us filing in afterward. My eldest brother drives toward West Enterprises while Kev is in the passenger seat, always Will's right hand. Sean and Dave took the third row while Cole is sandwiched in between Luke and me. We all ride in a somewhat uncomfortable silence. My brothers, no doubt, trying to figure out how to handle the situation. I moodily stare out the window while I try to reconcile Cole Harris' file with the man that I met today. Something doesn't add up; something isn't right. And I've never been one to appreciate and accept dissonance. If something is off, in my line of work, that unease can be the difference between my life or my death. But now is not the time to sort all that out. We need to get back to West Enterprises, away from any other potential threats like me, looking for opportunities to snatch the target away. After we all settle in, I will finally be able to give Cole Harris all further thought.

As we pull up to the house's driveway, Cole slowly begins to regain consciousness. Right on time, I say, but only in my head. I'm not sure how Will would appreciate that wisecrack, and then I'd have to explain how I adjusted the drug's dosage level once my plan turned into the West family plan. Cole begins to notice his surroundings with a frantic expression and quickly perks up. He looks over to me and then to the five men around us, not knowing their relationship to me, where we are or what's going on. I put a finger to my lips, signaling the need to be silent as we park in the West Enterprises garage, simply because I wasn't in the mood to answer his fifty questions. Let Cole think he and I have been kidnapped and are being held hostage. It'll keep him quiet, complacent and on his toes for just a little bit longer. Thankfully, Cole follows my lead as the vehicle doors open and we all pile out of the vehicle.

Will assumes his position out in front with Sean flanking his side, Cole in the middle. Dave is next to me while Kev and Luke bring up the rear. We walk through the breezeway, not breaking the stillness of the evening with words. I peel away from the procession and walk directly to the kitchen in search of a much-needed beer, considering I switched to water a couple hours ago while the rest of my brothers escort Cole Harris down the hall to our conference room located just off to the left of the kitchen. I don't catch his face, but I can hear Cole asking where I'm going as my brothers lead him down the hallway, separating us for the first time since we met at The Bailey.

As I take a long swig of my much-needed beer, I finally kick off my heels. I pull the hairpins out of my wig and carefully take off my wig and wig cap, putting them on the dining room table to put away after our impromptu conference room meeting. I shrug off my sweater, pulling my phone from its pocket before I head back to the kitchen to grab a couple of additional beer bottles for my brothers. I know they were sober tonight too, though I know a couple of them ordered a mixed drink. Even if we have differences about the work we choose to do, we're all similar to each other in the fact that when we're on the job, we're one hundred percent present and there.

I quietly pad barefoot with my normal black hair cascading in soft waves down my back to the conference room, following in after my brothers. After I cross the conference room doorway, I pass the beers to Dave and Kev as I look around to try to see the way Cole is taking in the room. The table and walls are white with light gray chairs strategically arranged around the table, which seats twelve comfortably. There are additional chairs lining the perimeter of the room if a larger group is needed to be accommodated. There is no artwork on any of the walls, it's incredibly clinical, a clear working space for West Enterprises. The room's only feature is the wall of windows overlooking the sandy dunes and the ocean beyond. I remember when this room used to be my father's home office, how this was where he planned how he wanted to form and structure his new, budding idea, West Enterprises Incorporated. A part of me misses that earlier time, things seemed easier then. But isn't that always the case when you're nostalgically reminiscing?

Will, like the pompous ass that he is, has already taken the seat at the head of the table, placing Cole at the opposite end of the table, facing my eldest brother directly in a power play type of move. Kev and Sean sit on one side of the table while Dave and Luke sit on the other side. Dave tilts his head toward the empty chair next to him but I subtly shake my head, choosing to stand off to the right of Will's shoulder, casually leaning a hip against the wall, all the while keeping a close watch over Mr. Cole Harris as I take another swig of my beer.

Cole Harris looks over to me, astonishment and confusion marring his handsome features, his brain still rousing itself from my knockout cocktail. "Alexis? What's going on? Are you okay? Did you change your hair?" he tentatively asks as the questions pour out of him.

"It's Alex," I automatically and stoically respond without an intentional thought, like I'm on autopilot or a robot.

Cole Harris stutters and stammers out, "Wh-what? Who are you? I thought you just started in our finance department this week. Right, Alexis? I thought we had a connection! How… How did I get here? Who are these men?"

"Well, you know, that's a really funny story and because of you, we're all in a bit of a pickle. But to make a long story short, I'm an assassin, contracted to kill you," I respond. Motioning to my family, I say, "These are my brothers and they are determined and contracted to save and protect your life. So, we're all at odds against each other, with you in the middle. Fun, right?"

While I'm talking, Mr. Harris' eyes look like they're going to pop out of his head. Continuing, I say, "I lured you in, got you drunk with some chemical assistance, and then I injected you with a tranquilizer to make transportation easier. After that, we all loaded you into one of our company's SUVs and drove to Long Island, which brings us to our current situation. Any other questions?" After I finish, I just passively stare at him, wondering if I'm going to need buy a vowel to get the next word out of him as his mouth opens, but no sound comes out.

I watch as Cole Harris' face goes through all the emotional stages people like me normally see when I confront people with their imminent mortality; denial, disbelief, fear and finally anger. "Geez, ease him into it, why don't you," Will admonishes sarcastically. I roll my eyes and shrug my shoulders. Classic Will, always trying to pick a fight or tell me what I'm doing is wrong.

Finally, Cole Harris lashes out at me, showing his fear affect by yelling out, "Who the hell are you? I meet you at a bar, do you even work for the same company as me? How did you find me? You're so cold and aloof now, but just hours ago you were warm and you were flirting with me, you two-faced bitch!" At the insult, I smile, genuinely amused. Enraged probably by my casual response, my target concludes by yelling, "So, which face are you?"

During his tirade, Dave, Kev, and Luke have become visibly agitated at the personal attack Cole is launching against me while Will shrewdly looks on and Sean sits back, quietly observing the interaction. Dave opens his mouth to interject and probably defend my name. But I pre-emptively lift my hand in the air, stopping my twin before he can get anything out. There are some battles a girl's got to fight on her own.

I predatorily come to stand in front of Cole's chair which he frantically backs up to where he's now stuck between me and the wall. I place my hands on both of the armrests, effectively boxing him in. Leaning forward to further encroach within his personal space, I calmly look Cole in the eyes and respond in a deadly serious tone, brokering no compromise, "This face. The so-called cold and aloof, or bitch persona as you so described. This is my true face. But I'm glad you enjoyed the other face, it's nice to know it's still believable in this day and age."

"You bitch," Cole spits out, the venom minced out with his words, "you lied to me."

"Hey!" Dave protests as he jumps to his feet, his posture bristling.

"You do not talk to her like that!" Sean roars out in an uncharacteristic display of uncontained self-resolve.

I calmly interrupt my two brothers with a bored expression on my face, "Guys, it's fine."

During my quick exchange with Sean and Dave, Cole has raised his hand at me, as if to punch or slap me in the face. Internally laughing while my brothers are coming toward me to intervene and protect whom from whom I don't know. Instead, I take my own action. I grab Cole's wrist, twisting it behind his back, forcing him to stand up before slamming his face into the wall so hard that the walls shudder at the impact. I strongly deliver a swift kick to the back of his knees and control his movements as he folds and deflates on the ground, his knees buckling and collapsing out from underneath of him. Luke and Kev have come over and together they roughly lift him up under his armpits, dragging him back into his vacated chair. Then, Kev and Luke take their post behind Cole's shoulders to make sure that he doesn't have another physical outburst again.

Looking at Cole who is so emotional that he is out of breath, I notice my heart rate hasn't increased, not even a single palpitation. Satisfied, I calmly address Cole, "Yes, I lied. People lie to each other every day. I doubt this is your first bout of deception nor will it be your last, so grow up and deal with it. The art of deception is an end to a necessary mean in my line of work. But either I was going to kill you or someone else was going to tonight. Instead, you're here and safe for the time being. And yes, I'm a bitch. But you'll be fine. So, make your peace and get over it. And when you're ready and you come to your senses, you can thank me and my brothers for saving your pathetic, worthless and wretched life."

My brothers cautiously nod in agreement as tension starts to recede in the room. My job and role for what I was needed in this room are both done, we all know it. Will starts to direct the conversation toward maintaining Cole Harris' safety within West Enterprises' walls, and the security measures that support that initiative while Mr. Harris continues to look shell-shocked through as my brother bloviates at him. I can't say that I blame him there, I'd be bored out of my mind too.

Taking my cue, I stalk out of the room and head back down the hallway toward the living room. I hear Dave following after me and brace for one of our stereotypical and predictable twin heart to hearts. "Hey, you okay? It was getting pretty heated in there... then again you weren't the one getting emotional. You very rarely ever do," my twin says with a small smile.

"I'm fine," I automatically respond. My short response is a signal to my twin to drop the topic, who gets my nonverbal communication immediately. We both cross the living room to the double doors which lead outside on the deck with views overlooking the Atlantic Ocean.

After a while, Luke comes to join us in the silence that only the night can bring. Dave and I turn as one to look at him with Dave breaking the silence, "So what now?"

Luke sighs, running his hand through his hair; another one of his tells to signal that he's stressed out. Our older brother sighs before he turns to look at us. "He'll be staying here. But we aren't under the illusion that fellow assassins aren't waiting for him to resurface or publicly show his face in order to take him out. Which leads us to you, Sissy. We need you to stay here with us. Help us guard and protect him, at least for the time being. You know better than all of us combined what the threats, angles and methods of attack other assassins will be trying to take against him. What do you think?"

I'm not surprised and was honestly wondering when they'd ask or subtly force me to stay and assist until we figure out what's going on and which contract to enforce. I look at Luke, then Dave, and promptly turn on my heel and head back inside.

I can still hear Will droning on in the conference room, just like when I had left, going on about living arrangements and filing a temporary leave of absence for Cole Harris' office job. I have a brief pang of pity for him as he had to sit and endure that dreaded lecture. I breeze into the room and abruptly stop Will's tirade of logistics and focus my attention on Cole Harris as Luke and Dave tentatively but quickly file in behind me. Given away by what I can only assume is my intense look, it would be the only explanation as to why Sean and Kev immediately jump to their feet to stand by Cole Harris, ready to handle a potentially volatile situation.

I roll my eyes at my brothers' attempts of protection and address the target directly. "Look," I start, "this situation is not ideal. I know, I get it. It's a huge inconvenience, a uniquely life-threatening situation. Honestly, and bluntly, it sucks. For you, for me, for everyone in this room. We get it. And it'd be nice to try to empathize with you, although my brothers will be the first to say that I do not have the capacity to empathize with anyone. Regardless, your life is in danger—"

"From people like you!" Cole Harris shouts as he interrupts me, testing my patience as his hands are fisted and his white knuckles show his rage given our current situation.

"Yes, from people like me." I placate him before continuing on with my point. "I'm the best shot that you have if you want to live. And my brothers are willing to put their lives on the line to protect you as well. I don't care if you give a shit about me. You've already made your feelings of contempt for me blatantly known. But... you do not spit in the face of

68

those trying to save your life, especially when those people are my brothers, my family. So say thank you. Be grateful. And appreciate them and accept the damn help they're freely offering to you. This isn't a game, nor is your life something to gamble with. If you don't like it, you could probably take your chances. We're not holding you hostage here, you're free to leave at any time. But if you leave now, you might last until the end of the weekend where you'd undoubtedly get a bullet lodged in between your eyes and your parents would have to fly out here all the way from California to identify and claim your body. Decide what you want to do now. We don't have all night. But if you're in, you're all in. And if you're out, then get the hell out of this house."

At the end of my uncharacteristically long speech, Mr. Harris visibly pales and grows silent. He looks at each of my brothers assessing the truth behind my words. To their credit, my brothers back my play and give nothing away, his gaze finally settling back on my face. I watch as he takes in my expression, his eyes darting between both of mine, looking for what, I'm not sure. "It's time. Make your choice, Cole Harris. No one else can make it for you," I command and challenge him. "Death? Or life."

Cole Harris nods and looks down, defeated as he reluctantly says, "Thank you, all of you. I readily accept your help."

Satisfied with his decision, I turn and take my final leave of the room. I grab my costume, wig and another beer just for good measure from the fridge before I head upstairs to try to get some sleep.

Each of us six kids had our own bedrooms growing up, so it was a believable and probable concept that this large, ten-bedroom house would later become the company's headquarters. I head upstairs to my childhood bedroom, passing by the rooms that belong to my brothers and four spare rooms for agents who need to stay at West Enterprises. Will's door is cracked open and even in the shadows, I can see the light from all the computer screens he has set up illuminating the room, creating chaotic shadows at odd shapes and strange angles. Luke's door is closed, but since he's the messy one, I know there are laundry, papers and other items laying around. Hurricane Luke has always maintained a perpetual residence in our house ever since we were kids, his bedroom known to home its wreckage.

Kev, the complete opposite of Luke, is the neat freak and minimalist of the family. He has his collection of boxing gloves in one corner near his closet with just the rest of the room containing a bed and a dresser. Sean's bedroom is dwarfed by the numerous stacks of books on every available surface and arranged all over the floor. His collection of stacks makes it difficult to navigate the small pathways of carpet left in his room, towers of books creating a path from the bed, door and closet. But he has his own filing system, even amidst the chaos; my youngest brother has always been the avid bibliophile of the West family.

Dave and my bedrooms are at the very end of the hallway, on the north side of the house which is closest to the ocean, across the hall from each other. When we were children, we were in our own little world at the end of the hallway with a clear path to the beach from below, accessible by my bedroom's balcony spiral staircase. Dave's room, much like his room in my condo, is decorated with the same light browns and navy blues. He thankfully is neater than Luke, with only a knickknack or two decorating his tall dresser.

Turning to the door on my right, opposite of Dave's door, I go into the sparsely decorated room that I call mine and look around. My white, queen canopy bed takes up the majority of the space, with just a dresser and vanity off to the side. The balcony French doors are draped in gauzy white sheers, which gently blow in the salt air during the day. As I was the only girl in the family, Dad had built a full bathroom for me, attached directly off my room, so I was spared the humiliation and disgust of sharing the hall bathroom with my brothers. I close my childhood bedroom door behind me and pull out a pair of sweatpants, flip-flops and a tee shirt from the dresser. It's not unusual for me to have a stash of clothing, shoes and toiletry items here, since this is headquarters and I stop over here a lot for work. In general, I don't have a lot of personal items, just the basics for the transient lifestyle I choose to lead. I quickly remove my makeup and jewelry and then proceed to pull my hair back into a loose ponytail, finally getting comfortable in my own skin and normal attire after a long day of costumes, subterfuge and conflict-heavy conversations.

As I walk toward the balcony off the sitting area in my room, I grab my staple beach bag with my beach blanket, handgun and a reusable water canister as I trot down the stairs to the beach in my flip-flops. I walk in the sand, cooled by the evening's temperatures, leisurely winding my way through the dunes. When I get to an area I like, I lay out my blanket before settling down, enjoying my position of halfway between the dunes and ocean. The shoreline is deserted for the night, the moon glinting off the sand and water. I observe the waves rolling in and take in the sounds and smells that seem to always calm me, even during the most turbulent times in my life. I watch the ocean's nightlife come alive under the moonlight, its creatures undisturbed in the dark hours around midnight. I see the small crabs skitter across the sand, digging for their meals in the glittering moonlight. Sandpipers flit about, getting their dinners before they make their way back to their homes, nested safely in the dunes. A flutter of wings draws my attention to my right where I catch piping plovers flying from their nests which is quickly followed by the iridescent reflection of the moonlight reflected off the eyes of a neighborhood beach cat chasing the endangered New Jersey species from their huddled nests. I hear the sound of the waves change and as my gaze is drawn back to the ocean. I spot a dozen arching dorsal fins moving parallel to the shoreline. This space, this environment here, this is my soul's home, my respite from the business of life, or in my case, of death.

When Dad was murdered, my brothers often found me watching the ocean at all hours, day and night. Sometimes, they'd join me as we shared and ruminated in our shared grief and disbelief in an understanding silence. My father was a compassionate man. He was always supportive of whatever his kids decided to pursue, even if he thought we should be doing other things with our choices and subsequent lives. He let us try everything and was there to help us learn through our mistakes. He never judged us, nor did he ever show any negative inclination to each of our individual lifestyles. My brothers would sometimes jealously state that Dad doted on me and that I was a typical Daddy's girl. And as much as my father loved me, I so equally adored him. He didn't bat an eye when I told him I wanted to be an assassin; I honestly think he was expecting it. He defended me to my brothers when I announced that I wouldn't be continuing in the family's tradition of security and protection, but instead would become the very threat that West Enterprises promised our clients would have to never encounter. My father celebrated my successes and grieved with me in my failures, he understood the long-term impact of diversifying his business' revenue streams. But most of all, he supported his daughter, even when it wasn't convenient or the safest choice.

My father is the one who taught me most of the skills I still use today, even though he's been gone a long time now. While he looked like a hardened, tough and weathered lifetime military man, I knew deep down he would have laid his life down for any of his children without any hesitation or regret, and that he'd do the same for any member of his team.

Thinking about how my dad wasn't what he physically appeared to be, I turn my thoughts back to Cole Harris. On paper, this man is supposed to be a spineless man-child who fears everything and everyone. Someone who could disappear and no one would miss him in their life. But the Cole Harris I met was the complete antithesis of the description given in his file. The Cole I met had confidence, charm, ambition and drive. This discrepancy gets me thinking some unsettling thoughts, what other targets could have had the same inconsistencies, and I just didn't take the time to notice them before I immediately eliminated them. Something close to guilt begins to encroach on my conscious and it takes everything in me to smother those feelings so I can retain whatever is left of my sanity.

I'm starting to spin. I recognize the signs, the self-doubt that is coming for me like a freight train. Regret starts to seep into my subconscious, that is, until I feel someone approach. I hear whoever it is noisily trudge through the sand, their steps coming closer to me. By the sounds and lack of stealth, I instinctually know that Cole Harris will be joining me shortly. My brothers would literally be dead if they were ever caught being this loud in their day jobs. So, I know, even when they're off the clock, that my brothers would still be conscientious of how much noise they were making, a beneficial casualty of our chosen professions, especially as stealth and silence were driven into our brains starting at a very young age following us throughout our entire adulthood.

I feel Cole come to a stand behind me, not saying anything and uncertainty hovering in the air around us. During the entire time he made his way over to me, I hadn't moved or acknowledged his presence. But he knows that I'm aware of his presence and he hesitates before finally asking, "May I?"

I finally look up at him, slowly raising my gaze to meet his eyes. I see the layer of fear reflected back to me, but deeper than that, I see curiosity. Intrigued, I make my decision silently known by moving over on the blanket to allow Cole the room to sit down beside me.

I immediately return my attention forward to the ocean. Forced conversations aren't my style. I give people the room, space and patience to share with me what they're thinking or feeling. Silence is a tool that seems to be rarely used any more. Many people store words in their arsenal for times of conflict. But I've found that silence is the most resilient and strongest weapon. Considering Cole sought me out, I figured he has something he wants to talk to me about. So, I give him the time for him to gather his thoughts, finding comfort with the silence the eastern seaboard offers. After a few minutes, I feel him turn and look at my profile, studying my face as he tries to figure me out while processing life-changing information given to him in a span of just a few hours.

"Look, I want to apologize. I can blame my actions on alcohol, shock, anger or any number of other emotions running through me right now. But I should have never taken my anger out on you. My parents didn't raise me that way and I only have explanations, no excuses. So, I apologize and hope that you can forgive me for my outburst," Cole says, his authenticity genuine and sincere.

Of all the things I thought Cole was going to say to me, this is not what I was expecting. I turn my body and my face toward Cole as I respond, "Cole. You don't owe me anything. No apologies, no explanations. What you're going through is understandable; I see it all the time. I see the fear, the regrets, the terror every day, without fail. I'm not mad. Just let your guilt go and we'll be all good."

Cole briefly nods and I can actually see his Adam's apple bobbing as he swallows, taking in everything that I've said and mulling it over. I'm sure his current situation and pending mortality is at the forefront of his mind, but we both allow the silence to enshroud us in the meantime.

"So... you're an assassin," Cole intentionally states after some time and internal deliberation.

I turn to look him in the eyes, noting the exhaustion etched on his face and his five o'clock shadow peppering his jawline. Cole's eyes seem dimmer, his shoulders look like the weight of the world rests upon them. And for some unknown reason, I feel the uncharacteristic urge to protect him. Ridiculous, I have never felt that urge before in my entire life, not even for my family. Everyone that I've ever known has been taught to protect themselves; us Wests were built to be self-sufficient. So I immediately dismiss those feelings just as quickly as that ludicrous thought arises. I turn my attention back to Cole's questioning face while I continue to ignore that silly, pesky and constant feeling that something is off about this job.

"Yes," I answer honestly, "it's what I do. It's who I am and it's all I have known for a long, long time." The sound of the ocean's waves crashing surrounds us, as we both grow quiet again.

"Would you ever want more?" Cole quietly asks after several more minutes pass, hope slightly tinging his voice.

I look over the ocean, slightly startled and caught completely off guard by his question. No one, not even my brothers, has ever asked me that question before. And even if they did, what would that look like for me? Would I even what more? What would more look like? What would I do with my life instead? When I was younger, I wanted fame, to be recognized. As I matured, I realized all the glitter doesn't turn to gold. Fame can become pernicious notoriety, being recognized turns into being closely scrutinized. So now, I treasure and protect my anonymity, fiercely guarding it and loving to live in shadows. The darkness is where the fun happens and I thrive in the spaces where the light can't pierce through. I consider my answer with the view of the ultimate paradox in front of me, the ocean. For the briefest of moments, I'm surprisingly thrown off kilter. Suddenly, a sense of peace washes over me as I finally realize the true question that Cole's asking me.

I'm not a normal twenty-something year old. I don't see my future drastically changing, either by my choice or circumstance. My course has been set for years now and it would take nothing short of a miracle for my path to be altered.

"Don't put your faith in me, Cole Harris," I bluntly begin. "This is what I've been doing for so long, it's hard to imagine doing anything else with my life. I'm one of the best at what I do, I don't know if I'd want to step away from that, I'm too competitive. And to be fair, I never thought I would live this long to have to ponder a question like this. In my profession, and specifically the type of contracts that I willingly take on, most people don't make it to their mid-twenties. I'm an anomaly in that sense. But it's pointless to dream of a life that can never be. Even when I decide to stop accepting contracts, when I step away from the job, I'll always have a target on my back. And anyone close to me will have that target too. My job will, then, become making sure they don't get caught in the crossfire that's intended to take me out. Fortunately, I don't have to worry about a long-life expectancy, nor do I have to worry about long-term relationships or commitments. The only people in my life are my family. And they all know the risks and how to protect themselves from being affiliated with me."

I stop my slight tirade as I notice his startled look. I take a deep breath, knowing that the conversation took a morose turn. "Don't try to change or save me, Cole," I say more gently. "It won't work. I'm well past rescuing, a lost cause. People, including some of my brothers, have tried to help me. Salvation is not in the cards for me. I've accepted that a long, long time ago. For me, there's no such thing as redemption."

"That's sad," Cole says with genuine sympathy in his voice as he meets my gaze, compassion lingering in his expression.

Cringing, I rearrange my face to a more neutral expression before I reply, "No, that's my life. It's my choice."

Considering my answer, I see his curiosity before Cole asks, "When did you start doing…"

"Contracts?" I finish for him when his voice falters and sputters out. At his reluctant nod, I reply, "I started when I was thirteen. I'm twenty-nine now; I've been doing this for the last sixteen years straight."

"I'm sorry," Cole quietly states, sympathy in his voice with perhaps a touch of pity.

"Don't be," I hastily reply, feeling rebuffed with his tone, "I've made my bed, now I have to lie in it."

Cole looks down and stares at his hands as he says, "I still believe that you're worthy of redemption. The girl I met earlier tonight? She seemed like she'd welcome any sort of forgiveness offered to her."

"Don't, Cole. Forgiveness isn't a part of my vocabulary, nor is it my destiny. Don't put faith, hope or love into me. It's not worth it. You'll only be disappointed at the end." I caution, although as I say the words, I feel something inside me splinter. Cole opens his mouth to reply but wisely stops when he sees the expression my face. I silently turn my attention back to the ocean as I recenter myself again.

Time passes. How much? I don't know, it doesn't really matter in the long run. But the silence is comfortable; I don't feel like the quiet needs to be filled with awkward filler conversation. All I know is that a good amount of time passes before Cole attempts to lighten the mood by saying, "Well, I thought you looked nice with all the makeup, jewelry and fancy clothes. But now looking at you without all of that, I realize that I was wrong. You're much more than just nice, you look fantastic, right here and right now."

I look over to him, shocked and amused. "Yeah?" I question, the corner of my lips tugging uncharacteristically upward, responding to the light teasing tone in his voice. He nods and gives me a megawatt smile, his charisma and confidence coming back, front and center.

The innocence and simplicity of this moment is not lost on me. I feel my shoulders begin to loosen and the tension lift from our spot on the shoreline. We begin to talk our way through the night, being careful to avoid broaching the subjects of assassins, contracts and killers. We chat about sports, new restaurants, trends and common topics until the sun's warm rays brush across the skies, ushering us into the dawn of a new day.

PART II

Alexandra West

Ever since that night on the beach, Cole and I have become something more than just coexisting during our first week together. The best way to describe our relationship would be to say that we've become companions, maybe even friends. There are moments of silence where I think he is going to say something about my chosen profession, either inquisitively or with judgment, but ultimately, he never does. What he would specifically say, I have no clue. But the silences still aren't awkward. I never feel the need to fill the gap with sound or to escape a social interaction which is unusual for me. I've always been content with solitude. But my brothers would always break my reverie with their own nonsense, filling the quiet with endless noise, showing their disregard for my beloved silence. But with Cole, I'm comfortable with not being alone. We regularly go on long walks on the beach and talk into the wee hours of the morning, since we're both confined to West Enterprises to keep Cole safe while my brothers and I try to figure out what's going on with Cole's contract.

Thankfully, Cole is determined to make the best of the situation, constantly trying to make me laugh and smile, and he actively seeks those moments out as if it's his own personal mission. And sometimes, he succeeds, though I try to minimize how much he sees my concessions. It feels weird to smile a genuine smile or to laugh at something that isn't sarcastic or condescending. It feels as if I haven't really laughed in forever, my laugh and smile rusty from disuse. In truth, I haven't really laughed since my dad passed away. But I find myself in better moods and that I'm more apt to smile ever since meeting Cole Harris. And you better believe, my brothers have noticed these changes in me too, especially Dave. I see the looks my brothers exchange out of the corner of my eye. I hear the conversations that abruptly stop when they hear me coming closer to where they're at. I notice the looks Dave gives me when Cole is around. I see the questions in all of my brothers' eyes. I ignore them, allowing myself to be present and not overthink my reactions. I disregard the changes in my personality because in truth, I'm just as unsure of my reactions too.

While Cole and I have chatted the days away, my brothers have tracked down the name of the third party who is targeting Cole. They have also identified other persons of interest that they deemed as a related threat too, fellow assassins. A couple of my old West contacts have started whittling down those names on their list, disguising the disposals as accidental deaths while eliminating our competition and minimizing the direct threat to Cole's life. We know that we're not in the clear yet, but we're getting closer. And because of that, we all seem to be feeling lighter, like the threat is finally lifting off our tired shoulders, like we can finally rest and breathe deeper again.

My brothers have accepted Cole like an old friend. Kev and Luke have even bonded with Cole, accepting him like a brother, which is completely in character for the types of people that they are. Sean, ever the observant figure, keeps his distance, just like he does with the rest of us as he tries to figure out what we're all questioning: why Cole has a price on his head to begin with. I still think that something bigger is going on, that there are larger players involved who are intentionally hiding within the shadows for this particular contract. From our gathered intelligence, Cole isn't a real threat to anyone, yet he's aggressively being targeted. I have dug into Cole's past and have found some interesting data about his parents and their personal and professional lives. Cole's dad runs a private security business in California, Cole's mother is a homemaker who frequents her local country club. But even looking into their history and business interests, there isn't anything current or recent activity that should warrant this type of attack on their son, especially on this coast. I know a couple of my brothers also agree with my concerns and raised their own questions. Dave, as always, stays near my side, making sure that I'm not going to bolt, or worse, act on my assassin instincts. By now, though, everyone seems to understand that I'm not going to honor my contract. I am now way too invested and intrigued to cut this narrative short.

My family, Cole and I have all fallen into a domestic routine where we would all cook, eat and hang out together, forgetting for the moment the numerous threats of the outside world waiting to bear down on us. Will and I are even beginning to overlook our differences and we are starting to enjoy spending some quality, older brother, younger sister bonding time together. Every night, we take our beers on the deck and shoot the breeze to watch the sunset together, reclining in Adirondack chairs and staying in the fading light until the darkness comes. It's become a tradition for all seven of us. Whatever we're doing, we pause and all go out on the deck together. Tensions fade and tempers subside as we're humbled by the light from the dying sun.

Cole attends my brothers' and my physical training sessions where the six of us spar with each other and work out. I think Cole is fascinated with my family's dynamic. His only child eyes are oftentimes the size of saucers as he watches us from the sidelines. Cole always is surprised at my strength and agility when I spar against my brothers. At first, Cole loudly protested when I was paired against Luke, the largest of all of my brothers. He kept going on about the size disparity and how I would be crushed. My brothers and I were amused, though I think Luke's ego got over-inflated while Cole was voicing his concerns. And then Cole was floored when I came out victorious. I couldn't quite place the expression in his eyes as he looked on. Pride? Intrigue? Fascination? Astonishment? I don't know.

However, the more time we all spend together, the more my brothers and I cannot understand why Cole is being targeted and hunted down. Will has done an entire background check and other research on Cole's life as well as a deep dive of Cole's family's investments and interests. Cole is an entry-level IT technician, without top clearances or access to his company's coffers of confidential information. He modestly lives alone and graduated college with honors, but not Summa Cum Laude or head of his class to spark ire with fellow students. Nor did he attract the attention of headhunter recruiters. He wasn't offered any headhunting jobs where he was in direct competition with other candidates, so there's no causation for rage or fury there either. So, why is there a sizeable contract on this guy's head? So far, all we know is that someone wants him dead, but we don't know why, nor do we know who. And if we can figure out the who and why, we hope the other details will succinctly and quickly fall into place.

One night in particular, Cole seems to be uncharacteristically on edge. Cole suggested that the two of us take a walk down to the beach, so I bring my standard beach bag with my gun and beach towel. We slowly meander between the dunes, find a spot and set up the towel for two.

"Alexis," Cole begins, "I know you and your brothers are wondering why I have a contract on my head." When I nod in agreement but do not say anything, my silence encourages him to continue, "I was trying to think about what the cause could possibly be, and I think I may have figured it out."

I pause and try not to gape at him in astonishment. This could be the first real lead we have had in days. I school my features and allow Cole to continue, "A couple weeks ago, I was hanging out with a couple of my friends and we were at a bar in the Bronx. My friends got drunk and I went to get the car since I was voted to be the designated driver for the night. I randomly looked down a side street and I think I witnessed a crime. I couldn't be sure, so I kept walking. No one was with me so I didn't want to stop and ask questions in a neighborhood I wasn't familiar with anyway. I mean, I wasn't one hundred percent sure, and the lighting was pretty bad, so I can't say with full confidence exactly what I saw. But now that I think about this contract and you and your family still not being able to connect everything together, maybe I did see something. I couldn't see who was involved or what really happened, but I guess that doesn't matter to them. I'm guessing they think I clearly saw them, so they…"

After he hesitates, I gently finish his sentence for him, "Need to eliminate the threat and minimize the risk."

Cole nervously nods and looks at me with a guilty look on his face as he resumes his explanation, "I'm sorry I didn't tell you sooner. I just thought of it earlier today. I just thought that it was that inconsequential, that it didn't matter. I swear I wasn't trying to hold out on any information from all of you. I just honestly didn't remember until today."

"You did nothing wrong, Cole, If this is the reason why you have a contract against you, it's because you were just in the wrong place at the wrong time," I knowingly state. "I'll tell my brothers so we can at least verify the threat, then narrow down who's targeting you and possibly eliminate the threat all together."

"You can do that?" Cole excitedly asks, hope slightly tinging the edges of his tone, his face lighting up with relief.

"Depending on the party, yes. My brothers can do the research. The elimination part is something that I would take care of, I just need to know who exactly my target is. Then I can anticipate the what, the how and the where factors," I answer matter-of-factly as I shoot a quick text off to my brothers' and my group chat.

"Alexis, I don't want to put you or your family in any further danger than what I already have," Cole says, putting his hands up to try to slow the conversation's momentum.

"Cole. This threat needs to end so everyone can get their lives back and not be stuck in this house like a prison," I firmly state. Cole looks down at his hands in the sand, hiding his face, but I notice his shoulders have slumped lower than the level they were at moments ago.

When he looks back up, multiple emotions cross Cole's handsome face. "I'll admit that I'm not sure if I want all of my old life back, but I do know that I don't want to lose the relationships I've made during my time here at West Enterprises," Cole haltingly admits.

Not knowing what to say, I diplomatically respond with a small smile on my face, "Let's just face all that if we get there, okay? We need to save your life first and foremost. That's the most important thing right now."

Cole nods in understanding and we both turn to face the ocean. I can still sense the unease radiating off him, so I gently rest my hand on his shoulder. Whether or not he is consciously aware of it, he immediately leans into my touch, his body communicating with me more than anything we ever discussed verbally. I file that away as I feel the muscles in his neck and shoulders release as he takes a deep breath while we stay gazing over the waves. We eventually both lean on each other, propping one another upright, soothed by the rhythmic waves and the calming quiet twilight.

***

After Cole felt comfortable enough to share his story with me, he and I seem to have gotten closer, more than I could have ever predicted. I don't know when the feelings started, not the precise moment in time, but I don't want to kill Cole anymore, which is a mass improvement for me. I like having him around, so much so that when this is all over, I may even miss him. My sense of duty and logic is starting to mess with what I can only guess is my thawing heart. I begin to withdraw into myself and everyone seems to take notice.

I'm trying to figure out what to do, I'm at the proverbial crossroads of life, having an existential crisis, and in this instance, unfortunately, no one can help me decide what to do next. My heart, of course, is finally rearing its ugly head during the midst of a contract, especially with all of my brothers closely watching my every move. In my desire to find solid ground, I stop interacting with my brothers and Cole, skipping meals and working out alone during odd hours of the night. Alone is how I have always been, even surrounded by my brothers. But now, since I've been hanging out with all of them and getting to know them on a deeper, interpersonal level, all this has only added to my deep level of confusion. Even Will is surprisingly concerned for my well-being. I see his looks out of the corner of my eyes whenever I hastily breeze through a room. I hear my brothers whispering about me when I leave or enter a room, the stilted and halted conversations abruptly cut off followed by the interminable silence. The chasm's gap grows every day, with every word not spoken and every gaze averted.

What my brothers all don't understand is that I am faced with a moral dilemma extending beyond Cole Harris' contract, but also that I need to reconcile my dark past with where I want my future to be. Two monumental decisions. And unfortunately, it's a decision that only I can make. My brothers don't understand how monumental leaving something that was a dream behind can end up being the best thing to happen for you. How everything can fall into place and surpass your wildest dreams. But to make that decision, it takes grit and courage. You have to make peace with your dream no longer being this esoteric and beautiful thing, that maybe it has turned into a nightmare without you even noticing. But this decision starts to cause me to begin to spiral, consuming me and creating scenarios of conflict that only exist in my head. Conflict which also leads me to scrutinize every contract elimination that I've ever done, and for the first time in my entire life, I'm second guessing myself and all of my decisions that I've made over the years.

Instead of focusing on those around me, I throw myself into figuring out the Cole Harris contract, disassociating through distraction. Something isn't right. To be frank, the entire situation isn't adding up, it hasn't been for a while now and we all know it. I know my brothers have spent hours trying to research and recreate all the possible scenarios that has led us to our current predicament. But no matter how much time and effort they've put in, they're still no closer to the answer than the day we brought Cole home from The Bailey. Cole Harris, on paper and in real life, is a diametrical paradox and he wouldn't be a target of this substantial magnitude based upon the information we already found. So, I make the decision that we need new details and information, there has to be something else that can help solve the why behind this contract. I contact a couple of police officer friends that I have in the Bronx and I confirm Cole's story. Cole was never interviewed as a witness by the police department, since he never came forward after the crime. I confirm to my contacts that Cole is safe and I promise my friends that he'd come in so they could take his official statement. Thankfully, there's no rush on bringing Cole in, the police already have the evidence they need for their case, Cole coming in would just be a formality.

All of this confirms that there's no official police report with his name on it, so where someone would get Cole's specific name from to target him is unbeknownst to me. My police department friends weren't even aware that there was a witness until I called and I had to talk them down from wanting to interview Cole immediately. The officers did confirm that the crime Cole briefly saw was indeed a murder, but the current investigation pointed to a drug deal gone bad scenario. Nothing that would trigger a contract where the payment for Cole's life is in the two-million-dollar range. What looks to be like a run of the mill drug-related murder where everything is cleared up, the case will end up being an open and shut case for the Bronx district attorney. And yet, Cole Harris is still caught in the crosshairs of assassins and being hunted like a nefarious drug lord. I know I'm obsessing about the details of this case and contract, but I'm trying to trust my gut. I know my family is concerned about me, but I need to understand why Cole is the target so I can trace back to whom the threat first originated from for this hit.

Late one night, I'm sitting on my balcony off my room, drinking a glass of white wine, my feet propped up on the railing. I hadn't joined everyone at dinner and had opted to watch the sunset alone instead of on the deck with Cole and my brothers, breaking the family tradition of a few rounds of beer in the dying light. I hear Dave as he comes into my bedroom, knowing full well that he is being louder than necessary for the sole purpose of not putting me on high alert. After a quiet but slightly conspicuous knock, I hear him come through the open French doors. I don't say anything or turn my head toward my brother as he takes a seat next to me in the other Adirondack chair. For at least ten minutes, my twin says nothing. But I know he took in the wine, my disheveled appearance and the shadows that have been lingering under my eyes.

The tension easily becomes insufferable. Dave finally breaks the silence. "You're off," he easily states after the silence has been unbearably uncomfortable.

"Don't, Dave," I harshly warn, trying my best to reign in my temper, "I'm trying to sort this all out."

"I know you won't admit out loud to feeling something for Cole, even though it's obvious to all of us that you do," Dave continues on as if I hadn't spoken at all. He continues after my blatant eye roll, "You're questioning your former contracts because maybe, just maybe, your dossiers on those targets were also incorrect."

When I don't reply and continue to stare out over the ocean, Dave comes to the realization of what I've been grappling with this whole time. "Lexi," he gasps out, "you really feel something! You're feeling guilt!"

I bristle but I don't deny his revelation. I know better than to deny it, Dave of all people would just see through that sad attempt. So, I settle with just looking at him, with an expression that I'm sure is mixed with anxiety, sadness, confusion and resignation.

"I haven't felt anything in years," I decidedly admit out loud, finally voicing everything that I've been trying to compartmentalize for days, but ultimately failing. I pause, futilely shaking my head in defeat. I take a deep breath before I continue on, "I can't. Not in my line of business, not if I want to stay alive. I have to do everything methodically and move on to the next contract without remorse or other emotions. I can't afford to second-guess myself either. Why do you think I accept so many contracts a year? Being that busy helps one not to have to think or feel, you don't have to process everything that you're doing. You're simply existing and surviving. But now that I've met Cole and have gotten to know him—I'm doubting my entire career and purpose—my entire life. What if I killed other innocent people just because a piece of paper said that that person deserved it? I didn't research into the person or complete a due diligence check. That wasn't part of how I was trained nor is it written in the procedures our company has in place for people with my specialized skill set. I just say okay, I do the job and move on to the next contract. The very monsters I thought that I was eliminating is the very thing I may have become."

Dave shakes his head. "You're not a monster, Lexi. You're human, a good human. You're allowed to make mistakes, even in your business. Don't be so hard on yourself. You can't change what you've done in your past, but you can change who you will choose to be going forward in the future."

I counter, glossing over his philosophical response as I say, "But what if this is the only thing that I'm good at? Killing people, eliminating threats?

What if, to assuage the guilt, I find that I don't have a place in the world outside of terminations?

Dave pauses as I watch him collect his thoughts. He seems to know, just as I do, the importance of what he's going to say next. Finally, my twin looks up at me, his eyes so similar to mine that it's like looking in the mirror. His expression is one of cautious admiration as he responds, "I know a little bit about a lot of things, that's what makes me dangerous. But you... you know the deepest parts of what seems like everything. You always have. And that's what makes you deadly. That's what makes you extraordinary. No matter what you choose to do, you'll never be able to dim your light or abilities. If you choose to stay within terminations or look beyond that, you will be successful. That I have no doubts about, and I'm sure our brothers share the same sentiments."

I look over at him and briefly nod. I feel like this is a decent reply to such a life-changing and startling revelation on my behalf. But I know that my twin means it, he's not just feeding me a line. Suddenly, I'm exhausted. Maybe it is the wine. Maybe it was the unusual regurgitation of all my feelings. Maybe, just maybe, this lifestyle isn't becoming of me anymore. Maybe I knew all along that one day, I'd eventually have to face all of these emotions and transform myself into the next iteration of who I am. Perhaps it's time to change. We all deal in the currency of time. But moving outside of the death business is a daunting concept to stomach. For me, death has always been easy. Living with my consequences, well that's another story entirely.

PART III

Alexandra West

The sense of people nearby cuts through my dreamless sleep. I usually don't dream. I actually can't remember the last time that I had anything remotely close to a dream. As I become more aware of my surroundings, I can hear the waves of the ocean below crashing into the beach while the seagulls fill the skies with their squawking to each other about their meals and territory. I can smell the salt water and coffee that has wafted up to the second floor, permeating through my restless slumber. I feel the warm breeze on my skin and the sun's rays glancing on my face. All of these normal smells and sounds have become like white noise when I sleep, so why am I awake?

Suddenly, I'm alerted to the fact that I'm not alone, my senses kicking in as I feel the presence of my five brothers, though I'm not sure which ones are the closest to me. From the sounds of their voices and quickly calculating their approximate distance from me to the hall, I figure that they're most likely hiding behind the barely cracked open bedroom door, positioning themselves right outside my bedroom door in the second-floor hallway. I can hear them all talking in low volumes with an intense sense of urgency tinging their words. As my brain clears, I zero in on exactly what is being said.

I can hear what Dave is saying as he enthusiastically effuses, "I spoke to her last night. She admitted to feeling, guys. She was feeling guilt!"

Will gruffly takes an audible sip of what I can probably only guess is his third cup of coffee of the morning before he asks with only a hint of barely contained disbelief, "What the hell do you mean, feeling? What, she's becoming human again?"

"Guilt over what, exactly?" Sean states in disbelief and realization, ignoring our older brother's sarcastic barbs, "She's feeling emotions!"

"Exactly, Sean. She admitted to feeling emotions. And she was always human, Will," I hear Dave reveal excitedly with only a slight tinge of condescension in his voice as he addresses Will.

Will gives out a humph as he mutters, "She's closer to being a robot than she is to being a human."

"Dude, chill," Luke responds to my eldest brother, the exasperation blatantly evident in his tone.

"Shit!" Kev exclaims. "She hasn't openly acknowledged feeling anything in years. Not since Dad died. Do you really think it's true?"

Dave remarks with a slight edge of doubt creeping into his voice, since our brothers are giving him the third degree, "Well, maybe."

"What do you mean, maybe? Is she feeling something or not?" Will exasperatedly asks, looking for definitive proof one way or the other.

Dave replies, "Last night, she talked about how she was questioning all of her previous contracts. She is having trouble reconciling her past with our current situation and her relationship with Cole. The file she received gave her information that she is finding inconsistent and that's been weighing on her mind ever since The Bailey. And we still don't know what her own intel report contained; we aren't exactly privy to that level of information. Lexi is struggling, sorting all the details out and dealing with the emotions that come along with it. But this is the most I have ever sensed that she was recognizing her emotions and allowing herself to actually feel them. She's unsettled, thinking she murdered innocent people like Cole, just blindly following orders. But she also can't go back in time to verify her intel was correct. She's stuck in her own version of purgatory." Silence pervades as all of my brothers consider Dave's words.

Kev breaks the silence, "Wow. Well, I truly hope this is true. She's been so out of touch with her emotions for years. And after Dad died, she pretty much shut down her emotions and became a workaholic. I know every time

I try to talk to her, she just puts on her emotionless mask and responds automatically, giving me the answers she thinks that I want to hear."

After some thought, Luke voices, "She makes a good point though, for herself and for us. We have all received files and have followed orders blindly. What if we've been wrong and some of the people we've protected over the years were actually the bad guys? I can only imagine her guilt, since she hasn't been saving people but…" I feel like I can actually hear the gears working and turning over in each of my brothers' heads as they all mull over Luke's words.

While my brothers have been discussing my levels of guilt and emotions, I have been quietly and inconspicuously pulling on a pair of shorts and a tank top over a hot pink bikini. I quickly tie my hair in a messy ponytail and grab my sunglasses and beach bag. I stuff all my items along with my standard 9mm and my recent book into my bag, a book about the last Russian tsar and his family. My plan for the day is to lounge and relax on the beach, away from all of my thoughts and my nagging brothers. I set everything by the edge of the balcony steps next to my flip-flops which have been sitting on the balcony from where I left them last night.

Right as Luke finishes up verbally mulling over his thoughts, I roughly yank open my bedroom door so quickly that the door protests from its hinges. I level a hard stare at each of my brothers with a cold look. I can tell that they weren't expecting my confrontation as their faces betray their shock, shortly followed by the slight reddening of their cheeks from their embarrassment.

My gaze settles and finally lands on Dave and hardens. "While I always enjoy listening to my brothers analyze my level of emotions, or lack thereof," I begin, "I hardly want to hear it outside my bedroom door when I wake up first thing in the morning. Since it would be rude of me to ask each of you to displace yourselves, I am going to remove myself from this overtly toxic situation and go relax for the day at the beach. If you follow me, do not for one second think I won't shoot. And no, I won't kill, but you know I always aim to maim. Sockets, joints, enough to put you out of work and in a hospital bed for a good amount of time, let alone rehabilitation time? Do not mess with me. Understood?"

I pointedly look to each of my brothers to make sure that they're clearly getting my message. They each respond by nodding their heads, their eyes wide with knowing that I caught them red-handed with their hands in the proverbial cookie jar. Sean and Dave have the decency to look contrite by looking down at the ground, unable to meet my eyes. Luke and Kev's eyes are full of what I can only guess is sympathy or pity; both of which I hate. Only Will has the gall to look me dead on, but I can't fully make out his expression. Understanding? Compassion? From Will, I doubt I'm guessing the right emotions, regardless of how far we've come in repairing our relationship.

I give a curt but dismissive nod before I walk toward the partly open double French doors leading to my room's private balcony. I'm mulling over each of my brother's reactions, especially Will's as I reach down for my beach bag and flip-flops. I'm about to shoulder the bag when it's then that I feel something like a sledgehammer slam into my body. Whatever it is hits me and forces me to take a couple of staggering steps back. Slightly confused, it's then that my brain is able to pinpoint the tell-tale white-hot pain radiating from my left shoulder. I look down to my left and see the bloodied entrance wound from a bullet. The wound is hot now, but I know from experience that it will soon burn like a supernova wildfire in no time. Thankfully, it was a through-and-through, but that does little to comfort me as I instantly grab my nine and pull the balcony doors closed, preparing for an onslaught of bullets as I lock and deadbolt the French doors. I know this will do little to stop whatever fight is soon to barrel its way into my childhood home, but I know it'll slow whoever it is down for a fraction of a second, buying my family and me some much-needed time. I run into the empty central hallway of the house and shut my bedroom door after quickly locking it from the inside. Again, a locked door won't do much in the realm of protection, but I'm going to need as much time as I can get, especially if this is what I think it is.

By the time I turn around, I see all of my brothers poking their heads out of their respective bedroom doors, curious at the commotion. Upon seeing my injury, my brothers have each reached back into their rooms and drawn their preferred weapons out, providing protection and coverage while I get to safety, even though we can't see our enemies at this exact moment. All of this has happened in silence, all of us communicating like a well-oiled machine, each of us knowing the value of silence and how to use it to our advantage. Each of my brothers quickly assess my bleeding shoulder before I interrupt them. My thoughts instantly have turned to Cole.

"Let's move," I quietly command with force. When none of them move, presumably due to shock, I smack Luke on the arm and firmly speak to all of them, "I'm fine. It's a flesh wound. A through and through. We need to cover Cole. He's the target. He's the job. This is what it's all about, this is the moment where we all have to fight." At the second mention of Cole's name, and by the end of my impassioned little speech, the freezing spell seems to lift from the five of them and we all move into action as a united unit.

Will and Kev take point as I'm assimilated into the center of the group due to my injury. Dave stands on my compromised left, providing extra protection, since I'll most likely be favoring my right until I'm patched up. Out of all of my brothers, my twin is the one who will accurately anticipate my moves, aligning him to best support my weakened side. Sean and Luke bring up the rear as all of our weapons are drawn. As we move closer toward the center of the house, we all take tactical positions as we close and lock all of the bedroom doors on the way, keeping low to the ground and on high alert. We head toward Cole's room, moving as a fluid unit, and enter his room only to find the space empty. Cole isn't here. Panic shudders down my spine as Kev methodically closes and locks Cole's bedroom door before we continue to move forward into the house and down the staircase.

We stealthily make our way through the common areas and broker our steps toward the back of the house. It's in the kitchen where we find Cole, standing at the kitchen counter closest to the deck's French doors, making toast with his back to us. How seemingly domesticated and normal, Cole's completely unaware of the brewing war which is beginning to steadily surround us. My heart briefly constricts, not wanting to strip him of this peace and contentment, but knowing if we want to all make it out of this alive, Cole's going to have to see the ugly side of what my family and I do, and he's going to have to see it now. Cole turns with a smile on his face until he sees our weapons drawn, our crouched stances and the blood freely running down my arm.

"Alexis, what happened—" he begins, concern marring his handsome features.

"No time," I quickly explain. "Let's go. We've gotta move. Now." I walk over to him with Kev and Sean flanking me as we provide coverage for him.

As we move toward Will, Dave and Luke who are standing just outside of the secret basement safe room door, Cole does a good job at masking his surprise as West Enterprises gives up an espionage secret unknown to outsiders. Luke enters his own personal security code on the door's electronic security panel and leads us down the stairs through the door disguised as a wall of photographs of the West family. While Will latches and locks the false wall behind us, the rest of us quickly descend down the stairs into the heart of the safe room. Cole looks around the space, taking in the miniature apartment-like room that is the formerly converted basement while the rest of us stay in motion. Luke, Kev, Sean and Dave automatically pair up and split up as they continue down the two main, separate hallways, making sure the area is truly empty. I go over to the stashed first aid kit, packing my wound with gauze with only a slight wince showing my discomfort. The entire time I'm keeping a watchful eye on Cole as I see this space just as he is for the first time.

The basement floor plan is divided into four main areas: security containment, the armory, personal living quarters and a functional professional area. The security area and personal living quarters branch off of the fully functional professional area, and the décor is in shades of grays. In the living quarters, there are four bedrooms and two full bathrooms off to the right, down the gray hallway that is softly illuminated. Going down the left hallway will lead you to the containment cells. While they're very rarely used, in case of an emergency, we have a cordoned off area where persons of interest or suspects can be detained. Each of the six, glass-walled cells contain a concrete-base day bed, a small sink, toilet and minimal linens. The hallway's security is top-notch with motion sensors and cameras strategically placed to alert of any breach of cell doors. The cells are placed crosswise from each other, so detainees don't have a direct line of sight into neighboring cells. The natural curve of the area's design helps to enhance the feeling of being sequestered while dim lighting illuminates the hallway's path. The last sub-hallway that is nestled in between the containment cells and the living quarters is the armory. Within the armory, all of our weapons, repair kits and go-bags are stored under biometric lock and key. Additionally, there is a mini gun range for target practice so live-in and special visiting agents can stay sharp on their marksmanship.

In the center of our bunker is the main hub made up of a sitting area containing an enormous navy blue sectional, large enough to seat twelve, a sizable table with benches placed further into the room in the left-hand corner and a series of TVs mounted on the wall. The minimalist kitchen is fully stocked and the pantry is full, the black granite countertops are clear and clean, positioned against the back of the room. All of the electronics and internet service runs on a different power source, separate from the house.

"There's no place like home," Dave mutters under his breath as he checks his weapons and cocks both of his guns.

Will rolls his eyes as he strides over to the wall of TVs. He turns on the screens while he simultaneously brings up all the cameras in the house, showing the multiple points of entry and the camera angles that cover them, searching for possible intruders and threats.

Glancing over to Cole, I fill him in, "It's soundproofed down here and there's full electricity with separate backup generators from the main power line. This area is off the blueprints filed with the county, so there are very few who know it exists outside of the West siblings and select West agents. Now, if you're going to be okay for a few minutes, I need to go clean this out." I nod to my shoulder wound and head toward the right hallway leading to the bathrooms.

"I'll help you," Dave quickly offers, taking a step to follow me.

I shake my head, still not ready to deal with my twin's invasion of privacy by oversharing my emotions to our brothers without my permission. I thought our conversation was confidential and my terse reply shows it. "I got it, thanks," as I turn away from my twin.

I turn to look over my right shoulder, glancing back at Cole who finally acknowledges in shock, "You got shot."

What a revelation, my sarcastic mind responds, my patience thinning because I know time is of the essence and I'm not one who enjoys the feeling of my blood dripping down my arm. "Yes, Cole. I got shot. A sniper got me." I patiently say. "This isn't the first time I've been hit with a bullet, and it probably won't be the last time. But it's nothing major. I'm going to go clean it out and bandage myself up. I'll be back in five. Make yourself at home, okay?"

During this time, Luke has gone to stand next to Will, discussing strategy, no doubt, as they both take notes on what they're seeing on the screens. Kev and Sean have finished clearing all the rooms, ensuring that no one has found our safe room and is now lying in wait, preparing to ambush us while we are reposed. I pass by Sean and Kev as I make my way to the bathroom, with the first aid kit I pulled from the kitchen in hand. My two brothers nod at me, Sean with a knowing smile and Kev with an older brother's concerned look. I go to the first bathroom down the hallway and close the door.

It's then that I take a good look at myself in the mirror. I look tired and on edge, but it's the flash and glimmer of fear in my eyes that scare me the most. Fear. I haven't felt the tendrils of terror for over fifteen years. I don't know if I'll remember how to deal with this, but I need to compartmentalize the emotion and put it away until the threat is neutralized. I shake my head and look at my shoulder, focusing on the task at hand. *Concentrate, Alexandra, there's work to do.* I keep telling myself that mantra on repeat as I pack my injury, hastily stitching myself up and securing gauze over the wound.

My shoulder, though stiff, is stitched and bandaged up as I make my way back to the sitting area. I know that I'll eventually have to go to the hospital to properly treat the wound and get antibiotics to combat a potential bacterial infection. I fire a text off to the medical staff at our preferred medical hospital and move to rejoin everyone in the main hub. I'll also need to eventually change out of a bikini. Thank goodness all of us West kids have a couple outfits stored down here, since it's not safe for me to go back upstairs to my bedroom. Will had switched the cameras to local news with the house's security views on constant surveillance in the bottom left-hand corner. I grab a drink from the small fridge in the kitchen and unceremoniously plop down next to Luke on the couch.

"Hey Sissy, you good?" Luke asks as he drapes an arm carefully over my good shoulder. I give my brother a wan smile as I readjust my position so my bad shoulder is angled out as I lean into Luke's side, using my older brother's build as leverage and support. Dave tries to meet my eyes, but I keep them diverted, focusing, instead, on the news and cameras.

Will looks over at me with something close to worry in his eyes. He looks at my shoulder, then my face. "You good?" he asks. I nod my head in confirmation. "Good," my oldest brother responds, something close to relief in his voice and some of the lines of tension around his eyes instantly fading.

Kev turns his attention over to me as he lets out an amused suggestion, "Hey, Lex, you may want to change. I'm not sure how tactically protective a bikini is."

I roll my eyes as I respond, "Duh, Kev. Good one." The tension in the room breaks with everyone letting out a round of chuckles, a much-needed distraction from the severity of the situation we have found ourselves in.

Getting down to business and redirecting our attention, Will gently commands everyone's attention before saying, "I may have some news. It looks like our unwanted guests are in the process of surrounding us, probably tracked our movements over the past couple of weeks and coordinated their attack from behind the scenes. Nothing is on the local police department's radar yet, but I'm thinking it'll only be a matter of time before they're here at our door. Kev already texted the local captain, letting her know that we may need additional backup. I'm guessing that there are multiple teams, working together, to take us down and try to get a shot off at Cole in the process, given the contract payment amount. That's why they took so long to launch their attack on us. There were too many moving parts to organize and coordinate, too many interested parties who had to reign in various alpha egos, especially when none of them are used to working with each other. Another point to consider is the fact that we're all aware of is that there are multiple contracts on each of our heads too, for various reasons. This only adds to further complicate our adversaries' current situation, since additional parties will be interested in exacting revenge on us. It's known by all that Alex West has partnered with the rest of the West brothers. We'll all be in the same place at the same time, a rare West occasion."

As we all nod in agreement and understanding, I stand up and walk over to look at the surveillance pictures Will had printed out and laid out on the large table. After a quick analysis, I explain, "It looks like three teams. You can definitely confirm that they've never worked together, just by looking at their sloppy formations. The larger of the teams is probably surrounding the south and west sides, with the second team taking up their positions on the east side to box us in. They'll probably try to get us to go toward the ocean where, undoubtedly, the last team will be positioned to pick us all off on the beach."

"How do you know all of that with just those photos?" Cole asks incredulously.

"Because," I simply answer, "it's what I would do." Cole's eyes widen to the size of saucers as I continue, "The six of us can't take them all down, no matter how strong we are. Especially with my injury and someone needing to keep an eye on Cole. We need backup. We need help."

Will nods in agreement as he continues to expand upon my very thought, "Call in your favors and contacts that you've each made over the years. These teams aren't going to go easy on us; we need to return the favor. They're still figuring out their strategy, thankfully, that buys us some much needed time. We got lucky with Alexandra getting shot, no offense. But they showed their hand too early, and now we know that they aren't ready. We have time, not a lot, but we have some time. Tell your contacts to come to West Enterprises, hot and fast. Everyone will need to use the old subway and sewer tunnels to enter West Enterprises, otherwise our allies will get picked off before they can receive a sitrep and instructions. Our lives are all on the line."

As my brothers start calling, texting and emailing their people, I text the one person I know who would never accept a contract on me or my family: Stephen Wallace. Steve is an old family friend, entirely vetted and trusted with our family's secrets. He was close with Luke growing up before they lost touch. I met and grew close to Steve later after I graduated from high school. Both Steve and Luke were gigantic mammoths of men who bonded over the ability to be able to roughhouse with minimal injuries when they were younger in school. But eventually Steve's career took a turn. Steve went through some pretty hard personal struggles, which redirected his life and career track into a groove that's now more similar to my professional experience. I hadn't met Steve until we were in boot camp together. It was in the mud and dirt where Steve and I came to an understanding, which then led to the close friendship that we have today. I shoot Steve a text, knowing that wherever he is, he'll do his best to get here in time.

AW: Hey. Are you in or near NYC?

SW: No. Upstate. Why, what's up?

AW: We have an emergency at West Enterprises.

SW: Shit, on my way. Can you hold them off?

AW: For now. Time is short.

SW: Casualties? Injuries?

AW: Nothing major. Shoulder: mine. I'm fine.

SW: Shit. Specs?

AW: Three teams, surrounding HQ. South, west and east. Funneling to the north shore. Known shots fired: north. Sniper.

SW: ETA one hour. Hold it down until I get there. I'll pick up Edwards on my way down.

AW: Got it, Wallace. Thanks.

SW: West?

AW: Yeah?

SW: Be careful. Stay alive.

AW: Always.

I look up at my phone and announce to the group, "Steve's coming, maybe with a friend. ETA one hour." Luke looks excited, like a happy Saint Bernard puppy dog thrilled at the prospect of seeing his best friend while Will audibly sighs in relief. "Status updates?" I call out and look around at all of my brothers.

Kev, seemingly answering for all of them, says, "We will have ground teams in two hours, consisting of twenty agents, but they're working on scrambling to be here for a quicker arrival time. Sean and Will called in some of their favors. Luke and I can't get ahold of our contacts but we're still trying. And Dave is still waiting to hear back from his old military buddies—"

"They're on their way. Add seven more to that count," Dave interrupts as he disconnects a call.

"With Steve and Edwards, that's twenty-nine. So, there's thirty-five of us," Kev concludes, nonplussed at my twin's interruption.

"Thirty-six," Cole boldly proclaims, inserting himself into the mix.

Will, smothering his chuckle, tries as politely as he can to ask, "Oh and you're our thirty sixth man? You do realize that you are the target and putting you on a team will only endanger yourself and all of us?"

Cole looks down at his feet, some of his bravado fading as he realizes the bigger picture. My heart goes out to him, Will is right but still, my older brother's delivery leaves much to be desired. Cole apologetically responds, "No, I didn't think about that. I guess we all know that I'm out of my depth. But I can't allow you all to risk your lives for me when I'm not willing to do the same for all of you."

Sean inquisitively asks, "Do you have any training? Weapons, fighting, firearms proficiency?"

Defiantly, Cole responds, "I took a couple self-defense classes."

Laughter erupts from my brothers as Kev regains his composure before he states in a gentler tone, "You would need to be the aggressor in this type of situation, not passively waiting for an attack. You have to be willing to take a life so yours isn't stolen from you. Do you understand what I'm saying, Cole? Could you do that?"

Cole silently shakes his head in the negatory sense as his posture slumps over.

"I'll cover him. He can be assigned with my team," I interject, surprising myself with my response. Cole's head, and all my brothers' heads for that matter, whips around so quickly I'm surprised that no one gets whiplash in the process. I am commanding everyone's attention in the room.

"Steve and I will take and cover him. He very well can't be a sitting duck. These teams are expecting us to leave him behind. We'd be playing right into their hands if we don't keep him closely guarded on a team. Someone needs to have his back, keep him moving around like a ghastly version of the city's con artist's shell game. And we need to wait for an hour or two anyways. While everyone else works on our strategic plan of attack, I'll teach him how to hold, handle and cycle weapons, a crash course of sorts into our world," I reason. My brothers look at me in astonishment, jaws soundlessly opening and closing, probably remembering this morning's hallway conversation, while Cole looks excited to be considered a part of our team.

***

After spending an hour in the gun range, I feel comfortable enough with Cole's skills to give him a loaded gun and a couple of extra clips. Cole has been able to quickly pick up some of the tips I showed him, efficiently mastering the basic skills of handling a weapon. I briefly consider if he would ever be interested in applying to be a West agent once all this nonsense is over with. Cole may have a future in the personal security business, maybe it's in his genes as his father runs a similar business on the West Coast. From my intel reports, Cole has never had any involvement with his father's company. I wonder if that's because it's hard to work with family or that he has a lack of interest in the security world. But I file those thoughts away, there's too much to already think about and get through first. When this is all over, maybe we can discuss that conversation over coffee, or perhaps a nice dinner. Wait what? Am I thinking of going on a date with Cole Harris? Well, that certainly is a new development. Maybe it's the adrenaline speaking, but I could see myself going out to dinner with Cole and having a great time. Well, first things first. *Focus on the job Alexandra, before you get too ahead of yourself*, I remind myself. I need to make sure Cole can go out in public again without a target on his back or getting a bullet lodged in his head. Cole, my brothers and I have to get through all of this and right now, that means focusing on the task at hand and on staying alive.

After we cleaned everything up in the armory, Cole and I walk back down the hallway and enter into the common area. As soon as we cross the threshold, I hear Kev address me by asking, "Is he ready?"

I nod before confidently saying in response, "He will be."

Kev briefly smiles at me before turning his attention back to the security screens with intense scrutiny, looking for any breaches to West Enterprises with Will and Sean. I turn to Cole, whose face is smiling broadly, proud of his accomplishments.

Suddenly, Cole's facial expression turns from excitement to anxiety as the hairs on the back of my neck signal a presence coming to stand directly behind me. A hand on my non-wounded shoulder signals that it is my friend, Stephen Wallace, as I feel a warm smile cross my face.

I turn around with an abnormally, out of character squeal to greet my old friend. "Steve!" I gleefully exclaim as I jump into his arms and embrace my old boot camp buddy.

Stephen Wallace is the definition of a tall, dark and handsome man. His coffee dark toned skin only serves to compliment his sharply attuned and striking gray eyes. Steve stands at 6'6" and his large, muscular build makes me feel like I'm a doll that's only two inches tall. But he's one of my closest friends from back in the day and I know that I can innately trust him. Steve knows all of my family's dynamics because he knows Luke. And for that contextual knowledge, I'm glad that he's here.

I notice Jace Edwards standing just behind Steve, a mutual friend that I have through Steve. I had spoken to Jace a few weeks ago, asking if he would be interested in joining West Enterprises. For the past year, I have been formulating a venture that I have yet to propose to my brothers. But it would expand the company's business to have a formalized segment of eliminations that would extend beyond me. Jace and Steve are freelancers right now, but both of their interests have been piqued at the thought of joining West Enterprises, specifically in the elimination line of business.

When I first met Stephen Wallace, we were running an obstacle course exercise during my brief stint in boot camp. My military career swiftly ended when I was drafted out of boot camp to do some off the books wetwork for one of the ABC agencies in Washington. But before I was plucked from the mud and grime, I was a young woman in yet another male-dominated industry with a chip on her shoulder and something to prove. We were running obstacle drills and were paired off against another person to instigate competition and fierce motivation. The group that I was a part of lined up in two separate lines to race each other throughout the course. Many of the other members were grumbling about how my smaller size would give me an advantage in the barbed wire section of the course. Other guys were condemning my participation, saying that a girl shouldn't be running with the proverbial big male alpha dogs, which of course pissed me off even more. But that type of anger only fueled me and made me feel like I had to double my efforts to prove myself to everyone. I never said it out loud, but I had my brothers to thank for that type of response, I grew up with them saying those types of things to me. So, these boot camp idiots were nothing compared to my family.

Steve almost initially reminded me of Will, actually. A large guy, judging me and looking down on me from over his nose without taking a second to assess before categorizing. I was still determined to prove myself

105

to those around me at the wise and mature age of eighteen, to show that I had earned my right and that I deserved to be there just like the rest of them.

As I got closer to the course's starting line, I looked over at the second line and quickly calculated with whom I would be facing off with. I see this huge man whose uniform identification said Wallace and cockily thought I had this win in the bag. An obstacle course like the one I was about the run needed agility where someone of a smaller stature could easily maneuver around in, comparatively to a larger and bulkier guy. Thankfully, I didn't show my cards and gloat like the rest of the guys were doing pre-course.

Ultimately, I did win in the end, but not by as much as I thought I would. Wallace, or Steve, could move surprisingly fast for a big guy. He and I were often neck and neck until we got to the obstacle where you had to crawl under the barbed wire in a foot of mud. Being smaller in this case had its advantages. I slid through that course like a snake on the hunt and ran to the last obstacle, which focused on core and leg strength. The obstacle required the runner to lift up various doors, dead weight style, to progress forward. Unfortunately, those doors and the weights of said doors increased the closer the runner got to the finish line. My smaller size and smaller capacity for upper body strength became my disadvantage as I started to struggle with lifting the increasingly heavy objects way over my head in order for me to continue to advance toward the finish line. I sensed Steve approaching the last door and I gave it all I had. Adrenaline got me the win that day, but I also gained a close friend and ally in Steve, and the respect of the men watching from the sidelines. The majority of them came up to congratulate me with genuine expressions and words, each welcoming me into the fold and accepting me as one of them. A few of them expressed that they were impressed with my final push to not only finish the course, but to win. Of course, there were a few that still grumbled about my gender, but I blamed that on them being jealous and misogynistic as I finished with one of the top five finishing times in the course's history.

From that moment at the finish line of the obstacle course, I knew Steve and the other guys that day admired me. I remember thinking a few times after that day that Steve may even have had a crush on me as we got to know each other and built our friendship. But I never doubted that he not only respected me, but honored me as well, regardless that our relationship never turned into an authentic, romantic connection. Luke had really liked Steve when he met him years ago, strictly by coincidence, when they were in high school. Neither Steve nor my brother knew that I was a connection between the two of them until I invited them both out for a weekend drink and they were reunited when we all met up at a bar in Greenwich. Based upon Luke's friendship and Steve's squeaky-clean record, I knew I'd have my brothers' blessing for my new friendship, partnership and alliance.

But unfortunately for my family, Steve wasn't my type on a romantic level. When my brothers met him, aside from Luke, they all liked him, and they also liked him for me. What my type is, still to this day, I have no clue. I'm still figuring that out for myself as I go. I've always been focused on my career and considering that I wasn't expecting to live this long, I didn't want any proverbial relationship loose ends. But I do think that if I ever decide to settle down, I believe that I wouldn't want that person to be in the same line of business as me.

I'm a lifer in this business, and I know that I'm jaded and cynical in a lot of different areas. Then again, how do you meet someone in this city? Usually, it's whom you work with, people in the office or part of your commute or routines that you form a bond with. So over time, I amended my relationship ideology to someone who isn't a fellow lifer. An agent, yes, but maybe someone who doesn't do exactly what I do, or what my brothers do for that matter. That may change over time, but I never felt the way that Steve maybe once felt for me. It would be unfair to either one of us to try to pursue a relationship that wouldn't be on level ground. I do have to admit though, Steve is beautiful, with a model-like face and an impressive physique. But my first memory of him is back to the time when he was muddy, covered in blood, being a jerk. Not exactly the image to stir loving emotions in this girl's heart.

Steve tightly hugs me back, enough so that my feet lift off the ground, the combined motion putting unnecessary pressure and muscular pull on my shoulder wound. Dave, ever my protector, notices my slight wince and tells Steve to reign himself back in. Steve releases me like I'm poison and automatically looks to my shoulder. "Are you okay, Aly?" he anxiously asks.

"Yes," I respond, rolling my eyes at the unnecessary concern, "I'm fine. And don't call me Aly. We've talked about this a few times now, that was my boot camp alias. Besides, you didn't have to drop me like a hot potato. I won't break, you know."

"Oh, I know," Steve begins to tease with an annoying smile and twinkling eyes. "I've seen you in worse conditions and you still kept going."

Resisting the urge to roll my eyes out of my skull, I ask Steve, "How'd you get in?"

"Who else," Steve says, continuing with his light tone, "your shadow, Dave."

I see Cole begin to posture as he shows that he's unsure of who Steve is. I shake my head in warning, motioning a slight head nod over to Cole. "Steve!" Luke interrupts, in classic Luke form, as my brother walks over and claps Steve in a man-hug before I can say anything else, more so to introduce Cole.

"It's been too long," Steve mutters during their quick embrace. Steve pulls back and looks around at our living space and nods a greeting to each of my brothers. "I came through the old tunnel system, noticed a few pulling up to the covert access point I used to get here by way of the sewers. Just so you Wests know. I brought Jace Edwards, Aly said that'd be okay," Steve explains.

My brothers all nod, shaking Jace's hand and thanking him for coming. Steve is one of the few persons outside the West family who knows there's a safe area below ground level, most of our agents don't even know this space exists. This space was specifically designed as a protective measure exclusively for the West family. Before today, Steve was the only non-West entrusted with codes down into our subterranean abode, even though he was escorted down by my twin.

"Edwards, good to see you," I say as I step forward and offer my hand to Jace Edwards, hopefully a future West agent.

Standing at one inch over six feet tall, Jace has to look down to meet my eyes, his blond hair falling into his face, just barely covering his piercing blue eyes. "Likewise, West," Jace responds as he firmly grasps my hand with his own tattooed hand.

From the reports we've internally run, I know Jace is covered from head to toe in ink, his body a work of art, expressing the pain of his past and the triumphs he's accomplished. Usually for covert agents, we try to be as unidentifiable as possible. But Jace Edwards would be an exception, that's for sure. He's not afraid to do the tasks and contracts others would hesitate to take on. Steve has shared with me that Jace has gotten out of multiple jams because he has mastered the ability to talk his way out of anything. Jace certainly would be an asset as he speaks multiple languages, his personality fluidly adaptable to whatever the situation warrants. Selfishly, the way Jace acts reminds me of me. And if I'm going to build the elimination side of West Enterprises, I'm going to need the right people in place so we can be successful.

I know today will be an audition of sorts, us Wests auditioning Jace to see if he wants to join West Enterprises full-time. I've seen Jace's skills in action, quietly watching in the background as he's done his work. Steve had identified him as a potential agent a year ago after the two men met in some conflict-ridden jungle overseas. Steve had jokingly referred to him as the male version of Alex West, since Jace can also turn off his emotions and brain to focus when he's on the job.

Now, Steve is watching our interaction with a slight smirk on his face. Steve knows that I've had my eye on Jace to help build out my side of the business at West Enterprises, and that although I've been watching Jace Edwards, we have never formally met until this point. I'm sure Steve planned this professional matchmaking session well in advance. I meet Steve's eyes as my friend morphs his face into a mask of innocence. I elbow his ribs as I pass by Steve, walking back over so I'm closer to Cole.

Steve's gaze finally finds and lands on Cole, who I now turn my gaze to as my attention has followed my friend's perusal around the room. What

I can't understand is why Cole is standing with a straight back and clenched fists, like he's about to beat his chest and attack Steve. Steve could easily kick Cole's ass in a second, training or no training. Steve has at least seventy-five pounds of pure muscle on him, let alone a good amount of height and experience. Cole doesn't know what kind of threat Steve really is. In return, Steve looks amused but he doesn't say anything. It's then I realize they're sizing each other up. For fuck's sake, now is not the time for a male testosterone-fueled pissing contest.

"Steve, Jace," I diplomatically begin, bringing the attention of the room back to center upon me. "This is Cole Harris. The intended target."

Steve thankfully wipes the amused albeit condescending smile off his face as he offers his hand which Cole begrudgingly accepts, both men clasping the other's hand in greeting. As Jace gives Cole a quietly assessing handshake, I continue by saying, "Will and Kev are working on the overall plan. You know, how we're going to all get out of this alive and in one piece. I just got back from giving Cole a crash course in murder." I hear a strangled sound from Cole's throat before I say, "I'm kidding, Cole."

"No, she's not," Luke says with a knowing smile and a teasing tone, his eyes twinkling with amusement.

Rolling my eyes, I return my attention to Steve and Jace as I say, "We're covering Cole. Others will be coming. I gave him a quick lesson on cycling a handgun. He's functional but will still need direct cover at all times. I need to repack my shoulder wound before all hell breaks loose."

"And you need to change," my eldest brother tosses in with a small smile on his face.

Looking down at the tee shirt covering my bikini, I nod as I respond to Will, "Cole and I need to clean all the weapons we shot in my quick lesson. And as Will so kindly pointed out, I clearly need to change. We'll be back in a few. Just yell down the hallway when you're ready or if you need us back early." I turn to face Cole, motioning him to follow me as the rest of our group continues planning our offensive attack while they bring Steve and Jace up to speed.

David West

I watch my twin walk away to the armory for the second time today, intentionally without me. The feeling of being unsettled has weighed heavily upon my shoulders since Cole and Lex's first trip down the hallway. Now I feel bereft and unmoored. I know she's upset about me sharing our private conversation from last night with the four guys. But our brothers need to know about her emotional evolution, especially with a battle closing in on us as fast as it is. Emotions can be a liability, especially for someone who is just starting to acknowledge those feelings for the first time in years. Her job, Lex's survival, has always depended on her deadening her emotional senses to do what she needs to do to survive.

When my sister was younger, she was told that she loved too deeply, too fiercely, too intensely. So she stopped. She turned off that part of her. To blend in, yes, but also to survive. Since then, she's done her best to hide those emotions. I know that sometimes she allows me to see the slivers that shine through. But underneath the tough and impassive exterior, I know that she looks for sparks and hope in the darkest and most dire of times. We were opposites, she and I, in that regard. But just as what's expected of us twins, we are always balanced.

None of us brothers are under the impression that her job is easy or safe. And whether my brothers will admit it or not, we all know she's been as successful as she has been over the years because she can remove emotions from a situation with practiced ease. Emotions popping up during a mission would be a dangerous liability, let alone for a mission that included elements of elimination. Lexi hasn't done a protection contract in a long while, and I'm sure she's concerned about how her defensive positioning could jeopardize Cole's safety and the viability of the mission's success.

Still, I don't like conflict, especially with my twin, and especially with the monumental task that's all coming for us. It is unnatural for Lexi and me to be out of sorts or at odds with each other in the best of situations. I notice the silence in the room that has followed with her departure. I look around at all the men in the room who are all closely watching me, waiting for my reaction and gauging my own emotional response. Sean gives me a knowing sympathetic look while Steve looks after her, his gaze tracking her movements. We all know that Steve romantically likes her but that she's never expressed any romantic interest in him. Poor guy. I turn my attention back to Will as he begins to go over and review our options to combat the threat looming outside and how we can keep Lexi, and Cole, safe.

Alexandra West

Even though I gave him a quick weapons training tutorial, I also made sure to show Cole some techniques on how to handle and defend himself if he were ever to find himself in a close quarter combat situation. He deftly handled the knives, moving his hands to match and mimic my routines during our quick session. I could see how he was dedicated to his self-defense training. I attributed some of his success to mastering those basics because of the skillset he had previously learned. I tailored my communication style with the syntax he would be familiar with hearing in those classes, although instead of teaching him to react, I was encouraging him to lash out and attack.

In our second stint in the armory, we reviewed what we had previously covered and talked about how if he would be comfortable enough to take a life in order to defend himself. I briefly war with telling him about my first kill, but I figure that's a different conversation for a different day. Instead, I quickly tell him how it may feel, what he should do in a forced, unfortunate situation. I instruct him to defer to me if that situation ever comes to pass. Unless I can't do it, I'll be pulling the trigger while Cole is able to dodge that moral, ambiguous quagmire. That's the least I could do, spare him the act of taking a life today. As we're finishing up in the armory, I can sense Cole wants to say something, but he's still choosing his words wisely. I focus on cleaning and reloading my weapons in patient silence while I wait for him to say what's on his mind, giving him the permission to take the time he needs for this moment.

"Alexis," he starts, "these past couple of weeks have been the scariest and the most intense weeks of my life. But if I didn't have you, I think I would've broken down or worse, that I would have been killed. I know this isn't the time or the place, but I feel something for you. I can't describe it. And maybe it's the fear of what's coming or the adrenaline talking. But do you feel anything for me?"

I briefly pause my cleaning as I think through his proclamation, but don't look up at him yet. I want to say my default answer: that I don't ever feel anything for anyone, it's just not who I am. But as I'm about to say those words, something holds me back. I suddenly come to the revelation that I do feel something, although I'm not quite sure what that something is. And Cole's right, now isn't the time. But maybe there is a future out there where I'm not alone, where I'm with someone who is my confidant, lover or best friend. Someone who knows exactly what I do and doesn't judge me for my past. Just maybe that could all be wrapped up in one person too.

Overcome with what Dave would call an 'intense emotional episode,' I look up at Cole and smile. "You're right," I slowly begin. "Now isn't the time. And to give some background context, this is the first time I've felt anything for anyone other than my brothers in a really long time. I still need to sort everything out, what it all means and put names and labels to these feelings. But maybe after this is over, we can grab a cup of coffee?"

Cole understandingly smiles as he nods. "I'd like that," he says before he leans in and gives me just a whisper of a kiss on my forehead. He breaks apart our contact, just looking at me with something akin to appreciation in his eyes.

Breaking the now awkward silence, I focus us back on our tasks of finalizing our weapon maintenance before we rejoin the melee in the common area. I think about the incoming invasion of West Enterprises, and everything we need to do to prepare in advance. I concentrate on weapons cleaning and say, "Cole, we need to clean all these guns if we're going to use them, and we don't want them to jam on us in the midst of everything." I'm at my limits with all these talks of emotions and feelings.

With a knowing look of understanding and endless patience, Cole gently asks, "How can I help?"

William West

I look around the room, knowing that I need to take the leadership role to get us all out of this mess. I also need to draw attention away from the growing tension between the twins. As unsettling as Lex and Dave's dissonance is, we need to redirect that energy in staying alive and maintaining the integrity of West Enterprises itself. This very threat could bring my father's, now my family's company down as well with destroying our childhood homestead.

I begin by addressing my brothers, Steve and Jace Edwards, "All right. As Lex said, the biggest threat is the south and west sides of the house."

Kev nods in understanding, picking up on my train of thought as he finishes my sentence, "Yes, and there's another angle to consider which is also on the east side. And the third team is probably stationed either on or by the water to pick us off on the north side, since that's the only area without an active team because they'd have to be on or in the water."

"And we'd know if they were already on the water because our US Coast Guard contacts would let us know. They're probably waiting last minute to get into position, as to not draw attention by the military," I finish in return for Kev, like we're playing tennis and volleying the conversation between us.

Nodding, Luke pipes up, "Exactly. If we can neutralize those threats around the house, we can then focus our energy of trapping those on the north side and reverse their plan on them."

"What about the house?" Steve is quick and wise to interject. There is a quick moment of silence after my youngest brother breaks the silence.

"The possibility of a home invasion is low, but it's still something that we all need to consider. The shot Lex took this morning was from a sniper, we all know that. From the angle, the bullet used and the angle trajectory, I know we all figured that out quickly. But where was that sniper stationed? Is that sniper still there? And where there's one sniper, there probably is at least a couple more," Sean suggests.

"Exactly. We need to ascertain where those snipers are stationed. We need satellite overlays to see who's lurking high up, even if they're in ghillie suits. That sniper shot is too close for my own comfort," Kev confirms as my brothers and I nod our heads in agreement.

Taking command of the conversation again, I continue, "There are many forms of security protecting the entrance to the house, both old-school and new age technology based. Electronic biometric screening, multiple layers of physical locks and barricades. A fully supported, self-sustaining surveillance system with multiple camera viewpoints. If people are going to try to breach the house, they would have to at least be as good as us. But we need to find that sniper, and any other sniper friends out there. You're right about that Kev. Or at least have a few snipers of our own to go up against them."

I think to myself that my sister is an excellent sniper and marksman, one of the best that we have at West Enterprises. I could always put her in that position. But she's also an amazing close quarter, hand-to-hand fighter, and we may need that too. We don't know exactly where the attacks will be coming from, she's a pinch hitter, to borrow a term from baseball. A week ago, I would have never admitted that she is one of our strongest utility team members, but now, it's all hands-on deck. I need to put my pride aside and do what's best so we all can stay alive. I shoot off an email to a friend of mine who has access to the satellite data above our heads. Kev is right, we need to find those snipers.

As the conversation is winding down, Dave finally asks the question I have been anticipating that he was going to ask. "Why can't Cole just stay here?" the elder twin says with a slightly petulant tone infusing his voice.

Before I can respond, Sean graciously and patiently interjects, "Because she's covering him. And all of us know that she won't agree to stay locked in a room. You of all people know that, Dave. Remember when we were kids and we'd all play hide and seek? She never stayed in one location for long."

I fondly remember those times, she was always tough to find because you could never keep her in one place for too long. "Exactly! She was always tough to pin down, since she was always changing her hiding locations, remember?"

Luke says as he echoes my thoughts, "She is fast too, a quick and agile runner."

Deep down, I know that she will be able to take care of Cole and herself. We all had to agree to that part of her plan, her covering Cole, that's how we got her buy-in. If we went back on our word, we'd never hear the end of it. And whatever trust she has in each of us would be decimated.

So, as I provide the strategic response, I summarize, "We'll have to divide into teams, each of us West siblings leading the teams so we're all on the same page while we pull our enemy's attention in multiple directions, drawing out their fire and splitting their teams and resources to allow her the time to safely move Cole around."

"Whatever the teams are, Lex and I are together. With Cole, she's going to need the extra assistance," Dave says, still sticking to his point and maintaining his sullenness.

Steve nods as he says, "Right. And she already let me know that Jace and I are coming with you, Dave."

Regaining control of the conversation, I conclude by saying, "I'll lead the east team and Luke, Sean and Kev—you will command the west and south teams. You three decide who will take lead on each of those teams. Now we'll just wait for everyone to arrive. Kev, we'll have to watch the covert entrances and let our teams in. Sean, do an inventory of weapons and see what else we need. Steve, you, Edwards and Dave barricade some of the weaker points of the house. Make sure that you're all armed when you go upstairs, watch each other's sixes. Luke, you and I will start drafting out the plans so when all the agents get here, we can show them the plan quickly and move out."

Everyone takes their assignments in, nodding and mentally plotting their missions. For a few blessed moments, there is an anxious but contemplative quiet silence. Until my right-hand Kev breaks the silence by asking, "And what if the house is breached and becomes compromised?"

I don't have any answers to that question, none of us do. But I have a sneaking suspicion that my sister will have some ideas for that soon.

Alexandra West

Finally, Cole and I emerge from our training and cleaning in the armory. I had taken the time to change into black tactical pants, a black tee shirt and have weapon holders lining each of my legs. I outfitted both Cole and myself with a bulletproof vest and we stashed additional guns and ammo into those compartments. My black hair is pulled into a high ponytail, braided and twisted in a bun so it's out of my eyes. We're dressed and ready for battle. As we enter back into the living area, we are greeted by all alpha males; the additional men stop what they're doing and observe our approach with shrewd and assessing eyes. As much as I can, I inconspicuously position Cole behind me in a protective gesture as their watchful eyes bore into us.

Some of the men I know, and conversely, they know exactly who and what I am. There are plenty of others who I don't know. Either way, it doesn't matter. If we're going to get out of this alive, it's all hands-on deck. And they all know the deal and they still came to fight. I am grateful for them, knowing they had to take some of the more inconspicuous ways to get to Long Island and into West Enterprises. I'm sure the tunnel system's pathways will have numerous dust-smudged boot prints after today.

I nod my acknowledgement to the newcomers. "I am Alex West, some of you may know me. Others may know of me. This is Cole Harris," I motion to my right. "He's the target and it's our job to protect him. Thank you for coming."

A couple men whisper my name in surprise, no doubt wondering what an assassin like me is doing in the same room as them. I see a couple of raised eyebrows going to my fresh shoulder wound, the extra bandage and padding showing through my tee, I'm sure concerned with my ability to hold my own in a firefight.

I proactively address their concerns about my ability to pull my own weight, immediately removing all doubt and uncertainty, "Yes, I'm an assassin. But first and foremost, I'm a West and a sister. Today, I'm on my brothers' side. Even if that means taking another bullet today." My voice hardens as I challenge the group in front of me, "If you have anything to say about that, say it now or keep it to yourself. I won't be as forgiving or accepting if you want to voice any concerns later."

Twenty-seven pairs of eyes look at me, shrewdly evaluating me before finally accepting my position. Dave comes to stand next to me as Luke slings an arm around my shoulder. I hear Kev, Sean, and Will also join me, coming up behind me, to provide a united front to the founding family's team dynamics. Dave and I silently exchange a look, communicating that all is forgiven for the previous infraction. We all understand the importance of being allies.

"Okay," I start, "Will, catch us up. What's the plan?"

After reviewing and revising the final plan, we all come to an agreement and begin to prepare. "Mount up," Luke cheerily calls out, which of course only annoys Will as the tension continues to build in anticipation and anxiety.

In the final plan, all of us split up into multiple teams as was the original suggestion during my brothers' initial planning phase. My team, consisting of Steve, Dave, Cole, Jace Edwards and two of Dave's military buddies are to be stationed inside of the house, the presumed safest point of the battlefield and the area least likely to be attacked. I'll be taking up a short-term residency in the crow's nest, looking for the damn sniper that shot me like a coward and for any of my sniper's friends. Satellite images have confirmed there are at least three snipers. That will be the first order of business, for me to take those three out so the rest of the teams on the ground will only have to worry about two-dimensional threats, not three. We're still getting satellite image updates for additional snipers, and I'm also tasked with keeping an eye out for other unspotted threats.

Before heading to the armory for my final pass, I hug Luke, Sean, Kev and even Will, silently giving them my love, just in case even one part of our plan goes awry. You never know what's going to happen in our line of work; all it takes is a nanosecond to make a grave error, and one day each of our luck will run out, as long as we stay in this line of business. I can sense my brothers' excitement thrumming through their veins, but underneath all of that, I can also feel their nervousness. I non-verbally share my affection and love for them all before I turn on my heel and head to the armory where I find my beloved my sniper rifle, with a good amount of ammunition to boot, I know that Will and six men headed to the east side of the house. Kev, Sean, Luke and everyone else will be heading to the south and west corners of the property.

In the privacy of only metals and powders, I quickly check and redress my shoulder bandage one last time before I start to load up, packing gauze in the wound and wrapping additional bandages to hide a point of vulnerability that an enemy could take advantage of under my shirt. I have the sniper rifle slung over my good shoulder along with both 9mms in my thigh holsters, knives along my ankles, two additional chest holsters containing glocks and a double shoulder holster, customized to carry two knives and two handguns. Lastly, I pick up my bag containing all my extra equipment, ammo and a few additional surprises that I decided to add in, just for fun. I feel armed and at peace, totally at ease with all the metal and explosives enshrouding my small frame. I come out of the armory to the surprise of my twin, Steve, Cole, Jace and the two other men from Dave's military days, their expressions showing the shock of my own arsenal.

I nonchalantly shrug my shoulders as I address them, "What? I am a woman who likes to be prepared."

"Damn, West," one of Dave's buddies named Russ Lange jokes. "I didn't know your sister was such a badass."

"You also didn't know that the infamous Alex West was my sister," Dave dryly returns, "until I showed you a picture of her, proving Alex isn't just a guy's name, you douche."

"And he's been drooling over her ever since, buddy. Well, more than drooling," says another man whose name is Mateo Rivera, as he playfully shoves Dave's shoulder.

I roll my eyes and try not to gag at all of the alpha male banter, not surprised or fazed. Growing up with five brothers, then being a master in a male dominated industry, this doesn't even spike my overloaded testosterone alarm. Looking at my watch, its analog face reads 17:52. Our plan initiates at precisely eighteen hundred hours.

"Are you ladies ready to go? Or do you need to primp your looks a bit more and grab a couple of tampons for the road?" I sardonically ask. Frowns and good-natured chuckles are my response, but the silence signals that I indeed possess the tactical command of the group.

I pause to fit a standard issued earpiece into my ear. I test the functionality by turning on its audio and am rewarded with the low hum of voices from the other teams. "And by the way, you're now in the company of two Wests, let alone four more on comms, so you're going to have to be more specific from here on out if you're looking for a West. Use either first full names or first initials," I command.

At the nods of my fellow team members, I turn on my mic and quietly test to check that the other teams can hear me on comms. My brothers respond, their voices signaling that we're all connected. The men on my team are also fitting and initiating their earwigs, surreptitiously testing the microphone before they nod to me in confirmation. I gather the group I'm leading, hoist my rifle higher on my good shoulder and lead six men up the stairs, away from our confined safe zone, directly into enemy fire. It's counter-intuitive, it goes against my gut, all of my prior training and every instinct. But here we go, from the fire right into the proverbial frying pan

**

At exactly eighteen hundred hours Eastern Standard Time, all hell breaks loose at West Enterprises. There is no other way to accurately describe it. We hear gunfire outside around the house as our teams meet up with the enemy teams per their assignments. I assume the enemy teams were instructed to prepare to mobilize and strike the house at the exact same time. I climb up to the false chimney which is now a crow's nest, something Dad had installed and converted for me once he realized that I enjoyed and excelled at being a sniper. Dad wanted me to have every opportunity and the ability to continue to practice and hone my skills of timing and accuracy.

Dad. In a rare and uncharacteristically sentimental moment, I take a second to remember his proud, smiling face. My father was always so supportive and strong, always pushing me further and challenging me to try new things. To incorporate new techniques and technologies into my style so that I could possess every advantage available to me. Dad was always making sure that I was the best I could be, setting me up for success and trying to remove any obstacles he could. He knew there would be additional challenges I would face in a male-dominated industry that he'd be unable to protect me from. Now, I know that my father was readying me for any setback I would eventually face. It's true he didn't know that he wouldn't be with us in our adult lives. But just like any good father, he was preparing me for a future where I would be strong, successful and where I would be able to survive. With the chaos surrounding us, thinking of Dad is the balm of calmness I need to center myself, since I can't hear my ocean waves over the pesky and interfering gunfire.

Feeling ready, I take a deep breath, set up my rifle, adjust my scope and begin to take aim. Not only am I searching for the sniper that got me and any others in the vicinity, but I'm also providing aerial support for my brothers and allies. I make sure that I continuously switch angles after every shot, so as not to immediately and conspicuously alert the enemy of my specific location. I need to buy as much time for myself and my brothers as I possibly can. I find the snipers immediately, based upon the satellite images from Will's contact in one of Washington's agencies. I quickly and clinically take them out, saving the one who shot me for last. Two quick rounds to kill zones allow me to sharpen my shot for my personal revenge. I line up my shot, pull the trigger and watch as my adversary's head snaps back, the scope glass shattering as a quick smile brushes my features. I scope the home rooftops and other high areas where additional snipers may be hiding, but I don't find any. Will's contact will be immediately patched into my comm in case any additional snipers are detected and located.

I turn my attention to providing air support to my brothers on the beach as I quickly take out the largest targets, our allies placing bright green marks on their faces and bulletproof vests, signaling to me that they are friendlies. I had asked them to do it in advance, just so I didn't accidently kill anyone by friendly fire and to minimize the risk of any other person on our team making that same mistake, since we had lots of agents who had never worked with each other before. That would be the last thing our family would need to deal with, accusations of me taking out West Enterprises allies, slipping back into my ruthless assassin ways. Looking over the property through my lens, I see that Will's team had neutralized the majority of the enemy threat and were moving toward the north side at the beach, to give our side a head start and assist with the north area, since there isn't a designated team for the smaller, lower-risk area.

It's when I turn my scope to the west and south sides that I spot Sean with a bloody face. I see the wound seems to originate from what looks to be a two-inch cut, starting at his temple, with blood glistening down the right side of his face. My younger brother is currently engaged in hand-to-hand combat with a foe that's slightly larger than him. Enraged on behalf of my little brother's plight, I wait for my opening to strike. I engage my laser pointer and flash it twice on Sean's opponent's chest, signaling that I need him to clear the line of fire. Once he gets the message and moves, I put a bullet in his adversary's kill zone, the body falling backward from the force of my shot. Sean doesn't look my way so as not to give away my position, but he offers a slight nod of gratitude before he moves on to the next opponent. I turn my own scope to the rest of my brothers, taking out six more foes in the process, using the same pattern of my laser to signal my impending shot. I'm taking out more people than I should, the enemy will be able to locate me easier than before, but my main focus is ultimately keeping my family safe, the rest of the blowback I can handle if necessary.

Once I confirm that the south and west sides are handled and the team starts also moving toward the beach, I search the horizon for additional snipers. As I'm panning back and forth over the rooflines, I see the tell-tale flash of the sun reflecting off a sniper scope. Triple Yahtzee. I zero in on the sniper, an adversary lying on the roof of one of our neighbors' house in a pretty decent ghillie suit. Just for fun, I zero in close enough I can see the shooter's finger isn't even on the trigger. With what I knew is a cruel smile, I put my bullet through the sniper's scope. With a satisfied grin, I see the weapon fall over the edge of the roof and clatter to the ground in my periphery as the sniper's body goes limp and drops from my scope's view. I take a final glance over the battlefield, sweeping over our three different teams as I see mass movement on the beach. I quickly dismantle my weapon and climb down from my perch to join the others.

"They're all convening on the beach. We need to provide additional support from above. Move now!" I command to the team.

Within seconds, all seven of us burst through the French double doors dumping us all out onto the deck, moving forward to provide additional backup from above. Instantly, we begin taking fire from our position by the doors. We all crouch down and surround Cole while taking cover behind the deck furniture, Mateo, Russ and Jace all take a step back into the house. Glass shatters around us and wood splinters rain down on upon heads.

"Where the hell is all this fire coming from? I thought they cleared this area!" Dave yells out to me over the noise as he fires a few shots, aiming in general directions.

"Apparently not. And how the hell would I know locations? I'm here with you!" I irritably toss back at Dave as I reload my gun and pull a bullet into its chamber.

Steve calls out, "Any great plans, Aly?"

I think as I fire off a few rounds of my own, mulling over our next move. I zero in on a plan, a crazy plan yes, but a plan nonetheless. I look over at Dave and ask, "Lucerne?"

Dave immediately understands my message, remembering a task force that we were both on together in Switzerland that got only slightly out of hand. And slightly out of hand is pretty good for our improvised ideas.

I smile as Dave and I look back at Steve. "Oh no. No, no, no, no, no. Not the dreaded Twin Power," Steve groans.

Jace and Dave's two buddies give Steve a confused look as my friend just shakes his head, buckling up for whatever idea Dave and I have. Dave signals his two friends to take Cole under coverage and head back into the house to guard him. I start moving down the deck stairs with Steve and Jace following, albeit just a half-reluctant step behind.

"Aly, what are we doing?" Steve exasperatedly asks, following my lead.

Yelling back, I answer, "We're creating a distraction so the other two teams can get behind whoever is left on the beach, leading to the enemy being surrounded," I patiently but urgently explain.

"Yeah," Dave yells as he catches up to us, "that way we provide support to our men down there and still get some action in the fight!"

I nod at Steve before I flash a grin at Dave. "You good Jace?" I call out, hoping Edwards is up to the task.

"Yes ma'am," is Jace's short response.

With a slightly crazy smile on my face, I look forward and brace myself. "Ready? Go! Go! Go! Go! Go! Execute, execute, execute!" I command.

The four of us draw fire to us as we stand up, breaking our cover. All enemy weapons automatically swivel toward our movements and position where we immediately begin taking fire. I see the telltale flashes of black Kevlar vests in my peripherals and start shooting at the targets' heads in front of me. I hit two and miss one which completely pisses me off, as I've been subconsciously calculating my accuracy percentages in my head. Ducking down, I edge around the corner and take out a couple target's legs before delivering the final kill shots. Now I feel so much better, my averages going back up.

"How many are left?" I yell, taking a quick cover to cycle my weapon, a fully loaded clip just feels so good.

"Twelve that I can see," Steve responds as he fires a few rounds before ducking down for quick cover. I throw a grenade in the direction over Steve's head, arching the device for maximum detonation coverage area, neutralizing the encroaching threat.

"Shit, when the hell did you bring grenades to the party?" Jace asks, surprised by my alternative methods.

"I come prepared. We like creativity here at West Enterprises, Edwards. Makes the job fun," I say with a sly smile.

After the grenade flashes and bangs, I wait two seconds before I quickly pop my head back up to take stock of what we've got left. While my head's up, I also look to see how my other brothers are faring on the shoreline. It looks like we've lost some men along the way and my brothers are taking the brunt of the shots now. I signal for Jace, Steve and Dave to go assist the family as I stay low, going back up the stairs to the house, firing a few defensive shots off. Right before I enter, I identify myself, so I don't get shot again, this time by friendly fire. I burst in and promptly shut what's left of the French double doors behind me.

"We're short on ammo, ma'am," Russ says, showing me his nearly empty clip. I snort at being called ma'am, but I easily hand off my bag of extra ammo to the team who has been holding down the fort from upstairs.

"Look, there are men down outside and it's getting heavy for our surviving team members. I've got Harris. You go help my brothers and I'll provide coverage from up here on the deck. Keep your heads down. Watch your six," I command and advise. The two men in front of me nod and grab the extra ammo and weapons before they leave.

I keep my 9mm, one glock, four clips of extra ammo and my sniper rifle with extra rifle bullets on my person. I hand off another 9mm I grabbed to Cole, ensuring that the safety is off and a bullet is in the chamber.

"Shoot at anything that moves, okay? Anyone on our team knows not to re-enter without identifying themselves first. If it gets to the point where you are down to a couple bullets, come up with me and I'll handle it. Got it?" I ask. Cole visibly swallows, his Adam's apple bobbing up and down.

But he bravely nods, putting on a strong front and taking a courageous stand.

As I begin to walk to the window, he grabs my arm and crashes his lips into mine before I can even react. He eventually breaks our connection, panting out his response. "For luck," Cole gasps.

I can feel my face soften as I softly concede and confirm, "For luck."

I move to the window overlooking the now bullet ridden deck and knock out the rest of the splintered glass as I set up my long-range rifle. I spy another thirty incoming adversaries along with the twelve or so left that my brothers are cleaning up on the beach. We have about twenty-five allies left on our side, so I start cleaning up the adversaries from my vantage point, trying to even out the playing field, not worried about my location becoming known to our enemies as I can easily shift to a new location. As I'm busy taking out the first five in the oncoming wave, my brothers get my warning message of their long-distance back-up and prepare for the coming onslaught. I eliminate another six, trying to give my brothers and allies the advantage. I'm also aware that I need to try to conserve bullets, so I'm now trying to use the same bullet for multiple kills, maximizing impact and efficiency.

Just as I am about to line up for my next shot, I hear shots being fired from just outside the front of the house. Taken aback, I wonder how the front of house was breached with all of our security measures that we have in place. I immediately disassemble my rifle and shove it in the antique cabinet stationed right under the window. The shots are being directed toward the front door, trying to breach the main entrance, so I yell for Cole to go upstairs and to stay behind me.

As I'm running up the stairs in Cole's wake, I say into my earpiece, "Is anyone on comms? Anyone at all? Come in! The house is being breached and I need back up. I have Cole, but it's just me and I'm running low on ammo. Can anyone hear me?"

I wait for a response from someone, anybody, as I back us into the hallway leading to the bedrooms, quickly unlocking the doors, as I stay low. I decide to tuck Cole into the hallway bathroom, midpoint down the hallway, just in case there's a breach from my balcony at the end of the hall. A team of what sounds like eight comes storming through the front door. I know that I need to conceal Cole and myself as much as I can, for as long as I can. I tuck us both into the bathroom and leave the door slightly ajar. I instruct Cole to get into the shower stall and stay low. I station myself directly against the door, crouching low, both listening for incoming footfalls and bracing the door in case they try to force the door open. Time is short.

It takes about three minutes before I hear multiple sets of boots climbing the hardwood stairs. I inconspicuously peak around the edge of the door as I quickly fire off several rounds, striking four fatally and wounding one before I duck back into the bathroom with bullets following in my wake. I am out of ammo with my nine, so I grab my glock and duck down low.

"Is anyone on comms?" I frantically address my family and our allies as quietly as I can, but I hear nothing, no response. Something must have happened with my earwig, this is strange, even to me.

I know that with every shot, I'm quickly running out of ammo and that even though I'm skilled, even I won't be able to keep the three remaining adversaries who I can hear are coming down the hallway at bay for long. My only comfort is the one who is already wounded, I'm pretty sure I got him in the lungs, not immediately fatal, but I can hear a man gasping for breath in the hallway, knowing that blood is probably mixing with his saliva at an increasing rate. But all of this is still not much a comfort as I'm down a gun and without back-up.

I motion for Cole to lie down in the shower so he doesn't get struck by a stray bullet as an unfamiliar panic settles deep into my bones. I turn the bathroom corner and quickly take out two of my three adversaries in the kneecaps with multiple shots. I get the guy that I had previously wounded in the neck before my glock notifies me it's out of ammo too. I grab my last clip, load it into the glock and start spraying bullets all down the hall. I hit the two targets who I previously injured their knees, their weapons dropping to the floor in deathly submission. The last target is 250 feet away and closing in fast when I realize that I'm now officially all out of ammo. I give

Cole another one of my knives, so he at least has two weapons and isn't completely defenseless in case I fail. I don't ask Cole for his gun; he needs to have a weapon just in case. Knowing that I have a one more target left with no extra ammo on me, I pull out my cell and fire a quick text to my brothers in our group chat, saying that I need back up ASAP, hoping they'll get my message digitally, since my earwig seems to be down. I pray my brothers can make it here to me, and Cole, in time.

Hearing someone approach a couple feet away, I grab my favorite knife, crouch down and aim to stab at my adversary in the legs. I don't know how, but somehow this adversary has anticipated my move. Pre-emptively, he manages to reach around the door panel and slams the butt of his gun into my back, pain radiating directly down into my spine. Pain sears and spreads through my entire body as I unceremoniously crash to the ground. He kicks my wrist hard enough for my knife to skid down the hallway, just a few inches out of my reach. I turn my attention to Cole, my ears pulsing and temples throbbing as I move my head, suddenly overcome with pure terror for his safety. His eyes meet mine and I can clearly see Cole's fear and distress on both his face and in the depths of his soul. *I need to protect Cole, it's my job,* I think to myself.

As I try to get up to go stand in front of Cole, to provide a barrier between the enemy and Cole, I hear our adversary shoot two bullets into my back. I can hear the shots being fired, since we're in an enclosed space, and the noise echoes off the tile floor and walls loudly enough to make me cringe, but I don't feel the bullets go through me. That's odd. I can tell by the guy's gun it's enough to put a decent size hole in a wall, let alone a person, even with a bulletproof vest on. I see Cole's eyes widen, his mouth is open and his lips are moving, but I can't hear any sounds, nothing from Cole, any weapons or the man standing over me.

I wonder if this is what death is like, silence in the absence of chaotic commotion. But then, it sounds like someone is slowly turning the volume up on the stereo as noise begins to slowly filter in, creating a din of undiscernible racket. Sound pierces through the haze as I faintly hear a disturbance coming towards us in the house, but it sounds like whatever is making the noise is miles away, not within the walls of the house. *Shit,*

Cole's dead if that's not my team, I reason to myself. I know that I need to get up, to finish the job and protect Cole just in case it's not anyone from my side on their way. But my arms don't seem like they want to work, all my upper body strength seems to have been zapped out of me. Thankfully, the thunderous noise in the house is my brothers. I recognize and can hear their breathing as they run up the stairs. I can see the edges of them round the corner of the hallway, weapons drawn and centered on the guy above me.

My enemy had also noticed my brothers' approach, but he still bends down and hovers over me. My own knife that I held just moments ago, the same one I attempted to stab him with, suddenly enters my side, ensuring my immobility as if the two bullets weren't enough and serving as a ghastly distraction to my brothers. I thought that knife was still just out of reach, apparently not, given its current location, lodged in my appendix. My adversary must have picked up the knife as I went down. I see but don't hear Kev mouth something, I take in Luke's shocked face and read Will's lips as he screams, "No!" But still, everything is muted which is more terrifying than I could have ever imagined. Sean's face is aghast, the blood having drained from his face. It isn't until I look at my twin's face that I understand just how dire my situation is. The anger I expected to see is there, yes, but the dread and horror that's on Dave's face seems to jumpstart my auditory faculties back to their full capacity.

Finally, I regain my hearing, the din clearing as I can hear every pin dropping sound in high detail and definition. I can hear a series of shots being fired, but they seem like they're still further away, all slowly coming closer, when I rationally know bullets are flying just a mere few feet from me. Suddenly, I feel a heavy weight crash down on my back, knocking the wind out of my lungs, quite literally taking my breath away. The sensation of being crushed to death overwhelms me; my opponent's weight and larger size, making it incredibly hard to breath. The pain sears from the two shots in my back as the knife digs deeper into my side from my adversary's dead body pressing relentlessly into me.

I faintly can hear Dave say, although I'm sure in actuality, that my twin's yelling, "Get him off her! Lexi. Lexi! Lexi stay with me; help is on the way. Just hold on. Cole! Are you okay?"

My hearing starts to get fuzzy again as I don't hear Cole's response. Everything seems to become muted, as if I'm underwater, currents pulling me deeper, my vision first dots with black marks, then darkness seeps in to a black abyss. I need to get to Cole. He's the job; I need to finish the job. I need my brothers to understand that sense of urgency.

I feel the relentless weight being shoved off me just as I begin to lose consciousness. I think I feel someone touching my back, but it feels like feathers lightly brushing over my skin. I can no longer hear anything again, even though my brain knows that I'm in the midst of loud conversations and chaos. I am suddenly surrounded by darkness and finally succumb to it, welcoming the pain-free sensations with open, awaiting and tired arms.

Cole Harris

Her eyes. I'll never forget that haunting expression in her eyes. Right before he shot her, Alexis was looking right at me. She was concerned, ridiculously worried, for my safety. I could see it all over her face. I know deep in my soul that she was trying to stand back up so she could get back to me, to protect me. And he shot her in the back like a coward, like she was an animal needing to be put down. In slow motion, I saw her fall. I saw him stab her, her body twitching with pain as the knife entered her side. The bastard then looked up at me with a sickening grin on his face, silently communicating with me that I was next as he rose to his full height. I watched as the small rivers of blood leave Alexis' body, creating a webbing pattern on the tile, settling and staining into the grooves of the floor's grout. I knew that with every second her blood flowed on the ceramic, her life was leaving her still body. I knew that I needed to get to her and stop the bleeding, or to at least stem the bleeding until help arrived. I knew in that moment that I would never be able to forget this sight, her willingness to die in order to save my life, how she hasn't moved since this jerk stabbed her in the side. But I didn't know how to get to her without dying myself. This guy took down one of the most lethal assassins of our time, if not in all of history. How did I have a chance to stay alive against him if even Alexis, or Alex West, can't?

Suddenly, it seemed like firecrackers went off around him, the explosions ricocheted violently off the metal, porcelain, tile and ceramic, creating a cacophony of strident pandemonium. Bullets, not firecrackers, my shock-ridden brain formulated. But where were they coming from? I realized that my enemy wasn't shooting at me, that the gunfire was coming from down the hallway. I watched as his heavier and significantly larger frame did a dance to music only the dying man could hear before he begrudgingly fell on top of Alexis in deathly submission.

I had raised Alexis' knife in self-defense, but I'll never be sure if I would have been able to summon the courage or the strength to stab him myself. I knew if it would've come down to it, it would have been either me or him. But I am not sure if I was ready to make that split second decision, to take someone else's life, even with all of Alexis' coaching and her brothers' warnings. But looking at Alexis dying on the ground, I knew she selflessly sacrificed her own life to give me the chance to protect and defend my own. I couldn't even move, let alone honor her sacrifice. She was on the hall bathroom floor bleeding out, and I ended up doing absolutely nothing.

I tried my best not to flinch as the muzzle of a gun, then a face breached the bathroom's doorway, but I know I failed. I met the eldest West's eyes as Will took in my position and his sister's, easily figuring out what transpired. Behind Will, I saw Kev's face as he noticed the knife wavering in my hand, positioned slightly above my head. With a look of compassion, Kev crouched down so he was eye-level with me before he reached over and gently took the blade out of my hand with murmured assurances while sheathing the blade in one of the compartments in his own vest. He silently assessed my physical condition, looking me over, but not seeing signs of any gaping wounds. His sister made sure that I was unharmed. Once he sensed that I'm physically unharmed, he turned his attention back to his little sister as Will moved to the hallway, staring down at Alexis' prone form.

Dave had run to Alexis' side and with help, had that bastard pushed off her prone form. Her eyes have since closed but her head is still positioned toward me. She is pale, too pale. There's debris all over her body, the lightly colored ceramic and tile flakes showing in stark contract with her black clothing. Blood is seeping out and pooling all around her, the red webbing the floor, her black hair shimmering in the glistening of blood. This has to be way too much blood for one person to lose, right? How many pints of blood does one human body hold? I can't remember. I'm hoping her attacker's blood makes up a high amount of that liquid red volume, but I sincerely doubt it.

I faintly hear Sean calling emergency services on his phone, his uncharacteristically quiet demeanor tossed aside, his voice booming and echoing against every hard surface. From what I've seen and since I've known him, Sean has always kept his emotions close to his heart, but not right now. The youngest West's distraught emotions are fully on display. Her brothers have made a makeshift bed for her from one of Luke's surfboards, talking about something I can't seem to comprehend or understand. They're trying to carefully shift her on the board, for what, I'm not sure. Everything isn't fully clicking or making any sense in my mind yet.

The next thing I know, Dave is in my face, yelling at me, but at first, I can't make out what he's saying. But then the fog in my brain lifts and the cotton falls out of my ears. I can make out everything he's saying to me now. Oh, he's blaming me for this. Dave's right, of course he is. My stammered out apology is hollow and it can't make up for the hole that's in my heart, let alone his heart or the rest of her brothers. Alexis took on the world for me, faced every threat and even started to change her life, her job and habits, just for me. And I couldn't even raise a hand to defend her, let alone protect myself. I don't deserve her, but I love her all the same. Wait. I'm in love with her. I'm in love with Alexis West. How am I going to prove myself to her and her brothers that I'm good enough when I can't even protect her or myself? How can I ask for her forgiveness if she never wakes up? How will her brothers forgive me for costing them everything?

David West

My twin is lying face down in a large pool of blood. Her blood, mainly. I inspect the gaping holes in her back and move to remove the knife from her side when Will quickly intervenes before I can extract the weapon from Lexi's body.

"No." Will stops me, "Don't remove it. If you do, she could bleed out. It may be the only thing that's keeping her blood and any internal organs from spilling out of her side."

"We need to flip her over, otherwise she could aspirate on her own blood." I gruffly reason.

"Dave's right." Luke solemnly agrees, his posture rigid and his words are clipped. "She can't stay like this."

Sean comes back from calling emergency services and his eyes widen as he takes in her too still form. Kev and Luke come over and help me lift her while keeping her head elevated as Will and Sean run to grab beach towels from the hall linen closet to serve as a pillow and blankets to keep her warm. Together, the five of us finish making the makeshift bed on Luke's surfboard. Lexi is still unconscious. At least we moved her to the hallway so when emergency services finally arrives, they'll be able to quickly transport her to the nearest hospital.

I look down at my sister, my twin. Shit, I should have never left her. I should have never listened to and agreed with her plan to split up. It's a classic, rookie mistake, especially as her attention was split between being the aggressor and defensively protecting Cole. She wouldn't be able to improvise or slip away the way she normally would if she didn't have backup.

This is all my fault, my thoughts swirling in the midst of my guilt and regrets. But wait, no. It's Cole's fault. He's the reason she couldn't fully fall back on her training, why she couldn't protect herself like she always has. He's the reason why my entire family and I are in this mess. He's the reason why my sister lies dying on the ground. Because of Cole Harris, Lexi had to split her attention so she could cover his incompetent ass. I swiftly look up, my eyes searching and finally zeroing in on his position, still cowering in the shower tub. My gaze is solely focused on him. I can't see anything else, almost as if I have blinders on. And suddenly, I'm angry, enraged beyond reason, so angry that all I can see is red. The ever-observant Sean seems to have accurately read my mood, since he had quickly positioned himself in between Cole and me, planting himself firmly in the bathroom doorway.

"Dave," Sean cautiously begins as he defensively puts his hands up to try to stop me, "this is the not the time nor is it the place."

I roughly shove Sean out of my way, only feeling a slight amount of remorse when my youngest brother's shoulder bounces into the wall with the force of my rage. I hear his grunt of pain, the noise trying to wiggle into my conscience. But I'm on a mission, avenging my sister. Moving forward, I lock onto my object of fury as I come face-to-face with Cole Harris.

"This is your fault," I begin, pulling Cole up to his feet and dragging him out of the tiled enclosure. I roughly poke my finger into his chest before I grab him by his shirt collar and unceremoniously yank him closer so he's in my face.

"You're the reason my sister was shot. You're the reason we're all in this situation and our home is damaged. This is your fault. Why the hell didn't you do something? We all knew you weren't ready for this. That you weren't prepared for all of this. We tried to warn her, but she had faith in you, in your confidence. And now look at her! Why did she take those bullets when we all know that they were meant for you?" I yell with vehemence and vitriol lacing into my voice as I barely have a grasp on the wrath that's trying to fully consume me.

"Because, Dave," Will answers for Cole, coming to stand behind me as he grasps my wrists and tries to get me to release the object of my rage, "it's what she does. She knew the risks and she still faced the challenge head on, just like she always has done."

"She's strong," Kev finishes Will's sentence. "She'll get through this, Dave. She's the strongest and bravest one of all of us."

The rest of my brothers nod their heads in solemn agreement. I pause and take a breath, trying to center myself and calm my raging emotions down. Looking back at Cole, I see his ashen face and I realize my mistake, my hasty anger lashing out at the one person, for whom Lexi risked everything for.

"I'm sorry," I tersely apologize as I quickly release Cole's shirt.

"No, Dave, all of you," Cole stammers out as he looks at all of us, emotion clogging his throat, "this is all my fault. I'd take her place if I could."

"Do not dishonor our sister's sacrifice, Cole Harris," Sean wisely warns Cole, his posture uncharacteristically rigid with tension and apprehension. Cole gives a nervous nod and immediately averts his eyes in submission.

Knowing that I've already reached and exceeded my emotional limit for the day, and that as soon as my adrenaline starts to wear off, I'll be a mess. To protect my privacy, I leave and stalk toward my twin's bedroom at the end of the hallway, going toward the last set of rooms. But the hallway is still enshrouded in uncertain anguish, the unknown chasing after my heels as I retreat to catch my breath. I'm about to take a left to enter my own personal sanctum when I hesitate for just a moment. I choose to turn, unlock, open and enter through the door on the right, using her bedroom door's secret key that we had designated in our own little hiding spot, nestled in a faux section of the door's panel.

The room still smells like her perfume. There are still remnants and echoes of the chaos from her being shot initially, with some blood droplets staining the carpet on the floor and her beach bag haphazardly strewn across the tile floor on the balcony. What a difference on how this day progressed for my sister, for all of us, from the start of this morning to now. I feel cold and so alone. Her energy, I can feel it waning, even with me being farther away from her physically. I'm used to being able to read her and feel her emotions, but I don't know if I would have ever been prepared to feel her potential death.

I relive memories of our childhood in my brain, images flashing in my mind's eye, like an old school thirty-five-millimeter film, colors rushing back to me in an intense photo reel. Old but good memories fill in my head, flipping through its footage from when we were kids to now. When we were eighteen, ready to embrace our adult lives together. A regular afternoon with us playing at the beach. The first time we both fired a gun. A random volleyball game at sunset with our brothers. I can't live without her, let alone live here at this house, work at West Enterprises, without her being here. We've always been together, no matter what, she's been my other half. She has to pull through, otherwise not only will she be gone forever, but I fear I will be lost too.

I can hear the emergency services' sirens quickly approaching, pulling me out of my reverie. I know someone will buzz them onto the property, so I'm not worried about rushing to do so. We still have a number of agents who are documenting the destruction and taking in evidence. I know phone calls are being made to families of West agents who were killed today. Facial recognition is currently running on all of our adversaries as we wait for what's next. Everyone outside of the West family knows what to do and they have already started to mobilize well before this moment. West Enterprises, the company, is in good hands.

I know that I need to return to the hallway. But I don't want to leave this space. I don't want to leave her room. I'm terrified that if I do, I'll lose my tether to my twin. That being in here is the only anchor to her staying with us. But the urge to stay doesn't outweigh the urge to be with Lexi. So I decide to get up, not tidying up or disturbing how she left things. I quickly go back to retake my place next to my sister's side. I don't intend on leaving her anytime soon, even in the hands of our trusted hospital.

Kevin West

Dave is completely devastated. You can tell that through his body language, his inability to look any of us in the eyes and his subtle aversion to our sister's still form. I can't blame him. I'm honestly struggling with it all too. And Dave, as her twin, he's going through all the emotions of grief in such a short amount of time. That's his twin. We make fun of them sometimes for their use of Twin Power and being able to, what it seems like from the outside, read each other's' minds. But we all know that their bond is something special, something indescribable and unique that the two of them alone share and understand. We all love Lex, but Dave is the one who truly understands her, knows her down to her core. I understand why he withdrew from us and went into her room alone. It was so he can feel closer to her, especially in this time of uncertainty.

This entire time, I have fixed myself next to her and have been holding her hand, albeit her hand is cold and clammy. But in the quiet before the next wave of melee, I choose to sit on the floor next to her, gently pushing hair out of her face, brushing debris aside and taking in the paleness of her skin. It's cruel, listening to her shallow breaths as she struggles to inhale and exhale each time. Her lungs rattle with blood and fluid from her injuries, and even in a state of unconsciousness, her eyes are clenched in pain. I can feel the unwilling tears begin to prick the corners of my eyes as I silently beg her to hold on.

I meant what I said before to my brothers and to Cole, that Lex is the bravest and strongest one of us all. Dad told us before his final mission that it was our job as her brothers to always protect her. No matter what. And all of us failed her and our late father today, even though I know we made the right, strategic decisions, the choices necessary given the insurrection against West Enterprises. But it doesn't make the feeling I have feel any better.

One of us West brothers should have stayed with her and Dave, especially since we knew that Cole was a liability, regardless of his good intentions and inflated confidence. Furthermore, we all know how often the twins have crazy ideas and unpredictable tendencies when they need to improvise a new plan, especially when their backs are up against the proverbial wall and their options are limited. Maybe we could have stopped them, or at least made them adjust their plans to a little more conservative lens.

Lex's team was originally comprised of seven individuals, including her. How did that team eventually get whittled down to two, with Cole Harris being that second person? Cole Harris, who is the target and who is incredibly inexperienced, acting has her backup. Thank God Will shot the bastard who almost murdered our sister right in front of us. Even so, if that guy ends up being the one who may still end up ultimately stealing our sister's life, my older brother may absolutely lose it. But if Will hadn't shot the guy, I most certainly would have gone a few rounds with him, aiming to do the most damage with every physical strike while keeping him alive. A bullet is far the better fate for her attacker than what I am currently imagining in my head.

I realize my anger is seeping out into my grip on my sister's hand, my grasp tightening on her metatarsals, but her expression doesn't change, there's no reaction. She doesn't feel it, or maybe it pales in comparison to a stabbing and two bullets that her body is still reeling from. Again, I keep asking myself why it was just her and Cole. Furthermore, how did any threat breach the house and bypass all of our security systems?

As I ask myself all these questions and then some, I hear a quiet sound. It would have been easy to miss if I wasn't right next to Lex, but I automatically know it's a moan. I instantly look at Lex's face. I'm startled to see that her eyes are open, but I can tell that she's unseeing, her gaze isn't focused on anything. She's staring at the ceiling, unblinking, her dark brown eyes glassed over, seeing things beyond the realm that us West

141

brothers are all in. This isn't a good sign. I know that this means she's going into shock. I quickly call for Will and tell Sean to get more bandages. We need to stop the bleeding before she exsanguinates before my eyes.

William West

"Will!" I hear Kev urgently call out to me, the anxiety and fear palpable in his voice. My head snaps up and I immediately run down the hall.

"Will," he says as I get closer, "we need to do SOMETHING! ANYTHING!"

"Emergency services are on their way," I automatically respond, the sight of my sister so pale is making me nauseous and dizzy.

"Will, that's not good enough!" the panic and sense of urgency in my younger brother's voice draws my eyes back to his face. I register Kev's fear before I look at my sister and notice that her eyes are open but unfocused.

"She's dying. Right in front of us, Will. Right now, she's in shock. We have to do something to stop the bleeding. We need to buy her some time until the emergency services team arrives," Kev frantically says, his eyes darting around to try to figure out a way to stop time.

At that moment, Sean comes running back toward us with towels and probably all the first aid kits he could have quickly collected, the kits stored and stashed in various locations all over the house. I gladly step away from the scene and turn toward the living room. Kev and Sean are taking command of the situation. I know that they're all counting on me to direct the situation, to be a leader. But I just can't. I try not to cringe as I walk away with an immense amount of shame that I'm feeling for leaving my sister on the floor and not doing anything more to help her. Hey, in my defense, at least I shot the guy that tried to kill my baby sister. That has to count for something, right?

I look around at the remains of the house, our childhood home and now our headquarters for West Enterprises. Broken glass, shattered picture frames and spent shell casings are everywhere, littering the ground and creating a grotesque mural of abstract, violent art. Splintered wood from former doors and window frames is scattered across the floor too, adding to the reflective metal and glass debris. With every crunching step that I take, I'm thankful that I'm wearing hard-soled combat boots. But as I look around me, at the house, my childhood home, my family's company, it's in shambles. Dad would so not be happy with me. And yes, these are all relatively easy fixes. The glass will be replaced, the doorframes realigned, the pictures put back over the spackled and repainted walls, but it will still cost money, time and help.

We also lost some good men today, some of our allies. I know after everything settles with Lex, that I'm going to have to make official phone calls to families and friends on behalf of West Enterprises, send condolences and try to provide answers in the face of uncertainty and mounting questions. That's the worst part of my job, but as the foremost leader of West Enterprises, unfortunately, it's something that I will have to do, it's my responsibility.

Lex once accused me of being heartless. I guess in this moment, I proved her right, that I am indeed. I thought we both were, although I would never admit that out loud to anyone. Before, I never wanted to be compared with her, I wanted nothing to do with my little sister. But right now, I'm standing in a house, surveying damage, while my sister is fighting for her life on the hallway floor. I really need to find a psychologist because I'm clearly having trouble prioritizing between the need to haves versus the nice to have preferences in my life. To be fair, I have never done well with blood, least of all a member of my family's blood. My little sister is always active and moving around. Her stillness mixed with all the blood is making me uneasy and queasy.

Dave and Lex were always in trouble when we were growing up, sharing their own little moments and communicating beyond words that the rest of us could ever understand. Motion, activity, running around, it's what Lex and Dave have always done, what they've always been. They never stayed in one place for too long. They were both always so busy exploring new things and taking on new adventures for them to become content in a single location. I think of Dave. I know that he's somewhere in the house. I just hope that he's doing okay. I hope he doesn't blow up with anger or devastation about Lex.

Lex... My little sister. She and I were finally starting to get along, to not only see each other's perspectives, but to also respect one another. After all these years, she was finally beginning to trust me. And then, of course, something catastrophic like this happens at the most inopportune of timing. We should have been with the twins, either Sean, Luke, Kev or I should've been with them. She shouldn't have been alone with Cole, without extra ammunition and without proper backup. And what happened to her comms as well, why didn't she call out her distress to us? We only got the text from her, saying that she was in dire need of backup. The moment all five of my brothers got her message, we all came rushing to her location as a single unit. There are a lot of questions we'll need answers for, questions that will have to wait to be asked until we get Lex to the hospital and fixed up. And here I am, the bastard in the other room. The man who's calculating the cost of home repairs and asking questions of technical failures instead of being by my little sister's side as she clings to her tenuous hold on her life.

Lucas West

I'm sitting with Steve and Jace in the kitchen. Thankfully, both of them came out of everything fairly unscathed except for minor cuts. Jace knowingly is quiet, deferring his thoughts and acting as an emotional support for Steve and the rest of us West brothers. Steve, well, he hasn't said a word yet, but then again neither have I. He already vomited twice in the kitchen sink. The first time was when he saw that jackass knife Lex in the side. Steve and Jace were with me when I got Lex's text. They came bounding inside with the rest of us as we caught the tail end of Lex's altercation. The second time Steve vomited was when my brothers and I put her on that makeshift bed, using one of my old surfboards as a backboard in order to stabilize her as much as we could.

I fleetingly am thankful that I applied a fresh layer of wax on the board last weekend before my weekly surf. There will be some resistance so she won't slide off, causing even more damage to her battered body. When we initially walked up, Steve, Jace and I could see the hilt of the knife still lodged in her side and blood was actively dripping from her wounds. I know my stomach turned when I saw how large the blood pool was that she was lying in once we moved her.

Steve's a really tough guy, but I have never seen him this distraught, ever. Steve's intense reaction finally makes me realize the severity of my sister's situation, making me jump to my feet, encouraging my compulsion to move and take action. If Steve's this upset, then that means this shit is real. This means that Lex's life really is in danger, it's on the line, and that she could go either way. Off goes my proverbial set of rose-colored glasses.

I look over to Steve and see him nursing a glass of water while Jace Edwards quietly watches the both of us, a silent observer, similar to Sean. I meet Edwards assessing gaze as he regards me warily. I stand up and begin to pace around the kitchen, unsure of where I should place all my pent-up fear and nervousness.

"West," Steve forcibly whispers as he continues to stare at the water level in his glass, "stop pacing. You're giving me anxiety."

"Sorry," I mumble, coming to an immediate halt. I need to do something, but I don't know what to do. How do I make this all better?

It seems like hours pass, but I'm aware that it's probably mere seconds before Steve voices in a slightly stronger tone, "I have never seen her look that bad, man. Never. Even when we were in training, and she lost thirty pounds. Or when we were overseas and she wouldn't eat any of the raw fish. Oh, and when we came back from the one job where her face was smashed in… it's never been this bad. She's never had this much damage sustained at one given time. I want to help but I don't know if I can go back down there. I feel so claustrophobic in that hallway."

Steve's words do the trick, as they pull me out of my existential crisis, halting my downward spiral and bringing me back to the task at hand. I regain my sanity and reasonably say, "It's okay, Sean and Kev are there. And Will's aimlessly walking around, going back and forth, vacillating between here and there. You can't have too many people in that hallway. It's too small of a space anyway. Maybe, we should look for Dave."

I know that I'm rambling and rationalizing my fear of being next to my sister, even though I really should be there with her. But what I'm really doing is just making excuses, shielding myself from the fear and pain that I know will confront me once I see her.

I turn to go search for Dave, but I halt at Steve's next words. "No, Luke, leave Dave be," Steve says firmly while looking downtrodden. My friend wisely explains, "We're all handling this in our own different ways. Besides, he's probably in one of their rooms. I can't imagine the pain he's feeling right now. It's like what we're going through, times infinity."

I nod in agreement knowing that my friend is right. The twins have always been the closest pair within the family. They seem to know what each other is thinking and feeling without having to say anything out loud, which was really infuriating when we were all kids, though now it's more fascinating. My other brothers and I were never part of the twin's club. I wonder now, in a daze, if Dave can physically feel what Lex is going through right now. I just hope that he's able to find solace in their shared space together.

I turn my attention back to the current life-threatening situation happening now down the hallway. My sister is in there, clinging to life. Sissy. Little Lex. I can hear Sean and Kev; I know she isn't doing well. She's fighting hard, but maybe this is something that is even stronger than her. Maybe she's finally met her match, and the one opponent she can't beat is Death itself. I can't see her like that. I can't have the last memories of my little sister be her facing death. She looked so pale, innocent and young when I first caught a glimpse of her. I haven't seen her look like that since we were kids.

She's seen a lot of life because of her profession and consequently experienced a lot of death. Is this all of our faults? Could we have prevented this? She was originally going to kill Cole. She was going to complete her contract like she has always done in the past. If she had, would she be dying in the hallway now? Would she still have second-guessed everything, leading to this very moment? Would she have sacrificed everything? If we had let her do her job, would we now be waiting for emergency services to arrive to try and save her life? If given the chance, would I go back in time and switch Cole to take her place, saving her and potentially fatally wounding him? Neither choice is optimal, morally sound or correct. But I love my sister. I would give anything for this not to be happening. I'd die for her. But instead, in true Lex fashion, she's dying for all of us right now.

Sean West

Fear and anguish have settled upon the remaining West Enterprises crew, like a thick fog where you can't breathe without wincing. You can feel it; it's palpable. Dave has withdrawn from all of us completely. Kev is by my big sister's side, vigilantly watching her vitals, almost to an obsessive, clinical level. Will has finally realized how much Lex means to him and now is being racked with guilt as he second guesses himself and the choices that he has made up to this point. My eldest brother has never done well with guilt and uncertainty, his indecision plaguing his ability to think clearly and triage the situation logically. Luke isn't holding his emotions together too well, but at least he hasn't puked like Steve has. Steve's friend is quietly watching and cataloguing, I sense a kindred spirit in Jace Edwards. And Luke wants to do something; he just doesn't know what to do. To be fair, none of us know what to do, except that we just need to wait for EMS' incoming arrival.

Emergency Services said that they'd be here soon, so where the hell are they? What's taking them so long? I look at my sister, someone who I have admired for my entire life. A part of me is deeply angry at her, at her need to win and her tendency to improvise plans. But I'm terrified she's slowly leaving us, fading away right before our eyes with each drop of blood and every exhale. I wonder if this second will be the last one before she is pulled away from us all forever. I see her chest slightly rise and fall. I hear her shallow breathing. I know she's fighting hard, just as she has her entire life. Her pallid face doesn't match the confident, self-assured and fiercely independent woman my sister has become, the woman that I have grown up with and watched.

When one is close to the end, thoughts oftentimes stray to previous memories or observations. Over the past couple of weeks, I have seen her open up to our family and Cole much more than she ever has in her entire life. She has made such great strides in just a matter of days to get in touch with her emotions, something we all have been trying to encourage her to do for years. But it took someone like Cole Harris for her to lower her guard, dismantle her defenses and to finally allow people in. It took a stranger for Lex to bring her emotions close to her heart and properly feel them. She is finally allowing herself to be free with her feelings and her personality. After all this time, she is embracing the entire human experience.

My sister has been smiling and laughing more, even when she's around us, which was also very rare. Now, Lex has been initiating conversations and some physical contact, slowly unravelling her protocols and knocking down the walls that she had built up over the years. Lex has finally realized that she can be successful in the protection industry, just as she has established her cemented and unrivalled success as an international assassin, as a testament to her strengths and adaptability. None of us brothers are disillusioned into thinking that she will join our side of the business, but she has demonstrated her abilities in our area and we're all proud of her. And the catalyst pushing her toward a new future can be attributed to, in a large part, in the form of Cole Harris. I look over at Cole. He has knelt down next to my sister, his face expressing his unspoken love for her. I know she loves him too, even though she hasn't admitted it. Maybe my older sister doesn't even know she loves Cole yet. I just hope she wakes up to hear him say it, so she can return the sentiment and continue to grow emotionally and physically stronger each day.

Kevin West

The ambulance finally arrives after what seems like ages. Sean runs to meet them at the door, buzzing the vehicle into the compound and leading the EMS personnel through the house. I go out to greet them, to take them to where they are needed most, to my sister. I can tell the fire and rescue teams are looking around the house, silent questions forming in their eyes as they take in the disaster zone that is our house and headquarters. I mentally note that I need to call their captains and give them a situation report or sitrep. All the personnel here today will also need to sign a non-disclosure agreement. I shoot off a quick email to our legal team to have them initiate those document deployments as soon as possible. I steer the emergency services professionals up the stairs and directly toward my sister, needing them to tell me that she's going to be okay and to keep their pesky questions of interest about our house at bay. I don't have the answers for those questions anyway, at least, not today.

Will, Luke and Steve have gathered near Lex, out of the way, further down the hallway, but still close by to keep a watchful and formidable eye over her. The EMS paramedics gently shoo Cole and Sean away from crowding Lex so they can get to work. They try to tell Dave to move but he doesn't budge, instead, he stares them down with unshakable determination. I know he won't move. He won't leave her. He never has in life, and he won't start now, not until one of them dies and they're separated in this life. The paramedics finally realize that arguing with my younger brother is fruitless and they wisely pick their battles. Instead, they turn their focus onto their patient at hand, my little sister.

Dave has subtly and graciously acquiesced, standing slightly off to the side but he watches over his twin like the guardian brother that he's always been. My heart goes out to him. I can't imagine his fear and distress. He's hiding his emotions very well, putting on a good front for everyone else's benefit. But us brothers, we know better. The paramedics are assessing the damage, sputtering out heart rates statistics, oxygen and blood pressure levels, all in clinical terms. They not so gently, in my opinion, roll her on a medical backboard to carry her out of the building. Dave follows right behind them as they walk through the house, the rest of us proceeding in their wake.

They open the ambulance doors and load her in. Dave immediately follows in to sit on the left bench next to one of the paramedics. Additionally, Will uncharacteristically rushes past me to join the ambulance team, claiming the seat on the right bench. Will, well that certainly is a surprise. I knew they were repairing their relationship, but for Will to jump in the ambulance with her is an intense move, even for him. I'm proud of him.

As the lights and sirens go off and the ambulance pulls away, Sean, Luke, Steve, Jace, Cole and I stand in a shocked daze, the adrenaline starting to wane off and reality beginning to rear its ugly head as we come to our senses in the middle of the driveway. I think about the state of destruction that is the house. I think of Luke's surfboard, covered in blood and impromptu towels. I think of the bodies of men all over our property, of the calls and conversations we'll have to make soon. Even though it feels like my family is falling apart, our family still has a business to run.

Luke snaps out of his haze first, breaking the reverie as he starts running toward the garage to get the SUV started. He must have swiped the keys from the kitchen as we were passing through and I was too caught up in Lex getting safely loaded in the ambulance to notice. Sean and I quickly follow our brother's path. Steve informs me in a low voice that he and Jace will be staying with the rest of the agents and that they'll start leading the efforts to clean up the house. Steve confirms that I'm comfortable with him gathering our agents and debriefing those that are here. It does take a village to keep everything running. I'm grateful that Steve is here to do what Will or I would normally be doing, but given the circumstances, neither one of us currently aren't even close to being in the right headspace to do so. I give Steve a grateful nod as I rush to the garage.

Luke opens the garage door and we all pile into the awaiting SUV, quickly buckling our seatbelts. Luke pulls out of the garage so quickly that the vehicle's tires squeal and faint wisps of smoke follow our departure. Driving like a madman, Luke steers us to the hospital while Sean texts Will, asking for their exact location.

We arrive in the emergency room to see Dave and Will sitting against the far wall, grief and exhaustion etching their features. The adrenaline has fully worn off, and in its wake, exhausted devastation take over. My stomach immediately drops like I'm on a rollercoaster and my heart lurches in my throat.

When we approach our brothers, Dave doesn't meet our gaze, doesn't even lift his head, and I can see his eyes are red around the edges, meaning that he's been crying. Something very atypical for Dave, he's not usually very emotional at all. Dave isn't like Lex with no emotions, but he is one to keep his emotions close to his chest and firmly in check. Will looks up and blankly parrots back to us that Lex is in surgery and that she's in critical condition. Between Will and Dave, they go onto share details about the events which transpired from leaving West Enterprises to getting to the hospital's operating room. Apparently, Lex flat lined in the ambulance, right in front of my older brother and Dave.

I'm completely in shock. I rationally know that my sister isn't invincible, but for her to flirt with death so closely. I would've never thought she would flat line. But Will's tone, as he tells us all of this, is empty, his eyes are glazed over. My brother, the one who always has a thought and who will put up a fight. It's shocking to see the light extinguished from his eyes, the fire behind his gaze is dulled. When he hears that our sister flat lined in the ambulance, Luke's knees buckle and it takes Sean and I reflexively having to catch him, purely based on instinctual response, in order to keep him semi-upright. Sean and I set Luke down on the chair next to Will, then Sean and I take our seats across from Will and Dave. In the silence and stillness of our corner in the emergency room, I realize the true gravitas of our situation. All we can do now is wait, pray and hope.

Lucas West

The next couple of days are absolutely brutal. Lex came through surgery better than the doctors or us brothers had initially expected, but the entire operation took over seven hours. At first, the doctors put her in a medical coma to jump-start the healing process. When the doctor came out and suggested a medical coma for the next forty-eight hours, I thought Kev was going to lose his mind, his control coming close to snapping and disintegrating. My older brother jumped up so fast and was in that doctor's face, it took the rest of us a couple of seconds to get our bearings and to intervene. Will begrudgingly but ultimately made the call to move ahead with a medical coma, much to Kev's dismay. Will sat down, defeated, knowing that it was the best decision for Lex but not being one hundred percent certain it was the right one. I know as the eldest brother, Will oftentimes has to make the hard calls at work and for him to make this call, it's like I can see the world settling its immense weight on his shoulders.

Kev is clearly pissed off at Will, his body language clearly sending warning messages for Will not to approach or engage with him. Sean takes a seat next to Kev and whispers something in his ear. Dave takes a seat next to Will and now I feel like I have to choose a side. The normal alliances are off-kilter and I'm the odd man out, wishing my sister was here to help even the score. Frustrated, I choose not to pick a side and turn around in search of a crappy cup of hospital coffee, one for me, and one for each of my brothers. I try to find the light in this situation, but all I can think of is my little sister's struggle to stay alive.

We wait fifteen minutes before Bonnie Hooper, the head of the hospital, sends her administrative assistant, Stephanie Cook, down to come and greet us. Ms. Cook gives us Bonnie's regards and on behalf of the

154

hospital, informed us that Bonnie, Stephanie and the hospital administration are all sending well wishes and a speedy recovery to our sister. Stephanie then ushers us into a private conference room right off the emergency unit's floorplan. My brothers and I appreciate the opportunity to be in repose as we wait, grieve and worry about the fate of our sister, away from the prying eyes of other emergency room patients or awaiting families.

It takes another hour before the head surgeon comes back out to brief us in the conference room. We're finally told that we can see Lex and tells us that she's still in the Intensive Care Unit and he's planning for her to stay there for at least a few more days. As soon as the doctor informs us that we each only have a limited amount of time to visit with her and that she's in room 517, Will takes off running to the stairwell, not waiting for the rest of us to catch up. The rest of us follow in his wake, taking the stairs two at a time to get to the fifth floor.

When the rest of us pile into Lex's room, Will's already there, holding her right hand, sitting on the edge of the hospital chair. Kev goes to her left side and gently brushes some of the long black hair off of her face. As Kev tucks a lock behind her ear, Dave pushes through and gently moves Kev out of the way.

"Lex, Lexi, do you hear me? We're here. I'm here. I'm not going anywhere," Dave whispers in his twin's ear. All of us are watching, but she never moves or even twitches a muscle to signal that she heard Dave.

Will's face is full of compassion as he follows up by saying, "Stay with us, sweetheart, you hear me? Stay here with us."

Sean and I sit at the foot of her bed and Kev settles over Dave's shoulder. We stay like this for hours, disregarding visitor time limits, protecting her now and subconsciously making up for when we didn't protect her during the insurrection at the house.

Sean West

I look at my sister's face. She looks peaceful, like she's at rest. I'm hoping this image will replace the last one I have in my head. The one where's she's lying on the floor in a pool of her own blood, her face scrunched up in pain. I'm not sure if I morally agree with her being induced in a medical coma, but if it helps her heal faster, then I'm okay with whatever it takes. The tension that was between Kev and Will before seems to have faded away as they both stare and watch over her, keeping a vigil over our sister's still form. Dave's face has more color to it, before he was deathly pale. Now Lex's twin's cheeks have some rosy hues to it. Luke is quiet, I know mulling over what happened and envisioning all the "what ifs" that could still happen. None of us are disillusioned into thinking that she's out of the woods yet, but we're hopeful. And I know my sister, she's a fighter, she's a winner. She'll fight death too, and she'll win.

Kevin West

It's been a couple of days already and my sister is still unconscious. My brothers and I all together made the decision to reverse the medically induced coma after forty-eight hours. Since then, Lex still hasn't awoken. The doctors have explained to us multiple times that she has to heal and will wake up on her own, repeatedly assuring us that in her own time, only when she's ready, will she regain consciousness. They encourage us to be patient, that the fact that she's stable and holding her own after severe trauma is encouraging. The medical professionals continue to tell us that she's doing well, considering everything, and the expert medical staff all expect her to make a full, albeit long, recovery.

Naturally, Dave is by her side around the clock, refusing to leave her even for the briefest of moments. The hospital staff graciously lent him a cot, since he refuses to leave. They even started to bring him meals, which he takes in her private, comfortable suite. The rest of us brothers rotate our visits throughout the day, coming and going in informal and unspoken shifts. Since she's in the ICU, normal hospital policy only allows a certain amount of people in her room at any given time. Dave is the constant and Cole is there frequently, but thankfully, the hospital has made exceptions for us, no doubt at Ms. Hooper's request. I'm sure the donation that West Enterprises made also influenced and inspired leniency by the medical staff.

Luke, Will, Sean and I each come separately and sit with her on an impromptu schedule. We hold her hand and tell her all about the house, about what's going on and the progress being made for the restoration and renovations. I know that I stay positive in my recounting of the house's status updates, sharing the things that have needed an overhaul and what we're doing to spruce up the place. Dave firmly believes that she can hear us, even though she remains motionless, her form so still, it's unnatural and unsettling. It has been very difficult for all of us to see her with tubes coming out of her all over the place and wires poking out of her pale skin. That's not our sister, not the sister we've known all our lives. But at least we know this won't be the end of Alexandra West.

When any of us are not at the hospital, we're at the house. We're sleeping, showering and eating, just going through the motions. Thankfully, Steve and Jace have provided us all with a great distraction: reconstructing and rebuilding our house. All the surviving men from our operative have been pitching in and helping too. Some have injuries but they, just like us, are all on the mend and are in the desperate need of a distraction as contracts are all halted until further notice.

Damaged windowpanes and door frames are getting torn down and replaced in record time. Wooden frameworks are being rebuilt and re-secured to the walls. Bullet holes are being patched, spackled and temporarily painted over. Our family picture frames have all been replaced and remounted on the walls. Our new TV is on its way. Will had it ordered the day after Lex got out of surgery. Painters are already scheduled to repaint the walls, doorframes and even the damaged crown molding. Slowly the house is becoming what we remember it with a few needed upgrades and modifications. The wounds from when we were breached beginning to heal and be cleansed away.

We stay busy, cleaning and rearranging the house, getting it ready for when Lex does come home. Will is obsessively reviewing all the footage from that fateful day and is trying to figure out how our enemies got past the house's numerous security systems. Sean is trying to figure out why her earwig died, the cause and how to make sure it never happens again in the future. Dave, when he's at the house for short periods, is consumed with reorganizing her room to how it was before the morning she almost died, scrubbing the carpet clean of her blood and personally repairing the splintered doorframe and damaged wall. I'm grateful that Luke has Steve and Jace to help him stay distracted and focused on reorganizing the house, my younger brother running point on that project. And me? I'm trying to be the supportive brother, checking in on everyone and keeping an eye on all the emotions coursing through the house and its repairs.

Nighttime is the only point in the day that we all sit down together, sans Dave, on the new deck and take the time to reflect. The deck was the first thing us brothers put together, reconstructed and re-stained by hand. We widened the deck and the subsequent stairway, just in case one of us needs to carry Lex to the beach when she gets home. The doctors were worried about her mobility in the beginning, and a wider deck allows for additional chairs and space as an added benefit. As we sit in the fading light, we also exchange childhood stories about Lex and Dave over beers, fond smiles matching our memories. We talk about how we think Lex will like the changes and upgrades that we've made to the house, some of them much needed and long overdue. We make a grocery list of foods she likes so when we know she's coming home, we can plan to go and stock up at the market in advance. Most of all, we're glad she seems to be pulling through and that she's on the mend, even though she hasn't woken up yet. But she will, it's just a matter of time. She gave us quite a scare, right to the edge of our seats, in true Alex West form. But she's strong, she's alive and she'll heal with us surrounding her. That is, as long as she just opens her eyes soon.

Alexandra West

Coldness. That's my first sensation that I feel after the prolonged and relentless darkness. A cold so deep that it seems to be deeply ingrained in my bones, emanating from my insides out. My next feeling I recognize is an insane amount of pain, probably the most pain that I've ever had in my life, if I think about it. But every instance I try to think about my medical history, all I feel is a stabbing pain in my head. Turning my attention to something I can control, I try to open my eyes but I find that I can't, at least not yet. Guess that's not in the cards for me right now. Instead, I try to get a sense of where I am at.

It's quiet, deathly quiet, meaning that I'm definitely not at West Enterprises. The only time the house would be this quiet is when none of my brothers are home. I hear medical beeps and smell the distinct scent of sterile disinfectants. Hospital? That's it, I'm in a hospital. But why am I here? Oh, right. It suddenly comes back to me in a series of high-speed mental flashes. Cole, my brothers, being shot and stabbed. I start to panic, feeling the need to get to my brothers and Cole, needing to know if they're unharmed, what happened, when all of the sudden, as if I summoned them based upon sheer willpower alone, I can hear some of them.

"You left her? What the hell, Dave?" Will bellows, my older brother not realizing how his voice is now painfully bouncing around in my skull.

Defensively, I can hear Dave snap back, "We were trying to save you, you asshole. We saw you taking fire and wanted to give you additional coverage, damn it!"

"We didn't need you to save us!" Will yells back, the sound seeming to echo in the stillness of the hospital hallways as the noise tumbles around in my head, making me wish my brothers were soft-spoken, instead of loud, brash ogres. Ouch, I definitely need an aspirin to clear up this headache. Before I can muster up the energy to try to open my eyes again to ask one of my brothers for aspirin, I hear Kev's calmer voice.

"Will, Dave, the both of you need to calm down," Kev diplomatically interrupts, "she's alive. She's healing, that's what matters. But we need to be patient.; The healing process, it will take time. Lex has already made so much progress in the time that we've been here. We got her here right after the attack and we got her the medical attention she needed in time, the doctors said it themselves. We won. She won."

Luke's voice sounds tired as he echoes what Kev said, "Yeah guys, the doctors said she is going to make a full recovery. And you know Lex. She's stubborn. She's not going to let that bastard win. She'll live, just out of pure spite."

I want to tell them that they're right. That I am going to be fine and that I know they're here, that I love them. I want to tell them I appreciate that they're all here in this moment and to thank them for saving my life. I want to open my eyes and see them, and Cole. I haven't heard Cole yet. Is he okay? Did that bastard kill him in the end? I hear the medical equipment beeps increase in frequency as I again try to desperately open my eyes while straining my ears to hear Cole's voice.

"Sean, what is it?" Dave anxiously asks, the conversation suddenly coming to a halt.

"Guys, I think she can hear us. Look at her eyelids, her eyes are rapidly moving underneath her eyelids. They weren't doing that before, or at any other time before today." Sean observes with slight astonishment in his voice.

Finally, the time has come when I need Sean to be observant for selfishly, my benefit, but yet, I can't do anything about it. I can't send a signal to him or the rest of my brothers that my youngest brother indeed is correct.

I hear the rustling of clothing and immediately know that my brothers are close, that they are here, surrounding me. I feel each of their essences, the connectedness of our family bonds immediately putting me at ease, alleviating some of my anxiety. I feel warm hands take mine and other hands find the uninjured parts of my body, just trying to make a physical connection with me. I struggle to open my eyes but alas, I still cannot seem to get my body to respond to my most basic of commands. I feel helpless, a feeling that I hate most of all, and I know that I never do well in this type of situation. I know my brothers need me to tell them that I'm okay, they need my absolution, but I can't do that, even though I am screaming it in my mind. I'm playing the silent victim, still and soundless in a tomb of conscious immobility. But as I sense them, I feel safe and content, I feel like I can rest. I feel a hand squeeze mine and instantly know it's my twin.

"Lexi, I'm so sorry," Dave begins, "I should never have left you. I should've turned back sooner. I should've been there with you, I'm so sorry."

"We all should've been there, sweetheart," Will quietly interjects, the regret tinging his voice.

"Just wake up, Lex. Just wake up, that's all. Okay, Sissy?" Luke pleadingly asks, desperation lacing his tone.

I struggle to open my eyes, but I can feel the darkness starting to pull me back down into the void, down to the abyss of pain-free oblivion. I try one last time to open my eyes before tendrils of deep peace reclaim me back into the nothingness of rest.

The next time that I regain consciousness, the world is quiet, all except for the machines incessant beeping, monitoring the progress of my health. I feel pressure on the edge of the bed and I know that someone is here with me. But my instincts kick in and I don't feel threatened. It's in that moment I know that it's Dave. I immediately and automatically know who it is after I take a couple of moments to reorient and center myself. He isn't talking to me, so maybe he's sleeping.

I use the quietness to take full stock of my injuries. The pain is less than the last time I was conscious, but it's still enough to cause some shooting pain to course through my body sporadically. I take a guess that I'm on some pretty heavy doses of pain medication, no wonder I can't stay awake.

I feel the warmth of the sun on my face, meaning that I must be near a window. I smell flowers, lots of flowers. Roses and lilies are the strongest scents that I can pick out. Who do I know that would send me flowers? My brothers aren't the hearts and flowers type. Maybe Cole? Cole, hopefully he's alive. My mind flits back to needing to know how he is doing. Before everything happened, Cole did kiss me. Maybe he sent the flowers to me? It's definitely not some secret admirer. Will would never let that type of scenario rest until he tracked down who it was and built a dossier on them.

I want to ask my twin about Cole and Steve, if they made it. I want to ask if Jace Edwards was chased away from the chaos that is West Enterprises, if my dream of starting my own team left with him. There are so many questions that I have and my twin is asleep. How am I going to wake him up? As I try to sort that all out, the darkness again calls my name. And similar to previous times, I don't have the strength to keep it at bay and fight it anymore. Sleep's coiling tendrils encroach upon my mind as I fall back into unconsciousness, entering a dreamless and weightless sleep without worries or a care in the world.

***

Once again, I am roused from my sleep by a voice urgently talking to me. At first, I can't make out all the words, just the low timber cutting through the din. Then I realize that the speaker is my eldest brother, that Will is talking to me. He's reminiscing about when we were kids, before Dad died and our world was forever changed.

"You and Dave were off in your own world as usual. And Dad was trying to get you guys to come back to the rest of us. I was so mad at you two. All Dad wanted to do was to take our family picture, just like he did every year on the first day of the summer when we all went to the beach together. But you two wouldn't come over for the picture," Will pauses, remembering that day clearly in his brain.

He takes a deep breath, my eldest brother overcome with days gone by before he continues, "Everything seemed so much easier then. Our relationships, our daily responsibilities, our lives. Everything was simpler. You and me, our dynamic back then, we were simpler. I wish, now, that I could take back all of the anger from our relationship that's separated us, all the instigation that I infused, which has only intensified over the years. I realize now that it just isn't worth it anymore. That animosity we've carried toward each other for years. It's just not what's important, not in the long run."

I feel something wet drop against my arm. For a second, I can't figure out what it is until I realize it was a tear. Will is crying! I haven't seen him ever cry, even when Dad died, in the quiet of our house, at the funeral or after it all in the stillness of grief.

Will suddenly grabs my hand, holding it tight, almost to the point to where it hurts. With thick emotions lacing his voice, Will urgently whispers, "Just hold on, Lex. Okay? Hold on, honey. I know you can make it through this and we're all here for you. Just stay with us Lex. Just open your eyes.

Can you do that? Can you open your eyes for me, sweetheart? Just for a second? So I know that you're okay, so I know that you can hear me."

As he's speaking, he has intensified his grip on my hand to the point that it feels like my bones are about to be crushed. Wanting to let him know that I can hear him, and on a side note, that he honestly is about to break my hand, I try to funnel all my energy in squeezing his hand back.

I hear his gasp and I know that he felt me listening, even if it was a pithy acknowledgement. "Lex, can you hear me? I'm here. I've got you, sweetheart," Will urgently responds.

I try to squeeze my brother's hand back again, but I am getting so tired. That one squeeze seemed to drain all of the energy out of me. Since when did squeezing hands take all of my physical effort? When I get out of here, I'm going to need to work on my strength training and improve my grip strength again. As exhaustion settles in and the darkness comes back to reclaim me, pulling me back under, all I hear is Will's voice as he says, "I'm here, Lex. I'm here with you."

William West

"I swear," I emphatically say, "she squeezed my hand. She knew that I was there. She heard me. Lex is in there, guys, and she was trying to communicate with me."

Luke looks at me, his gaze full of concern and doubt as he leans his hip against the newly installed black granite kitchen counter. When I arrived back at West Enterprises, I practically rushed in, barely taking the time to properly turn the SUV's engine off. I yelled for all my brothers to join me as I effusively recounted my experience with our sister in the kitchen.

"Are you sure?" Sean hesitantly asks, the hope in his voice faint, but still seeping through the proverbial, doubtful cracks.

"Yeah, man, no offense, but you haven't slept much in these past couple of days," Kev dryly comments.

Shaking my head, I firmly and adamantly say, "Yes. She was undeniably with me. She heard me, and she knew that I was there. I know what I felt. I'm sure of it. I'm not going crazy."

I look around at my four brothers, my eyes begging for them to believe me. I need them to believe me, to make it real. I need Lex to forgive me. I need her to wake up so I can apologize to her directly. In my mind, if my brothers believe me, I'm one step close to getting to say that I'm sorry to her.

Dave, seeming to understand my desperation, gently responds, "I believe you. I can feel when she's present with me and when she's not during my visits."

I nod, understanding how hard it was for Dave to leave her side. But we all have been encouraging him to come home to sleep, shower and eat. He is drastically losing weight, wasting away at her bedside and not really smelling like roses either. This is the rare time where Dave's at the house, that he's showered and has already taken a quick work video conference call that he couldn't reschedule.

"I'm going back over there," Dave continues, "I'll keep you posted on her progress." We watch as Dave walks toward the garage with his shoulders slumped, almost as if he has the entire weight of the world bearing down upon his back. I know the feeling.

As I turn my attention back to Sean, Kev and Luke, they are all nodding in unison agreement. Luke gently suggests, "C'mon, Will, let's go grab a couple beers, sit on the deck and talk about Lex and all her mischief."

Knowing my three younger brothers are all doing this for my benefit, I nod in appreciative concession. We all grab a beer from the fridge as we walk onto the deck, just as the sun is about to set upon the distant horizon.

Alexandra West

I wake up, feeling someone crawling in the bed next to me, the covers pulling taunt against my frame. It's Dave again, I can immediately tell this time. He starts holding me, just like he did when we were kids and I was scared that Dad wasn't going to come home from one of his business trips.

For a while, he's silent. I can tell he's going to say something. I don't know if he knows that I can hear him, but he begins talking anyway. "Lexi, I'm so sorry. The doctors tell me that you're fine, but I want you to say that to me yourself. I need you to open your eyes. I need to hear your voice. I need to see your smile and hear your laugh."

I desperately want to ease his misery, but I am still trapped inside my own body, imprisoned in a state of confined silence. He goes on to tell me all about the construction going on at the house. Our men and my brothers have been rebuilding, remodeling and fixing everything. I'm glad. I don't want to come home to a house reminding me of my latest injuries and our family's failures. I hope they get the bloodstain out of that hallway carpet. As if reading my mind, Dave tells me what a difficult process cleaning blood out of carpeting is. In the end, they will be replacing the carpet with laminate vinyl plank flooring. Thank goodness. That carpet needed to be replaced for years. It's just a shame that I almost had to die for my brothers to update that part of the house.

My twin then goes on to tell me Will was adamant during his last visit that I could hear him, that I was trying to converse with him non-verbally. I wish I could smile. Who knew Will and I would be getting along! By Dave's tone, he is just as surprised as I am. But I'm glad that Will had Dave to believe in him. I knew out of anyone, Dave would understand.

Before long, I start to feel the fatigue that I've become so used to start to settle into the corners of my consciousness. As I start dozing off, Dave begins to tell me about the completed deck reconstruction. I try to focus on his words and stay awake, but I slowly succumb and slip into the world of welcoming rest and dreams, feeling safe with my twin by my side.

David West

As I exit my sister's room, a nurse stops me in the hallway. Apparently, Bonnie Hooper, the head of the hospital, and the doctors want the entire family to meet with them here at the hospital. My twin still hasn't woken up yet, it's been quite some time, probably too long of a period for her to be unconscious. Everyone's concerned and on edge, so I call Will and tell my brothers to get down here as soon as possible. They arrive at the hospital in under ten minutes, a new all-time West family record. I know their speedy arrival is based out of fear and concern for our sister. I didn't give them details because I honestly didn't have any to provide.

We are all standing outside of Lexi's room, looking through the glass at her motionless form while we wait for the doctors and Bonnie Hooper to join us. Thankfully, they took some of the tubes and wires out of her since her healing is progressing, but it is still an unhinging sight. Lexi has never been that still in her entire life. Seeing Lexi on that bed, not moving and looking so small is so unnatural, it's frightening.

It's in our contemplative silence that the doctors walk over to us and lead us to a meeting room nearby. In it, we find that Bonnie Hooper and her administrative assistant, Stephanie Cook are already seated. We all sit down and warily watch the team of doctors parade in, silently waiting for one of them to begin speaking. The silence seems to unnerve them and to pervade into self-consciousness, manifesting in nervous ticks and the shifting of limbs. For us, silence is an automatic reaction commonly used in interrogation techniques, regardless of which side of the table you find yourself sitting on. It's a part of our agent training from day one.

Finally, the doctors inform us that even though she hasn't woken up yet, we can take Lexi home. We all give a questioning gaze to the team of doctors. That's when Bonnie graciously steps in to clarify that medically, Lexi is a normal, healthy, twenty-nine-year-old woman. At this point, she needs to rest and to take it easy. She can do that at home in a place where she is comfortable. What is not being blatantly said, the communications between the lines, is that Bonnie is making an exception for our family. The doctors all know we work for and run West Enterprises, as we have all been in their hospital at some point in time, needing to be patched up. Because of this, all of the medical staff know that we have basic medical training and will immediately bring Lex to the hospital if her condition were to suddenly worsen. They believe she'll recover faster at home, in a safe, familiar environment. One of the doctors mentions something about her psyche being able to heal better at home, how that may be the spark to get her to regain consciousness faster.

The doctors already initiated the paperwork in order for her to be formally released into West Enterprises' care. The hospital will be sending medical equipment over this afternoon, the transport being handled by a couple of trusted registered nurses who will also ensure Lex is properly monitored, having all she needs that would be comparable to here in the hospital. We only have to wait another couple of hours, a few grains of sand in the greater span of time before we can finally bring her home. We all nod in appreciation and file out of the room, lost in our own thoughts, afraid to finally feel relief.

We go back to stand at the threshold of Lexi's room. After awhile, we watch as the nursing staff disconnects all the tubes and wires from her, putting gauze on her skin over the various IV locations she has had. They redress her wounds, and the nurses bring in a backboard with the intent on lifting her from her bed to a gurney where she'll be loaded into the transport vehicle. Us West brothers all look at each other and nod, understanding what we need to do. We file in the room and motion for the nurses to leave. We will carry her out instead of using a gurney to the awaiting transport ambulance, not letting anyone else near our sister.

The five of us brothers load her in the vehicle, the awaiting medical team securely strapping her in after exchanging momentarily looks of disbelief and confusion. After the paramedics secure her, we all crowd into the ambulance, sitting along the bench walls. The paramedics go to say something but once they notice the expression on Will's face, they wisely refrain. Kev gives the house's address and we all get underway. Luke texts one of his buddies, telling him to come to the hospital later and to pick up the SUV. Dave's gaze is intently watching Lexi's face. She's becoming more expressive, her face twitching every now and then. We're all hopeful that she'll wake up soon, once she's finally home.

William West

She's home. Finally, my little sister is home. I feel like I can actually breathe a little easier with Lex being under the same roof as me. We are able to keep Kev's promise, that she'd come home. I rationally know that she's still unconscious and has a long way to go to a full recovery, but at least she's here and we don't have to worry about going back and forth to the city. Stress I didn't realize that was stacked on my back seems to fall off my shoulders the minute the ambulance parks in the garage.

We decline help from the paramedics, carrying our sister up to her bedroom on the backboard. I pick up her prone body from the board and carefully cradle her to my chest as the rest of my brothers prepare her bed, pulling the comforter and sheets down, fluffing her pillows. I gently lay her down in the bed and carefully brush her dark hair out of her face. Kev pulls the covers up to her shoulders while Sean opens her double doors so she can hear and smell her beloved ocean while feeling the cool sea breeze waft over her face.

The sun's rays gracefully dance into the room, the light beams moving and shining across her face. I take a moment to notice the light playing off her ornate table lamp, the glass creating prisms of color and shapes on the wall behind the bed, myriads of art decorating the soft white walls. I feel at peace now, just because of these small moments with my family. I look down at my little sister and feel the corner of my mouth tug up ever so slightly. The color has returned to her face, she seems to look healthier than when we were just at the hospital an hour ago. Happy with her being home, I turn and quietly leave her be so she can rest and ultimately open her eyes.

I grab a beer and go grab an Adirondack chair, sitting on the deck. The afternoon sun is shining, and the ocean looks like it spans across the entire horizon, leading to an endless eternity. I take a deep breath, inhaling the salt of the ocean and the wood of the house's renovations, feeling a relief so deep, my soul is satisfied. Lex is safe. She's here. She is alive. Dad would be happy, he loved her so much. A feeling of much needed peace washes over me.

After a few moments of enjoying my revelry in silence, Kev joins me on the deck, grabbing a chair next to mine. He looks over at me with a knowing gaze as he intuitively says, "You can relax now, brother. She's home. We got her home. The house looks great. And she is going to be fine."

"I know." My voice showing my relief as the tension leaves my shoulders. I let a silent moment pass before I reflectively say to my best friend and brother, "I hadn't realized how much she mattered to me. It took me almost losing her to spark the desire to have a healthy relationship with her again. I only hope that she can forgive me once she wakes up. I am responsible for her, and all of you, you know that. Dad told me to look after her, after all five of you, right before his departure for his last mission."

"Will, you did protect her. You were there, you helped her. You got her home. If you want a relationship with her, then when she wakes up, start one with her. Be ready to compromise as this relationship, just as any, needs to be a two-way street. You guys have always butt heads, but only because you're both a lot alike. And there isn't anything wrong with that, but you each need to realize that you've both been right and wrong over the years. And to let those mistakes stay in the past so you can forge something better for the future," Kev gently and advises with sage wisdom.

I nod, knowing that my younger brother is right. I know what I must do when Lex finally wakes up. And I hope against all odds, she'll want a peaceful relationship with me too once the dust settles.

Sean West

The house's atmosphere has lifted considerably since Lex's arrival back at the new and improved West Enterprises. Everyone seems to be in a lighter mood. There are extra bounces in everyone's steps as we all move around the house, finalizing the last of the repairs. Lex has woken up a couple times, only staying conscious for a couple minutes at the most and she's barely lucid. But the doctors are saying that she's on the mend, that this is good progress and we're heading in the right direction towards healing.

I'm so grateful that my sister's back at the house, that way we can all stop in and visit with her instead of driving back and forth. All that travel becomes taxing after a while. She's only had one moment where she spoke and that was to ask for Cole. Since Lex's hospital stay and all the chaotic renovations at West Enterprises, we had Cole stay at a hotel nearby, here on Long Island. He had around the clock protection from our teams and we were constantly texting him with any updates that we had on Lex. At Lex's question, we immediately let him know that he should start to make his way over to West Enterprises. We made sure during the renovations process that we had all of the West kids' bedrooms ready, as well as a few guest rooms ready for those working around the clock and those, like Cole, who may be a permanent visitor.

To his credit, Dave still has never left his twin's side, fearing he won't be there when Lex finally wakes up fully. He's taken to eating his meals in her room. I don't blame him, the rest of us pop in so often, we usually tend to take our meals in her room too. We toggle between us brothers cooking or ordering take-out.

Those moments when she wakes up, though fleeting, are some of the brightest moments in the house. Will is on edge, waiting for her to wake up completely, wanting to talk to her, to ask her finally for the redemption he thinks he so desperately needs. Kev has to remind him multiple times a day that he needs to relax, to give her time and to be patient. She probably won't want to talk about relationship repairs right when she wakes up. She's still healing and will want to know what's going on and what happened. Will begrudgingly agrees every time, but I can see the laughter in Kev's eyes, as he continues to remind our usually stoic and composed brother to wait and practice exercising patience. Luke's mood has also significantly increased since her arrival. He's joking around more and trying to make us all laugh. He's getting back to his version of what is his normal state versus his level of quiet distress that he was constantly dwelling in while Lex was medically touch and go.

To this day, I still can't believe how close we all were to losing her. The doctors said that she was right on the knife's edge of life or death, that her demise was imminent. But she decided to stay. Lex ignored how easy it would be to go to the other side and to be with our parents. If she had decided to go the other way, we would've lost her forever. There was a lot of damage she physically sustained and she had lost a little over five pints of blood by the time she was admitted for immediate, emergency surgery. I can't imagine our family without her. She has changed us, made us a stronger family, stronger individuals and agents. She has unintentionally united us to all be better to each other. When she wakes up and after she heals, all six of us Wests should sit and talk about our family's dynamics and relationships going forward. Maybe even take a family vacation. That has never happened before in the history of the West family.

PART IV

Alexandra West

The first sensation that I feel is warmth on my face, like the rays of the sun. Next, I mentally register that I can hear waves. I can smell the ocean. I piece together that I'm home, I'm no longer in a hospital room. Good, because I'm not a fan of being in hospitals, never have been. But how did I get here? When did I get here? I'm missing something and my memory is drawing a blank, unable to fill in the gaps. I have always hated not being able to piece my timelines together. My mind flashes as it remembers the smells of the hospital before I fast-forward to small bursts of barely being conscious at home, with my brothers. My brothers were to ones to bring me home.

I slowly open my eyes, silently celebrating the achievement of finally being able to visually see the world after how many failed attempts at the hospital, and then those blurred attempts in my room that were too fast and fleeting. Everything is bright at first, like a wall of white light, and I fight the urge to close my eyes again to ward off the glare. As the brightness dims and my light sensitivity subsides, I make out the outlines of my bedroom's curtains, walls and minimal décor. I see a fuzzy image of my beach bag to the left of the French doors. My vision continues to sharpen as I take in the white sheers that frame out the balcony which are blowing in the light breeze, looking like they're performing a dance with predetermined choreography to a song that only nature can hear. Yes, I'm definitely home, my brain registers its confirmation. But how am I not in the hospital? I decide I'll figure that out later. Sinking a little further into my pillows with relief, I make a mental note to thank my brothers for getting me back home.

Suddenly the feeling of being so thirsty is overwhelming, to the point where I can't think of anything else. It feels like I haven't had water in years. I go to rollover and stand up to get out of bed, but I am met with the solid form of a sleeping figure seated by my bedside, with a head resting on a set of folded arms next to my hip. It's then that I take stock that this someone is also holding my hand. I follow the hand in my mine and my eyes travel up the arm, coming to rest on this figure's shoulders and head. As I study the figure more, my eyes slowly come into focus. It's after a few moments that I finally recognize Cole Harris. I need to get his attention. I need to get a glass of water.

"Cole," my voice barely a whisper, my tone raspy with prolonged disuse. "Cole, wake up. I need water."

Cole slowly looks up and realizes that I am expectantly staring right at him, waiting for him to move. His ocean blue eyes widen as he starts yelling for my brothers. I cringe at the yelling and immediately cover my ears, the noise abrasively resonating around in my skull. I try closing my eyes in the process, to ward off an incoming headache and fight back against the sound. I open my eyes and look up after the commotion at my bedroom door ceases and Cole falls silent. All five of my brothers are standing in my bedroom's threshold, looking like they've seen a ghost. I look at them and quietly request water again. Kev thankfully rushes off, running to the kitchen to grab me a glass of water while the rest of my brothers slowly file in, never taking their eyes off me, acting if they make a sudden move, that I'll disappear just like a wisp of smoke.

Dave is the first to snap out of his trance and he comes around to sit behind me so I have something to lean on while I stay somewhat upright. Man, my abdominal muscles must have wasted away for however long I was out. I appreciate my twin's knowing that I need to ground and brace myself against a solid foundation. Kev returns with a glass of water which I chug in only a few gulps. After I finish, I lean back against Dave, silently seeking strength from my twin as well as catching my breath. I'm sore, but not as bad as I remember the couple of times when I was conscious in the hospital. But I still feel like I've been hit by a bus.

I open my eyes as I hear the rustling of clothes, of movement coming closer. I watch as my eldest brother slowly approaches me, as if I'm a feral cornered animal, ready to attack at any given moment.

"Lex," Will starts in a low and uncharacteristically hesitant voice, "I'm so sorry. I failed you, and I promised I would never—"

I gently interrupt him, "Don't, Will. Please. I heard you before. It's okay. We're good. You have nothing to apologize for, brother."

"You could hear us?" Luke asks incredulously, my brother's jaw comically dropping open. If this wasn't such a serious moment and if I didn't think I would wince with the pain, I would've started laughing.

I nod as I continue, "I think so. I couldn't tell if it was real or if I was dreaming. But it doesn't matter anymore. I don't blame any of you for what happened. What's in the past is in the past. I'm just glad that you were there to kill the bastard and get me the medical help I so very clearly needed. Just tell me the prognosis. Also, can someone tell me how long have I been out?"

"Fifteen days, Lex. You've been out for fifteen long, agonizingly brutal days," Sean answers, heavily emphasizing fifteen.

Slightly surprised, I had no clue I was out for that long. As I take a closer look at my brothers, I notice they all seem to have lost weight and none of them have shaved in a while. I see the shadows and bags that surround their eyes, the exhaustion that seems to be weighing down their spine and limbs.

"And you're going to be fine," Luke quickly interjects, anticipating my next question. I turn my attention on him as he gives my prognosis, "You'll be sore and you're still healing, but the doctors cleared you to come home and recover here. You'll need some minor physical therapy, but that's nothing we can't handle here. We weren't sure if you wanted to come here or go somewhere else. This was closer but wherever you want to go, we can grab your bags and take you there now."

"No," I answer, interrupting Luke's anxious babbling, "I'm fine with being here. I'd rather be with all of you. Just help me up, I want to go sit on the balcony. I want to feel the sunshine on my skin."

My brothers and Cole scramble to help me stand and we slowly move together toward the balcony as a unit. My legs feel like they haven't been used in ages and I'm not as steady on my feet as I would like to care to admit, but thankfully no one seems quick to point that fact out. They get me seated and I lean back into one of the Adirondack chairs, completely shattered and exhausted. Dave brings me my sunglasses and motions for everyone else to leave. He grabs another chair and sits down, right next to me. I smile at him, embarrassed at being so exhausted from such little exertion.

It's nice in this moment to be alone with my twin, the understanding we have passes between us without having to say anything out loud. I think I'm actually too tired to speak and am grateful for our Twin Power with the accompaniment of the beach's soothing sounds. Dave takes my hand, understanding that I'm fatigued and not filling the silence with needless conversation. We both turn our attention back to the glittering ocean as my eyelids begin to droop closed and my skin warms from the beautiful, afternoon ocean sunshine.

***

I wake up, still warm from the sun's rays. I immediately note that it's later in the day, the sun is beginning to set. The warmer colors are beginning to be painted into the late afternoon sky, the sun like a bright ball of light, slowly fading away for the day.

"That was a close one, Lex, even for you," I whisper to myself, taking a moment to reflect and admit not only from my brothers' haggard appearances, but also how I feel, at just how close I was to the other side.

I don't remember feeling or hearing Dave leave, but before he left, he had tucked a blanket around my legs. For that, I'm grateful as the early evening chill is starting to roll in and I resist the urge to shiver. I roll my shoulders, grimacing through the pain, my shoulders stiff from being in a bed for over two weeks. I choose to test my legs and stand, holding onto the banister for additional support and balance that I wish I didn't need. I immediately feel exhausted and sit back down. But I have this burning and unrelenting desire to sit on the beach to watch the sunset. I want to feel the sand between my toes. I miss feeling the breeze blow through the dunes and hearing the waves crash on the sand. I need to feel that sense of calamity and peace beneath and around me, to be a small part of it all. It's been way too long, and I'm craving the sense of being grounded, of being a part of the Atlantic shoreside again.

As I begin to formulate a plan on how I am going to get down to the beach, I hear Cole enter my bedroom. Perfect timing. I honestly have no idea how I could've gotten down my balcony's stairs, let alone through the heavy sand to the dunes. Now Cole can help me because right now, with all of my injuries, I admittedly can't get down there by myself. I start to pull myself up again, but my arm strength seems to also be giving out on me.

"Alexis," Cole says as he rushes over, concern etching his handsome face as he notices my efforts to stand up again.

Cole tosses the towels he had in his hands when he walked in onto the bed, his free hands now steadying my shoulders as he helps me back down to a seated position. He notices my flushed face and my uneven breathing. Man, I need to get back into shape, this is ridiculous!

"What are you doing? Are you okay? What can I get you? Where's Dave?" Cole rushes out all in one breath, his questions coming out like rapid fire, giving me only a slight case of whiplash.

Putting my hand up to stop the beginnings of his interrogation, I ignore his questions and urgently reply, "Help me get down to the beach. I need to see the sunset on the beach. Please, Cole."

For a brief moment, I can see him questioning my logic and sanity. To be honest, if I were him, I'd probably be concerned about my own mental health as well. Even I could hear the desperation in my voice. I was released from the hospital and just woke up from a comatose state. And now my sole focus is getting to the beach? I can see how someone may be concerned about me. Maybe I hit my head or something. But all I know is that I need to see the sunset and catch up on the moments I missed while I was unconscious on the shoreline. But I could rationally understand if he thought that I was going considerably insane.

"Cole, please," I repeatedly plead, "I need help to get down to the beach. I can't do it alone."

I watch Cole's expression as it wavers, but ultimately, he nods in understanding and grabs my beach bag. He stuffs the bag full with a beach blanket, an insulated water bottle, my medication and the bunch of towels he brought in with him. He slings the bag over his shoulder and comes to stand in front of me. I briefly toy with asking him to grab one of my stashed handguns, but I think better of it. I need to pick my battles wisely and the beach is the end goal.

"Ready?" Cole asks, his nervousness of being complicit in my crazy plan present in his tone.

I eagerly and enthusiastically nod my head, slowly pulling myself to my feet, tightly gripping the handrail so I don't fall backward. Before I can take a further step to head toward the stairs, Cole slips his arms under me and lifts me up. I instantly start to protest. I need to try to get to the beach myself, for either my pride or ego, I can't say.

Cole absent-mindedly interrupts me and says, "You and I both know that you can barely stand, let alone walk down those stairs. You're still really unsteady on your feet. So if we're going to the beach, you'll have to make this concession and let me carry you for once. Okay?"

Admittedly, I stop protesting. Cole's right and we both know it. He mutters more to himself than to me, "You need to put some more weight on. You lost so much while you were in the hospital." I smile at his caring nature as we start descending the stairs, and I hold onto Cole tightly as he balances me and the beach bag.

Once we get onto the sand, I'm expecting him to let me down and for me to try to walk. Man am I ever mistaken. He continues to carry me over to my favorite spot, just past the dunes, so we're overlooking the waves. He gently lowers me to the ground and helps me plant my feet onto the warm sand. He checks to make sure that I can stand on my own and that I'm steady before he pulls the blanket out of my bag that's been hanging on his shoulder and lowers it on the sand. He lays down one of the three towels in a pile and pulls my medication and water thermos out too, setting those aside on the blanket. Cole comes back to me and helps me sit on the blanket, making sure that I'm comfortable on top of one of the towels. He takes a seat behind me, allowing me to lean back on his chest for support. He grabs the other two towels and wraps one around my shoulders and drapes the other one on my legs to keep me warm. I'm impressed that he thought of all this through, quite on the fly too.

Improvisation is one of the greatest skills a successful West agent possesses. Maybe Cole would consider joining West Enterprises as an agent one day. But I tuck that thought away as I take in my view of the Atlantic Ocean.

The sun is starting to set, and it'll start to get even cooler than it is right now. With Cole sitting behind me, this allows me to take some of his extra warmth for my own. We watch the sunset in companionable silence. Each gazing at the brilliant yellow ball lowering down slowly, pastels brightening the early evening sky. The sky looks like all the colors have been painted in the form of a rainbow. The vibrant hues of red fading and bleeding through to the oranges, yellows, green and blues until the deep purples and dark violets of the night are all that's left in the sky.

I sigh, truly content with nature's simplistic beauty. I missed these moments, the space in time right before twilight and the sun has fully set have always enchanted me, even as a child. Minutes of silence pass as the stars begin to dot the evening sky, the lights sparkling and shining high above us. I shiver and immediately Cole's arms are around me, providing additional warmth.

After a moment of pure contentment, I heave myself up so that I'm sitting, using my rusty abdominal muscles as I wrap the towel tighter around my shoulders. I lean forward, stretching out my back muscles as I stare intently, looking at the night's ocean. I've always enjoyed the light show that reflects off the ocean's surface when the moon comes out. How the sky and the ocean seem to be competing with who can shine the brightest. I wait for the moon with anticipatory glee, soothed by the evening's beautiful predictability.

I feel Cole move so he's sitting next to me. Out of the corner of my eye, I surreptitiously watch him as he looks at my profile, studying my face, for what, I don't know.

"I just wanted to say thank you," he starts, "for saving my life. I will never forget what you did, nor the image of you bleeding on the floor to protect my life, even if that meant you giving your life up for me. I will forever be in your debt, Alexis. I could never repay you. But my promise to you is that I will live my life every day in a way that will honor your sacrifice. And know that I will be forever grateful for what you did for me."

I take in his words and consider them carefully. I realize that I honestly didn't want him to die, nor did I want anyone in my family to be hurt. I felt relieved when I woke up and was told that no one I loved was critically harmed. Then I realized I said the L word, even if it was only in my head. Wow. I'm officially admitting to myself that I'm feeling emotions. And that action hasn't consumed me in an eternal inferno like I had originally thought that it would.

All this time, I thought if I allowed myself to feel emotions and to express those emotions openly, I would be so overwhelmed and not be able to function in any realistic capacity. That somehow, I'd become weaker, more vulnerable, and I of all things can't or won't be vulnerable. But I'm starting to get in touch with my emotional side and I don't feel like I'm drowning. I don't have the floods of guilt that I always thought would overwhelm my senses for all the things that I've done in my profession, and in my life.

I've never lived my life as a saint, staying close to the shadows and using my anonymity to my advantage. I have always liked the dark; I've always had more fun and thrived in the shadows. Instead, I feel a happiness and gratitude for being alive and for being able to see another sunset, and for the possibility to spend another day with my family and friends.

I take a breath as I realize all of this and slowly exhale. This is all truly liberating! I am thankful for having five brothers who fiercely protect and love me, even if they do overprotect, smother and frustrate me at times. I love my family and I also have the same intense need to protect them back.

And there's grace in being given a second chance. I can help repair the relationships that I have with my brothers that have been fractured for too long. It's a choice that I get to make, because of them making the decisions and taking the necessary actions for me to be here today.

I feel something for Cole, although I don't fully understand it, at least not yet. However, I know that I need to get this off my chest and that in turn, Cole needs to hear what I have to say.

"Cole, I need to stop you right there. You don't owe me anything. In fact, I'm the one who owes you everything. Yes, I may have played a part in saving your life. But you, Cole, you... you have saved my soul. I didn't feel many emotions before you, or if I did feel them, I immediately suppressed them, depending on which of my brothers you choose to ask. Before you, I muted everything. Every high, every win. Every good memory, every achievement. If I didn't allow myself to feel the joys of life, the profoundness of the lows wouldn't be able to drown or crush me. I know that essentially I was deadening my human experience, operating solely in survival mode. The thing I thought that I loved and wanted most was the very poison that almost became my utter undoing. But getting to know you and building our relationship over the past few weeks, I feel myself opening up not only to you, but also to my family members. I would have died that day in a heartbeat if it meant that you or my brothers would have escape unharmed. And I don't regret the choices that led me here to right now. You have to know that. Thankfully, it didn't come to that. But you have restored my ability to empathize with others and to have compassion, something that I have been missing for many years. So, it is I who needs to thank you, Cole. I appreciate everything you've done for me. I am the one who could never repay you," I quietly confess to the man who has changed everything.

Cole, looking in my eyes, smiles and looks down at the sand. When he looks back up, his azure blue sky eyes are suspiciously glistening. "I like you, Alexis West," Cole admits. "I want to get to know you better. Maybe when you're feeling better, we can go out to dinner on a date or go on that coffee date we talked about."

"Did you ask my brothers for permission?" I ask teasingly, the corners of my mouth turning upward.

187

Cole chuckles, "Yes, in fact I did. I felt like I was gearing up for a battle before I asked, especially when I asked Dave. But they already said it'd be fine."

Sighing, I say as I shake my head with amusement, "Don't worry about Dave. I'll talk to him. He'll come around eventually."

Cole smiles before tentatively continuing, "So… is that a yes? Would you ever go with me? On a dinner date, or coffee, if that's less intimidating?"

I feel a genuine smile light across my face and look Cole directly in the eyes as I respond, "I'd love to go on a date with you, Cole Harris." The smile that breaks out on his face fills my soul as I nestle back into him with a sense of tranquility.

Who knew that all it would take was the same target and two competing contracts within the same family to spark emotions and compassion within my soul? The target that I was supposed to kill ended up saving my relationships with my brothers and helped me to establish a new, possibly romantic relationship with a great man. More so, Cole helped me see the benefits of tapping into my human emotions, that feeling something didn't make me weak. It, in fact, makes me stronger. Connecting with people could become one of my greatest weapons and strengths, as a sister, friend and professional. I wonder if my parents are looking down from heaven and seeing all this play out. I wonder if my mom and dad are proud of how much that I've developed in such a relatively short amount of time. I wonder if Dad had any help in pushing us all together in the end, as if he knew that it'd take something like this to bring us all together again as a family.

I start smiling as I hear and sense my brothers coming up behind us to join us for our evening traditions. I finally feel complete. I have all the important things in my life, right here with me. I look up and see them all smiling down at me, with their own individual versions of brotherly love radiating off each of them. They brought their own blankets, plus an additional fleece blanket for me, along with multiple bottles of beer and a picnic basket presumably full of food. They planned this, of course; Cole and my brothers planned this out of love. Love for me. Of course, they coordinated this without my knowledge, but I can't be mad at them. I smile back up at them as they all start to settle in around us.

Dave comes to sit on the other side of me, looking at me to make sure that I am comfortable with everything going on. Luke brings the fleece blanket over and tucks it around my legs and waist, knowingly helping me to ward off the evening chill. Will briefly checks my temperature, his wrist softly placed against my forehead, making sure that I am not running a fever or that I'm at risk for an infection. As Will pulls away, he gives me a rare smile and kisses me lightly on the forehead. I nod at Dave and Will both, as they finally settle down with the rest of us as we look at the various stars and constellations lighting up the now midnight blue sky. I take a deep breath and feel the peace settle over us all.

I take a moment to reflect upon my journey thus far. I realize that I'm not the same Alex West I was a month ago. And that knowledge isn't as scary as I thought it would be. I can't say that I miss her, maybe pieces of her, yes. But overall, I'm content with who I am now, maybe content with who I am for the first time in my adult life. I feel reborn, like a phoenix rising from its ashes. And with the cosmic change within my psyche, I wonder if I look different. Any external proof to reflect the changes going on inside me. But I know that type of change isn't visible, at least not yet. That may come with time.

If I'm capable of this type of change, I need to sustain it by continuing to head toward the right direction, to be the woman my brothers, Cole, Dad and Mom always thought and hoped that I could be. A lightbulb goes off in my head as I realize I can change something simple, something that could signal all the changes swirling inside of me.

"Oh, and guys?" I ask, figuring I'll let my brothers and the man I'm falling in love with be the first to know, that they deserve that much.

All six men drag their eyes away from the sky and look at me expectantly, not rushing me or my thought process. "I'm glad I'm here with all of you as Lex, not Alex or Alexis West or anyone else. Just… Lex," I shyly say.

Cole broadly smiles as my brothers' expressions transform to happiness and joy. They all realize the weight and impact of what I just said, reading between the lines. I'm still Alex West professionally, but I am no longer Alex West to my family and close friends. I'm just Lex. A sister, a friend and a companion who is on their side too.

My heart beats. The stars twinkle. My lungs expand. My muscles relax. Weight seems to lift off my shoulders. We all look out over the ocean, to the paradoxical waves ahead as a comfortable silence settles upon us all once again. I am home. I am surrounded by the ones that I love and hold close to my heart. This is the peace, hope and redemption that I've been searching for all my life. And I have found it right here. Along all, it's been with my family. It was right in front of me all this time. They were waiting for me to see it for myself. And in return, they were preparing themselves to accept me and to provide their unconditional love back. All I had to do was to accept them and let them in past all my barriers and walls. Now that I've done that, I have finally found love for myself.

HARRIS, COLE

Name: COLE HARRIS

Age: 30 Years Old

Height: 6'2"

Weight: 192 lbs

Physical Characteristics: Blue Eyes, Brown Hair, Average Build

Employer: West Enterprises, Inc.

Employment Status: Probationary Period

Role: Intern Agent (Temporary/Contract)

Specialty Area(s), Select All That Apply:

    ___ Behavioral Analysis/Profiling

    ___ Company Admin (Finance, HR, Legal, Training)

    ___ Foreign Diplomacy/Politics

    ___ Forensics

    ___ Intelligence Operations

    ___ Investigations

    ___ Other

    ___ Security: Combat/Weaponry

    ___ Surveillance/Covert Operations

    ___ Threat Analysis

    ___ None of the Above

    X__ Unknown, To Be Determined

PART I

Cole Harris

The sun slowly begins its customary descent to the horizon as the sky changes from its brilliant bright blue to hues of red, orange and yellow. It's mid-June here in the city, and the beach at Long Island was sweltering hot earlier today. Now the temperature is thankfully finally beginning to cool off in New York, directly correlating with the retreating sun. The ocean breeze is beginning to pick back up, offering a much-needed reprieve from the intense summer heat, giving way to the cooler temperatures from the Atlantic Ocean.

Having been raised in California by the water, I have seen my fair share of sunsets and beaches. But being here in New York with the West family, these afternoons have hands down become my favorite time of the day. Just watching the sun give way to the moon and stars, gradually trading off its reign in the sky for some rest provides my soul with a peace that I never thought existed. A sense of serene completion settling upon my soul every evening.

I turn my attention to the sun's finale, its tendrils skating across the sky, its brilliance highlighting the cumulus clouds lingering in the atmosphere, throwing them into all of the colors on the spectrum. Like many other things in life that take time, the sun slowly disappears and allows the moon and stars to illuminate the sky as it darkens from warm hues to the cooler tones of deep purples and blues. But what makes these moments so special isn't just what I'm seeing day after day, but it's with whom that I'm seeing and experiencing these moments with. Her.

I turn my head to see if my woman, Lex, is watching the sun's dying rays. She's what has made these moments special, along with nature's beauty highlighting the facets of her face. Every day since she's come home from the hospital, Lex has insisted on watching the sunset along the shoreline as a way to get back into her regular routine, which has resulted in starting yet another family evening tradition. At least one of her brothers and myself have been joining her for months now, along with our nightly habit of sitting on the deck with beers to decompress from the day's activities after we walk back from the beach.

I look down at the woman that I love who is still napping with her head in her arms, her back and body getting some of the day's last sunrays and warmth. Dark hair covers her shoulders, black wisps gracing the bright red towel that she's resting upon. Lex enjoys lying on the beach, soaking up some tanning time, letting her brothers and I know that beach time is an integral part of her recovery. Whether or not this is true, none of us have the heart to suggest otherwise. And we do have to admit that she's in better spirits as she regains her strength.

As my eyes gaze over her form, I slightly cringe as I look over at her back, the scars that are still bright and noticeable pop out to me on her skin. Her shoulder scar is now just a pucker of skin, the one where the sniper got her in her bedroom. The knife wound that almost cost her life has healed over and is now just a thin, raised white line on her side. The two darker marks on her upper back are where she took two bullets just for me. I can't help but stare at the myriad of her recent scars. I also notice that there are other ones too, older scars which are all sure to have their own stories and tales to tell. Her scars don't tan, and in the dying light, they take a mesmerizing pattern, showcasing and illuminating the story—this is Alexandra "Alex" West.

Even while she's asleep, I know that Lex is always protecting me. At the slightest sound, I know she would wake up, alert, ready to take on the world again for me. She's slowly gaining her energy and confidence back and it's truly a beautiful process to behold. Although all of us call her Lex now, with the exception of Dave who still calls her Lexi, she is now professionally known as Alexandra, Alexandra West. We all have mixed feelings about this complete, about face change. But we're trying to support her, so none of our concerns have been raised by anyone. Physically, she is still healing, with the doctors' reaffirmations that she is making good progress towards a full recovery. Professionally, she has redefined herself and her missions, taking smaller protection contracts instead of her previous elimination tendencies under the persona of Alex West. Relationship wise, she's building and rebuilding strong ties with her family members. Emotionally, though, I'm not sure if she's started her mental and emotional healing yet.

It seems like ages ago, but then again, it seems just like yesterday since the nightmare of my life being turned upside down had finally concluded with a violent, reverberating bang. In reality, it's only been a couple of months since West Enterprises Incorporated was attacked, all because they offered me shelter, assistance and security. Since then, I've helped them with the rebuilding of the West family home and headquarters, offering my assistance in making needed technological updates around the house and a necessary overhaul of the security systems so a breach on the house will be less than likely to happen ever again.

We discovered the West house's security system was remotely hacked by a sophisticated outside source. Will expertly and diligently followed the hacker's trail through the dark web, which took months to accomplish. This security breach allowed teams to break in and enter, resulting in Lex's hospitalization and the house's demolishment, also resulting in the upgrades and renovations. Together, Will and Kev found the hacker from their dark web activity. Kev went after him on a solo mission, some twenty-something year old in eastern Europe, where he was able to utilize his MMA skills to exact some well-deserved revenge. We haven't spoken of it since his return, but the trip seemed to be therapeutic for Kev. Although I'm not at the point yet where I approve of taking a life, I noticed that Kev was struggling with his bottled-up emotions, grief and anxiety.

Each of the other four West brothers have been managing their own grief and anxiety in different ways after the West Enterprises breach. Will has channeled his emotions into creating a custom, brand new security system on a closed network, with around the clock maintenance and scans unique to West Enterprises, all from scratch because of the security incident. Luke has been in the kitchen, trying new recipes for Lex as she regains her appetite. An added benefit is that the rest of us all get to try his culinary creations, though he hasn't mastered the art of cooking for one. But growing up in a house of six kids, I can understand why he cooks for an army, with all the rest of us benefiting. Some of his dishes are wins, other meals that Luke tries are graciously accepted as losses. But the larger West still maintains his positive optimism and has found a creative outlet for his feelings. Sean has focused his energy on contingency planning. Because of the youngest West's strategic efforts, the family's company has hired a team of technicians stationed at headquarters in Long Island as well as individuals located around the world to solely support and monitor the house's security system around the clock. Will admitted that he was getting lax with some of the company's security protocols and that he hadn't made any significant updates in quite some time to keep pace with the rapid and evolving advancement of technology. Now, there are West agents and contractors exclusively dedicated to protecting West Enterprises' assets, including the West family members themselves. Dave's emotional obsession has been ensuring Lex's personal items that were damaged in the fight were either restored or replaced, his strong attention to detail skills coming to painstaking, anal retentive levels. All of us, me included, have focused on various distractions, either as an avoidance technique or as therapeutic release. All efforts to just try to cope with the West Enterprises attack, but more importantly, with almost losing Lex.

Lex's brothers, Will, Kev, Luke, Dave and Sean have all welcomed me into their lives and are teaching me some of the basics of being an agent. They're teaching me techniques for self-defense, attack methods and general insight and knowledge of their daily lives. I quit my job in Manhattan a couple weeks ago, knowing that I could never go back to some dull nine to five job, not when I know that there's excitement and yes, even danger out there, just lurking in the shadows. I also wanted to be closer to Lex while she has been recovering. I'm starting to feel more confident when handling weapons which could be seen as a good or bad thing, depending upon who you ask. Lex has been showing me some highly aggressive attack maneuvers, giving me advanced lessons, which her brothers probably wouldn't approve of since she's still in recovery status according to West Enterprises' employee files.

My Lex, she really is a great teacher. She's patient and willingly shows me how to move, think and act like an agent. She lets me practice, coaches me through areas where I could improve and encourages me when I master a skill. She's recovering and getting stronger too, probably using our sessions to help strengthen her own skills as well as to share her knowledge and insight of her former life with me. But when the topics or questions get too close or too personal about her time as Alex West, she immediately retreats into herself, putting some guarded walls back up around her. But at least they're not as tall as they used to be. She's still coming to terms with who she was and who she wants to be now.

***

After the dust had settled and we knew that Lex was going to pull through with a projected full recovery at West house, I had called my parents, who currently reside in Newport Beach, California. I briefly explained the situation, leaving out the whole part where I had had a contract to kill on my head, and effusively described Lex to them. My mother was excited, as most mothers are, when their only son expresses interest in a possible mate. My dad, on the other hand, wanted to know more about Lex, her family history and what she does for a living. I told them the bare minimum, stating that Lex is in the security business and that she saved my life due to me unknowingly witnessing a murder, though I didn't mention that last part. I also didn't mention West Enterprises, her brothers or her role in the family business. None of the West family members had explicitly said that I couldn't disclose that information, but I still for some reason I chose to keep it close to the vest. Call it intuition, but I followed my gut. I kept the conversation focused on the fact that Lex is the reason why I am still alive today.

Both of my parents seemed satisfied, my dad mentioning that he wanted to meet Lex in-person so he could thank her properly. I easily agreed, I want them to meet Lex too. But not yet, it's still too soon, especially while she's healing, let alone an airplane ride wouldn't be the most conducive given the physical rehabilitation she's been going through. Lex and I haven't defined our relationship yet and I don't want to spook her. I know how I feel about her, but I don't want to come on to her too strong and freak her out. And right now, her focus should not be on me, but on herself.

But I don't tell my parents any of that internal dialog. Instead, I vaguely answer that we'll come out and visit soon and suggest for them to hire personal security for the short-term to ensure their safety. Initially they protested and insisted they could take care of themselves, asking why in the world would they need security. I couldn't give them the full details, choosing to say instead that since I was almost killed, I was feeling jumpy and wanted the peace of mind knowing that they were safe. But when I did not alter my stance or back down, they eventually relented and agreed to look into personal security and protection, just as a precaution. I continued with saying that I didn't believe there was an imminent threat, but that I'd prefer for them to be overly cautious in case any groups would try to use them as leverage over me. They, thankfully, agreed without questioning too much of my lackluster logic, I'm sure blaming my reactions on post-traumatic stress and assuaging my fears.

I found out later that because of the affluent area of Orange County and my father's standing within their community, my parents were thankfully able to quickly secure a personal security company, and they had installed a state-of-the-art security system based off of the recommendations that I gave them, all of course without me having to mention the West family's input. My mom insisted that I immediately come home multiple times, even though I told her I was fine and safer in New York. The full realization of the threat finally breaking through on her conscious and her motherly instincts reared its overly protective head. I understood that she just wanted her only son home, to be close to her and my father. My dad forwarded me money from my trust fund so I could take the time off from work to really figure out my life and career next steps. As much as I didn't want to admit it, the financial security of knowing that I had funds to live from until my career and personal goals stabilized soothed the inner storm of personal survival anxiety, allowing me to focus on helping Lex heal and to take the time to decide what my next steps should be. While the Wests hadn't mentioned anything about my recent financial dependence upon them, it made me feel better knowing that I could contribute or live independently apart from them if there ever was such a need to, like if Lex decided that we should perhaps but inevitably part ways.

After reassuring my parents that I was taking all the necessary precautions to ensure my safety, I ended our conversation, promising I'd visit soon and that I would call if anything else came up. As I ended the call, I saw Lex watching me from the conference room doorway where I had stepped away, searching for some privacy. Lex had been silently observing my mannerisms and behaviors, something that she's been teaching me to do. She had heard the whole trust fund comment, to which I was instantly embarrassed about. She has never been one to come to quick conclusions or judgment, so she just stood there, waiting for an explanation, but only if I was willing to give one to her. I confided in Lex about how my parents are very well off and after my grandparents passed and being an only child, I had a sizeable trust fund at my disposal. My dad had wanted me to become a lawyer and my mom wanted me to pursue a career in the field of medicine. Instead, I went and got a degree and a job in the Information Technology field, which can also be seen as a lucrative field with plenty of job security.

While my parents supported me in my decisions, I knew they always thought that I could do greater things with my life. I just wasn't sure what I wanted my personal greater mission to be. My dad reiterated multiple times as I started my career that I could retire anytime I wanted to and live off the trust fund, that it was that large, in order to pursue a medical or law degree full-time at my own pace. While I have always been grateful for the financial security and flexibility my family has provided for me, I still wanted to do something impactful with my life, on my own. Not saying a lawyer or doctor wouldn't be impactful, but I never felt like that was authentic to who I was and who I wanted to be.

Dad never seemed to understand my drive to make something of myself, independent from the family's money. My father definitely didn't appreciate my decision to move to the other side of the country, all the way to Manhattan in order for me to find and then follow my dreams. Dad had reasoned that there were plenty of West Coast technological firms that I could work for, especially highly visible companies located in the prestigious Silicon Valley. What Dad didn't understand was that the companies in Silicon Valley knew my family's name. They'd hire me right on the spot, regardless of my qualifications or skills, and that I'd be their monkey, required to perform at the drop of the hat to impress their investors or shareholders. I moved to New York to escape the Harris name, to make it truly on my own talents and abilities.

Everyone says that time is the healer of all wounds and wrong doings, and I guess that is really true. Months after the initial shock of my move and abrupt career change, my parents have been fully supportive of my decisions without doubting the charting of my own intentional path that I have been envisioning for myself. They may not understand all that drives me, but they still encourage and support me. Regardless of their initial uncertainty, my parents know that I'm pursuing something I am passionate about, something that I want to do for the rest of my life.

I told Lex everything that day, from the trust fund to my family dynamics. Lex nodded with empathetic understanding, just as I knew she would. Her eyes carried no judgment. Based on what I told her, she now has a deeper perception and respect for my willingness to share my personal information, along with my bravery to chart a new course for my life. She and I have that in common, choosing a new path, even with one already pre-paved that has minimal risk and obstacles which lie right in front of us. A path leading away from predestined and easy futures, filled with uncertainty and obstacles. We both know how frightening, alone and scary charting your own path, a whole new path, can be. How easy it is to fold back into what you used to be, what you were once good at and know through and through. But ultimately realizing that that path is something you cannot authentically travel down any longer takes bravery and courage. To find and chase your dream, it takes determination and character.

***

Lex stirs on the blanket beside me and shivers ever so slightly, pulling me back to the present, on the beach with the woman that I'm falling in love with. I move to pull a towel over her shoulders when her eyes suddenly pop open, instinctually taking in her surroundings. The muscles on her back ripple with her subtle upward motion, her pupils constricting as her eyes dart to uncover an unseen threat lurking just out of sight as her head and chest rise from the cooling landscape. Upon seeing me and the darkening sky, her body relaxes back into the sand. Lex smiles when she realizes that there is no threat at this moment. I give her a few minutes to gather herself before I nudge her, signaling that it's time to head back home.

We walk back to the house in companionable silence, each smiling our goodnights as we separate to go to our respective rooms. I walk through the doorway of my guest room suite, decorated in the coastal tones of green and blue. After I tuck into bed, I think about how much my life has changed in the past couple of months. Yes, there's been imminent danger, but with that came an exorbitant amount of love and friendship.

***

On most mornings since her return, Lex sleeps in until around eight. The rest of her brothers are up and moving around well before seven. I've gotten into their routine of rising early and I decide to regularly go for a run on the beach, taking advantage of the early morning before the heat tries to slowly murder me. On my way out, I usually grab a quick glass of water and put on a healthy layer of sunscreen. This morning, I take the deck stairs smoothly, jog to the water's edge and start to push myself until I find my perfect stride and pace. I see some families and parents who have already set up an early camp on various points on the beach, settling in for a typical June day at the shore. I dodge children here and there, careful not to splash them as I barrel by. After a mile, I turn around and loop back. I run all the way up to the dunes, the soft sand slowing my progress but working my core strength and testing my endurance. More families line the beach now, meaning that it is probably getting close to being later in the morning.

I jog up the stairs to the French double doors of the deck, entering into the cool and refreshing air-conditioned house. Lex is in the kitchen, preparing an early lunch for everyone. She smiles at me before refocusing her attention back to cutting some fresh bread. With a silly smile on my face, I run upstairs to take a quick shower, feeling invigorated and mentally awake.

As I'm getting dressed, I notice that my phone has an unread notification message, so I grab it on my way back downstairs. In the hallway at the halfway point to the stairs, I stop point blank. I received a text from Mom, asking if I wanted her and Dad to come out and visit in the next couple of months. I don't know what to initially say, so I've just stayed frozen in shock. Right now may not be the best time with everything going on at West Enterprises, Lex's recovery and my own indecisiveness for a visit. I don't respond but mull over how I'm going to answer my parents, trying to imagine the upstream and downstream impacts of the myriad of responses I could send.

Suddenly, the hair on the back of my neck raises when I feel someone's eyes on me. Looking up, my eye's crash into Lex's calm and confident gaze. She's at the top of the stairs, carefully watching me. She quickly assesses my emotional state before she gently motions for me to follow her back downstairs, all without saying one word. She knows that I'll tell her when I'm ready. And I know she won't pressure me to divulge my thoughts until I am indeed ready to share.

I take her outstretched hand as she finally says, "I was just coming to find you. It's lunchtime."

The ease of her voice and the normalcy of it all is just the soothing balm I need to recenter myself so I can eventually make a decision. I descend the stairs with her, hand in hand, in a perfect state of much needed calamity.

As we walk toward the kitchen, I can smell Lex's cooking wafting up to my nose. She is great in the kitchen, just another gem that I have found out about her. Apparently when the family was younger, they would all cook together every week as a tradition, meaning all of the West brothers are not only talented agents, but tactful in the kitchen, something their mother wanted for each of them before she passed. Some of the West kids are defter in the kitchen than others, Lex and Luke being the two with the most skills and who are more open to trying new things.

We enter the kitchen just as the front door opens. In walks Lex's twin, Dave and the eldest West brother, Will. Luke and Kev, the third and second oldest brothers respectively, come in from the deck outside after playing one-on-one against each other in the volleyball pit that's located just off the bottom of the deck's staircase. Sean, the youngest of the group, turns off the TV in the living area, the daily news-halting mid-sentence as he comes to stand at the kitchen bar. Lex resumes her position in the kitchen and starts dishing out lunch, a baby spinach salad with mandarin oranges, sliced almonds and small pieces of crumbled bacon. She had a fruit salad and a homemade vinaigrette dressing for the salad, which she instructs Sean to carry to the dining room table after she slips a serving spoon into each of the bowls. She hands Kev the flatware and napkins as she tells Luke, Will and Dave to take a set of filled water glasses to the table. I help grab some of the plates when she's done arranging the salad and place the plates on the table. She brings to the table an artisan cheese platter with French bread and olive oil with spices mixed in for dipping.

I sit at my place on her left with Dave at her right. Will is at the head of the table, sitting on the other side of Dave. I sit opposite of Luke with Kev across from Lex and Sean is seated opposite of Will. Without any hesitation, we all start to dig into the salad, silence falling over the room as we all eat as if we haven't had any food in weeks.

Luke finishes first and complements Lex on the salad, fruit and charcuterie board. She nods her thanks as she continues to eat, a small smile and a slight blush grace her face, the only sign of her taking her brother's compliment to heart. It's taken her a couple of weeks now to get her full appetite back since her hospitalization, but judging by how much she's been eating, it looks like it thankfully is starting to resume back to normal. Dave reaches over and squeezes her hand as the twins share a look the rest of us can't read or understand, but they both smile as they disengage from their own language to continue eating.

Will, who is much gentler with Lex than when I first met him, looks over at her with a worried look in his eyes. Her head is down, her gaze solely focused on picking at the fruit bowl in front of her, completely unaware of the concerned looks being passed around the table by her brothers. Will in particular looks uncomfortable with her lack of engagement. I can't say that I blame him there. We're all worried. Lex hasn't been the same since the shooting. Sure, she's regaining her strength, working out every day and getting physically stronger and back in shape. But she hasn't been her normal, spitfire self. Her silence echoes and yet resounds in the empty gaps, reminding us all of how she used to fill the spaces with caustic and sarcastic comments or her dry wit. I remember when she'd go toe-to-toe with all of her brothers, especially Will. It was always noisy and boisterous in the West Enterprises household, particularly during times of conflict and disagreements. Now, Lex has become a lot like Sean, observant and reserved, without making many comments, but her eyes are full of questions and insight.

Will gently asks her, his tone soft as he directs the daily question toward his sister, "Lex, what are your plans for today?"

Lex looks up at him, pulling herself out of her own head and responds, "I was thinking that I'd go to the beach."

All of the West brothers' heads nod, anticipating this answer. They know this has become a daily routine for her and that this would most likely be her response.

Dave volunteers, "I was going into the city to scout a job. Kev and Luke were going to come with me, but I can stay if you want some company, Lex."

"No," the West sister softly responds, "I'm sure Cole and Sean will join me, and Will may drop by to check-in, as he now has a tendency to do as of late. Just find us on the beach afterward and join us. But bring a round, would you?" As she is speaking, she has stood up and has begun to methodically clear the table.

Everyone notices that while she's been eating more, there's still a good amount of food that she hasn't touched left on her plate. I know Luke will finish her leftovers, but we all share a concerned look. As Luke shovels in her remaining salad and side dishes, I rush to stand up, helping her with her self-designated task and the rest of her brothers quickly follow suit. Soon, the seven of us make quick work of cleaning up the dining room and kitchen. As she walks to her bedroom to change and get her beach items together, I turn to Lex's brothers at the subtle clearing of multiple throats.

"Keep an eye on her, Cole," Luke starts, his tone low but cautious.

"Yeah," Kev chimes in, "something is going on with her. Dave, has she said anything to you?"

Dave answers, "No, not yet. Maybe I'll try to talk with her tonight."

"Or maybe," Will interjects with a tone of older brother finality, "she'll come to us on her own terms, in her own time, in her own way."

I'm slightly surprised that those words came from Will's mouth and so are the other four Wests, judging by their shocked reactions. But I understand what the elder West is getting at. She needs to trust us. Once she comes to us, we'll know that her faith in us is fully restored and that all trust has been completely rebuilt. Sean and I nod in agreement with the eldest West.

"She's tough." Will continues, "she's been through worse."

"But nothing has questioned her morals, character and career choices before," Luke counters in a slightly exasperated tone.

We all fall silent as we hear her coming down the upstairs hall. She joins us with her staple beach bag slung over her shoulder, a loose white tee shirt and jean shorts covering the majority of her bright bikini with flashes of hot pink peeking out near her shirt's neckline, the bright color highlighting her summer tan. Lex hugs Dave, Kev and Luke before grabbing a water thermos and heading to the deck. The three brothers yell their goodbyes over their shoulders as they head toward the breezeway to the garage.

Sean and I each grab ice packs from the freezer and Sean quickly pulls a cooler from the garage. We pack the cooler with snacks and pre-made sandwiches as we quickly follow Lex as she has slowly descended down the stairs to the sand below. Will goes back into the conference room where he's working on a presentation, with the promise of joining us once he's finished on the project.

As we walk toward the water, moving in between the dunes, the sand is getting hot and the sun that is beating down on us is intense. A couple of seagulls soar high above our heads as the Long Island beach is now filled with families and fellow beach enthusiasts for a typical summer day at the shore. Lex has turned toward a small open area, thankfully large enough for a couple beach blankets and our cooler. I help my girl open and lay the blanket down as Sean parks the cooler close by. Lex instantly sits down in her spot in the middle of the blanket with Sean and me taking our informal seats on each side of her as we all stare out over the ocean. My woman sighs in content and pops open her water thermos as she links her arm through Sean's. I'm struck by their similarities as Lex rests her head on her younger brother's shoulder, her black hair mixing with his brown hair.

"How are you feeling today, sis?" Sean quietly asks after a long pause.

"I'm good, I think. At least, I'm going to be good," Lex softly responds, her forehead creasing to a slight v as she contemplates her answer.

Sean nods and points out, "We should really lather up. Dave will kill me if you got sunburnt."

The youngest West siblings both share a smile before we all shift around to grab the suntan lotion from Lex's bag. We pass around the suntan lotion, silently lathering up as we coat our skin and finally relax in the rays.

We settle into our routine of lying out in the sun for the rest of the day. Sean and Lex talk about what they observe, playing a little version of the I Spy game, quizzing each other to see who is the more observant agent. After a while, a group of guys come up to us and they start talking to Sean. The youngest West casually greets them and strikes up a nonchalant conversation, but it's clear that Sean doesn't know them. The group of guys are paying attention to Sean, but I catch their eyes straying, no doubt their attention is partially on Lex. They may be even trying use Sean to get to Lex. We've seen that happen numerous times over the summer. It always appalling, the guys who try to get close to her when there the two, or sometimes all of the West clan are surrounding her. Luckily, Sean and the rest of us are wise to these audacious games as this is an unfortunate but common occurrence that happens multiple times every week. Lex never pays those guys any mind, choosing to steadily ignore them.

Today, Lex had taken off her tee shirt and shorts when we first sat down, revealing the hot pink bikini, matching her bright pink toenail polish. Now, she stands up and stretches as she asks me under her breath if I can reapply sunscreen to her back. I agree as she secures her sunglasses back over her eyes and she sits back down, handing the suntan lotion to me before turning away from me and so I can easily reapply the lotion to prevent sunburn.

We have fallen into a routine, and we are each in our own minds and worlds, when all of the sudden, one of the guys in the group talking to Sean gasps and caustically exclaims, "What the hell happened to your back?"

Sean and I instantly turn our attention toward the speaker as he is openly staring at Lex's back. We're immediately the aggressors, ready to defend Lex and make plausible excuses like we usually do to protect her.

Only today, Lex doesn't seem to want to avoid the truth. She just seems over the stories and the excuses, almost taking a laissez-faire or an indifferent tone when she responds.

Lex calmly looks at the questioner and asks, "Which part are you referring to?"

Sean and I are taken aback, she hasn't been this blunt or forthright so far this summer, the echoes of her former self ringing in my head.

The questioning guy looks closer and notices her shoulder scar as well as the two bullet scars over her shoulder blades. The guy's eyes widen when he sees the rest of her scarred back, zeroing in on all of the older scars that create a web of white, untanned skin.

"All of them?" he belligerently asks, totally unaware of who he is talking to, or just not caring, so secure in his entitlement and privilege.

"The holes are from bullets, the line here is from a knife. The rest I can't say without seeing them for myself, but if you really want, I can take a guess at each of them," Lex answers smoothly without emotion or inflection of tone, the only thing giving away her amusement away is the slight twinkle in her molten chocolate eyes that she allows only Sean and me to see.

"How the hell did that happen?" another guy asks, his eyes wide, never losing his focus from her back.

I toss a look at Sean, wondering if she's going to give these guys the whole truth. Her brothers and I had gotten so used to deflecting these types of questions without the slightest engagement from her over the past couple of weeks. But Lex addressing things head on, now we're in uncharted territory.

Before Sean or I can say anything, she flatly shrugs while she answers, "A couple people were mad at me. You should see what I did to them. They were lucky to come out of that argument with what I left them with. This is basically me walking away with just a few scrapes."

We watch as the gears in these guys' heads start to work, trying to figure out what's true and false. Lex, to her credit, doesn't crack a smile as she brazenly meets their eyes with disinterest and distance, similar to how she used to carry herself as Alex West.

We can see the moment everything clicks when as a whole, the entire group of guys take a collective step back, saying their hasty goodbyes to Sean, before turning on their heels and swiftly walking away. Looking back at Lex, the expression of amusement and a glimmer of laughter and glee have returned to her eyes. Sean is openly smiling and nods his approval, silently laughing at her humor in killing two birds with one proverbial stone.

"I'm going to take a walk," Lex quietly announces, brushing off the intrusion of the guy group to her routine.

She looks to Sean and me, silently asking if we want to join her. We both nod and stand up, stretching out our muscles under the hot sun's rays. As a team, we collectively walk toward the water, listening to the ocean waves relentlessly crash against the shore and the rest of the summer beach day sounds and smells filling the air and taking over our senses.

After our walk amongst the waves, the three of us return to our beach blanket. Sean tosses us some oranges and sandwiches from the cooler before pulling out one of his books. I smile as I watch Sean let the rest of the world fall away from him as he instantly becomes engrossed in the book's story. Lex has taken her seat and is staring over the water in deep contemplation as she slowly eats her orange. I am seated next to her, leaning back on my forearms, watching her as the waves signify how time marches on.

As we were walking up and down the coast, I noticed that some people were staring at Lex, some candidly and some more inconspicuously. Whether it was her bright swimsuit, her beauty or the scars that mar her tanned skin, I don't know what drew each person's attention, but I felt protective of her all the same. I noticed Sean was always trying to shield her scars from prying eyes, using his own body to protect her and stand in between prying, curious eyes and his sister. Lex, as usual, didn't seem to notice, or maybe she just didn't care. In a very Alex West determined manner, she just kept walking, owning and wearing her battle scars like the badges of honor they are.

"I'm going to take a nap," Lex quietly states, breaking the comfortable afternoon silence.

Sean tears his attention away from his book and nods at her in response. "I may or may not be here when you wake up," Sean kindly informs her.

"That's fine, that's what I figured," Lex says knowingly, "I know you're all scouting for a job." She turns her attention to me, the question forming in her eyes.

"I'll be here," I respond to her question before she can vocalize it in a reassuring tone.

She smiles and lays down on her front, resting her head in her arms, the sun's rays warming her back while she uses her towel as a pillow, her hair fanning over the towel like a dense palm tree. After a couple of minutes, I subtly note her breathing has changed. Now it's deep and steady, signaling that she's asleep under the summer sun. Sean and I both dutifully watch over her as she sleeps.

"I always forget how young she is. I'm reminded of that when she's asleep," Sean murmurs.

"You're younger than she is," I teasingly point out.

"Yes," he immediately and automatically agrees. The silence stretches out as he ponders his response, before carefully continuing, "But she's seen and done far more in her lifetime than all of us five West brothers combined. But in spite of that, in her heart, she's not the sum of what she's seen. My big sister... she's so much more than that."

I take his words in, knowing that there's an uneasy truth behind them. She's seen violence, war and darkness where her brothers have tried to offer hope and light to the targets of their contracts.

Sean's phone vibrates and he reads his text, looking up at me and silently motioning that he's going to make his way back up to the house. I nod, knowing that another one of her brothers will be out with us soon. Since the shooting, the West brothers have made sure at least one of them is with her, if not all five of them, at all times. They are just starting to review new contracts and scout jobs since West Enterprises is now back up and fully functional. Not to mention the fact that Lex is becoming more independent and stronger as time continues on, so her brothers are all feeling more confident with leaving her for a while as they get back to work and to reassume business operations. I lower my arms, stretch out as my back touches the warmed towel and straighten out my legs, allowing the sun to soak its warmth into my own skin. I lazily look over at Lex, content with her slumber and I smile. This is what peace is, this gift of freedom. We've come so far, but there's still so much more to go, together.

***

In the beginning when Lex and I first met, I was afraid that she'd think I was the stereotypical privileged trust fund kid, born with a silver spoon in my mouth, expecting the world to be handed to me on a silver platter without any effort on my part. When we were at The Bailey and I thought she was Alexis from the finance department, I made sure to charm her with my New York stories, all without mentioning who my parents were and steered clear of any conversational topics revolving around money. I didn't want to mention that my dad was a successful businessman on the West Coast. Or that my mom is the queen of her local country club. Nor did I want to say that I grew up in the world of money and then be asked what my bank account balance was. I had had enough of that in the past when I dated women on the West Coast. Those women only dated me for the dollar amount I represented, they were never interested in truly getting to know me.

I just wanted to fit in with my peers and be normal. Normal with Lex. But how wrong was I to prejudge her and compartmentalize the viewpoints I thought she would have about me into a narrow, ill-fitting box. I ended up prejudging her, doing to Lex the exact thing that I didn't want her to do to me. Lex deserved more from me than what little credit I initially gave her.

At no point while we were getting to know each other did Lex judge me or care about my background. She wasn't interested about my bank account or access to liquid funds. As time wore on, I learned that I was the one that had the lesser bank account, so money and my fears around women and money became a moot point. Lex only saw me, Cole Harris, and nothing else. When she decided not to honor her contract and kill me, she became a friend and ally. Lex and I would talk for hours, sometimes about unimportant topics and other times, we'd have serious and deep philosophical discussions. She stood up for me and defended me when it came to her brothers. And believe me, the West brothers all together are a formidable and intimidating unit.

In all my thirty years of life, I haven't met anyone quite like her. She has no fear. Lex is confident in her decisions and actions. She doesn't second-guess herself. Lex holds herself accountable to the highest standards. From the stories that I've heard about her over the past couple months, both from her family and her close friends, she is a deadly, formidable rival, an excellent marksman and chemistry connoisseur while she operates as West Enterprises' only bank rolled assassin.

As time continued on, I observed many instances where Lex came forward effortlessly as a natural-born leader. During the attack at West Enterprises, she immediately commanded the room of alpha males without any doubt and had no problem putting everyone in their place for the good of the mission. She strategically mapped out the plan of attack, located weaknesses in the plan and communicated those concerns. She made sure that when she created teams, she aligned each individual's strengths to compliment the team's dynamics. Lex knew each person who was an ally, showing the depth of her knowledge and research. She didn't have time to read reports on each of the agents called to West Enterprises that day, she already had known those characteristics and traits, or she picked up on them while everyone was preparing and loading up. It makes me wonder how many people's skills, abilities and qualities are locked away in her brain, a treasure trove of tactical, strategic and execution knowledge.

Another characteristic I admire of Lex's was how she wasn't afraid to step into the middle of gunfire to do what was right, even if it cost her life, pain or a long recovery time. I watched as she fought her way back from extreme blood lost, where every breath she took caused her extreme agony. She never complained, not even for a second. My Lex just brushed off all our concerns and continued moving forward, looking to her future on the horizon. I heard later that she contacted every person who came to West Enterprises that day to thank them for their service to the company and that she reached out to the families of the agents who were lost to express her gratitude and respect. She did all this without fanfare, not looking to be recognized for her strong leadership.

But most of all, I admire her strength, compassion and resilience, and I have told her so repeatedly, especially after she came home from the hospital to begin her recovery. I told her that I liked her more than friends, on a romantic level. I remember her smile when she shyly admitted that she liked me too. We still haven't gone out on that dinner date yet or even grabbed a cup of coffee, but I'm in no rush. I don't want to push her beyond her limits, considering she hasn't left West property since her return. I'm a patient man and if all goes to plan, she and I will have all the time in the world to go out on all the dates life and time can afford us.

I'm enjoying exactly where we are, this moment here, right now. I'm reveling in how we're learning all about each other and building a solid foundation for the future. We do see each other every day, as I currently am residing at West Enterprises. For her sake, I'm trying to take this slow and I don't want to mess up my chances with her. I could definitely see myself falling for her even more, as if I haven't started too already.

***

Waking up, I see that the sun had just disappeared from view as Lex starts to stir from her slumber right on time. Will had come down to sit with us right after Sean left. He had brought his laptop and worked while I took a light nap. He nudged me about fifteen minutes ago, saying that his laptop was about to die and that he was going to go back up to the house, to plug in his device and finish his work. Lex just missed him, but I know that we'll be joined soon, and I choose to enjoy these stolen moments with her.

Lex sleepily opens her eyes, her dark lashes blinking rapidly a few times, taking in the darkening sky, before she turns her lazy attention toward me.

"How long have I been out?" she asks, her voice still gravelly from sleep as she stretches her arms over her head.

"About four or five hours," I respond, smiling down at her upturned face.

Looking alarmed, she quickly sits up, noticing her surroundings and fully taking in the darkened sky. There are only a few people left dotting the shoreline, strolling the beaches, trying to gather the last rays of the day as the majority of today's beach goers have already packed up and cleared out about an hour ago. Hastily, she pulls her tee shirt back on as the evening air has ushered in cooler temperatures and we watch as a couple, hand in hand, walk past and head away from us.

As she's staring out at the darkened sea, Lex quietly says, "I don't know how to be Alexandra West, Cole. I don't know what that means."

Startled, I turn my full attention toward her, knowing questions are beginning to form in my eyes but being so shocked at her vulnerability, I'm failing to have those questions cross my lips. I never would have thought that that admission would ever leave her lips.

"That's really what has been bothering me lately," Lex softly continues, "I know you all have been talking about it, wondering how I'm doing, why I'm so quiet, how I'm so different. You're all trying to get an idea of what's going on in my head. Well, that's the sum of it. Now you know."

I avert my eyes from her, knowing that I'm non-verbally confirming her statement and I don't want her to feel like I betrayed her confidence. But her brothers and I have been concerned about her mental health.

After a pause of silence, she continues, "I put Alex West to bed. I put her in a grave. But now I don't know who I am, or who I'm supposed to be. I was Alex for so long, I don't remember who Alexandra was, let alone is. The last time I was Alexandra was well before my dad was killed, even before my mom died. Dave, Will, everyone, they all seem to expect me to easily slip back in being Alexandra; to make a smooth transition to another lifestyle and persona that I barely remember. But no one has defined who Alexandra is or what she stands for. There's no direction, no compass pointing me and telling me what my next move should be. All I have is Alex. And if I can't be that, then who am I supposed to be now?"

After a couple minutes of silence, I finally respond, "I don't want to fully speak on behalf of your brothers, but I truly don't believe that any of us want you to switch to a different personality instantaneously, or even completely. You'll come into your own with your personal beliefs and perspectives shaping who the new Alexandra will be. It will take time, Lex, we all understand and know that. Keep in mind that you still are healing from the shootout and now you're going to reshape your entire perspective. Something like that doesn't happen overnight. You have to give yourself a break and allow yourself to take your time. And maybe, just maybe, Alex West doesn't have to be in a grave, but merely reigned in. With the qualities of Alex, maybe there's a way to merge that with a newer version of you."

"Then why, Cole, have all of my brothers kept this new contract under wraps like it's a secret? The details, locations, everything. It's like they are all waiting for me to snap back into Alex and they don't want to tempt fate. So in response, they aren't telling me directly that one, there's a contract, and two, what it's about. This is why I don't feel like I have the luxury of time to define myself!" she says, exasperation marring her beautiful features.

Surprised by her rare emotional outburst, I carefully and tactfully try to share my perspective, "I don't think they are trying to be conspiratorial intentionally. They're probably worried that you aren't physically one hundred percent yet, and they don't want to push you before you're physically ready. But if you think that they're hiding things with true intent, talk to them about it. Tell them how you feel and listen to what their motives truly are. You may be surprised."

"Surprised about what?" Will asks from directly behind us.

Startled, Lex and I both turn our heads around to see that all five of her brothers are standing a few feet away, keenly interested in our conversation, waiting for our response. I am always shocked at how stealthy all six Wests are. I'm even more surprised her brothers surprised Lex. She doesn't surprise very easily. She must have been distracted to miss their approach.

Lex shakes her head and stands up to greet them, and taking her lead, I follow suit. She walks over to Dave, helping him lay out additional blankets for her brothers to sit on. She then takes the bottle of wine that's in Will's hands, kisses his cheek and walks back over to me, sitting down. The rest of the clan sits down around us as she deftly opens and pours the wine into the cups Sean had brought down with him. Luke pulls fresh deli sandwiches from his bag while Kev produces different bags of chips, the logos signaling that they stopped in the city before coming home. We all choose our respective sandwiches and chips as we sip on the crisp white wine. All of us are highly focused on watching the stars twinkle in the dark canopy of the sky above, looking like a tapestry of sparkling lights.

As we munch away under the nighttime canopy, Luke lightly asks, "So, what were you guys talking about as we came up to join you both?"

219

My gaze automatically swings to Lex. This is her call, these are her opinions and feelings, not mine. She doesn't say anything in response, continuing to eat in silence. To my dismay, five pairs of eyes automatically turn to me, waiting for me to fill in the gaps.

"It's not my place," I simply explain, trying to hide how uncomfortable I was by being put on the spot.

"Lexi?" Dave tentatively asks, calling her by his nickname, the concern evident in his voice.

Lex looks up at her twin, meets each of her brothers' gaze and looks at me with gratitude. She looks up at the sky, most likely centering herself and gathering her thoughts before she returns her level gaze to her brothers.

Lex lets out a deep sigh before starting, "I feel like you are all treating me with kid gloves, like I can't handle anything. I know that you don't want to involve me in any jobs right now, that you're all concerned about having me on the front lines. But I already feel lost, trying to redefine who I am and what I'm supposed to be doing with my life now that I essentially killed off Alex West. I don't have anything to keep my mind off how to be Alexandra except for going to the beach with Cole. No offense Cole, or the rest of you. But this not doing anything or being part of the family business is driving me mad. I feel like it's almost as if you don't trust me, which then makes me doubt if I should trust myself, which leads me to being reluctant to reinventing and redefining myself."

As she's talking, a couple tears had gathered and fell from the corners of the West sister's eyes. Lex didn't seem to notice that her emotions are bleeding through, but her five brothers certainly have and they all look terrified. I guess they don't know how to handle their usual non-upset sister, and yet they can handle her when she's murderous. Oddly ironic, but I keep that thought wisely to myself.

A curtain of shocked silence covers our little group. Luke has to physically shut his mouth, since his jaw was dropped open repeatedly as Lex was talking. Kev can't meet anyone's eyes as Sean scoots closer to Lex and puts his arm around her shoulder. I watch as I can see Will clench and unclench his jaw, the tension on his face easily distinguishable. Dave looks over at me with something I can't quite place in his eyes, but if I had to guess, it'd be anguish.

"I'm frustrated because now I'm questioning every decision and contract that I have ever made or fulfilled. I'm doubting if I have made the right choices for my entire career and my entire life," Lex continues but talks softly enough that I wonder if she's more so talking to herself rather than the rest of us. "Six months ago, everything was cut and dry, black and white. Now, I'm in this whole gray spectrum and I don't know what's up or down. You all know how much I hate ambiguity. And to top it all off, I feel like you are all intentionally keeping secrets from me about work and the business, shutting me out. I feel lost, out of the loop and unsteady. And I don't know how else to put myself back together, let alone puzzle out all the pieces that comprise my new life now," she finishes, her confession complete.

While Lex has been speaking, the desperation grew in her tone, her voice gradually raised to a clearly audible level and her face became increasingly flushed. None of us really knew the depth of what was going on in her head, not even Dave who looks stunned and ashamed. And now we each realize that we have been inadvertently walking on eggshells around her with the intent of protecting her, but in reality we have alienated her and contributed to her sense of loneliness and isolation. Luke reaches over to grab her hand while Dave takes her other hand in a soothing manner.

"We didn't know," Kev starts, dragging a hand through his dark hair, one of the signs that the older West is stressed, "which isn't an excuse by any means. But we are so sorry, please know that that was never our intent."

"How can we make it up to you? How can we help you gain the clarity for the direction that you need?" Sean asks, his gray eyes searching her face.

Lex just looks down at the sand, breaking eye contact while she shakes her head. She doesn't know how they can help her, which is even more heartbreaking. Lex, who normally has all the answers, has nothing left to offer and the unsettling veil of uncertainty lapses over all of us.

Will goes to say something but stops himself just in time as he readily takes in her defeated posture and her uncharacteristic loss for words. As a unit, the five West brothers scoot closer to surround their sister as I, the outsider and anomaly, move back and look on.

***

Over the next few days, the West brothers have rallied around Lex since the night on the beach when Lex shared her heartfelt confession. Will and Lex had met a few times to go over the most recent contract the company had accepted, the new job Lex was upset about not being included in. Apparently, she found some flaws in the original operational design plan and helped to reconfigure the target extraction course of action, to keep everyone safe and still stay under the radar. The job which Lex tells me about as she learns the details, seems like an easy contract for this team of experienced agents. Dave, Kev and Luke will be going in and doing the actual extraction, since they're the lead agents while she, Will and Sean will observe from a safe distance, providing technical support and backup if needed. I had told her that I wanted to become more involved with West Enterprises, so she is letting me shadow her while she's slowly integrating back on the job. I am not allowed to carry a weapon since I'm still in the learning phases and I don't have the proper clearances, but I have her and she's certainly weapon enough.

As the days continue to move closer to the extraction contract date, the Wests meticulously review the plans, scout locations remotely and plan various contingency exit routes. They are anything but meticulously methodical, where each West comes to the table with different viewpoints, strengths and experiences. Witnessing all six of them together is quite a sight to behold. They previously decided that tomorrow, on a Saturday, would be the best date for the extraction job once they ironed out all of the last-minute logistics. Satisfied with the plan, we all grab a couple of beers and head to the deck to relax and view the sunset. This ritual has become religious to Lex, a daily requirement, where the entire family makes every effort to join her if she's not on the beach.

Ever since Lex was able to regain her independent mobility after she came home from the hospital, she always wanted to watch the sunset. Maybe she needs to see the day ending, giving way to night. Or maybe she wants to witness the beauty of everyday nature. Whatever her reasons, it's during the sunsets that seems to be one of the only times she looks to be at peace, not tormented by the changes and upheavals happening within and around her. I note her relaxed shoulders, small smile and calm demeanor. I know her brothers also have seen these changes in her during these precious moments of time. We all have collectively and affectionately dubbed it as the "Sunset Effect."

On the deck at sunset the night before the extraction, Kev and Luke are chatting away while Sean listens with quiet intent. Will is silently reacting to his brothers' whimsical discussions with a small smile tugging at the corners of his lips. Dave and I are talking about weapon handling and how I can improve my techniques. The West family is in repose, something many people aren't privy to seeing. We're all relaxed and joking around when Will suddenly silences all of us with a subtle look and small gestures. We look at him expectantly, with quick and questioning gazes, noticing his attention is not on an immediate threat, but that he's staring intently at Lex.

We all turn to look at her and see that she has fallen asleep, with a smile on her face, just as the sun drops from our view. I smile; she truly is gorgeous and looks so serene while she slumbers, the last of the sun's rays for the day highlighting and playing across her delicate features. Apparently, I'm not the only one feeling the same sentiment about the woman I'm falling in love with.

"She looks so much younger when she's asleep," Kev softly comments, the adoration clear in his voice.

"I just said that to Cole a couple of days ago on the beach." Sean affirms, looking at me for confirmation.

As I nod in agreement, Luke interjects, "This is one of the few times when she looks like she's at peace, like whatever demons are hunting and chasing her are kept at bay."

Will nods and looks directly at Dave and me, "Has she talked to either of you about anything else that's going on inside that head of hers?"

I shake my head as Dave replies, "No. But she does seem anxious about this upcoming job. I don't know if it's precontract anxiety, getting back into the swing of things, fear of getting hurt again or her just being unsettled. Lex is usually never nervous before a contract. But she keeps saying that something is off, that something doesn't feel right to her. But she can never figure out what the problem is, never put her finger on what exactly is making her uneasy. So, she doesn't want to voice it, whether or not for our benefit or if she doesn't trust herself, that I'm not sure of."

"Does she think there could be an issue with other assassins on location?" Sean queries, curiosity lacing his voice.

Dave shakes his head, "She's gone over that and read the file multiple times. She doesn't think an assassin would even take a job like this. The pay isn't big enough nor does this target pose as an imminent threat which would require someone with a high sense of urgency wanting him dead. Our contract is just to offer protection for a few weeks, something we normally see, and it seems safe to me. Still, Lex can't shake the feeling or sense that something is off."

"We thoroughly planned this extraction through and we went over it multiple times. We went over our specifications, contingency plans and did a background check on our target. I'm sure we'll be fine," Will says, almost dismissively. The eldest West's tone reminding me of when I first met the West family. I see the hesitation in Dave and Sean's eyes, but they eventually acquiesce and nod their heads in agreement as well.

"Listen, I trust her instincts. Let's review the plan in the morning before we go," Kev diplomatically says. I know that Kev is trying to keep the peace and provide compromise for both sides, for which I admire him.

Kev continues by saying, "I just want to double-check everything. Dot our proverbial i's and cross our t's, so to speak. We did our homework, let's check to make sure that it'll get us high marks. It never hurts to be prepared and double-check our plan."

Lex slightly stirs in her chair and we take that signal to finally quiet down and turn our attention back to look over the horizon. The rest of Friday night passes like a flash of light, twilight barely registering on anyone's internal timetables.

***

Saturday morning comes quickly enough as all the Wests are up and organizing for the day well before I come downstairs for breakfast at seven in the morning. There's a buzz of excitement with a small hint of nervousness in the crisp morning air. Overall, everyone is in a positive mood. Luke, as always, is cracking jokes and even Will is laughing at his brother's playful antics. Since it is summertime in New York, the brothers are dressed in lightweight polos and tee shirts paired with shorts and sneakers. Lex is dressed in a sundress and slip-on shoes, her hair pulled back into a casual high ponytail. Sunglasses are the go-to accessory for all of the family members, each with their own individualized pair completing everyone's outfits. Although it doesn't look like it, each of the Wests' sunglasses actually leverage the upgraded technology initiatives Will is passionate about. By using the small cameras attached to each pair of sunglass frames, the live feed is streamed back to West Enterprises to be reviewed in real-time. Later the recordings will be archived for legal and contextual purposes.

Underneath the airy clothing, each West has multiple weapons stored and hidden away, both obvious and innocuous in appearance. But that doesn't mean the technology ends at the sunglasses. All of their clothing has been custom made, the fabric lined with movable Kevlar to provide additional protection, since the meeting place is in public and out in the open. Considering this contract is what Will considers a minimal threat, other teams and assets have not been called in for additional support. The seven of us, we all reason, should be support enough.

All of us will be heading to the historic Bryant Park, situated in the heart of midtown Manhattan, just east of the tourist trap and ever-popular

Times Square. Tactically, the seven of us are arriving to Bryant Park in a variety of different ways. Lex and my entrance point is at the intersection of Sixth Avenue and 42nd Street after being dropped off right as we get off the bridge, taking the metro to the park, a popular spot for locals and tourists alike, so we'll be able to blend in with the weekend crowds. Sean's entrance is from the south, as he'll be dropped off just west of Times Square. The youngest West's quick strides will carry him east to the location. Will plans to park on a side street two blocks west where he will walk east to the park's southwest corner entrance. The four of us will be on comms while the other three West brothers take that lead and arrive conspicuously together in a black SUV.

With the summer sun shining high above us, Dave, Luke and Kev load into one blacked out SUV while Will, Lex, Sean and I head into the city in a similar SUV. Will has taken our vehicle as the lead SUV so the four of us can get situated and stationed in our appropriate areas before Luke, Kev and Dave arrive for the meet. Lex and I are playing the role of a young couple having a romantic lunch in the park. Will is posing as a photographer, capturing the beauty and history in still life while Sean is reading a book on the lawn with some Starbucks coffee he picked up from the store across the park.

Once we're in our designated places and are settled, Lex fires off a quick text to Dave. We inconspicuously watch the West SUV pass and park one block up twelve minutes later. All three brothers exit the SUV and enter the park, a football in hand. The three are pretending to play a game of tag football with the element of monkey in the middle, where Luke is in the middle. Lex thought Luke being in the middle was quite apropos.

Behind Lex's darkened sunglasses, I can tell that even though she's turned towards me and we are carrying on our conversation, her line of sight is always on her brothers. I take a quick survey of the park, my gaze roaming over the entire expanse. I try to see what Lex sees when she takes in the over nine-acre area that we're positioned in. Her eyes are casually dodging between each cluster of people as well as noting everyone else in the park, observing them closely, but her gaze never lingers for too long so as not to draw attention to her. She uses her keen situational awareness skills and clocks people as they walk around the park's perimeter, keeping an eye out for unusual levels of intense interest. If my senses weren't on such high alert and I didn't know the clandestine world that West Enterprises regularly operates within, I never would've guessed, as a civilian, at what was about to go down: a protective extraction assignment.

Everyone is in position and the mission is set. Now we're just waiting for the mark to arrive. Our target is a male in his mid-thirties named Townsend. All of the sudden, Lex's spine straightens and her head tilts up ever so slightly. I unobtrusively turn my body to see what caught her attention. Following her line of sight, I spot Townsend, who I recognize from his file's briefing picture. Townsend is walking into the park with a group of his friends, five other guys about his age, height and weight class. They start playing football just as they do every Saturday, and after about ten minutes, one of Townsend's friends invite Kev, Luke and Dave over to join them. This was the plan, this is Townsend's routine and he's falling for our proverbial trap. The mission is for the three Wests to make friends and infiltrate the group, separate Townsend from the rest of his friends and extract him safely back to West Enterprises Headquarters for further protection protocols.

Things seem to be going well between Kev, Dave, Luke and Townsend's group. Will, even, comes over to take a picture of Lex and me during our picnic, keeping his eyes focused on the scene through his camera lens, but also on the situation unfolding just out of earshot, directly behind us. Instinctually, Lex and I move in closer to each other, smiling together as our shoulders briefly touch. Will nods, a smile on his face, as he lowers the lens and focuses on the camera's screen to view the picture. He moves on farther down and continues to take shots every so often, all the while keeping a watchful eye on his three brothers.

I know the eldest West is also taking shots of people in the park, just in case there are additional people here to pick off our mark. During the planning phases, Will was upset over the lack of cameras in this particular area, hence the photographer façade. Lex explained to me that he'll take the photos and analyze them later with facial recognition software, to categorize and store them for future reference or to further follow-up in case there are people of interest he catches on film. I catch Sean subtly looking up a couple times every few minutes to insouciantly observe his surroundings. Everything seems to be like it's going according to our prepared plan, and I hope everything continues to fall in our favor.

As the game of impromptu football comes to a natural close, Lex suddenly starts fidgeting. "Something isn't right, Cole," she nervously says, her hands wringing and her gaze darting around the park.

Her leg is bouncing as she starts fiddling with the hem of her dress. I frantically look around the park before I turn my gaze back to her as Lex asks me, "Something's different, something has changed. Can you feel it?"

"No," I worriedly answer, looking around and shaking my head, trying to keep my tone low and the energy level calm.

"What is it, Lex?" Sean has taken note of Lex's change in demeanor and softly speaks his question into our earbud comms.

Will's head pops up and begins to make his way back toward us, taking rushed pictures so as not to break his cover. Kev and Luke hear the observed change in their sister's behavior too, subtly changing their stances to a more aggressive posture.

Lex abruptly stands up and walks directly toward the group of guys, bee-lining straight for Dave, breaking protocol and her cover, immediately changing our plan. Without taking her eyes off Dave, Lex shakes me off as I try to block and stop her. I see Will scowl out of the corner of my eye while the other four brothers look discreetly concerned.

"She's never broken her cover or protocol before, Will. Something is off," Sean whispers to the eldest West as they stand shoulder to shoulder, still trying but also failing to each maintain their individual covers.

Regardless of Will's feelings, he's intently watching over his little sister, ready to swoop in if needed, waiting to see how she'll play her cards, the concern clearly etched on his face. Lex is heading to her twin with determination and undivided focus, a true force to reckon with. I have to jog just to keep up with her quick pace, but I'm still several steps behind her.

"Hey," Lex says as she comes up next to her twin and touches Dave's arm.

"Who's the babe," one of Townsend's friend asks.

I bristle at the word babe, but I try to hide it as I come to stand behind Lex, only slightly out of breath.

"I don't know. At least, I don't think I do," murmurs Dave, cocking his head in confusion, questions forming in his eyes.

After observing the twins for a while now, I can tell that they are communicating through their Twin Power as waves of anxiety pulse off Lex. I feel Will and Sean come to stand behind me and join the huddled group.

"Hey, are you okay? Can I help?" Townsend gently asks, something akin to concern lacing his tone as he focuses in on Lex.

"Why is it that men like you always seem to think that women like me would ever need your help?" Lex's voice drips with hatred as Townsend reaches for her shoulder.

I'm taken aback with the amount of vitriol and vehemence in her voice, unsure of where it's stemming from. We're the ones offering Townsend protection after all, he isn't one of her old, contracted hits.

I quickly turn my attention back to the scene unfolding in front of my eyes. The very minute Townsend touches her shoulder, Lex instantly changes. The best way I can describe it would be that her composure snaps and she explodes. Her anxious demeanor instantly changes from a passive observer to the blatant aggressor as she whips her head to look Townsend dead in the eyes. Lex spins on her back heel, grabs Townsend's wrist and uses her momentum to pin him to the ground. When he fights back, she snaps his wrist, effectively breaking it, and I cringe when I hear his wrist bones crack.

All this happens in just a matter of seconds. I look at her brothers who all immediately broke their covers as they watched Lex take down a guy who outweighs her by at least a hundred pounds. All of her brothers are openly staring at her in shock, no doubt probably regretting or doubting the prudence of her involvement with this extraction contract.

I look at her face and see her genuine surprise. It's clear by her expression that this wasn't her initial intent, but her instincts kicked in and years of training and experience took hold over her ability to logically see reason. She immediately releases Townsend, who at his full height stands about a good foot taller than her, but Lex's speed and strength are remarkable, along with her taking him by complete surprise. To see her in action is both terrifying and incredible. I start thinking of how close I came to seeing this exact scene moments before my own untimely death. That this could have been me if Lex hadn't changed her mind about my file. While we are all gaping at Lex's reaction, we didn't notice the swift movement of Townsend's team, surrounding us in what seems like an instant.

"Well, well, well. If it isn't the little sister trying to play the hero. Guess your shady brother taught you a thing or two after all," Townsend condescendingly spits out, his voice changing from gentleness to a more menacing tone with the slight edge of pain flitting through.

"We're looking for Alex West, have you seen him?" Townsend's one friend states, long gone are the jovial overtones, now his words are menacing, getting right down to business.

Will, taking the lead, replies, "What do you want from Alex West?"

"Alex West is dead," Lex automatically and tonelessly says, without any life, like it's become the default, automated response that she's been preprogrammed to spit out at the mere mention of her former alias's name.

I covertly gaze her way and notice that her face is blank. I know that she's someplace far away, somewhere else far removed from the rest of us here in Bryant Park. I'm not the only one who has noticed her remark, her brothers zero in on her, all the while keeping their eyes on the now adversarial team.

"Alex West isn't dead and we all know that. Your brother just disappeared, like he always does from time to time. We need his help. Now," Townsend spits out with venom.

"So, you put a contract on yourself so we would take it and get Alex to help you?" Kevin asks with a slight edge of disgusted disbelief.

"Why would we ever want to help someone like you?" Dave snarls, his shoulders squared, his dark brown eyes almost black.

"Because if you don't," a third member of Townsend's squad speaks up, "we'll take your sister as hostage until Alex arrives."

"You're not taking her," Luke hotly but firmly interjects.

"Wanna bet?" Townsend taunts as his entire team covertly point six guns at all of us males while Townsend snakes his arm around Lex's neck and draws a knife from his pocket, firmly pushing it into the soft flesh of her throat. Lex doesn't even blink, she doesn't even flinch. Her face has become replaced with the mask I recognize, the mask she wore when I first met her, the face of a cold-blooded assassin. Dread begins to fill my senses. I'm not sure of what the play is now that the mission has been completely compromised and flipped on its end.

"What, little girl, are you scared?" Townsend's voice drips with sarcasm as he taunts her.

"No," Lex simply replies, her voice as empty as her expression.

She takes a look at each of her brothers, looks at me and then stares at Dave. Dave's stance changes ever so slightly, signaling that she is about to make some kind of move and that her twin and brothers should be able to anticipate and appropriately respond.

"Why not? We have your brothers surrounded. I'm going to force them to watch me as I filet their darling sister's throat right here in Bryant Park," Townsend snidely remarks as he continues to berate her, tightening his grip on her throat, lifting her heels slightly off the ground so she's on her toes.

"Because, I'm the thing that people are usually scared of. I'm the nightmare," Lex easily says in a restrained voice, but still not showing any fear or any emotion for that matter. She's absolutely fearless.

Before Townsend can say anything else, Lex manages to swiftly grab the knife, using speed and surprise to her advantage in a mocking, you didn't learn your lesson type of way. Lex shifts her position so that she's immediately out of his grasp. She seizes control of the hand that's holding the knife before she twists Townsend's wrist and drives the knife deep in his chest, a couple inches from his heart which I have no doubt was intentional. In that split second, the rest of the Wests have disarmed the rest of the Townsend crew without causing a scene or drawing undue civilian attention to our group.

I stand, frozen in shock, unmoving, which is a direct dichotomy to all the action that rapidly unfolded around me. The Wests all spoke a language that I had no clue even existed. Boy, do I have a lot to learn. Lex, along with her brothers, are so fluid, so graceful and expeditious. Every move was calculated, intentional and deliberate. There was no flourish or extra fanfare, just efficiency maximized at its finest. Lex's hand is still around the knife's hilt where she's controlling Townsend, diabolically twisting it ever so slightly, causing Townsend to grimace in pain, but ultimately keeping him and his crew in check.

Everyone here knows that she could've killed him, why she didn't is yet to be discovered. Maybe she's curious, maybe she's bored, who knows. I spot a small ribbon of blood trailing down Lex's neck, from where Townsend pressed the knife's blade on her throat and I can feel my own anger spike despite our tactical and offensive advantage. Lex's voice has now taken on an edge that is both bored and furious, a tone and mindset I know to be a dangerous combination for her. Dave takes a small step toward her, but to protect her or Townsend, that I'm not sure of.

Lex finally addresses Townsend as she uses the knife to pull him closer to her face, forcing him to lean down to her eye level, "What the hell do you want? And before you say anything, I am Alexandra West. You may have known me as Alex West. But as I so graciously pointed out before, Alex West is dead. And your assumption of my gender, that Alex West is a man, truly shows what a sexist misogynist narcissistic chauvinist that you really are. So I will ask again, what the hell do you want from me?"

On the last eight words, she reiterates her intent by twisting the knife and pushing the hilt deeper into Townsend's chest, eliciting a strangled scream from him. Some onlookers finally turn their attention to us but thankfully, the West brothers have created a circle around her, providing their sister with some much needed privacy.

"Stupid bitch. I should have killed you when I had the chance," Townsend spits out as he grimaces in pain.

"You're right, you should've. And now, you'll never get the chance again. This is the last time I'm going to ask you Townsend, because frankly, I'm getting bored and I hate repeating myself. What do you want with Alex West?" Lex dryly reiterates with a few slight twists of her wrist again.

"I want to hire Alex, umm, you, to kill someone," Townsend gasps out in pain while his replies to her question.

"Not interested," Lex says flatly.

"But you're Alex West," Townsend quickly and incredulously responds.

"Correction, I am Alexandra West. Alex West is dead. Or weren't you listening?" Lex hisses out, her patience clearly thinning. She continues by condescendingly concluding, "And what part of 'not interested' did you not understand? The 'not' or the 'interested' part?"

As she says the words not and interested, she gives the knife a few final twists to the point that tears are freely running down Townsend's face.

"I understand, I get it! Please! Just let us go and we'll never bother you again," Townsend pleads.

Lex narrows her eyes and smiles an evil, unsettling smile that doesn't quite reach her eyes.

"If I ever see you again or if you ever make a threat against me or my family, I WILL be the last thing that your eyes see before they close and you go on to your next life in hell," she concludes, finally ripping the knife out of his chest and taking a step back.

Townsend collapses to the ground, clutching his chest as he tries to catch his breath. I see that his shirt is quickly soaking up blood, the stain increasing with every passing second. Townsend's hand, which is covering the wound has blood running down his arms. Lex looks on dispassionately and for the briefest of moments, I fear that she's become Alex West again.

After a beat, Lex subtly nods for her brothers to let their respective charge go. The five goons Townsend brought with him all gather around him, helping Townsend to stand up. She watches as all six men retreat, stagger and run south, a couple of the men supporting Townsend as they leave in quick haste. She unceremoniously wipes off the knife blade in the grass, throws it in her bag and turns to face her brothers. They are all staring back at her with expressions ranging from shock, pride and uncertainty. I realize that they probably share the same concerns as me, with the ease of her reverting back to her Alex West persona. I know Lex noticed my behavior and that she's picking up on her brothers' unease as well. I see what I think is a flash of disappointment and doubt in her eyes before she strengthens her resolve and squares her shoulders.

"What? I didn't kill him or any other guy from the team. For me, that's progress," she lightly reasons.

When her brothers don't say anything, she shrugs and walks back toward where we parked the first SUV.

***

The start of the drive back to West Enterprises is incredibly awkward and tense. Dave, Lex, Will and I are back in our original vehicle while Luke, Sean and Kev decided to commandeer the SUV they drove into the city. Will, while driving, is arguing with Dave, who is defending his twin from the front passenger seat. I look over at Lex, wondering why she hasn't weighed in on the conversation and I'm shocked to find that she's just silently staring out the window, watching the people walking along the sidewalks as we're stuck in some typical afternoon Manhattan traffic.

"She compromised the mission." Will is yelling, his voice reverberating in the compact cabin space.

"No, she didn't," Dave interrupts as he corrects his eldest brother. "She saw a threat and made a move to neutralize the situation. She made the right move! It wasn't a true contract, it was a threat, Will. A trap! The mission was compromised from the start, she is the reason why we were able to keep the casualty count low today," Lex's twin reasons.

"She made it into a threat! And she blew all of our covers," Will stubbornly counters.

"We're not compromised. Kev ordered a team to tail them, some of the best guys we have," Dave reminds Will, trying to calm the eldest West brother down.

Dave concludes, "And we broke our own covers. She didn't give us away. We made that choice ourselves. Regardless, this doesn't feel like it's done and over with. It feels like the beginning of something bigger. I just don't know what or why, but it's just a feeling."

Will shakes his head in frustration and looks out the window as we stop at yet another red light. I see Will gripping the steering wheel so hard that his knuckles have turned white with suppressed emotions. I look over to Lex, wondering what she's thinking. I know she can hear everything going on and that she has already noticed the doubts we all let flash over our expressions.

As if she knows that I'm looking at her, she glances over to me and tilts her head toward the street before she gives me a small smile. In a flash, she grabs her bag and jumps out of the vehicle to the sidewalk. I scramble after her, crossing over the bench seat while quickly figuring out her message a second later and hastily joining her. I hear Will yell after her, asking what she's doing while Luke yells out from the other SUV's driver's side window, trying to get her attention.

People part around her as Lex looks at them all blankly, raises a hand in a gesture of goodbye and turns on her heel as she begins to head north, immediately getting swallowed up in the city's weekend tourist crowd. The five West brothers all look toward me as I shrug my shoulders, communicating my choice to follow her lead. As the drivers behind both brothers start to angrily honk their horns, since the lights have turned green, the West SUVs are forced to move forward while I nod and run after Lex, understanding their wishes for me to continue to keep my eyes on her.

**

At first, I can't find her. Even with my six-foot two height, it's hard to spot her smaller frame in the hordes of people taking advantage of the beautiful afternoon weather. Finally, I catch a brief glimpse of her, her dark black hair bobbing with the tide of people. Her pace isn't rushed and her movements seem calm and relaxed. I double my pace as I maneuver around and in the crowds of people to get to her. Lex's phone is ringing when I finally catch up to her, slightly out of breath, a seemingly common theme.

She answers, talking immediately, before the caller can even get a word out, "Dave. I'm fine. I'm going to the apartment. Meet me there later."

She hangs up without letting Dave get a word in edge wise and turns toward me.

"We're going to the apartment. Let's hail a cab," she states without emotion. Lex walks to the corner, lets out a loud, ear-splitting whistle and raises a hand to hail a cab.

"What apartment?" I dumbfoundedly ask, trying to keep up with her brain and turn of recent events.

"Mine," she answers flatly, not giving any additional context.

"You have an apartment here in the city?" I ask, still processing all the changes and new information.

Lex just looks at me with an almost wearied expression on her face. Moments later a cab pulls over and she gives the driver the address. The cabbie nods his head in understanding and we are whisked away uptown. Lex continues to silently watch the city rush past us from the taxi's backseat window as we head to her place.

I'm still wrapping my head around the fact that Lex has an apartment located outside of West Enterprises' footprint. I thought she lived at West Enterprises exclusively, on a full-time, permanent basis. I hadn't heard of her living anywhere else from either her or her brothers. I know that she hadn't left her childhood home during her recovery once she released from the hospital, so it never struck me as an option for her to have a residence separate from her family's company.

But the more I think about it, the more Lex having an independent living space makes complete sense. Of course, she wouldn't put all of her eggs into one basket. She is too strategic to make that rookie mistake. I had only seen her at West Enterprises' headquarters, but that doesn't mean West Enterprises is her only permanent residence. I was aware there was tension within the West Family before I came into the picture. There seems to be some deep-seated issues, and something fractured this family a long time ago. Perhaps the West family rift was about the death of their father and the specific circumstances of how he died. No one has talked about it and I don't want to pry, it's not my place. But maybe it was because of that conflict that Lex sought refuge in the city far away from her brothers, needing separation from the memories that haunt her.

Getting lost in my own thoughts, I wonder what Lex was like before her father passed. How was she different from the woman she's become now? Was she more like the Alexandra she's trying to be? Was there an innocence in her dark eyes when she saw the world? Was she ever vulnerable, was she ever comfortable with showing her vulnerabilities? As I keep picturing what Lex could have been in comparison to what she is now, my gaze keeps flickering to steal glances at Lex. She's still staring out over the streets of Manhattan, her eyes unfocused, her face partially hidden by the curtain of her black hair.

In what finally seems like eons, the cab has pulled over in front of an impressive apartment building located in the Upper East Side. Lex elegantly gets out of the cab while I'm scrambling and trying to rush to keep up, a seemingly common theme within our dynamics.

Lex walks up to the doorman, a middle-aged gentleman, and greets him with a smile. Wow, he gets a rare Alexandra West smile? The doorman nods at her with a smile on his own face and turns a questioning gaze toward me.

"He's with me," she responds to his silent question, the casual way she answers his unspoken question is an attestation to the personal level of their relationship.

"David may be coming over later. Feel free to let him in, but no one else, for now. Not until you have further instruction directly from me," Lex continues and instructs in a commanding yet friendly tone.

The doorman nods with a patient understanding and opens the door for us as she whisks on by.

"Have a good evening, ma'am," he politely replies.

Lex abruptly stops in her tracks and turns around with a playful smile on her face. "George, as always, it's Elyse," she says with a warm smile.

"Of course, ma'am," he states with his own wink and smile while she rolls her eyes good-naturedly.

At the beginning of their conversation, I would've guessed that they are comfortable and familiar with each other. They seemed to have made this exchange often; the conversation exchanged in a witty way, exuding a seemingly effortless manner and habit. My suspicion is confirmed, they know each other, and Lex is comfortable enough with him to trade inside jokes. She smirks before she turns on her heel and strides through the lobby before stepping into the waiting elevator and hitting the button on the door panel. After I surreptitiously look over the exterior of the lobby and elevator, I quickly enter the elevator before the doors close and look at the elevator panel and notice the "Penthouse" button is brightly illuminated.

"Lex, you don't have an apartment, you have the penthouse suite! How long have you lived here? And why did the doorman call you Elyse?" I ask my questions in rapid succession with disbelief tinging my words after the elevator doors close.

Lex shrugs her shoulders nonchalantly. "I would never use my full legal name. It would put everyone who lives and works here at undue risk. And to your penthouse question, twelve years. Well, I've owned the building for twelve years, although legally this place is owned by one of my shell companies, so it can't be tracked back to me. I decided to buy the complex as an investment, real estate in New York is always a smart, long-term plan. I rent out all the lower levels, live on the top floors. Why? Is me being a pseudo real estate mogul a deal breaker?" she teases.

I just smile and shake my head, glad to see that the playful side of Lex is starting to come back out after the Bryant Park incident.

The elevator chimes a light tone, notifying us that we've arrived at our destination. The mental doors open to an ornate lobby which I move to stand in the middle of, gawking at the sight of the elegant opulence that I've been transported into. Lex keeps moving forward, unimpressed with the beauty and art as she steps up to the distinguished entry doors. She enters a set of digital codes into the security pad against the wall, successfully completes the biometric scan and opens the heavy double doors with a manual key. Three different types of locks for my woman's residence, I can't say that I'm surprised at her precautions.

I take my first step into her sanctuary from the foyer and my jaw drops to the floor. Her apartment is huge, but the term apartment is a massive understatement. By the looks of it, she has at least the top two floors of the entire building as her apartment. Her open floor plan is enhanced by the two-story floor-to-ceiling windows showcasing a beautiful view of the city. Immediately drawn to the windows, I walk over to them and see that I'm looking over the city skyline, buildings from downtown creating a metal landscape.

"The windows are privacy tinted, so no one can see you. There is also thermal heat signature masking, new technology a friend of mine wanted to try out to minimize snipers or anyone tracking internal body heat movements from any distance. Since I remodeled my living spaces, another friend of mine in the public sector looked the other way. He owed me a huge favor considering I'm the one that took out his biggest competition who was trying to slander him in the press. Because of my connections, there are no official blueprints on file with the city, minimizing oversight of the layout from any prying eyes. There are minimal ways, if any, a threat could infiltrate my defenses here," Lex offers.

I'm too busy trying to close my mouth to worry about threats or to offer any type of thoughtful response.

"Do you want anything to eat? Drink?" she asks, her voice cutting through my shock, directing me to more manageable and digestible decisions.

"No, I'm good for right now, thank you," I manage to murmur out, suddenly finding my voice but still in a state of astonishment.

Suddenly, the doorbell rings, startling me from my trance. Lex hurries over to the door and looks at the screen that I previously walked by and didn't even notice, but now I'm just registering as a camera view of the penthouse's elevator lobby. I see Dave looking right at the camera, smiling and waving his hand. With a smile mirroring Dave's, Lex quickly lets him into the apartment.

"That was fast," Lex greets her twin as she shuts the door behind him.

"Yeah, I got out at the next corner and hailed a cab, too…" Dave drifts off, staring at me.

I was about to step forward, but I hesitate when I see the expression on his face.

"You brought Cole here?" Dave asks, incredulity lacing his voice.

I try not to take offense to his tone or his shocked facial expression, but I'm still confused as to why me being here has taken Dave by this level of surprise.

"Yeah, it's no big deal. What else was I going to do? Leave him vulnerable on the corner for Townsend to pick off or worse, use him as leverage?" Lex sarcastically pushes back, immediately brushing off her twin's concern.

She walks toward the kitchen as Dave watches her walk away. Then he turns his attention to me, studying me, making me feel uncomfortable for just being here in Lex's place.

"I'm the only other person who has ever been here," Dave softly explains so that his sister can't hear our conversation. "Even the rest of the family hasn't been to her apartment yet. Some of them may know about it, but for those that have an inkling, they would also know they aren't welcome, that they're persona non grata, and they won't have access until she decides to green light each of them."

"To be fair," I interrupt, "it's not an apartment, it's a penthouse suite."

"Yeah, well, you know how my sister can be modest at times," Dave good-naturedly laughs at my comment, clapping a hand on my shoulder, and in that moment, I instantly know that we're good.

Lex walks back over to us with two beers in one hand while she sips a glass of white wine. She hands us the beers and invites us to move deeper into the apartment towards the casual sitting area.

After a few minutes of silence and sipping on our respective drinks, Dave turns toward Lex and asks about the proverbial elephant in the room, "So, what happened today?"

Lex pensively stares out the window, the silence stretching out. I don't know if she's actually seeing anything, the cumulus clouds or roving crowds, or if she's just lost in her own thoughts. Finally, after a few moments, she turns her head and sighs, seeming to know that this question would eventually come up sooner or later.

"I don't know," Lex finally and honestly responds, "I knew something was off before we even left West house. I kept saying that over and over again in my head, even when we were in the planning stages. But it wasn't my op, and I didn't feel like it was my place to take over a contract you, Luke and Kev had agreed to. That sense of dread was only enhanced once we got to the park. And then I saw it: Townsend's body mannerisms, his non-verbal communication. All of Townsend was completely off. He was too cocky, too aware for a civilian. He was the definition of the antithetical archetype. Their regular game should have been casual and for fun. It wasn't. People don't go to Bryant Park to play football. They go to read, relax and enjoy the greenery. Football is for Central Park, there just isn't enough room in Bryant Park to play a proper game. And just by watching them, I could tell that Townsend and his men were just like us, hyper-focused, aware and extremely calculated. They were going through the motions. I was just concerned for all of our safety. I couldn't focus on anything other than protecting my family. The whole thing with Townsend, that was pure instinct. Like a switch, something automatic that kicked in."

"Knifing someone in the chest is instinctively automatic for you?" I yelp out.

Dave looks at me, amused while Lex meets my eyes.

"Actually, that was pure anger. He was threatening the family. And he had a knife pressed into my throat. He pissed me off. Those twists at the end were for good measure, albeit maybe a little much, but slightly warranted in the midst of the situation," Lex admits with a small smile.

"It was still a bit harsh Lex, even for you, especially in public," Dave admonishes.

"No, it wasn't Dave," Lex vehemently responds, her head snapping back to her twin, her smile instantly gone. "You and the guys secured the area. They set the trap, which is an unacceptable action by anyone in our business. That's the low of all the lows. I had to get that point across to Townsend and his crew. And I had a friend of mine disable all cameras in the area before we even arrived," Lex shares with us.

"All of them?" Dave incredulously asks.

"Yes, traffic cams, ATM surveillance, everything within a five-block radius. He also blacked out cell usage, so camera phones or any live streaming platforms couldn't and didn't catch our actions or identities. We are in the clear," Lex states matter-of-factly. "Have Will search through the recovered footage, he won't find anything," she confidently continues, the challenge in her voice subtle but strong.

Before Dave can continue his line of questioning, his phone starts ringing. He immediately silences it, but notifications start following, the chimes loudly interrupting the previously calm reverie.

Lex raises an eyebrow while I venture to ask, "Who is it?"

"The family," Dave simply answers.

Looking at Lex, he gives her a knowing look.

After a minute, she nods and responds, "Fine, invite them. It's about time that they've finally seen the place."

Dave texts who I can only assume is the family group chat, telling them to come over. "We have fifteen minutes before they're here," Dave advises.

"Okay, let's get to work," Lex responds, lithely standing with the New York skyline in the background, the light from the buildings framing her silhouette.

***

In the next ten minutes, Lex checks out all the rooms upstairs, making sure that they are clean and organized up to her standards. She had called down to George, the doorman who we met earlier, stating that there were four more additional men on the way and that they were authorized to come upstairs. I notice she doesn't refer to the four Wests as her brothers.

As if she read my mind, she says as she hangs up, "To protect them, and specifically, to protect George."

I nod, immediately understanding and internally smiling at her compassion for George. I don't know his story, but I have a gut feeling that he's been a much needed, constant factor in her turbulent and unconventional life.

Dave and I were commanded to clean and straighten up the first floor. As we're hustling and trying to meet her exact standards, I ask Lex's twin, "Why is this such a big deal?"

"I'm the only one who's been here, besides Lexi and now you. She's never invited the rest of the guys over. I'm not even sure who even knows the fact that she has an apartment, let alone where it is," Dave ponders aloud as he fluffs a couch pillow.

"Will probably is aware of all the details and the exact location," Lex says as she comes down the stairs, "The others? Probably not. Dave, do you mind going to the lobby and greeting them? I'm not giving them the codes to my fortress just yet."

Dave inclines his head with a smile and gives her a comforting hug. Dave nods at me before he turns toward the front door, walks to the elevator foyer and closes the front door behind him.

After Dave's gone, Lex turns to look at me and fully explains, "This place is my retreat, my own personal sanctum, from all the craziness that is my life, both at work and my family's volatile relationship dynamics. The less people who know about it, the better. It's safer that way for everyone involved. Dave has a room upstairs, but other than that, he is the only person who has been in my apartment before today… and before you."

I nod my head, understanding the importance of the privacy and sanctum that she finds here, as well as this space being her personal refuge from the storms of her job and life.

I've always known that Lex is a private person, especially when it concerns her family. They're all in the business of secrets and confidential information, and knowing Lex, she protects and guards her personal information fiercely. I'm an only child, but from what I've seen of the West family dynamics over the past few weeks, I can only imagine how six siblings can be in each other's personal business in a normal family, let alone in a family that all works for the same company and lives very similarly secretive lives. I've even seen the small looks on her face when she feels that Dave is encroaching upon her personal space and sanity, resulting in her tending to shut down and disengage from everything around her.

Lex continues, "Most likely, this whole Townsend situation and me having an apartment nonsense will end up turning into a classic West family argument, full of fireworks and posturing from both sides. Don't worry about it, it happens all the time with us. It's just how we communicate. My advice? Just keep your head down and don't antagonize anyone. You didn't do anything wrong. If any heat comes your way, I'll handle it. Okay?"

I nod my head and she half smiles. She's about to reach for my hand when the doorbell rings, interrupting our moment. Going over to the lobby's monitor together, we see all five of the West brothers. Dave is looking directly into the camera again with a knowing smirk on his face. But the rest of the brothers are looking around the elevator lobby, in various states of shock, their mouths agape as they take everything in. I can't fault them for that, the lobby is gorgeously decorated and beautiful, and I'm sure that I myself had the same facial expression moments ago when I first walked in.

Lex sighs and mutters something under her breath that I can't quite catch as she physically braces herself before reluctantly unlocking the door. Upon the door cracking open, the movement lets all five alpha males to step in the entryway, right in the midst of her peaceful sanctuary. Ready for an argument to immediately begin, I am shocked to hear only a resounding silence echoing through the moments that follow.

"Come in and make yourselves at home," Lex politely welcomes them and steps aside, allowing her brothers to enter the rest of her home.

Dave comes to stand next to Lex while the four Wests brothers are staring open-mouthed at her apartment, edging closer inside to the point where Lex can finally close the door.

Luke looks back at Lex and is the first to start and say, "Sissy! Since when did you have…?"

Lex holds his gaze, nods and ignores his fractured sentence.

After ten more minutes of silence where the brothers explore both floors and each room, everyone finds their way back into the living area where Dave, Lex and I have been seated, waiting for the others to join us in their own time. Lex had wisely grabbed additional beer bottles for the rest of her brothers, which all four men take advantage of when they eventually find their seats around us.

"Wow, Lex," Sean starts, "this place is gorgeous."

Luke and Kev nod in agreement, still looking around. Lex gives a slight but wry smile, acknowledging their sentiments before turning her attention to Will, waiting for his comments of approval. This small moment speaks volumes about how far Will and Lex have come and how much she truly values his opinion as her older brother.

"Is it safe?" Will gruffly asks, his overprotectiveness showing through when it comes to the safety of his little sister.

"It is, but of course you already know that answer. We both know that you were always aware of my exact location at all times," Lex counters and her comment reaffirms what I assumed, Will always knew but he respected her privacy, even when they were at their worst in respect to their relationship's health.

"I knew you had a place, I just didn't know the specifics, like how to get in, defensive strategic measures, all of that," Will admits with a smile.

Lex nods and looks around her apartment, maybe trying to see it through her brothers' fresh perspective and new eyes. "It works for me," Lex simply says. All five brothers nod in easy agreement.

"I'm just surprised that Cole saw your apartment before we did," Luke says jokingly, breaking the silence and tension with his characteristic quip.

"In all fairness," Lex replies, "I didn't necessary plan for him to come and see this place today. And there was less than an hour gap between Cole coming here and you guys inviting yourselves over. So, I think we're even, no?" She's smiling and joking back with her brothers now.

The room's atmosphere seems to have lifted, the tension breaking and shoulders relaxing. As Lex stands up and starts to head for the kitchen, Will opens his mouth to speak.

Before he can get a word out, Lex silences him by putting her hand on his shoulder as she's passing by and knowingly says, "Afterward. Let's make dinner, just like old times. Together. Then we can talk about everything later. Okay?" Her voice, somewhat defeated and unexpectedly vulnerable, triggers something on Will's face.

Will looks up at her, trying to decipher her expression. After a moment, the elder West nods and places his own hand on top of hers in a sign of consideration and compassion.

Will's understanding concession is a small, quiet gesture in the grand scheme of time and their lives, but it means so much more than what is initially on the surface. It's a symbol of how much Lex and Will deeply trust each other. They innately understand each other and they're not afraid to compromise when needed, even if that compromise is something as inconsequential as a conversation after dinner. They're both committed to working together toward a common goal. It's really amazing to see how their relationship has grown and blossomed to become stronger over the past couple of months. From what I've heard about Will and Lex's dynamic over the past few years, they were always combatively at each other's throats without ever compromising. The two siblings could never see eye to eye, let alone agree to any form of common ground.

Lex nods and gently extracts her hands from under the eldest West's palm. She meets all of her brother's eyes before she heads into the kitchen. By silent instinct, all five brothers follow in her wake. Again, I find myself on the outside looking in, watching but not fully being a part of, at least, not just yet. The family West is a formidable unit: loyal, dedicated and strong.

***

"That's not how you chop garlic!" Lex squeals as Kev attempts to gracefully chop garlic. In actuality, he has butchered the garlic beyond its original or intended form. Lex had put a few pieces of garlic out on a cutting board for Kev's kitchen assignment. But the West brother who is proficient in the MMA ring has met his match: cutting and slicing garlic pieces into uniformed chunks, ultimately making a mess. Laughing, Lex shows him how to expertly hold the chef's knife and how to properly chop the garlic for the homemade Alfredo sauce she has been preparing. She patiently watches him as he focuses on his task, both of them smiling with sibling love.

Sean and Luke are in charge of slicing and seasoning the zucchini while Dave is cooking the pasta. Will was put in charge of grating the cheese from the fresh Parmesan cheese block Lex picked up at a local cheese shop. I was promptly told that I was to supervise all activities in the kitchen, a polite way of saying that I was the guest of the night. The former tension that had blanketed over the group when they first arrived has dissipated into peals of laughter, the random reminiscing of childhood stories and an air of playfulness that is unique to siblings. *So*, I think to myself, *this is what the West family looked like before their mother and father died.*

Lex quickly chops up the remaining garlic into uniform and perfectly sized pieces, efficiently adding them to the saucepan already simmering on the stove. She adds in cheese, cream to taste and Kev's hacked garlic before finally telling us all that the sauce is done after it has boiled and simmered after a few minutes. Dave plates the pasta with Sean and Luke adding the steamed zucchini on top of the pasta.

Kev holds the saucepan for Lex as she covers each plate's pasta with a healthy dose of the aromatic white cream sauce. Will is right behind Lex, grating fresh cheese on top of the Alfredo sauce, pasta and zucchini. Sean and Dave had already grabbed silverware and napkins as they had previously set the dining table for seven. Every so often, one of the siblings bumps into each other, but for the most part, they all seem to know the choreography of the making dinner dance. Like a well-oiled machine only slightly rusty from time, I see how the Wests were and the potential for what they can become again.

Each person grabs a plated dish and a wine glass or a beer bottle before heading toward the open dining area, located adjacently next to the kitchen. When everyone is seated, the five West males start to ravenously dig in. I pause with my fork in mid-air, watching the scene unfold around me. Lex has a small smile on her face as she sits at the head of the table. I'm seated in between Luke and Sean with Kev directly across from me, Dave sitting to Lex's right and Will on the opposite end.

Reading Lex's body language, she is pleased that her brothers are devouring the meal that she commandeered. She meets my eyes and I give her a smile and watch as a slight blush spreads across her cheeks. I suddenly feel like I'm being watched. I look over and see Kev's small smile on his own face. He noticed Lex's and my non-verbal exchange. He picks up his beer bottle and tips it in my direction, I slightly incline my head as he smiles. I turn my attention back to the meal, enjoying every morsel and the company surrounding me.

After a while, when all the plates are empty and we're sipping on wine and beer, Sean comments that the fresh flowers on the glass dining table are a nice, decorative touch.

"Thanks," Lex responds, "my cleaning team makes sure that I have fresh flowers on the table every week."

A welcomed silence descends over the table, everyone content with the meal and company.

"This is honestly the first time I've ever used this table. Normally I eat in the kitchen or in the living room," Lex quietly admits out loud.

"How often are you here, Lex?" Kev casually asks without any judgment tinging his voice.

"It looks like you're rarely here, Sissy. No offense, but it seems like it's barely lived in. And it's so clinical, no personal touches that I can see," Luke adds on as he looks around.

"If I'm not on a job and not at West Enterprises, then I'm here," Lex simply answers.

249

Will audibly gasps and says, "You're here alone? For all that amount of time? This place looks like you just moved in!"

"No, well, sometimes Dave's with me. His room upstairs is the only decorated room in the whole apartment," Lex says with an amused smile tossed over in her twin's direction.

"But I hardly doubt," she diplomatically continues, gently redirecting the conversation, "that we're all here to talk about my décor and living arrangements. Why don't we all adjourn to the conference room down the hall and discuss the matter at hand? Shall we?"

We all nod as we take our plates back into the kitchen. Lex tells us to leave them on the island countertop while she shoots off a quick text.

Looking up in explanation, she says, "My one cleaning representative lives downstairs. She said she would gladly come up and clean the kitchen."

"We can clean up, it's not a problem," Sean offers as he moves toward the kitchen sink.

Lex holds her hand up, replying, "I don't pay them as much as I do to not have the convenience of immediate assistance if needed. It's fine. My staff are compensated fairly."

As if on cue, the doorbell promptly rings and Lex excuses herself to answer it. She has a warm smile on her face as she speaks to the woman in a different language. Spanish or Portuguese, I think, I can only tell that it's one of the romantic languages. I didn't even know that Lex spoke any languages other than English, but it makes sense considering all the traveling she's done.

I pull myself out of my thoughts and reverie as the brothers all head down the hall to the right, passing the front doors on our left and I quickly follow along in their wake. Toward the end of the hall, the conference room is on the left. Opening the door, Lex leads us into the room, switching on the lights by the door, allowing us to see the last remnants of the city's sunset from the room's windows. *What a gorgeous view of the west side of Manhattan,* I think to myself. As I turn to tell her just that, I see her peacefully staring out of the window, her eyes chasing the silhouette of the fading sun. There's a small smile teasing the corner of her lips and her eyes seem to be full of serenity.

As if she feels my gaze lingering on her, she looks over to me and softly asks, "Beautiful, isn't it?"

I stare at my woman, taking in Lex's gentle complexion and her calm gaze. I answer without thinking, "Stunning," although I'm not just talking about the view of the sunset anymore. I'm looking at her, admiring her beauty, elegance and grace.

Dave quietly clears his throat, noticing my romantic overture. Lex and I both reluctantly take our seats, the quiet moment in the sunrays ending with the setting sun. Lex sits next to me as she positions herself across from Will. Kev has appointed himself at the head of the table in an uncommon and uncharacteristic display of leadership and perhaps, impartiality. Sean and Luke are seated on Will's side of the table while Dave sits on the other side of Lex. And so, we're all queued up for the next West saga, as I internally brace myself for the intense discussion that's sure to follow.

Lex and Will are silent, looking at each other, waiting to see who will speak first. The rest of the brothers all seem to be on edge, waiting for the first side to strike, their eyes darting between Lex's and Will's faces, everyone seeming to grow increasingly more uncomfortable with the silence as the minutes tick by. That is, everyone except for Lex. She looks calm and cool, like she is in her element. I suppose that she is.

"Is Townsend still a threat?" I tentatively ask, unable to stand the silence any longer.

Six heads swivel my way, surprised that I said anything, that I was the one who started the conversation. I am fully aware that I am out of my depth here, and I am slightly surprised at my own brazen question. But someone needs to start this conversation and get it going, and I'm more than happy to be that person. Lex, with amusement in her eyes, turns and looks at Will, expecting an answer.

"We're not sure," Will carefully answers, "we tracked down everyone who was with him in the park and neutralized those threats. Since they made a direct threat toward the family, they had to be terminated."

I'm shocked but Lex is amused as she lets a slight smirk light up her face, "Wow—look who is doing my job now. Maybe I should spruce up my resume and prepare for some competition.

Luke doesn't meet his sister's eyes as he says, "You have absolutely nothing to worry about, Sissy. It was necessary, but none of us enjoyed it. I don't think we have the stomach for eliminations."

Lex good-naturedly rolls her eyes as she refocuses the discussion back to the mission at hand, "And Townsend?"

"We haven't been able to locate him," Kev begins, "but we consider him a direct threat to your safety."

"Why Lex's safety?" I continue on with my bold streak and ask the group, trying to shirk the feeling of falling behind from the group.

While Will good-naturedly rolls his eyes, Sean patiently explains, "Because he has seen her face and knows her true identity now. He knows Alex West isn't a male, but a female. He could also identify all of us as members of the West family. That alone is a cause for immense concern. But it seemed like Alex West was the target of his rage. So, this puts her life at risk. And depending on his intent, Townsend can sell that information quickly for a high profit on the black market. She has made a lot of enemies in her career. Those enemies would all be vying for that information, regardless of the cost, to exact some revenge on her or indirectly, on us."

I gulp down my anxiety and look to Lex for confirmation.

Lex meets my gaze head-on, unafraid of what could become an inferno for her to manage. "It's true. I wasn't well-liked in my previous work. Shocking, I know," she flatly says.

There are a couple of chuckles and knowing smiles passed around the room, effectively dissolving and breaking some of the room's tension. But it doesn't solve the problem at hand.

After a beat, Will continues on with a more relaxed tone, "I'm not sure I'm all that comfortable with all that we know about Townsend. There's more to him than what we're seeing and what our research has come up with so far, that's already been proven after today's interaction. He has a solid source, someone who knows a lot about the West family. Sure, he thought Lex was the youngest of all of us, not Sean. He didn't seem to know about our specific order of birth. And he made assumptions about Lex's gender. But he was able to identify all of us as West siblings by sight. That alone, is a serious breach of our personal information and security."

"I've been tracking him," Luke quickly interrupts and offers to the group, "and he pops up here and there all over the city. I need to get a lockdown on his location, but his patterns are all erratic. It's almost as if he's hunting."

"For what?" I can't seem to stop from asking the horrific question for which I think I already know the answer to.

"For me," Lex definitively says, sighing, pushing away from the table, "Townsend is hunting me."

There's a nervous unease that suddenly fills the air and settles like a wet blanket in the conference room. Lex goes to stand in front of the windows, staring outside and a sense of unsettledness pulses off her in waves.

"We need to be proactive here, even though I know none of you want to hear that," Lex bravely continues on as she speaks to the window, "if we don't neutralize this issue, it's going to quite literally blow up in our faces. Where is he, Luke?"

"Lex, what are you planning?" Kev tentatively asks, his face drawn in wary concern.

"No! You can't do what I think you're going to do," Dave exclaims, his eyes wide and his jaw tense.

I look at him, questioningly. But Lex doesn't enlighten the group.

"She's going to act as bait for Townsend to draw him out," Dave answers, filling in the blanks for the rest of us, the fear fully evident in his voice.

"Obviously," Lex flippantly confirms as she sits back down, "but I also know that I have five brothers who would go to the end of the earth for me. And Cole? His training is coming along well. This can be an assessment of his skills and what we can work on to improve, to prepare him to become an agent."

Sean starts, catching on to his sister's line of thought, "Lex, no…"

"Lexi, don't do this," Dave says over Sean's statement.

Luke has reached over to grasp her hand as he begins, "Sissy…" Lex gives Luke a small smile before she addresses the objections.

Although she is talking to all of us, Lex is only looking at Will when she firmly declares, "You know this is our best play, our only true play. I won't have this family pay the price for my sins."

Will looks at her, his eyes pleading. "No, Will," she continues, "I've got to go in alone. He knows all of your faces. Townsend will be on high alert and if he sees any of you, we may not get him in time, or he could disappear forever. And we'd all live the rest of our lives in fear, wondering if and when Townsend will make his move against us. I can't let that happen. And I know, deep down, neither can you."

I can see the gears in Will's head turning as he mentally debates his sister's points and their merits, weighing them against his brothers and his own personal feelings on the matter.

"This is the only way. I won't let us all live in fear," she softly and gently says.

"Don't let her do this," Kev hollers, standing up in anger, a stark difference in volume from Lex's quieter voice.

Luke and Sean look at Will, expecting him to immediately veto Lex's plan. Luke is still holding onto Lex's hand with a grip so hard, I'm afraid that he's going to break her bones. Will looks at all of us, his expression is admittedly defeated as his eyes settle back onto his sister's face. He has made his decision, and it's not putting Lex's safety's at the forefront. My stomach drops, my fear palpable.

"All right," Will says reluctantly, not meeting our questioning eyes, but still looking at Lex, "Luke, give us the last coordinates. Lex, go get ready. Call our contacts and see if we can get additional ground teams to station at the primary location."

Lex smiles a grin that doesn't meet her eyes and gives Luke a light kiss on the cheek as she disengages from his grip and leaves the room. The minute Lex leaves the room to go upstairs and prepare, all hell breaks loose in the conference room.

"How could you agree to something like this?" Dave bellows, his face livid with rage, his emotions directed only at Will.

"Will, did you really think this situation entirely through?" Sean queries with an unusually slight edge in his voice.

Luke questions, "How the hell can we keep her safe without being there to protect her?"

"She can't go through with this. She's still recovering from all of her injuries. Dave, you have to go talk some sense to her," Kev strongly states over the voices of questions before he turns to Dave's red face.

"She has to go. She has to be the one," I confidently but quietly state, thinking no one will hear me over all of the yelling. But I'm surprised when all five heads turn my way as the room becomes deathly still, waiting for me to further explain my logic and reasoning.

Man, that's an intimidating sight: all five, strong, dominant males turning my way. Not just males, but Lex's brother, all asking me how we should be responsible for Lex, their only sister, who they all love and care for. Where I'm willingly putting their sister's safety on the line, where I'm agreeing that she should knowingly walk directly into the line of fire. That she's the sister for whom they would all die for and they have the experience and expertise to make these types of decisions whereas I don't. For Lex, though, I need to speak up.

"We all know that she won't let any of you take a bullet with her name on it," I bravely continue, "and she feels compelled to do this. And her instinct is not to kill him, at least I don't think that's her first line reasoning. She could have easily done that in the park, but she didn't. She showed restraint. That is a big step for her, right? She let him go, but she won't make the same mistake twice if that means that any of your lives are threatened."

I pause, an internal debate warring in me before I decide to continue, "Look, she told me that she was struggling with how to be Alexandra and how to leave her Alex West persona behind. Her offering to do this, I believe, goes toward what she thinks are Alexandra values. What Alexandra would do and what matters to her. And that's family. She's looking for absolution and redemption. And we, who love and care for her, need to support her in as she grows."

Sean finally starts nodding in agreement with me. I can see that Kev and Luke are slowly coming around to the same understanding, even if they don't like it. Will seems pleased with the additional context, but I can tell that Dave is still irate with Will.

Sensing his ire, Will looks over to Dave with sadness in his eyes. "We can't stop her, you out of all of us know that the most," the eldest brother starts, "and even if we were to try, we would fail. Cole has a valid point. Even with her striving to be different, to be Alexandra and to redefine herself, she can still outsmart us all. We just need to protect and support her, to make sure that she comes home safe."

"I'm not letting her take any more bullets for us, William. You of all people should know that about me," Dave says stubbornly, staring Will down and throwing his eldest brother's words back in his face.

Will gives Dave a slight nod and a small look of understanding before Dave rushes out of the room, presumably to try to talk some sense into his twin. Will sighs, closing his eyes for the briefest of moments. It's in that instance I can finally see how leading West Enterprises and managing the intense family dynamics which play into the professional and personal lives all of the West siblings have taken its toll on the eldest West.

Luke gets up to follow Dave but stops at Will's voice who advises, "Let him go, Luke. He needs to get everything he's thinking and feeling off his chest. She of all people will understand him. And Lex is the one that needs to hear it. Lex will get Dave to concede as to why we have to do this her way."

Luke slowly sits back down in his seat, looking slightly deflated. I turn my attention back to the rest of the men and am shocked by what I see. The exhaustion and worry that is etched in Will's face are the same expressions reflected in the faces of Kev, Sean and Luke. I'm surrounded by an encompassing feeling of being overwhelmed and at an utter loss as to what to do next.

It's comforting to see that Lex's brothers are rallying around her, even when they don't agree with all of the decisions being made. But isn't that what family is? You don't have to always agree nor do you have to be happy about someone else's choices. But to know that there's still the love and support to back and guide your way, that there's someone who will be in your corner no matter what. It's comforting to know that you have someone to help carry you when you don't have the strength to do that for yourself.

Will looks up at me and says in a challenging but authoritative tone, "All right, Cole Harris. Our sister seems to think that you're ready to join our agent ranks. Let's prove her right. What do you have?"

PART II

Cole Harris

Fifteen minutes later, all seven of us have devised a plan that we can all tentatively agree upon. It may not be the best one, but at least we think it's a plan that will keep Lex safe which is everyone's main objective and priority. The decision includes texting Steve Wallace, a family friend who I met during the West Enterprises attack, who is also close to Lex and cares about her safety. Luke shoots off that text, asking for assistance and thankfully, Steve is still in town and is up to helping us out, based on Luke's Hail Mary request.

The plan is a ruse where Lex and Steve are pretending to be on a date, heading to Cedar Local which is a bar in the Financial District, located in Lower Manhattan. Townsend has been recently seen frequenting this establishment through our research and reconnaissance that has tracked his movements, so there's a good chance that he'll naturally be there. But just in case he's not there tonight, Lex and Steve will be able to move around to various bars in the area under the guise of a self-initiated bar crawl. Even though I wanted to accompany my girl, I knew that it was best for me to sit this one out. Townsend has already seen me with her in Bryant Park and could easily make me.

And I also know that I'm no match against Steve's skills and years of agent training. Besides, Lex and Steve have operated on missions together before, so that synergy will be beneficial to our mission's overall success. Our primary goal is to protect Lex at all costs, even if that means that she's on a fake date with another man.

When the time comes for Lex and Steve to leave for the city, Dave goes down to the building's lobby and brings Steve up to the apartment as Lex is descending the stairs, ready for the mission. As I look up to her, my breath stops and my heart skips a beat. She's in a tight but classic little black dress that she paired with blood red heels. Her dark hair is down, straightened, with dramatic smoky makeup and bold eyeliner accenting her beautiful eyes. She paired her look with painted ruby red lips, the kohl, powder and wax highlighting not only her beauty, but her fierceness too. She looks stunningly gorgeous. She notices me staring and smiles a little smile that I like to think is just for me. Luke lets out a long and low wolf whistle while Will assesses her outfit and nods approvingly.

"Damn, Lex," Kev says with a brotherly grin, pride seeping through in his voice.

"Seriously," Dave mutters under his breath as he comes back into the apartment with Steve in tow, his tone giving way to him not fully approving her attire, or the mission.

"Aly, it's been too long. Nice place," Steve jests as he greets her with a bear hug that encompasses the smaller West's frame.

Once she returns his hug, Lex leans back from Steve's embrace to assess his gray slacks and black button up shirt with a clinical, agent eye. Steve casually has his sleeves rolled up, perfect for blending in and assuming the watering hole personas they'll be embodying. The two of them look beautiful together, like two models who just stepped off the page of a magazine, looking dark and mysterious while being incredibly strong, resilient and in-tune with each other. In a flash, I'm green with envy. They look perfect together, a match made in heaven. Invigorated and gorgeous, two beautiful people coming together to form the ultimate power couple.

"I'm the luckiest guy in the world with a date like you on my arm," Steve continues to joke, unaware of how his playful behavior is grating on my nerves.

Kev chuckles as Will shakes his head with mock derision. I'm surprised with how jealous I have become of Steve for being able to take her out like this while I stay behind. I'm aware that this isn't a real date, but I can't seem to stop the claws of bitterness from gripping my heart.

I try to play down my emotions but I'm sure Lex can see them written all over my face. She comes over to me and kisses me on the cheek while a get a waft of her expensive and luxurious perfume.

"I heard you put this all together, Cole," Lex begins.

I nod, not trusting my voice to verbally respond. I don't want her to hear the undertones of jealousy and envy in my voice.

"Dave told me all about it; seems like a really solid plan, good job. I trust you," she concludes.

"Don't jinx us yet, save all that for the end of the mission, Sissy," Luke says with a half serious, half-joking tone.

Lex rolls her eyes at her older brother and looks back into my eyes. "Don't worry," she whispers, "everything will work out and I'll be okay."

I nod and she smiles her smile just for me as she winks before she turns away. Lex hugs her brothers and takes Steve's arm as they exit the apartment. As the mission begins, I have a sour feeling that I created the opportunity for Lex to permanently walk away from me.

***

Steve and Lex arrive at Cedar Local around seven, right on time. Steve has a button cam on while Lex has a GPS locator sewn in the hem of her dress. We are all disbursed in separate vehicles surrounding the area, acting as surveillance and providing additional backup if needed. I'm paired up with Will, parked a block away. Sean is with Kev around the corner while Dave and Luke are in the last SUV parked by the bar's entrance.

Going by the feed from Steve's button cam, Cedar Local looks busy and the noise level is pretty intense considering it's a Saturday night and Cedar Local is located in the Financial District of the city. Usually bars, restaurants and clubs on the weekend in this area aren't as busy, since most employees have gone home for the weekend. But Cedar Local is almost filled to capacity, creating cover for Lex and Steve, but acting as a challenge for the rest of us running surveillance and serving as tactical back-up.

Will patched into the security cams installed within the establishment, providing us with additional angles of perspective that we previously didn't have access to. I refrain from asking how Will got the access, knowing that the oldest West is both squeaky clean and a highly accomplished hacker. With the added cameras, we are able to see everything from a bird's eye view, tapping into the feeds to keep eyes on the bar, the sitting area, the main entrance and the makeshift dance floor. Will immediately starts running facial recognition software on all the patrons in the building as the rest of us wait for a hit, or for Lex and Steve to encounter an obstacle.

Speaking into the set of walkie-talkies, Will commands, "The power couple is in the building. Everyone be alert. Hold on my count."

The power couple, I think to myself, *what a code name.* They certainly look the part, and I briefly wonder if Will read my mind when he assigned that code name to Lex and Steve. Would Lex's brothers ever call us a power couple too, if I were to officially begin to formally court her? What if we made our small but growing relationship public to her family? What would they think, would they even approve?

Shaking my head, I let those thoughts fall away. I need to focus on the mission, now isn't the time for these types of thoughts. Lex went to bat for me, vouched for me. I can't let her down with unnecessary distractions. A lot is on the line for me at West Enterprises, and for Lex's confidence in me. So I force myself to look back to the camera screens, tracking their movements, as I focus in on Lex. Lex and Steve are headed toward the bar to order a round of drinks, getting our night, and mission, underway.

Stephen Wallace

Aly is looking smoking hot tonight, but I need to remember that this is strictly business. Besides, there seems to be something going on between her and the Harris guy. I'm not sure how I feel about that, but she seems happy. She's smiling and seems more relaxed than I've ever seen her in a long time, so I'll just have to continue to view her as just a little sister and nothing more. We had our chance a long time ago and we had an amazing time. But it doesn't do well to stay devoted to a ghost or to be in love with a memory. Playing the "what if" game is always dangerous terrain to navigate, especially when you work with each other. And besides, that was the end of what could've been and unfortunately, that moment passed a long time ago for us.

When we walk into Cedar Local, all the eyes in the building swing to us. The males are taking in Aly while the ladies are checking me out. Everyone looks like they want to eat us, or at least score a piece of us. I know we look good, that's why we're here, why we were the two agents chosen for this assignment. Part of the goal is to draw the attention of everyone in this establishment. In doing that, we'll be able to draw out Townsend if he's here today and make our extraction play. Completely in sync with each other, we go move toward the bar and each grab a drink.

"Bottoms up," Aly playfully says. I don't worry about alcohol tolerance; I know we both have high tolerance levels and we both know to signal to each other if either of us getting close to ours. After we swig our drinks, we move onto the dance floor. We're both dancing and chatting with those around us, making conversation with new friends, drawing more attention to us, acting like a flame that's drawing in all of the proverbial moths. It's tough to dance with her and keep things platonic, it always has been. A small part of me wants to finally show my affection for her, since we're playing a couple. It would go along with our cover story; we're on a date after all. Some may view it as suspect if I didn't fully act the part. But I restrain myself as much as I can, keeping my hands on her waist as I try not to stare at her lips too often.

Aly isn't my girl, she's not mine to take. I've seen how she and Cole exchanged glances before we left and I'm not stupid. I know there's something there between them, and if she's happy, that's all I've ever wanted for her. So tonight, I'll just try to keep my jealousy in check and contained.

After we've been dancing for a while, Aly motions to me that she wants to grab another round of drinks. I could use some water myself. I steer her back to the bar, guiding her away from the dance floor, keeping my hand on the small of her back as I use my body to block any pushes or shoves from unaware dancers.

As we approach the bar for another round, Aly nudges me and mouths three before she gives me her bombshell, megawatt smile. Tearing my gaze away from her mouth, I scan to my right and there Townsend is, conspicuously watching us, or more accurately, intently staring only at Aly, completely out in the open, not trying to hide his gaze. His expression has anger boiling on the surface, but I catch glimpses of other emotions as they flit across his face. Desire and curiosity vacillate in flashes on his face, his eyes tracking Aly's every movement. Townsend is enthralled; Aly has always had that effect, enchanting and entrapping those who draw closer to her.

Upon a further scan, I quickly note a compression wrap encompassing his wrist. I can blatantly see the almost hidden extra padding from the bandages on his chest from the knife wound Aly drove into him at Bryant Park. Deciding to stay inconspicuous and unsuspecting, I keep my eyes roving and settle my eyes on the TV and some basketball game that's being broadcast on the chosen channel. She whispers in my ear, stating she's going to the restroom. I smile and nod, my eyes never leaving the TV.

Before I know it, Aly's walking over to where Townsend is standing, the complete opposite direction of the restroom. Keeping my cool and maintaining an air of casual indifference, I get out my phone and shoot a text to Luke. There's been a change of plans. Just like old times. Classic Aly, calling an audible mid-mission. Some things just never change.

Alexandra West

I walk up to Townsend who since I first spotted him, is now sitting in a booth. I decide on the direct approach, already annoyed at the prospect of wasting any of my time. Pretending to be coy, I register his initial reaction of surprise before he smiles, looking me over appreciatively with a disgustingly predatory glint in his eyes. Ugh, men. I take the seat across from him, cross my legs and stare him down. He noticeably grows uncomfortable with my direct approach and silence after only a couple of seconds. Eventually Townsend shows his weakness by breaking the silent tension first.

"Alexandra," he purrs after he regains his composure.

"Townsend," I flatly respond, already bored and unimpressed with his opening line, just waiting for this drama to end.

"Mark," he says with a hint of conviction, but with a slightly earnest quality in the tone of his voice.

At the raising of my amused eyebrow, he continues, "My first name is Mark. Mark Townsend."

"Congratulations, you know your name," I say sarcastically, "so, what do you want Townsend?"

"You. And only you, Alexandra. It's always been just you," Townsend smoothly replies as he starts to try to infuse charm and charisma into our interaction.

"Wow. You said the word 'you' a lot in one sentence. So, why me?" I simply ask, trying hard not to recoil at his response.

"I need your protection. I need you to kill someone who is after me. I want to take the offensive stance," he responds.

"And if I don't?" I query, curious at what his boundaries are.

"I will put a contract on that guy over there pretending to be your boyfriend," Townsend says.

I immediately look over at Steve. He goes to make a move toward us, but I subtly shake my head. He pauses, confused, but takes a step back, instinctually trusting my non-verbal communication.

Behind him, there's a guy I recognize from various mug shots that I've seen over the years. I briefly remember him as being an associate from previous contracts that I had eliminated as Alex West. This thug has his eyes zeroed in on Steve's back. Damn, Townsend is serious enough to have planned a little in advance. He already contacted an assassin, albeit an unsuccessful one, and has this guy queued up in Cedar Local. That's pretty brazen, even for someone like me back when I was in the game. I know Steve can handle himself, but I don't want to take any risks with any of the civilians who are also in this bar. These people are relatively innocent. I have never believed that anyone was ever fully innocent. But nevertheless, these people don't deserve to get hurt because of any personal grudges someone has against me.

I refocus my attention back toward Townsend and calmly ask, "What's your extraction plan?"

"Leave with me, exit by the bathroom," Townsend easily answers without a second of hesitation, almost as if he knows that he's got me.

"Just you?" I ask, wanting to make sure the plan is clear.

At Townsend's nod, I look up at the cameras and incline my head. Townsend follows my gaze, paling when he realizes that there is a live video feed from the bar where anyone could hack in and access with the right skills. Skills my eldest brother just happens to possess.

Analyzing my options, I quickly decide on the best move for Steve, my family and Cole. I swiftly stand up and move toward the restroom. Just like I expected him to, Townsend is following right behind me, just like a lost

269

little puppy. I hear Steve calling after me, trying to get to me through the crowd but I keep moving, grabbing Townsend's hand as I hastily pull him along, forcing him to quicken up his pace.

Townsend motions me toward a motorcycle parked, hidden in the shadows. He hands me the extra helmet as I again note that he came prepared as I watch him quickly put his own helmet on. I hop on the cycle, sitting behind him, holding on. I'm not taking any chances with innocent lives. I already have enough blood on my hands. I don't need to up my body count.

Stephen Wallace

"What the hell happened?" Dave bellows at me the second that I quickly exit Cedar Local and get to Aly's twin's SUV, only to have to face off with the other four angry West brothers who have also gathered and are also highly skilled agents.

"How could you let her go?" Will roars in my face.

Luke is standing by my side in a subtle show of solidarity, but I can tell that he's pissed off at me too. I know that he's my only other ally in this family, other than Aly. But when it comes to his sister, I don't even rank on that scale of importance. Aly is his only priority right now.

"Steve, what happened?" Kev asks, in tones softer than Dave and Will, trying to get a rational explanation amidst all the emotion.

"I don't know. One moment she was going to the restroom and the next minute she's confronting Townsend head on without any backup. They chatted for a couple minutes and then she looked over at me. But when we locked eyes, she shook her head and signaled for me to stand down. Then she walked out the back door with him. I tried to follow her, but she used the crowd to her advantage. She evasively changed the play on me," I exasperatedly explain.

"She would have only done that if she thought that any of us were in danger," Sean wisely interjects.

"Sean's right. Townsend had to know that we were here. At the minimum, he did his homework on us or at the very least, Alexandra West," Luke agrees as he nods his head.

"But how the hell does he know anything about her? About us? We just confronted him at the park earlier today!" Will hotly asks.

When no one answers, Will continues in a more principled voice, "None of us from the park were in Cedar Local. He never actually saw us."

We all take a moment to try to sort out the details before I remember a small moment that passed, a detail that I had brushed away in the wake of Aly's quick departure.

"When Aly went over to him, she was careful to not look directly at me. She was in my line of sight the whole time, yes. She made sure that I could see her at all times. But she didn't make eye contact, she didn't acknowledge me. But there was one moment. She looked at me before her gaze quickly darted over my shoulder. After that, she was gone, that's when she made her exit. There must have been a threat, someone behind me. I didn't even look around me because I was so focused on her," I say apologetically, the defeat becoming a burden as I feel a pit in my stomach opening up, guilt assuaging my senses, telling me that this is all my fault.

Cole sighs, "It's not your fault, Steve. We should've been in there with you. This was my call, my plan. And maybe that glance was of no significance."

Will suddenly pulls out a laptop from his pack and starts frantically typing. "But maybe it was. Our sister doesn't waste time or effort on something that doesn't matter. I'm checking security footage to see if there was something we initially missed during our first pass. And as a point of good news, she still has her GPS tracker in her dress. We need to proceed carefully, but at least we still have her location," Will excitedly states, typing as he talks.

"Start tracking her, Will. We need to get her back. Now. Then we can figure out what the hell happened once she safely returns," Cole takes command with his adamant response.

Alexandra West

Townsend takes me to Queens. I can't think of the last time I willingly went to Queens. At least we're at Five Points, but still. Townsend leads me up to the third floor, passing a bunch of artists camping out and lounging along the walls as we ascend the way up. Five Points isn't inhabited legally, but a lot of squatters take residence in the old building, especially those who are artists, taking refuge amidst the concrete and steel. They've turned a disused, old building into a piece of art, colors bursting on the walls so there are no blank spaces.

Eyes casually flick to our position, expressions disinterested and immediately redirected back to their own business. They probably think we're a couple, considering Townsend is holding my hand, pulling me along. Gross. I know that we wouldn't be recognized, not with our helmets on. But at the fleeting thought of any romance, my thoughts immediately redirect back to Cole. Then I think of my brothers and Steve. I wonder how they are all holding up, considering my disappearing act. My brothers are used to working as a team whereas I'm used to operating alone, our different working styles clashing but benefiting us given my current predicament. Will is probably pissed, upset and maybe just a bit worried, but to be fair I'm worried about them too. Townsend showed his hand, that he was prepared to hire multiple assassins or teams to get what he wants. I need to nip this in the proverbial bud. I need to stop Townsend before he can hurt my family and friends.

Suddenly, Townsend halts our steps and stops our progress near a corner when he motions that we will take a step into the shadows of the night, allowing for some privacy. He pulls off his helmet, signaling me to

273

let me finally pull off mine. Taking a subtle deep breath of fresh, albeit Queens oxygen, I run my fingers through my hair and drop the helmet to the ground.

Taking a casual position by leaning against the derelict wall, I level my gaze at my opponent, patience already thinning and fraying at the edges. "What do you want, Townsend?" I ask with a slight edge in my voice.

"First, I want you to call me Mark," he asks of me with a condescending tone. To add to the uncomfortable feeling, he takes a step closer to me, invading my personal space.

"Not going to happen. What else?" I bluntly continue.

I proceed with caution, unsure of Townsend's end game but I know that I'm getting too close to my own patience breaking and ultimately striking out against him. This situation feels like he's either trying to make romantic overtures at me, or that he's purposefully trying to antagonize me. But he can't be that easy, that predictable, right? So what's his angle? What are we doing here?

"I want to finally see the face of the person who killed my brother," Townsend's tone suddenly changes, becoming more menacing and letting me hear the anger rippling underneath his calm and playboy façade.

Ah, so there it is, his real motive. Townsend's game is finally revealed: revenge. How predictable. But we're not on my turf, I'm almost quite literally boxed into a corner where I don't have a way to quickly communicate with my family. And I'm trying to turn over a new leaf while also happening to be completely isolated in a borough that I'm not very familiar with. The hair on the back of my neck instantly goes up and I lean a fraction of an inch back on my heels, instinctively trying to put some distance between us and coiling my muscles for my impending attack.

"What was his name again?" I ask, buying more time and instantly detaching my emotions from the situation, switching back into old habits where I purposefully bait my mark's anger.

"You don't know his name?" Townsend incredulously asks, careful to not let his voice thunder within the building's walls, which would only draw attention to us as he steps closer to me, eliminating the final inches of space between us.

"No," I say flatly, "I've killed a lot of people in my lifetime. What was his name?"

"Dale Townsend," the surviving Townsend brother replies, hatred acidly dripping from his voice.

"Oh yeah, now I remember. From Spring Valley, New York, right?" I say nonchalantly with a blank expression on my face.

I can tell that my aloof attitude is antagonizing him even more to the point where I'm becoming amused. I need him to be angry. Because it's when in anger that he'll make a mistake and give me a chance to do what I swore I would stop doing since I came home from the hospital: killing targets. But right now, it's him or me. We both know it. He's out for blood. Wow, will this be the first self-defense kill that I've ever had? I guess that there's a first for everything, who knew? Who would've thought I'd ever need to kill anyone in self-defense, let alone in Queens!

I can see the toll that my actions are taking on Townsend's emotions and mental stability. He takes a moment to ground himself as I watch him take a deep breath through his nose, his nostrils flaring. As much as he's trying to get his wits about him, I can tell the exact moment when his humanity finally snaps.

"What is wrong with you, you cold-hearted bitch? How can you say that so casually, like it's what you just had for dinner? Dale's death has been haunting my dreams, the grief permanently grafting its tendrils to my conscious. Dale's death has also ruined my family. Devastated our friends. And you're standing there, unaffected? My mother committed suicide because of Dale's death! My father bankrupted his company, just so he could continue searching for you, to avenge my brother's murder and my mother's suicide," Townsend finally yells out, not caring about the somewhat curious glances searching for us in the obscure shadows of Five Points, his voice echoing and fading as it moves through the concrete hallways.

"I don't really have affect, but it's something that I'm aware of, and that I need to work on," I reply, brushing off his anger and accusations before I drive the proverbial knife in deeper.

"Your brother died because he was selling some major government secrets, definitely a big no-no, resulting in some lucrative and heady payouts. It wasn't personal for me, if it's any consolation. Nothing about my job is ever truly personal. I don't remember who ordered the hit off the top of my head, but I'm sure you could figure it out if you really wanted to. You seem smart enough," I condescendingly explain with a shrug of my shoulders.

While I am talking, I let Townsend back me against a wall, his aggression unknowingly propelling him forward. Instead of being on the defensive, I know that I will be planning to use the unyielding wall as my impromptu weapon, since I left all my guns and knives back at my apartment. You have to be resourceful in my line of business.

I can tell Townsend is slowly absorbing this information. He probably hasn't heard my side of the story, and I don't think he wanted to know that information either. People generally don't want to see the ugliness that lies in the ones they love.

"Wait, it's coming back to me." I pause while I act like I'm remembering, "I remember, yeah. The hit came from within our country's borders. Someone in one of the alphabet soup agencies, CIA I think. I believe the wording of the hit was along the lines of your brother being called a terrorist and that he committed treason. But he was unfortunately beyond the grasp of law enforcement's claw of justice. They caught your brother, caught him in his lies. But instead of going through the arduous legal system, which costs a lot of time and money, they put out a quick contract, much cheaper and efficient. I remember, I had just finished a job and took your brother's contract just for fun."

At that last sentence, with my intentional goading and provocation, I see Townsend internally snap before he makes his opening physical move toward me. I had prepared for his swing, using his momentum to my advantage, I push Townsend face first into the concrete wall. I kick the base of his spine in as I hear bones crunch under my heels. He blindly swings a fist around and catches me under my right eye. I have to admit, I'm a bit surprised with his skill level. A little bit of West Enterprises training and he could've taken a considerably different path in life. I hear the knife cut through the air before I feel it slash my arms and deeply slice into the soft flesh of my left cheek, a trail of blood flowing down to my chin.

Relying on my past persona's training, I plant my left foot before striking out with my right foot, aiming for his head as I lean my upper body downward, slanting my body at a diagonal angle. I make my intended connection, my foot landing squarely in his right eye socket with the tip of my heel digging into the front of his skull after piercing his eye. Before he can scream in response, I swiftly lash out and punch his throat, silencing him as my blow crushes his windpipe. One of his hands goes to his eye, the other travels to his throat. I use my momentum and honed strength to shove my palm into his nose in a severe, upward angle. He dies instantly as the bones in his nose crush and splinter into his brain, a classic case of momentum and the laws of physics. I am left standing, blood slowly coursing down my face and from my arm due to the open knife wounds, my dress dusted with concrete flakes.

Knowing that I can't just leave an easily identifiable body here, nor can I walk out of this building with blood physically running down my face and arm, I strip Townsend's jacket off his body and clean him of his identification, cell phone, keys, a lighter and other personal effects that could be traced back to him. I take his knife and pat him down for any other weapons, which thankfully I don't find. I don't have the luxury of being able to hide them on my person in this dress. I slip into his jacket, shrugging it on to hide my bloody arm and change the size my appearance. I grab the helmet I wore into the building and roughly shove it on my head and walk out with Townsends helmet in my hands. I descend the stairs, forcing myself to slow my pace, to blend in with the other patrons of Five Points. I need to be unnoticeable, untraceable. Just another shadow in the dark, a gray man that will be instantly forgotten about. Don't draw attention to yourself and you're immediately a faceless body in a crowd.

Once I get outside, I toss Townsend's helmet into a nearby barrel before lighting it on fire with the victim's own lighter. I add the other personal effects minus the wallet to the blaze, destroying all traces of Townsend's evidence that he brought with him. I watch the flames dance and I slowly back away from the alight barrel as others nearby are attracted to the flames, the flickering mesmerizing and hypnotic. I stand closer to the shadows, slowly moving in the direction of Townsend's bike. I know that no human noticed me inside the building and no human outside took notice of me walking away.

All of the sudden, I feel a gaze lock directly on my location, the hairs on the back of my neck raising automatically in response. I slowly turn around to see a small black cat watching me from the shadows, her yellow and jade green eyes seeming to iridescently glow and dance in the opaque night. This little cat, maybe eight or nine pounds, watches me with a fixed, knowing gaze. Her body is relaxed as she is sprawled out on the ground, her tail slightly flicking with her thoughts. I instinctually feel that she knows exactly what I did upstairs and what I just extinguished into ashes.

The little minx stands up and stretches, arching her spine before she causally walks over to me, taking her time with the supreme air of indifference that only a feline manages to encapsulate. I hear a little trill vibrate from her throat as she holds my gaze, her black tail subtly flicking while voluntarily curling over the top of her back. The black cat blinks one more time with glowing green-yellow eyes of wisdom before she casually turns and saunters away.

For the briefest of seconds, she pauses and stops before she looks at me over her shoulder for one last time. Then the moment passes and I'm dismissed. Using her coloring to her advantage, she slowly fades into the long shadows that stretch across the ground at odd angles. She knows how to use the shadows and dark angles to her advantage, just like me. In my gut, I get the distinct impression that she's saying see you later. I shake out the guilt and unease from my feline interaction. I determinedly stride back over to the motorcycle, revving the engine to head home. I leave Queens, and the little black cat with the curled tail behind.

Feeling the cycle roaring with life underneath me, I let my thoughts of Five Points fall from my shoulders. Before I shoved off, I had texted an old friend of mine who owes me a favor, telling him where the body is and asking him to dispose of it permanently. He knows not to ask questions and to make sure nothing at Five Points can be linked back to me or my family. He'll quickly get on the scene and erase any biological evidence that I missed, as well as he'll make sure to take care of any surveillance evidence that could have captured me in passing.

Thankfully, the residents at Five Points are good at keeping their mouths shut, so I'm not worried about eyewitnesses, let alone any of them coming forward to the police. Besides, I was in a helmet whenever I was in the dim, quivering light. And my interaction with the deceased Townsend doesn't even tip the scales of interest for those inhabitants. Some gnarly activity is known to happen in that building, so a screaming match by a presumed couple wouldn't even spike those people's interest. To err on the side of caution though, I mentally make a note to have Will double check the security footage feeds as an additional precaution when I return home. I wouldn't want this getting back and tarnishing West Enterprises Inc.'s reputation. And I'm not quite sure how to compartmentalize me killing a former target when I was supposed to leave Alex West behind and be Alexandra. I turn my attention back to the road, enjoying the motor roar beneath me, relishing in riding a motorcycle again and silencing out my other thoughts. It's been a while since I've felt one with the road, so I immerse myself in that feeling and push all the others aside.

Knowing my twin, Dave would have brought the entire family back to my apartment to wait for my return. That's our private, twin protocol whenever our plans go awry. If we're ever separated, personally or professionally, we meet back at my apartment. Even though Dave usually uses the doorbell when he comes to visit me, I did give him his own key and he has his own personal set of security codes for the various access panels that make up the security system of my private sanctum. Dave would have had to enter in the building, get in the elevator and insert his key before entering his set of codes. But I know in my gut that that would've been exactly what he did. And George, my doorman, also knows Dave personally, and knows that my brother is allowed access to my apartment at all hours of the day and night. So I head back towards the Upper East Side.

I can imagine all of my brothers, Cole and Steve setting up a mini-command center, tracking my movements from my GPS tracker like I knew they would once they got settled into my place. I'm willing to bet base camp is set up in the conference room that I rarely use. Once I get to my underground garage, I steer the motorcycle into one of my designated spots and calmly enter my apartment building through the garage, knowing that at this time of night, I won't see any of the doormen or staff. I just enter my code to get into the building and then swipe my keycard to gain access to my apartment, helmet in hand. Then, I enter my floor number to access the top levels once I step inside the elevator and am whisked skyward.

When I feel the elevator starting to rise, I take off Townsend's jacket and lean my hip along the elevator's railing. The adrenaline rush is starting to wear off and suddenly, I feel the exhaustion of the night starting to sink in all the way down and settle into my bones. I regressed into my Alex West persona, something that I promised myself I wouldn't do. I can physically feel the disappointment with myself, my pride and ego hurt. What is the most disconcerting was how easy of a seamless transition it was for me to go back to Alex West, how natural it felt and even more so, how much I enjoyed it. All of my years of training were to be Alex West, all of my talents and strengths honed were to strengthen and enhance my alter ego. I didn't have any time over the years to learn how to be Alexandra West.

No wonder I feel like I'm failing miserably. I take a steadying breath and focus on what needs to be addressed right now. My face is starting to hurt, and I need to clean and bandage my arm. I can only imagine what I look like: bloody arm and face, a dark bruise forming under my eye, hair a mess and my high heels with blood on them in hand while carrying a motorcycle jacket and helmet that aren't mine. I need to make sure all digital traces of me in Queens tonight are wiped. I need to confirm with my contact that all physical evidence of me is gone. I need to figure out what I'm going to do with Townsend's motorcycle and what traffic cam footage I need to review to secure my anonymity. I have plenty of time to throw myself a pity party and commiserate with my failures later. Right now, I need to take care of my injuries, finish the job and see my family and Cole.

William West

Dave was insistent after we got in our SUVs outside of Cedar Local that we immediately come back to Lex's apartment. I had always known her address, that she spent a lot of her time above the clouds. So much of the work that she does requires her to see the dirt and darkness of humanity, it only made sense that my slightly starry-eyed sister would want to distance herself from the ground and dredges of humanity. As I stepped back into her refuge, I again notice the lack of personal touches, an unfortunate side effect of the business that we're all in. My gaze is immediately pulled to the windows overlooking the city. I completely understand why she comes here to seek solace and to recharge her batteries.

I turn my attention back to Cole, the mission leader of the day. I notice the sag in his shoulders, a classic posture of defeat. I feel for him, being the head of a mission is a huge responsibility, let alone when Cole doesn't have the experience to help influence his decision-making. Thankfully, my brothers aren't giving Cole a hard time yet, but tensions are rising and it's only a matter of time before all my brothers' patience boils over.

Before I can offer to take the lead, Dave announces, "Let's set up a command center in the conference room. We'll use the resources Lex has in there to support our home base."

Well, you can't argue with that logic. Turning on my heel, I follow the rest of the group down the hallway.

The tactical, albeit temporary, command center is buzzing with activity and nerves in Lex's conference room. I smother a smile as I think about how she modeled her own formal meeting room using the same configuration and technology as the conference room that I created back at West Enterprises. It's in that moment where I realize the strength of the bond Lex and I have always had, even when we were at our worst. My little sister still respected me enough to take the expertise in what I created at home and to duplicate it into her own home. My heart is fuller with that knowledge which only fuels my desire and need to find her.

Alexandra West

The elevator finally lets out a soft whoosh as the doors open to my apartment's lobby. I enter in the codes on the access panel and wait for the green light to illuminate so I know that I can turn the door handle. I carefully drop the helmet, jacket and my heels by the door as I quietly pad down to the conference room, drawn down the hallway by the noisy commotion coming from that area of my apartment. The volume racks up in intensity with every forward step I take. I open the conference room door and immediately immerse myself into the chaos and a noise level that's so intense, I only react in a measure of self-preservation. I immediately cover my ears, my aching head already beginning to throb with new vigor as the cacophony of acoustics bounces around in my head.

If my brain wasn't ringing and reverberating, I would have laughed at the sight that befalls me. All five of my brothers are running around the confined space with Steve hovering over Will's shoulder and Cole working with Dave on some project. Their attention is so focused, they don't notice the door opening and closing. They're all talking over each other, the din resounding.

"Hey," I try to yell over the pandemonium, but again, my energy is waning. Gathering what little strength I have left, I yell again, trying to raise my voice over the commotion.

Suddenly, it's silent, like deathly silent. The strict dichotomy from the previous ruckus is dizzying at best. All seven guys stare at me as if they're seeing a ghost, finally noticing me standing in the doorway. When no one speaks, I resign myself and sigh before I automatically slip into agent mode and provide my situation report,

"The threat is neutralized. Body is located at Five Points in Queens. Clean up is being taken care of as we speak. His motorcycle is downstairs, parked next to my car. Will, I'll need you to double check to make sure that all cameras are wiped from Cedar Local, Five Points and here. And someone needs to get rid of that goddamn bike," I conclude.

I wait for a reaction, for someone to say something. While I was speaking, no one was moving. "Okay, I'm going to grab a glass of water and clean myself up," I cautiously inform everyone.

I turn around and leave the conference room as I head to the kitchen. I open the cabinet where the glasses are stored and grab one, filling it with filtered water from the fridge. I quickly grab a dish-towel and fill it with ice to try to stay the swelling of my eye. As I'm about to head toward the open sitting area, that's when I hear the thunderous sound of feet coming my way. I continue on and gingerly make my way to the set of sofas, careful not to get blood on any of the fabrics. It takes all of my patience to remain composed as my brothers, Steve and Cole descend upon me.

Cole Harris

I rush over to Lex, overwhelmed with relief and concern. She looks like crap, but she's alive and still standing, well, at this moment, she's sitting, but she's here. I hug her, holding her close, realizing just how deep my feelings are running for her and her safety. Slightly shocked at my feelings' intensity, I pull back but I don't let her go.

Lex seems to understand, her eyes patient as she says while smiling, "Cole, I told you. Everything would be fine. I'm okay, I promise. It looks worse than it actually is. But it's all just superficial. It'll heal soon."

She puts her hand on my cheek and smiles an exhausted smile, reassuring me in her own silent way. Lex then turns to her brothers, each of them expertly assessing the damage with a clinical eye while they each lean down to hug her. Finally, her gaze lands on her friend as she leans forward and hugs Steve.

"Aly," Steve utters, crushing Lex into his chest, "I am so sorry."

Shaking her head, Lex confidently interrupts her friend, "It's fine. I knew what I was doing. I should have let you in on my play though. For that, I'm sorry too." She leans back into the couch and looks at us all with a tired half-smile that doesn't quite meet her eyes.

"If it's all right with you all, I need a beer, I need to shower and then I need to go to bed. In that exact order. Then I will tell you all about what happened tonight, but it can wait until tomorrow morning. Everything is in place to clean up the situation. We'll get finalized reports first thing in the morning," Lex summarizes.

We all nod and watch her as she walks toward the kitchen, with Dave following her. When she pulls the fridge open, I'm shocked to see how the bright white light of the appliance fully illuminates her face. The softer lights of the room were kinder to her wounds, where in the harsher light, the forming bruise and gash stand out against her pale skin. She swiftly grabs a bottle of beer and opens it, handing another to Dave. She walks over to the windows alone, drinking her beer and looks over the city below her.

I tentatively walk over to her and begin, "Lex, I'm so sorry, I—"

"Don't," she softly but smoothly interrupts my haphazard apology, "I'm fine, really. Truly, I mean it. I'm going to bed. We'll chat about all of this tomorrow, okay?"

I nod, seeing just how drained she really is and hearing the pleading undertones in her voice. She smiles and kisses my cheek, leaving me by the cityscape windows to ponder my own thoughts. She drops her quickly emptied bottle into the recycling bin and kisses each of her brothers' cheeks before giving a final hug to Steve. Lex slowly takes the stairs and walks toward the hallway and out of sight into the master bedroom. We all hear the closing of her suite door echo in the deafening silence of her penthouse.

The rest of us decide to turn in early as well. It was a busy and hectic day and now that her brothers know that their sister's safe, they can all relax and enter a sedated state. They all have a round of beers together, sitting on her couches having hushed conversations. Together, we decide that Sean will bunk in Dave's room with Luke and Kev crashing in Lex's guest bedroom. Will opts to go back to the conference room to begin scouring surveillance videos. I'm sure the older West is anxious to protect his little sister. Steve and I decide we'll grab blankets and get some shut-eye on the couches.

As I lie in my makeshift bed, I can't sleep. My first, planned mission that I was responsible for leading and executing failed. Lex was injured. My subconscious berates me with decisive vitriol. *Oh Cole, it's because this isn't your world. You don't belong in a world of assassins, spies and secrets. You weren't trained for murders, missions and contracts. You only know how to fix computers and write basic code.* It takes a moment for me to get my wits about me before I can silently admonish the devil sitting on my shoulder.

Lex has faith in me. And she came back in one piece. Lex trusted me, a well-known and renowned assassin who has been in this business for her entire life trusts me. Her brothers didn't stop me as I took the lead, and this is what they do as their day jobs, this is their family's legacy. Sure, I made my mistakes, including that I should have known more about Townsend. And in the future, I will need to be able to anticipate Lex and Steve's moves, especially when she tends to improvise in unknown situations. But I will learn from these errors and ensure that it never happens again. I look to the future, knowing that I will inevitably make more blunders but with each fault, I will learn, adjust and succeed. With those thoughts slowly quieting the turmoil in my head, I'm able to finally close my eyes and rest.

***

When the sun wakes up, I get up too, considering the fact that I've been up for an hour already. I figure that I won't waste additional time, as I wasn't going to get any more sleep anytime soon. I put a pot of coffee on and stand by the windows doing my best not to disturb Steve's sleeping form on the couch opposite of my temporary bed. I find peace in watching Manhattan as it wakes up and becomes illuminated with the rising sun's rays.

"Couldn't sleep?" I whirl my head around at Steve's voice. I didn't even hear him approach. Man, I have a lot to learn about this covert world.

"Yeah," I say, self-consciously normalizing my breathing, "I guess not. To say it was a rough night would be a massive understatement."

Steve knowingly nods and looks out the window as he takes a stand next to me. After a few minutes of silence, Steve begins, "When I first met you, I thought you were weak, a liability. But Aly saw something in you, even from the beginning. She still does. And last night, you proved that you had her best interests in mind. I respect that. The West family is a tight knit group, dedicated to their line of work and even more loyal to each other.

They're all tough to crack, even harder when they're united as one family. For all of the years I've known them, personally and professionally, they're an incredibly private bunch. They don't let strangers into their midst, they keep things close to their bulletproof vests. But they've quickly welcomed you into their inner circle. I hope you understand that gesture means more than you could ever know."

I silently nod my head and watch as my reflection moves its head in sync with mine. I don't know how to respond, so I continue to gaze out of the window. I'm still silently doubting myself and my self-identified lacking agent abilities.

"Cole," Steve says. At his pause, I instinctually know that he's waiting for me to turn and look at him, so he can fill the silence with the rest of his thoughts.

Steve smiles with wisdom and surprising understanding, "You're doing well. Better than an average civilian would be faring in this type of situation with the limited training that you've had. You have a great teacher, but you're also a quick learner. This mission was a success. You have some learning points to study, yes. But overall, you did well and handled every twist and turn with agility and responsiveness. Don't doubt yourself. She didn't."

I nod and smile, knowing that I have his respect and maybe even a blessing for a relationship with Lex, although I think the latter is pushing it. "Thanks Steve, that means a lot," I honestly reply, feeling more confident than I had just a few moments ago.

That is, until I hear a crash coming from upstairs. Steve's body language immediately goes to protective mode as he bolts up the stairs in a matter of seconds. I quickly hurry after him, not yet possessing Steve's grace and agility, but knowing that one day I could.

When I crest the stairs, I see that all five West brothers and Steve are all crowded in front of Lex's closed master suite door. Dave is frantically pounding on the reinforced steel door while the rest of the brothers are calling out to her. I can't hear if Lex has answered over the noise, but I'm sensing the brothers' increasing panic, so I'm guessing that she hasn't responded to them yet.

When Steve catches sight of me, he pulls back and stands behind Lex's siblings, a worried look still marring his face. I walk up in the midst of five distraught brothers while inconspicuously pulling out a key. I move forward to unlock the door. I absentmindedly recall when Lex had given a spare key to me when we first arrived at the apartment from Bryant Park, my very first time here.

At the time, she had said, "This key unlocks my bedroom door, just in case something was to ever happen and you need to get inside. Hold onto it, okay? Don't let anyone else know that you have it, even Dave. Keep it on your person at all times, make sure it's hidden too."

I briefly wondered if she thought something would happen to her, feeling the need to give me this key to cover all of her bases. I know that she's a strategic thinker, but I doubt she ever imagined the fallout from last night's mission would be the situation where I'd be using her key.

As the door slightly pops open, Dave looks at me as if I have three heads.

"What?" I ask, trying to tamper the defensiveness in my tone, "I'm helping. She gave the key to me."

Temporarily accepting my answer, Dave nods and steps aside to let me take center lead on going through the doorway. I grasp the handle, take a deep breath and push open the door fully.

The first thing I see is glass. There's shattered glass all over and around the carpeted floor, halting all of our progress for a moment, as we need to readjust our footing to navigate further into the room. My gaze quickly sweeps over the room as I look to the windows, to see if the glass was the source from an external intruder who breached the windows. No windows are broken, nothing looks out of place. The glass fragments almost look like they once were a vase, there's a slight coloring mixed within the glass shards and I think that on some pieces, I see the etchings of a faint floral design.

But where is Lex? Will heads straight for the bathroom with Dave and Luke, while Kev, Sean and Steve move toward her walk-in closet, verifying that there are no threats lurking in the shadows. I follow after Will's lead, stepping over and around the glass shards, my gut telling me that something isn't right, but I don't know what the problem is yet.

Will swiftly opens the bathroom door with so much force, I briefly wonder if the door came off its hinges. It's then that I see the sight that breaks my heart and takes all of our collective breaths away. Lex is huddled in her walk-in shower, tucked away far in the back corner, sitting on the tile flooring. She's wearing a tee shirt and pajama shorts as she hugs her legs to her chest, forming her body into a small ball huddled against the shower wall. The water is still pouring all over her, but she doesn't seem to notice the rivers snaking down her skin. She is shaking and looks as if she's been crying for a while, her eyes are that red. Lex is crying?

At this point, Steve, Sean and Kev had made their way into the bathroom behind us. All of us are staring at the sight before us for a moment in stunned silence. This is the first time I have ever seen any vulnerability from Alexandra West or from any of her professional personas. Normally her confidence, intelligence and self-assured traits are on full display like a heavy set of armor. But now, her protective shields are down. I look around at her brothers who seem shocked as well. It isn't until a soft unguarded sob escapes her lips that everyone starts moving forward into action to figure out what's going on and what they can do to fix the situation.

Without a moment's hesitation, Dave immediately strips off his sweatshirt and slips his shoes off, hastily placing all of his electronics on top of his personal items pile and enters the shower in just his jeans and tee shirt. He unceremoniously sits down, right next to Lex, silently pulling her into his arms. Even though he is soaked in a matter of seconds, it's in this moment where I can truly see the unbreakable bond between the twins. He doesn't say a word and neither does she. They don't have to. While he might not know everything that's going on inside of her head, I can tell that he feels her pain. His eyes are filled with the depths of grief as he surrounds her smaller form with his arms, as if he's trying to protect her with his own body from the demons haunting and hunting for his sister. She leans into him, still shaking, keeping her eyes downcast and focused on watching the water swirling and spiraling around the drain. She seems to understand that he is going to be her armor in her moment of weakness. Instead of fighting it, she just readily accepts it.

It's in this moment that I'm jealous of their relationship. Growing up as an only child, I often longed for siblings. Someone to bond with other than my parents. Sure, I had plenty of friends. But what I really wanted and longed for was exactly what I'm witnessing right now: someone who knew me so well on a primal level that words didn't need to be spoken for me to be seen and understood.

During the twin's soundless exchange, the other four West brothers have all emptied their respective pockets, following Dave's lead. Will reaches into the shower stall next and turns the water off. He grabs a towel from the rack before he too enters and drapes the terrycloth around Lex's shoulders. He sits on the other side of her, rubbing her arm closest to him to increase blood flow and generate warmth. He gently moves the hair out of her face and silently rubs her back. Will has never been explicitly affectionate with Lex, or with anyone, from what I gathered and observed since knowing the West family. Their relationship has definitely improved, the dynamics shifting. But what surprises all of us next firmly cements the repairing and healing nature of the relationship between Will and Lex.

In a gesture that amazes us all, Lex moves from Dave's arms and latches on to Will's embrace. As she settles next to Will's form, Lex freely lets the noise of her sobs surround us, the haunting symphony bouncing off the tiled walls, resonating within all of our beings. Without hesitation, Will fully wraps his arm around her thin shoulders while his other hand is grasped tight in Lex's two-handed grip. He is whispering to her in low tones now, words that I can't make out, and maybe I shouldn't. Sandwiched in between Will and Dave, she looks so small, so young and helpless.

Will's words seem to have an eventual calming effect on her as Lex's sobs and shaking start to slow down and soon, cease to exist. Luke, Sean and Kev are hovering nearby the shower door entrance, respecting the scene in front of them while showing their family's love and support.

After some time, Lex finally looks up and meets Will's expectantly patient gaze. Her eyes are pleading as she says in a small voice, "I killed someone last night."

Will nods but he doesn't respond, intuitively knowing that he needs to wait for her to continue.

"I killed someone, Will. But I'm trying to be Alexandra, who isn't like that. She isn't Alex. How can you stand to be around me? I haven't changed, even though I've been trying so hard, and I've been telling you all that I've been working on changing. I feel like I've been lying to you, to all of you. I'm still the killing machine that is Alex West."

As Lex explains, her voice continues to rise various decibels, but what's unmistakable is the shame and pain nipping on her conscious.

"No, no, no Sissy," Luke steps into the shower in order to interrupt her, crouching down and turning her chin up so she meets his eyes. The largest of the West brothers' humility and compassion is on display.

As Luke kneels in front of his sister, the water from the shower floor immediately absorbs into his sweatpants. "Sissy, you were defending yourself, that's different, we all know that," Luke says as he gently takes her hand.

"But I—" Lex goes on to say, hesitation and uncertainty lacing her voice. But if I'm not mistaken, there's also a buried layer of hope.

"You reacted and you took care of yourself. You did what any of us would have done, what Dad taught us to do in a situation like that," Kev says as he takes his step into the oversized shower and sits down on the watery floor so he can look her directly into his younger sister's eyes.

"It's okay, Lex," Sean finishes for all the brothers, also kneeling in front of her, completing the circle of Wests, "I understand what you're saying, I hear you, but know that we aren't mad at you. We saw the footage before Will permanently wiped all traces of it. We saw that your actions were clearly justifiable, classified as acts of self-preservation. Any court of law in this country would attribute that to self-defense. You didn't do anything wrong. We aren't mad at you. If anything, we're proud of you."

Lex vehemently is shaking her head during this exchange, but at Sean's last words, she freezes. She looks over at her twin and timidly asks, "Dave?"

Her voice is so unsteady, so unsure. She looks like a scared little girl, needing consolation and reassurances from her brothers, so very different from her normal façade.

Dave gently nods, kisses her forehead and pulls her closer. Without saying another word, the West brothers have forgiven Lex for the transgression she thought she made, even though there was nothing truly to ever forgive in the first place. Lex finally found the redemption she was looking for, and it was in her family's arms.

As the scene unfolds, I unobtrusively look over to Steve. This is clearly a West family discussion and I feel like we're invading this exclusive moment. I look over to the doorway, he follows my gaze and nods in understanding. This scene should be private for the West family. We both agree and can appreciate that. We silently creep out of the suite, shutting Lex's bedroom door behind us before we both head downstairs. I beeline for the coffee pot while Steve silently grabs two mugs. I look at him and see that Steve's eyes are haunted and distracted.

"I have never seen her cry, Cole. In all my years of knowing her, it hasn't happened… until now," Steve quietly murmurs, still in a state of shock as he prepares his coffee on autopilot.

"And she welcomed her brothers' embraces, that has to be a monumental step forward for the West family," I muse out loud, more to myself than anyone in particular.

Steve nods as we grab our filled coffee mugs and sit on the kitchen bar stools, contemplating the morning's events together in silence. Here I thought that Steve and I would have too many differences to ever have a proper conversation where both parties could come to agreement, let alone an understanding about one other. It seems that my previous assumptions were grossly incorrect and solely based on my own prejudices. With a jolt, I recognize all of this with a humbling and sobering reflective thought.

***

After about an hour later, Luke slowly descends the stairs, grabs a mug and fills it with coffee before he adds a splash of cream. Steve and I are just looking at him, expectantly waiting for him to speak and provide us with an update of what's going on upstairs. He looks exhausted, his pants are still slightly damp and his usual joking nature has been doused and muted.

Finally, Luke turns to us and somberly says, "She's okay. She's asleep. Apparently, she didn't sleep last night. She was up pacing in her bedroom all night, replaying the situation with Townsend in her head over and over again until she couldn't take the stress, guilt or pain anymore."

I see the lines of worry creasing his face, the slump in the older West's shoulders. His normally bright face looks dim and pale, uncharacteristic for Luke.

"Want to help me clean up all the broken glass?" the West brother asks.

Steve and I nod, knowing that Luke needs to feel like he can contribute to something, to do something to make the situation better or easier. Steve and I both have felt that much ever since the moment we saw Lex soaked to the bone on her shower-tiled floor. And from what I know about Luke, he could really use the distraction. Steve seems to understand my exact line of thought as we both get up, grabbing trash bags and gloves so we don't cut up our hands.

Luke, Steve and I slowly ascend the stairs as I remember just over an hour ago running up the same steps, scared for Lex's life. We walk into the bedroom and see Will and Dave on either side of Lex as she soundly sleeps in her bed. Lex's hand is wrapped in Dave's while her head rests on Will's shoulder. Will puts a finger to his lips, signaling to be as quiet as possible.

"She just fell asleep," Dave whispers, providing an explanation.

Steve nods as we start quietly cleaning up the glass with the added assistance of Kev and Sean's help, who quietly join our efforts. Within minutes, we have all of the glass picked up. The carpet is now drying from a light washing and the trash bag has been placed in the hall to be taken downstairs.

We all just stare at Lex, taking in her pale complexion and the dark circles around her eyes. Her bruised eye is a brilliantly deep shade of purple now, but the outer edges are beginning to turn to the sickening shades of greens and yellows. Her arm has been freshly bandaged, the dressings clean and secured. The cut on her face is healing, beginning to scab over, just as the rest of her will follow suit in time.

Will's phone vibrates from the bathroom as Kev goes to retrieve it for him. Kev offers it to him, but Will shakes his head and looks down at Lex, kissing her forehead and pulling the blanket up to cover her shoulders. Dave adjusts her pillow and kisses her forehead before slowly moving to the edge of the bed to stand up.

Will finds me and pointedly looks at my coffee mug. I nod, silently understanding that he needs a cup of caffeine. I make my way back down to the kitchen, grabbing the trash bag and dumping its contents in the bin before I head over to the coffee pot to prepare the eldest West a mug of coffee. I hear the rest of the entourage slowly follow in my wake, leaving Will and Lex in a quiet, peaceful state together as she slumbers into a state of oblivion and rest.

Alexandra West

I wake up as I hear the crescendo of traffic of the populous island and the city's life bustling down below. For the first time in a long while, I feel safe. I try to remember what happened before I fell asleep. Memories come barreling upon me like an unrelenting freight train. Oh yeah, it's coming back to me now in high-speed flashes, like picture stills. Townsend, Five Points, tiled floor, breakdown.

It's then that I suddenly realize that I am overheating, feeling trapped and suffocated. Panic immediately begins to set in. I frantically start throwing back the covers in an effort to quickly cool down.

"Whoa, whoa, whoa, Lex. Hold on" I hear my older brother's voice exclaim, taking me by complete surprise.

For some reason, my memory hasn't filled me in yet on how this new development came to be. Surprised, I look over at Will and am immediately confused as to how I got into bed, all tucked in. Not to mention that he's been here long enough that Will is sitting on top of my comforter with a fresh steaming mug of coffee in his hands.

Coffee. My sole focus of caffeine stirs me to awkwardly leap towards him as I quickly grab his mug and down its contents before he can say one word. It's still hot, with a hint of cream, just the way I like it. That's something else Will and I recently found out that we had in common. I place the now empty mug on the nightstand and turn to Will expectantly, trying to fill in the missing pieces in my brain. It's then that I notice how tired he looks, my eldest brother's always groomed hair is mused and his clothing is wrinkled. And if I'm not mistaken, it's still the same outfit that he was wearing last night.

"What happened?" I tentatively ask, not sure that I want to know the answer. But the need to satiate my curiosity overrides my pride.

Sighing, Will starts to explain, "We heard a crash in here this morning and came in to see the remnants of a shattered vase all over the floor. You were in the shower, crying. We sat with you until you fell asleep in the shower. I carried you here and Dave tucked you in. You've been asleep for a couple hours now."

I automatically nod, starting to remember the rest of the memories, my mind jolting with his prompting and the caffeine, every detail that he's outlining and then some.

My older brother pauses, then asks quietly, "Are you all right, Lex?" The care and concern are etched deeply in his expression.

My face softens as he conveys a rare look of compassion. I'm not sure if I am, but for his sake, I nod.

"Thank you," I manage to whisper out, suddenly touched by his loyalty to take care of me while he's being the somewhat overbearing and overprotective big brother. His actions remind me of the version of him I knew before we both grew into the adults that we are today.

Will gruffly clears his throat and continues, "You have six worried men downstairs, all concerned about you. You better go see them before they storm back up here. Besides, I was up all night scrubbing cameras. I'm gross. I need a shower and a shave."

I gently smile and nod in my understanding as I slide out of the bed and pad into my closet. The clothes I'm wearing are still a little damp, so I change into one of Dave's tee shirts and a pair of gym shorts.

"There are extra toiletries in the guest bathroom. Dave probably has some clothes in his room that you could borrow."

"Don't you worry about that. We had agents rush over a set of our go-bags. Are you sure you want to walk around barefoot? What if they didn't get all the glass?" Will cautiously asks from the doorway, right as I emerge from the closet. My older brother warily eyes the floor as I walk into the bathroom to freshen up.

"I trust them," I state simply, casually tossing my answer over my shoulder.

Pulling my hair up into a messy bun and splashing cold water on my face, I walk back into the bedroom, ready to leave.

Together, Will and I walk out of the master suite door and head toward the stairs. Will assumes the first position in what I used to believe was a passive aggressive, power struggle move. But now, knowing what I do, I realize that it's because he cares about me and wants to protect me. I'm used to Dave's stifling protection. I know that I will eventually become sick of Will's overprotectiveness too. But for this moment right here, I enjoy the unexpected display of brotherly love and I don't question or call attention to it.

As we progress closer to the landing of the stairs, I can see my brothers waiting at the bottom of the steps for me, all with tentative smiles on their faces. I allow myself to smile, to truly smile, the first grin that I allowed to cross my face in a while as I begin to descend toward my family. I look past my brothers and in the kitchen area, I see that Steve and Cole are also watching my progress, inconspicuously looking for signs of distress. Cole looks like he's been worried out of his mind. Steve looks like he's also slightly on edge too, but to his credit, I know that he's been a quiet support to Cole while I slumbered and healed.

I smile a shy smile at Cole and nod my head toward Steve. Cole brightly smiles in return and I can see his shoulders visibly relax. Steve nods back at me before shooting an amused, sidelong glance at Cole with a knowing look on his face. I realize right then that Steve has picked up on my relationship with Cole and in that small gesture, he's letting me know that he's happy for me. Pleased, I turn my attention back to my brothers, my remaining family members, as I'm welcomed into their warm and steadying embrace.

Cole Harris

Her smile is brilliant, truly magnificent, so much so that I didn't realize how much I needed to see that to restore the faith I have in myself. *This woman trusts me,* I think to myself. I watch the West brothers fold Lex into their arms, each sibling asking how she is feeling and subtly checking her for other signs of any physical damage. Thankfully, the bruising on her face shows various levels of healing. While she was sleeping, Sean had bandaged her arm and thankfully, those bandages survived while she slept. Lex is officially on the mend, but then again, we always knew that she would physically recover. Lex is a survivor. And the fact that she'll be okay is the only mantra replaying over and over in my mind, calming my racing heart when the anxiety and self-doubt inevitably creeps in.

I will never forget the fear and unease of seeing her so broken in that tiled shower stall, the image will forever haunt my soul. Lex walks up to Steve and kisses him on the cheek. They share a knowing grin before he pulls her into him and kisses her forehead, his eyes closing in silent relief over the fact that she's safe.

Before I know it, Lex is standing right in front of me, a small smile gracing her face. "Hi Cole," she shyly says, her voice abnormally unsure and tentative.

I know that she's testing to see if I'm okay with her actions from last night. But also more importantly to our relationship, her emotions from this morning.

I smile a huge grin and reply back, the tension in my voice fading away as I easily respond, "Hey Lex."

She hugs me and whispers a thank you in my ear. I squeeze her a little tighter before remembering her injuries and quickly let her go, instantly searching for a new bruise or blood seeping through her arm bandages.

Lex pulls back, openly laughing and shaking her head. "I won't break, Cole," she teases in a playful tone, "but I will fade away if I don't get another cup of coffee and some food in me."

"Yeah," Will remarks dryly, "Lex already downed my coffee upstairs, so I'm going to need a fresh refill too."

Luke and Kev laugh while Steve claps a hand on Will's back. Sean smirks and Dave chuckles as the room's mood lightens, the fear and worry lifting from all of our shoulders. We begin to make breakfast and get the coffee unceasingly brewing as a united team.

After breakfast, we all take turns as we quickly shower, change and freshen up. When each of us finishes, we all find ourselves downstairs on the sofas, waiting to hear about last night's tale from Lex herself. Lex graciously and patiently regales us, walking us through her thought process and the progression of last night's events. She answers each of our questions, explains her rationale and gives us a clear insight of what really happened in Cedar Local and Five Points, Queens. We have all arranged ourselves around Lex's spacious living room, postures relaxed, signaling a state of repose as her words sink in. Eventually the questions subside, a comfortable silence taking over, the story told and the storyteller finished in regaling us about her adventures. Lex has slipped into a silent spell, the gears in her head grappling with concepts, trying to figure something out.

"What is it, Lex?" Kev asks, closely watching her and calling her out.

She shakes her head, as if she's trying to put her finger on the answer but she still can't work out the problem's solution.

We all wait for her to speak, knowing that she won't until she's ready, until she has a decent certainty level in her head. A few minutes pass before she looks up at all of us, her mind ready, her resolve organized.

Finally, Lex says, "Townsend knew that I killed his brother. He hunted me down to get vengeance."

"Lex," Luke interjects in a kind voice, "I know it may feel that way, but this isn't your fault."

The concern is clearly displayed on Luke's face. I infer that he's nervous she'll have another bout of self-doubt and he's doing what he can to prevent that.

Lex looks at him with a forgiving smile on her face as she shakes her head. "No," she continues, "you guys don't understand. Mark Townsend knew for an absolute fact that I killed his brother, Dale Townsend. Mark said those exact words to me, confidently and fully assured. He wasn't making any inferences or looking for me to confirm or deny his assertion. He knew me by name. Well, he firmly knew that Alex West killed his brother. When I mentioned why he was killed, he didn't look the least bit fazed or surprised. Actually, that was exactly when he snapped and finally attacked me."

Will's jaw had become clenched during the last part, but he patiently asks his sister, "Why was his brother killed?"

"Dale Townsend was selling government secrets to some United States' enemies that he obtained from one of the ABC agencies. Off the top of my head, I don't remember which one. But if it matters, we can check the files and confirm the agency and details," Lex casually explains as she shares the contextual background.

"But that doesn't make sense," Sean asks with an elevated tone, "I mean, how would Townsend know those level of details if he wasn't directly involved in the contract?"

"Those are details that are never given, not even to us as the organization managing the contract price and terms negotiation. They aren't given to anyone except to the person who accepts the assignment to complete the contract," Kev adds.

"And he knew the reasons why and he still wasn't surprised," Steve finishes the thought with a musing tone.

Not fully grasping the situation, I ask, "What does that mean?"

Finally, Dave speaks, his tone laced with anger, "It means that Townsend was just a necessary end to a mean, a pawn in a larger chess game. Lex's life is still in danger. There's a bigger fish out there, specifically targeting and hunting her. It means, Cole, that West Enterprises has a leak, or a mole, or both, whose sole purpose is to destroy and kill Alex West."

***

After the initial shock wears off how dangerously precarious the situation we're all in truly is, we all start moving and getting to work. While Luke reviews all of the footage from the night at Cedar Local, Sean and Dave are calling some of their government contacts to see exactly what information and government secrets Dale Townsend stole and sold. Steve and Kev are doing physical safety checks at West Enterprises while Will checks the company's mainframe, looking for breaches or weaknesses that could be the source of a data breach. In the midst of all of this, Lex has pulled a recliner over to the window and is quietly sitting in silent thought, overlooking her cherished city.

As I come to stand behind her, she addresses me, always surprising me with her sense of hearing and anticipating my movements.

Lex softly speaks to my reflection in the glass, "It's beautifully unique, this city. I've been all around the world and have traveled to countless gorgeous cities. Cities full of life, history, the arts, culture and sports. Cities where their country's honor is strong, their antiquity storied. But to me, there's nothing in the entire world like New York City. The pride, the devotion, the loyalty. Those attributes are not easily replicated. I love this city, it is my home. It's the foundation of my entire being, of my heart."

I nod in an understanding agreement. I too share a love for this city, even though I'm not a native resident. The city draws you in and pulls at your heart, adding you to its enduring life source.

"Cole, this is bigger than we all think it is, I can feel it in my gut," Lex voices, referring to the matter of Townsend and not being comfortable with the unknown amount of players at the table.

I look at Lex, her face upturned, looking at my face, gauging my reactions and searching my expression for what, I don't know. But I trust her gut and her instincts. They haven't been proven wrong yet.

I nod and smile, saying more confidently than what I'm honestly feeling right now, "We'll figure it out."

She nods, mirroring my smile and my reassurance as she turns back to her city and we watch the teaming of life and activity from high above, completely removed.

David West

I'm watching my twin and Cole as they look out of her apartment's windows together. I can tell that Cole is crazy about my sister. I mean, who wouldn't be? Admittedly, she is pretty great. I know that I've always personally thought that. But Lexi seems to be slightly off. I can feel the tension pulsing off her in thick waves. Before I can go over and sort out what's going on with my sister, I see Will walking in my direction, halting my progress.

Will comes over and asks me in hushed tones, "Dave, can you call some of your military buddies who work for the alphabet agencies in Washington? I think we are on the trail to found out who is behind all of this and I need government access to confirm."

Of course, my twin's ears perk up at Will's excited tone, even though she didn't appear to be actively listening and Will was speaking in a quieter tone. I can tell by the way her back instantly straightens and the slight tilting of her head toward our conversation that Will has her rapt and undivided attention. I subtly incline my head toward Lexi and Will quickly looks over, realizing the mistake he just made. I know my eldest brother was trying to keep his information closer to the vest. Will likes to wait until he has firm details and facts before he presents his findings to the family, he always has. Will nudges me toward the door, trying to quickly get out of Lexi's earshot. We're too late, we both know that. But we make a last-ditch attempt to escape her interest and Vulcan hearing.

With a determined look, Lexi strides right over to us, puts her hands defiantly on her hips and directly asks, "Who?"

I see Will mentally calculate if he should withhold any information back from Lexi. But judging by my sister's fiery determination, my brother makes the wise decision to clue her in.

Will slightly hesitates and looks over my shoulder, to the rest of my brothers, to make sure they're listening in as well. Kev nods and Will turns back to Lexi and pauses before he responds, "El Diablo."

My twin's eyes widen with surprise as she mumbles out, "Well shit. At least this will be fun."

"Who is El Diablo?" Cole tentatively asks, basing his tone to a cautious level after seeing the distress on everyone else's faces.

Lexi faces him and explains, "So, El Diablo is translated to 'The Devil' in Spanish, right? And this guy truly is the devil incarnate, or at the bare minimum, the direct spawn of Satan. He's never been arrested to date, but he has done some pretty atrocious things on multiple continents. And what he doesn't directly do, he indirectly has his hands in the proverbial pot. Multiple countries have warrants out for his arrest. Interpol has been after him for years, same with the CIA and FBI, all for different crimes. Additionally, there are multiple open contracts on his head, some of them have been open for almost two decades. But no one can ever get close enough to complete the hit."

I pause, trying to rapidly absorb all of this information. I have always heard of El Diablo, but I thought he was more of a myth and legend. I should've known what a grave misconception that is, considering my own twin was thought of being a myth as well.

Lexi takes a breath before she continues as she addresses all of us, "El Diablo first started his career in Spain, sometime in the late eighties, killing over a hundred people. But that was just his three-year ramp up period. Then he set his sights on the rest of Europe and murdered his way across the continent, heading towards Russia. When he finally reached Eastern Europe, he racked up over a thousand deaths in a span of six months. He's started as a contract killer, growing his network into an empire that included everything from drug running and money laundering to human trafficking and the mysterious disappearances of people he declared were his enemies.

His personal network is now run like a dictatorship: all those who raise their voice against him are killed in conveniently accidental ways or they are arrested and sent to prison for life, never to be seen or heard from again. But none of these actions have ever directly traced back to him, let alone there's never seems to be any proof of evidence that seems to stick in order to hold him accountable of his crimes. I'm sure it also helps that he has blackmail information on many high-powered individuals and leaders on a global scale. El Diablo oversees a large group of contract killers, thugs and various informants who enjoy the hunt, people who enjoy torturing and the actual act of killing a target. Along with mixing in other activities El Diablo's has vested interests in. He's a very dangerous man. Few people know what he looks like. There are only a few pictures in circulation, which contain grainy subpar images of him from years ago, nothing clear, identifiable and concrete. Every law enforcement agency is after him, but he's a ghost."

Will jumps in and continues, "Arresting him is like catching smoke in a strong breeze. Some say that El Diablo doesn't exist. Others say he was killed a while ago and that his empire is being run by his surviving family members or a designated right-hand man. I still believe that he's alive and thriving, pulling the strings of destruction. In all fairness, he makes Lexi look like a saint."

Cole's eyes widen at the thought of something worse than Lexi, but he doesn't know at heart, she wasn't ever full of hatred and malice. Even at her worst, she was just following orders. El Diablo is and he's proud of it, he wields his vitriol like a weapon. We all take a moment to let the weight of our now-named adversary settle over us and allow the information Lex and Will just shared with us to sink in.

"Aly and I thought we saw him once. He wasn't our main target, he just happened to be there. But we're not entirely sure that it was him either," Steve chimes in, breaking the contemplative silence.

"Yeah," I interject, "I saw Lexi talking to this guy one time who compared her to El Diablo. She gave him fifteen stitches, a broken jaw and four cracked ribs. And he was one of our own West agents. Lexi may be badass, but she's not evil like El Diablo."

Lexi looks over at me with an amused look as she remembers the incident I brought up, "Oh yeah. I totally forgot about that night."

We share a chuckle together at the memory from a couple years ago. At least, she can smile about it now. That night and for the weeks following the incident, she would practically bristle whenever that encounter or El Diablo was brought up. I had to pull her off of the guy that she was so mad at, and I took some blows to my abdomen while she was still swinging, catching me by accident.

"Anyway," I continue on with my explanation, "El Diablo could be a myth, could be a group of ten guys acting as one, trying to make themselves appear larger than what the organization actually is, or it could be the largest network of underground, criminal activity in Europe, striving to reach its tentacles across the pond to the States."

"And now, they are solely targeting Lex," Cole flatly states.

"But how? Why now? Did you ever take a contract against him, Lex?" Steve asks, trying to figure out why Lex is on El Diablo's radar.

"No, that was one target that I always avoided. I never had great intel on him specifically anyways. And I'm not into suicide missions, I'm too competitive with my win percentages," Lex quickly responds.

"Then why you, Lex? Why attract your attention onto him by directly targeting you. And as a consequence, the scrutiny and probing of West Enterprises?" Sean's question hangs in the air.

We all think for a second before Luke suggests, "If I'm remembering correctly from reading the files, the Townsend family has money. My guess is that Mark probably paid El Diablo for information on his brother's death. El Diablo has his hooks in a lot of people's mouths, even in this country. If there was a contract and he saw how Dale Townsend died, El Diablo probably could put two and two together and he figured out that it was you, Sissy."

"El Diablo does know my work," Lexi says reluctantly as Luke sighs, not wanting to give confirmation but knowing that we all need to know what we're heading into. "It probably doesn't help that I've killed a couple of his guys for fun when I was on vacation," Lexi continues as she casually lets out that admittance.

"You what?" Kev incredulously exclaims, my normally composed older brother momentarily losing his highly regulated cool.

Lexi nonchalantly shrugs her shoulders as she looks at our four brothers. Steve doesn't even spend the energy to act or look surprised, maybe he was in on it too. Oh well, that's another conversation for a different time.

"And," Lexi says before she hesitates, the rest of our brothers leaning in expectantly. My twin looks at me and I give her a brief nod.

Stiffening her spine, she divulges, "And El Diablo tried to recruit me a while ago. We never met in person, but he sent a letter to one of my strategically difficult, but not impossible to find, addresses. He addressed it to Mr. Alex West, so he didn't know my true identity then. Obviously, I said no. But there aren't many people who say no to him and live to tell the tale about it. And that could have spurred a personal vendetta against me to the point where he did start to dig around into my identities and try to find out who I really am."

I knew that our family would be shocked. I'm not surprised with the jaws that immediately drop and the eyes that widened so much that I begin to worry that they'll pop out of my brothers' skulls.

Deciding I should continue on with keeping the conversation focused on protecting Lexi, I interject, "Exactly. For El Diablo, this is a win-win-win situation. He gains money from the Townsend family, he loses an enemy and the embarrassment of the great Alex West turning him down. And it's an easy job in his books."

Lexi nods and looks away, getting lost in whatever thoughts are running through her head. She has been struggling with something for a while and hasn't talked to any of us about it. It's time to bring whatever that is out of the darkness and into the light.

I walk over to her, gently putting my hand on her shoulder and turn Lexi toward me so that we're facing each other. Looking down in eyes that eerily mirror mine, I gently say, "Lexi, what's going on?"

My brothers' ears perk up as they listen intently to our conversation. I wonder if they even knew that something was off or if it was another case of Twin Power. And I know that Will's interest is definitely piqued considering the fact that my twin and I are vocalizing our conversation instead of easily using our twin telepathy. Cole and Steve also lean in, clearly interested in her response.

"How do I be Alexandra?" Lexi quietly asks, her eyes stormy as she meets my gaze, her eyes searching between my own for the answers she's so desperately seeking.

I'm instantly rendered speechless, the air sucked from my lungs. No one else in the room responds, seemingly stunned and frozen by her question.

Speaking louder, my younger twin continues, "How do I be Alexandra West against someone like El Diablo? He's looking for Alex West. But Alex West is dead. How can I survive all of this with just being Alexandra?" Lexi has commanded all the attention in the room, her questions hanging over us, unanswered and unresolved. My sister's gaze is trying to reach each of our brothers, but no one can fully meet her eyes head on.

Luke starts as he struggles to formulate an answer, "Sissy… it's okay. You know, you can do—"

"I can do what?" Lexi interrupts, the distress clear in her voice, desperation echoing around her.

We all collectively take a step back, stupefied by the emotions filling her voice. Normally, Lexi is in full control of her emotions, usually to the point where she never shows them. To see them on full display, as well as being able to sense her uncertainty and fear, is definitely a shock to me. I can tell that she's about to unravel, that she's about to come undone.

Taking a brave step closer to my sister, Cole gently holds her hand and looks into Lexi's eyes before he calmly asks her, "What's going on, Lex? What is really happening here?"

Sighing and sounding defeated, my sister explains, "It's like I told you earlier, Cole. I don't know how to be Alexandra when in all actuality, right now, we need me to be Alex. Alexandra isn't a cold-blooded killer, at least not the version of her that I want or need her to be. But with El Diablo threatening us, a cold-blooded killer is exactly what we need—it's what he's looking for. And it's the only way for all of us, any of us, to maybe have a shot at surviving this. I don't know how to stay alive if I go in as Alexandra. My process will be different. My techniques will be different. I wouldn't be going there to kill, but to what, just disarm him? I'll be shot dead before I even reach the doorway. All of you will be executed immediately right after me. Or if El Diablo really is still alive, I'll watch him torture all of you before he kills you while I'm forced to watch. He'll maximize my suffering. He'll do all of this, all because I choose to be something that I apparently am not any more at my core. Alexandra is a good human being, at least that's I want her to be, that's what I want for her. Alex is not, she operates more in the gray space. How do I be good when facing the dark evil that is El Diablo?"

No one says anything, even with her looking around at each of us, pinning us with an intense stare. We are all standing in front of her, but none of us have the answers she so desperately needs.

Lexi shakes her head and mutters, "I'm going to go take a shower."

We all watch her as she dejectedly climbs the stairs with her shoulders slumped, as if she is the only one capable of supporting the entire weight of the world on her small frame. Innately, I sense her fear: that if she were to crumble, so the world would fall with her.

Cole Harris

I watch Lex walk away, my heart breaking for her. Her brothers look at each other, seemingly lost and reeling from Lex's confession. We all knew that there was a major crux of the issue, something that was holding her back. But none of us, let alone her own brothers, could anticipate this, nor can we fix this for her.

"You knew about this all along," Luke turns to me, not asking, but confidently stating the fact.

All of her brothers look at me as Steve raises his own eyebrows but thankfully says nothing.

"Yes," I cautiously begin, knowing that they would see through any lie I attempted to throw at them anyway. So I opt to go for the truth.

"She spoke to me about it a couple days ago. She volunteered the information all on her own. She told me that she was conflicted and that she was trying to sort everything out in her own way. But I got the sense that she would have preferred to announce her struggle once she had a solution, but this El Diablo forced her hand," I finish, waiting for a barrage of questions and accusations to begin flying at me.

"Why the hell didn't she tell one of her brothers?" Will angrily interjects, the outburst masking his sense of betrayal.

"Least of all to her twin," Dave mutters in a tone I realize is anger trying to mask the deep-seated hurt simmering just below the surface.

"Why didn't you tell us about this sooner?" Kev asks, trying to school his tone into a non-accusatory and partially diplomatic manner, but failing as his older brother instincts have kicked in.

"It wasn't my place to tell her concerns," I simply state.

I wanted to protect her, yes. I also wanted her to know she could trust me, that I wouldn't divulge her secrets, that they would always be hers to tell.

Sean nods, accepting my respect for her privacy while Luke is studying and scrutinizing my expression as he mentally analyzes my explanation and actions. Sighing, I turn toward the windows, looking for the peace Lex so often finds while she overlooks her city. I know that trying to convince the West brothers on any topic about their sister is a hopeless cause. She's the only one who can change their minds, so I feel lost, with my back up against the proverbial wall.

Sean, Luke and Steve walk up next to me to stand by my side. I feel a brief sense of comfort knowing that I have some support in this impossible situation. Soon, the rest of Lex's brothers join us by the windows, melancholy settling in around us.

"We don't blame you," Kev says after a while, "I'm sorry if you felt that we were. I'm glad she's that opening up to someone. We all know that she's an extremely private person, by nature and profession. We just want her to know that we're here for her too."

"She knows that," I quietly respond, looking to provide some comfort as we all look at the people bustling and teaming below us.

"Do you think I'm pressuring her to be something she's not?" Dave asks to no one in particular. No one immediately voices an answer, the same thought weighing heavily on each of our minds. "I want her to be Alexandra so much. For her sanity, for the business, for all of us. But what if it's too late for that? What if the Alexandra, we knew growing up, is no longer alive? Dad's death, her career, all those factors have changed her into the woman that she's become. Why aren't we accepting that? Why aren't we okay with that? Are we forcing her to be something she isn't, someone she doesn't want to be, just so we can be happy, even though it's at the expense of her mental health? If she were to inhabit Alexandra, it could mean her life would be stolen away from her because of how her mindset would completely have to shift. So, are we just pushing her to be Alexandra so we can feel more comfortable?" Dave finishes, out of breath, rushing his words out with fervent emotions.

We all take in his words and consider them, taking the moment to self-reflect on the pressures we didn't intend to force upon Lex.

"Maybe," Sean honestly voices, "I mean, we all want her to soften her approach and to be more comfortable with opening up to us. Maybe she thinks that in order to be the more personable sister we want her to be, she has to completely give up her old life and redefine herself from scratch."

"I honestly never minded the fact that she was an assassin for the company," Will begins, "I just gave her a hard time about it. I know. Why? I don't have any good reasons for my behavior anymore. Maybe I thought she could do better, or I didn't like the fact that she was willing to go against the company's biggest source of revenue. I've been too hard on her for too long."

Dave gives Will a sidelong glance as small smiles creep on the two brothers' faces. "We all were hard on her because she was different from us. From what she used to be before Dad. And who are we to tell her what she should be, how she should act? There's a fine line between being overprotective brothers and being entitled control freaks," Kev begrudgingly admits.

More silence ensues as guilt lowers its cloud over the West brothers.

"We need to make this right. We need to go and apologize to her," Luke states with finality, calling us out of our ruminating stupors and moving us all toward action.

All the brothers seem to be on the same page as they turn toward the stairs as one, ascending the stairs to Lex's bedroom in silence. Steve and I stay and wait downstairs for the brothers to receive the redemption that only Lex can provide.

William West

All of us five West brothers approach our sister's master suite door and knock, listening for Lex's quiet approval for us to enter. She's sitting by the windows, staring over the darkened city, her hair damp from a recent shower. She has a hoodie draped over her shoulders with a pair of sweats and a tee shirt on. Her eyes are red from crying and my brotherly instinct drives me over to her, hoping to protect her from the demons that she's been battling alone in silence, all this time. I've always thought that my sister was the strongest one in the family. It's in this moment that I realize part of her strength means that she suffers and bleeds all alone, in solitude.

I immediately engulf my little sister in a hug and she surprisingly leans into me, grabbing onto the front of my shirt with both of her hands. I hear her voice coming out in the midst of her waves of sobs while her emotions physically rack her small frame. She hasn't openly reached out for any emotional support from any of us since Dad died. Between right now and finding her in the shower earlier, I feel at best unsettled. I'm sure there's a shocked expression that has taken its place on my face.

Dave sits on the other side of her while Sean, Kev and Luke surround us from the front, filling in the cracks and forming a half circle. She cries for minutes, which seems to turn into hours. She eventually becomes quiet, her breathing evening out and her small frame ceasing its shaking.

"She fell asleep," Luke whispers.

I nod in understanding. I could tell the exact moment that she nodded off as her grip on my shirt loosened, her body slumping onto my shoulder as her muscles relaxed and loosened.

Kev gently picks her up while I support her head as my younger brother moves to lower her on the bed. "She's lost weight," he says, his tone sounding surprised, incredulity seeping into his voice.

314

"What?" Dave asks as Luke quickly strides over and gently takes her sleeping form from Kev's embrace.

"Damn," Luke says looking over to us as Kev turns down the bed. Luke gently places her in the bed while Sean tucks her in.

"She lost all that weight and none of us even noticed? Even if she was trying to hide it from us, we should have noticed... I should have noticed," Sean mutters more to himself than to the rest of us as he pulls the sheet and comforter up to cover her shoulders.

"What did we do to her?" Dave voices out loud, asking no one in particular.

We each have the same thoughts running through our heads, all fueled by guilt, regret and remorse. Is this our fault? Are we slowly killing our sister's spirit, or worse, her?

We all walk out of her room in silence, each feeling horrible for inadvertently hurting her. Dad's voice rings in my head, reminding me that it's my job to take care of all of my siblings. To take care of Lex. It's what my father wanted me to do before he died. I failed both my father and my little sister.

We join Steve and Cole downstairs in heavy silence. They both look at us all with questions in their eyes. Sean miserably shakes his head, signaling that now is not the best time to ask what's going on. The youngest West is right, they can ask but I don't think we even know the first place to begin to try to give the answers they're looking for or the answers that we need. Time to focus on what we can control: the job.

"Okay," I say exhaustedly, looking around the kitchen island at my family's faces, and at Cole and Steve, the two people Lex loves outside of our family. They're all looking to me, waiting for my direction, explanation and guidance.

Assuming the reluctant leadership role, I say in a resolute tone, "Let's start planning this operative. Our main objective is to protect Lex."

Alexandra West

I wake up, my brain hazy, groggy and feeling emotionally exhausted. How did I get here? Oh yeah. Shit, I cried in front of my brothers. Again. Twice in a short span of time. I need to make sure this doesn't become a habit. My brothers must be freaked out. I can't say that I blame them. I'm perplexed at my own recent and uncharacteristically extreme display of emotions.

I take immense pride in my ability to put on an emotional front, a mask, where nothing or no feelings could ever hope to penetrate through and break my stoic façade. It has been one of the strongest facets of my armor, well, it used to be an advantage of Alex West's armor. Now, I feel like I'm nothing more than a scared little girl, looking at her brothers to have all the answers for my multitude of questions.

Is this what being Alexandra feels like? Do I want this type of fear to constantly rule my life and my choices? Questions fill my mind as I contemplate the future, how to balance being Alexandra and differentiate between me as Alexandra and me as Alex. I know that my family needs me to be Alexandra on the emotional spectrum, but they need the skills and talents of Alex, for this case and maybe for the family business as a whole. Self-doubt is a dangerous and slippery slope for anyone, let alone a West Enterprises agent. What is the middle ground between Alex West and Alexandra? Is there even a breaking point between the two? And if I figure out the balanced point, can I live with that choice? If I don't, what firestorm of vengeance and hatred will reign down on my family? What battle do I need to choose? Will I be Alexandra West or Alex West?

I know the decision that I need to make, the strategic choice that's best, but I can only imagine what my brothers are going to say. How they'll protest my decision. Ultimately, I'm most afraid of them being disappointed in me. They saw what I could be as Alexandra West and they know what I was when I embraced my Alex West persona. I need to convince my brothers that this is our best play, our only legitimate play.

Mentally preparing myself for putting back on my proverbial Alex West armor, I pull my hair in a ponytail before I slowly and quietly make my way back downstairs. I hear Will's voice first as he is planning out the operative with the guys against El Diablo. From the discussion that I have stepped into, it sounds like they have made great progress. But they're missing their biggest weapon, their greatest asset.

"Count Alex West in," I say with authority, my voice clearly ringing out across the room, interrupting their planning and catching them slightly off-guard.

My family, immediate and extended, all turn towards me. Not only surprised with my silent approach, but also to hear my confidence. No doubt they immediately begin questioning my logic and abilities.

"Lexi," Dave starts, trying to gauge my mood as he steps to me.

"No," I interrupt, already knowing what my twin is going to say, "I need to do this. El Diablo wants to meet Alex West, so we're going to give him Alex West. But this time, I'll have my family backing me up. A tether and tie to keep a piece of Alexandra with me." Silence follows my declaration and rationale.

"Are you sure?" Sean asks without judgment, only curiosity.

I nod. I know that I have to do this, to resurrect Alex West. And I think that my brothers all know that too. But with my family there, they'll be able to make sure that I don't go too far off the deep end where I wouldn't be able to come back from my Alex West persona. Will, Dave, Sean, Luke and Kev will all make sure that I'll be able to look at myself in the mirror when this is all over and maybe I'll find Alexandra West, someday again in the future.

"Just keep me honest, okay?" I ask, hinting to them that they are my safety net.

My brothers, Cole and Steve all slowly nod as I walk up to the kitchen bar where they're all gathered around, standing over a pile of blueprints, surveillance photos and plans. I come to stand in between Will and Cole.

I surprise Cole by taking his hand and I look up at him, meeting his eyes. "Thank you. For letting me tell them in my way, on my terms," I genuinely say.

Cole nods as my brothers' eyebrows collectively raise. I rest my head on Cole's shoulder and look at my brothers and Steve with an amused smile on my face. It's good to know that I can still shock them when I want to.

I turn my attention back to Will and say, "Okay, brief me on the plan."

Cole Harris

Will runs through the plan with Lex interjecting at some points, making slight adjustments and improvements during the briefing. Overall, she seems satisfied with the planned operation as we discuss the various options over a light lunch. Lex had called to have lunch catered once she realized the magnitude of our plan and the time that we needed to commit to reviewing all of the details. While waiting for our lunch to be delivered, Will had found El Diablo's encrypted message to the infamous Alex West online by sifting through thousands of message boards and posts on the dark web.

El Diablo is asking for an in-person meeting at the old defunct City Hall subway station, located here in the city. We study all of the relevant traffic cameras and various angles over our sandwiches, plotting our entrances, exit points and where various teams will be stationed to protect and provide additional support for Lex's face-to-face underground meeting. The Wests and Steve call their respective contacts and pull in their favors, directing everyone available within a fifty-mile radius to head toward West Enterprises to be briefed before we all converge upon the island. Dave, Steve, Will and Luke decide to go scout the location in advance and meet up with us later while the rest of us head to West Enterprises to stock up on supplies before we gather our support teams and move out.

Lex, Kev, Sean and I pull up to West Enterprises which is still under some minor construction since the security breach and subsequent attack a while ago. Lex enters her codes as we pull into the driveway and park in the garage. Kev and Sean are busy talking to their various contacts on their phones as we step into the filtered light of the breezeway that connects the garage and house. I look over to see Lex as she stares at the building's exterior, suddenly becoming quiet, before she starts to move forward again into the house.

As we all enter the family home and company headquarters, Kev immediately begins preparing for the influx of agents. Sean, noticing Lex's quiet behavior and out of character actions, focuses his attention solely on her and motions for Kev to stop moving for a few moments. Lex doesn't seem to notice Sean's gaze, Kev's sudden stillness or my facial expression of concern.

Almost as if she's automatically being drawn to something in a trance-like state, where the subconscious prevails over the conscious state of mind, she moves upstairs and down the hallway, almost as if she's floating on air, stopping in front of the bathroom. She stoically looks down to the missing flooring and the faint outline of her blood pool stain on the underlying wood, the actual blood cleaned up and hauled away with the carpet a long time ago. I hear a slight intake of breath and am surprised when I realize that it came from me, as I'm the only one who closely followed her down the hallway. Kev and Sean are both standing at the entrance of the hallway on the second floor's landing foyer, quietly watching our exchange.

Lex suddenly looks up directly at me as if she's snapped out of whatever trance she was in by saying, "I don't regret it, Cole. I'd do it again in a heartbeat if I had to. Because it means that you'd still be here with me. I wouldn't give that up for the world."

I am always amazed at this woman: her bravery, resilience, strength and loyalty. I nod and smile, not needing to fill the space with any words. Instead, I open my arms for her as she steps into my embrace.

She holds onto me and adamantly whispers in my ear, "You have changed my life, Cole Harris. Don't you ever forget that."

Pulling away, she smiles up at me, with the smile that I like to think she saves just for me.

"We have a lot of work to do," she says, transitioning her thoughts back to the mission.

And with that, Lex immediately gets back to business, turning on her heel and heading back downstairs to the kitchen as she hears the sound of people entering the house, prompting me to quickly follow after her.

By the time I get downstairs, Kev is escorting fifteen agents inside and they come to a stop in the kitchen. Lex had grabbed a glass of water and now turns her attention to the newcomers, shrewdly assessing them one by one, as she finishes the glass of water.

"Good to see you A-West," one agent says as he walks further into the house, bringing up the rear of the group.

"Quick recovery, nice," another guy who I recognize from the West Enterprises' attack comments with admiration.

"Nice to see you upright, ma'am," the leader of the unit says, evaluating Lex's commanding stance with an appreciative nod.

To her credit, Lex graciously bows her head in acknowledgement before she turns to Kev, efficiently asking, "Briefed?"

At Kev's confirmation, Lex goes to pull out her phone to make a call. After a couple moments of silence, she ends the call with a deep frown creasing her eyebrows.

Sean notices her expression and is quick to ask, "What's up?"

"Dave isn't answering his cell. I'm trying Will now. Kev, call Luke. Sean, call Steve," Lex barks out her commands, the atmosphere of the room becoming tenuous and arctic.

After a minute, she looks at her brothers, me and then to the men assembled in front of her. In her eyes, I can see the brief flicker of fear and anxiety, but I also see the simmering stages of fury and rage beginning to brew. Lex knows something is off. She called it from the beginning when we first started discussing Townsend, El Diablo and our strategic plan. She was right, of course. And now her wrath and anger threaten to consume El Diablo and anyone else who stands in her way of getting her brothers and Steve back.

Lex immediately takes command of the room, her body becoming straighter and her tone sterner, as if she's embodying a renowned and historically powerful four-star general. With everyone's rapt attention and full control of the room, Lex addresses the assembled men, "Gentlemen, we have been compromised. My family will never be the ones paying for the mistakes that I've made in my life. Call everyone and anyone you know who will help. I will personally make sure the compensation is worth their investment, risk and time. I want my family back, alive, in one piece, today. Anything short of that is non-negotiable. And I will do anything or go through anyone in order to get them back. Understood?"

Lex is staring the recruited agents dead in their eyes, making sure that they understand that if they become obstacle, they will be instantaneously eliminated. Lex is making it personal because this matter is personal to her, this is about her family and the family's company, West Enterprises. A series of "yes ma'am's" resound around the room as each West agent pulls out their phones to reach out to their contacts and various networks.

Suddenly Lex's phone rings, breaking through the din. She looks at the incoming number, her face hardening as everyone immediately freezes around her, instantly silenced, waiting for her next move.

"West," she curtly answers, after placing a finger to her lips as she puts the call on speakerphone.

"The iniquitous Alex West. I was wondering when you'd finally answer my call. It has been a while, hasn't it, my dear. It's a shame, really, that you sent your brothers to take your place. Only a coward sends others to die for them. But alas, here we are," a disembodied voice dispassionately sighs over the line. "Of course, we're a very accommodating organization, so we made sure our arrangements were flexible enough to include four additional burials sites instead of just the one I reserved for you," the voice continues on.

During this time, Lex had motioned to Kev to track and trace the geographical origin of the call as the voice continues to goad her, "Do you want to see your brothers alive?"

"Obviously. Stop wasting my time. When and where," Lex commands, her patience beginning to unravel.

"City Hall station, two hours, just like the message said," the voice taunts, "I have one request, before you hang up on me. A request that I think you'll be highly interested in. One where I'm willing to sweeten the pot, as a one-time exception for you."

I immediately get an uneasy sensation, having a familiar feeling about what's coming from the Bryant Park debacle, but still wishing it to just be a figment of my imagination. The rest of the men around me seem to get the same feeling too, some shifting from foot to foot while others visibly look rattled, everyone uncomfortable with the growing silence.

The disembodied voice finally announces, "You are still a source of embarrassment for me, when you turned down my offer to join my empire. This one-time offer is just between you and me. Are you ready for it? Your life, Ms. West, for all of theirs."

"Done," Lex interjects without hesitation or batting an eye, cutting him off with a finality that brokers no contest as my greatest fear comes to fruition. Her brothers look like they're about one second short of crying out in indignation, the gathered agents look unsure and uncomfortable of what the next steps are.

"I'll be there in one hour. I know your guys didn't start digging yet, so why don't you dig one more grave. If I'm going down, I'm taking you with me," she says, venom dripping from her voice.

"Oh no, Alex West. You're the one who is going to die today, I only bought a one-way ticket for that train. But I'm a man of my word. If you come and give me your life, I'll spare theirs. Your life for theirs. Only one will have to die today," El Diablo's voice jeers.

Lex aggressively ends the call and in a bout of anger, she throws the phone across the room so hard that it slams into the wall with enough force to shatter the device. I think I see her shoulders slump slightly, the exhaustion and weariness of the constant conflict between Alexandra and Alex wearing her down. But just as quickly as I think I see her vulnerability, she straightens her posture, fixes her face with a menacing look and resolves herself to a new plan. An Alex West plan.

Turning to fully face the group, finally looking at all of us head on, Lex announces, "There's been a slight change in plans."

PART III

William West

"I hope she doesn't come for us," Luke mutters under his breath as he futilely pulls against his restraints.

The acoustics at the old City Hall terminal are phenomenal, so we could hear everything our captor said to Lex. We could even hear bits of her responses through the phone. I chuckled when she told El Diablo to dig another grave for himself, quietly thinking to myself that that's our Lex.

Similarly, none of us are under the assumption that he can't hear anything we say. Knowing that, I keep my voice low and my vocal tone deep. "She will," I quietly say with resignation.

I know my sister. She'll come for us. She keeps her word. And she protects her family.

Steve asks gruntingly as he tries to break the binds that are wrapped around his wrists "Is she ready? Is she ready for all this?"

"I don't know, but did you hear her voice? Did you hear the words she was using? Alex West is back. And she's beyond pissed," Dave states with finality.

I realize that today will mark the first time that we all will witness my sister in action, as the infamous Alex West. Only this operation has taken a turn, where her has been family taken away from her. I can only imagine her rage. The enemy has finally figured out that we're her kryptonite and is doing his best to leverage that against her.

"She's coming," I say with certainty. "She's coming because we put her in this situation. No one else knew that she had a family. No one else knew any personal details about Alex West until we pushed her to be

Alexandra," I reason, regret filling my voice. We forced her hand and now she's going to be the one paying the price.

Continuing on, I say, "Lex would execute contracts, be debriefed here and then spend the rest of her time at her apartment before Cole came into her life. She kept her personal and professional lives completely separate for this specific reason. No one put it together that we were her family until now. She kept her life a secret, to protect all of us. And then we asked her not to be Alex West. We're the ones who asked her to be open, to show her face and to be vulnerable. We forced her hand and the Alex West we knew was forced to fold her cards. We did this to her, and to us. She knows it too, but she'd never say that we're to blame. Still, she will come for us."

Luke, Dave and Steve all look at me, shocked at my easy acceptance of blame and our involvement in the situation. I finally feel connected with my sister, after all this time. Where I implicitly understand her motivations, what drives her and moves her forward, for the first time in our adult lives.

I try to shrug my shoulders, diverting attention from my soliloquy and say, "We all know how she is and that's she's coming for us. So we have to be prepared for when she does arrive and how she'll approach this situation."

Luke nods in agreement, saying, "We need to make her plan easier. Dave, what do you think her moves will be?"

Dave takes a minute to contemplate his twin's anticipated actions before he answers, "As Alex in this current situation? I don't know. I haven't truly seen her as Alex before, none of us have. And no one has ever seen her when her family is being threatened, as Alex West or Alexandra West. But regardless, it'll be fast, bloody and intense. We need to be ready to move, to provide whatever assistance we can in advance of her incoming assault."

Great, I think. We're all bound with heavy duty rope on our wrists, even though I'm grateful that our hands are bound in front of us. But what complicates things is that we each have one foot locked in a chain that's bolted into the concrete wall. But if there's a chance that we can help Lex, I know that we need to do all that we can do to at least try.

"How can we help her?" I ask.

With a cunning smile on his face, Dave lifts up his foot to show us his stash of thin razor blades hidden in the treads of his boots. "With these," his eyes gleaming with glee and just a tinge of malevolence as he gets to work, handing out razor blades to each of us so that we can use them to cut our way through the ropes on our wrists.

Once our wrists are free, we then use the corner of the blades to slowly but quietly pick the locks to our ankle cuffs. Alex West is coming, it's only a matter of time. It's our job to do everything we can to make it easier for her to get us out of this situation.

Cole Harris

A sort of organized chaos has erupted at West Enterprises since El Diablo's taunting call. Lex's mind is working a mile a minute and the rest of us are all scrambling to try to keep up with her vigorous pace. Our plan has changed at the drop of a dime and Lex is handling it all with the intelligence and the awareness of a highly trained and lethal operative. The rest of us are notably impressed at Lex's ability to adapt and change so quickly and effortlessly. Her sole focus is getting her family back, especially her twin.

There are short moments where you can see the pain in her eyes behind the simmering rage, determination and her strategic mindset. That anger is a sight to behold, but only when you are auspicious enough to catch it. She is back in complete control of her emotions at all times, but that rage below the surface is sure to come out the minute she makes physical contact with El Diablo. In this moment, I am thankful that I am her ally instead of her opponent. I can only imagine what the end to my life would have looked like if she hadn't changed her mind about saving me. It would've been absolutely terrifying.

Since El Diablo's call, Lex has changed her clothing and is now wearing all black. Black fitted pants and a slightly loose onyx shirt paired with dark obsidian combat boots. Her long hair is pulled back into a thick braid, away from her face, completing her guise: tactical and aggressively intimidating. Her weapons of choice line her thighs and ankles, on clear display, the muted metal of her firearms and the menacing glint of her silver knives a testament to how fatal she truly is. Alex West, the true and authentic Alex West, is wholly frightening.

Lex's demeanor has changed too, her body language is different: aggressive, hardened and confident. Gone is the woman who was just hours ago holding my gaze with soft eyes. Lex's eyes now are glacial, shrewd and untrusting. Her body language is that of a warrior, preparing for an offensive attack and impending physical impact. Her anger is felt by all of us in surges, her temper being shortened by the circumstances. I can tell that she's doing her best to reign her fury in, to not let her wrath impair those around her. The majority of us leave her be, either afraid of her short temper or understanding that she wants to save it for the man who stole her family away from her. We all have no doubt that she'll get her family back. It's just a matter of time and how bloody it'll end up being.

The rest of the brothers and I have changed into black attire as well while the other recruited West agents came in already wearing black or dark camouflage. We've been monitoring the situation from the various cameras Will, Dave, Luke and Steve were able to position prior to their capture as well as other cameras we were able to hack into. Lex watched her brothers and Steve's ambush footage only once, swearing under her breath the entire time. When it was over, she walked over to a wall and punched it so hard, she broke through the drywall but thankfully missed a stud and a broken hand.

"I'll just add that to the list of repairs," she muttered under her breath before she stalked out of the room, but not before commanding us to watch it again to look for any of our enemy's weaknesses and opportunities that we can take advantage of.

We have been able to precisely locate where the guys are being held and where El Diablo has strategically but defensively arranged his men to stand guard. This El Diablo guy knows that she's coming, but what he doesn't know is the level of fury that he has unleashed on all the somewhat innocent men he has employed for this particular job. We're all aware that she will stop at absolutely nothing to get Steve, Dave, Luke and Will back. And to top it all off, she's now gunning for her adversary's blood as personal revenge.

As we're finalizing our plan, more agents trickle through West Enterprises' doors. Kev and Sean are there to immediately greet them and quickly bring them up to speed. A few of the new arrivals have openly gawked at seeing Lex. In those moments, I'm subtly reminded that her reputation precedes her and that it's a dangerous reputation that she's cultivated over the years at that. Once everyone has assembled in the common areas on the first floor, Kev asks me to help him bring up additional weapons and ammunition from the safe room's armory so we can stock up and prepare for all of those who are presently on our side.

Silence has fallen over everyone as we all know what our next step is: it's go time. In these last few moments before we all deploy, the woman I have fallen in love with finally resurfaces for the briefest of moments. Lex takes command of the room, voicing her gratitude to the West agents standing before her, knowing what she's asking of them, all in order to save her family. Lex is a natural born leader, where people look to her for direction and who are loyal to the point of death. I'm reminded that her leadership style is eerily similar to her eldest brother's when he takes charge of situations.

All of the West personnel assembled around Lex nod as she gives her instructions, understanding the lengths that she will go to get her brothers and Steve back. Lex reminds everyone of the operation's logistics, that their mission is to first rescue and extract the four captive agents. She and an elite team will be doing the killing on behalf of West Enterprises. I can tell that some of those assembled here are relieved to hear that they are here to only save, not eliminate, their postures subtly relaxing when she announces that specific aspect of the mission. There are other agents, those whom I recognize from previous interactions, who look crestfallen at the prospect of only performing in an extraction scope, without their involvement on the elimination piece.

After Lex's thanks and debriefs everyone, all of the agents start to file out of the room, heading toward the SUVs and vehicles parked in the garage and on the driveway. Sean, Lex and Kev hang back, all of us looking at each other, bracing for what's ahead.

"If there are any signs of movement that isn't friendly, immediately neutralize it," Kev instructs.

I nod, understanding that this is a big step for me, being accepted as an equal operative agent to save the members of the illustrious West family.

"Remember, we don't know what we're walking into or how our own men are doing," Lex objectively begins, trying to set expectations from the beginning for us to anticipate the worst-case scenarios. "We need to be prepared for anything and everything. Turn off your emotions as best as you can. It will help you get the job done. We can worry about tears, emotional trauma and medical attention later," she advises while meeting each of our gazes.

The West brothers and I all nod in understanding and read between the lines of what she is choosing not to explicitly say. That Will, Luke, Dave and Steve could all be dead or worse, inanimate puppets in El Diablo's grand master scheme to psychologically torture Lex. I can only imagine if that's what Lex finds, how her fury will engulf, consume and wash over everything and everyone around her. If that happens, I'm not sure if we could ever get Alexandra back. Grimly discerning the gravitas of the situation, Sean and Kev each kiss Lex's forehead in a silent goodbye and walk toward the garage as they rearrange their weapons on their persons.

Lex and I walk through the breezeway and to the garage in silence. "You're going to see things that you're not going to like," she starts, breaking the silence, "I'm going to do a lot of damage, you'll see a lot of the old version of me. I'm not going to hold back. I can't. Once I get my hands on them, each and every one of El Diablo's men will be dead. They have my brothers, Cole, and one of my closest friends. These men, they have my family. I'm coming back home with them, one way or another. I just need you to promise me that you'll be here when it's over. That you'll help me pick up the pieces if I break during the process," she finishes, looking for me to grant her the permission that she needs for her to get her family back in her own way, whether that's as Alexandra West or Alex West.

I nod and fold Lex into my embrace, taken aback at her asking me for permission to be an agent, to be a sister. I keep those thoughts to myself as I reassure her, "Go do what you need to do, love. I'm not going to judge you. You got this Lex. Take El Diablo down. Finish this once and for all. And bring them all home."

Lex nods, a small smile crossing on her face as she presses a light kiss to my cheek in what I refuse to be a goodbye. In a flash, she slips right back into agent mode and hops into her designated awaiting SUV as I find my seat in a different vehicle and buckle in.

***

After arriving near the defunct City Hall subway station's above ground entrance, we inconspicuously drive to the nearest pre-determined parking location to access the decommissioned underground train tunnels. Lex and her brothers specifically chose this time of day, using the onset of dusk and its longer shadows to our advantage.

The various tactical teams silently creep to their strategically predetermined checkpoints where they will be stationed to provide support to Lex and her brothers, the leaders of the front offensive teams. Based upon our plans, I know that Lex has accessed the tunnel systems through the Brooklyn Bridge City Hall Station alone, just as El Diablo requested on his dark web message. She plans to walk right into the thick of things, catching El Diablo off guard. She's hoping that this will give her the slightest chance at having the upper hand.

My team and I are stationed in the abandoned tunnel system just beyond where the brothers and Steve are being held. Along with the other teams, we're all waiting for Lex to signal when she's in position, using the curve of the tunnels to our defensive advantage.

Never subtle or particularly quiet, we hear Lex loudly shout out, "El Diablo, I'm here, you pathetic bastard. Give me back my family. Now."

Her voice echoes in the empty tunnels, off the unforgiving concrete and stone, bouncing and resounding toward our locations. It takes a moment for me to orient myself to gauge distances and approximate locations based upon her voice's sound waves.

"You'll get them," we hear the same disembodied voice from the phone echo and ricochet off the walls in response, but from how the sound is reverberating, we can tell that he isn't directly in Lex's immediate vicinity. At least, not yet.

Of course, this jerk is using the acoustics to his advantage, just like us. He's purposefully making it extremely difficult for us to pinpoint his exact location from where we are waiting for him, nestled in the shadows.

"Right," Lex sarcastically spits out, "too bad that I already know your plan, Moreno. Oh, that's right. I know who you are, Sergio Moreno. Props to you, though, on trying to keep your identity a secret all of this time. You're almost as good as me. Almost."

On Lex's signal using El Diablo's legal name, the tactical teams start to slowly move in, still hugging the shadows of the old tunnels for cover as they converge on the central point. As we're moving forward, we meticulously watch the placement of our feet and make sure our weapons don't make accidental contact with any of the old pipes or debris coating the walls. We all are overly careful that our advancement isn't heard through the acoustic tunnels, moving stealthily but quickly to our various secondary positions.

When we encounter any hostile enemy, as a team, we swarm and silence them efficiently. From our angles, we are still in the shadows but now we are close enough where we can clearly see Lex. My attention is also drawn to Luke, Steve, Will and Dave, who each have chains on their ankles that are attached to a wall. The four men are about twenty feet away from Lex on her left. Dim light filters into the open space from the grime caked on windows that haven't been cleaned for some time. Not once has she looked over to the four men chained to the wall, nor have they openly acknowledged her presence. They are too busy looking at the red dots that have miraculously appeared on their chests, pining them in place and effectively neutralizing them for the moment.

"Snipers," Sean whispers in my ear, "they're directly above us. We can't move any closer to get our family without alerting them of our position and tactical strategy. We'll need to neutralize them."

I notice that Lex has a few red dots pointed on her torso too. Worried, I look at Kev, the tactical commander in lieu of Will being incapacitated and Lex acting as the designated distraction. Kev and Sean share the same grim expression, acknowledging the additional complication before they turn in sync with each other and look at me.

"We're moving upstairs. You stay here, get closer if you can and provide coverage when all hell breaks loose, got it?" Kev says in a whispered rush as Sean already begins to climb the stairs.

I nod as I watch the two brothers seep back into the shadows as they signal for a team to follow them as they climb up the metal stairs then head toward the access ladders, which will lead them to the catwalks that line the ceiling. Lex knows where all of our teams are positioned and what their intentions will be. Since she knows what our side's next play will be, she begins to loudly speak, knowing she needs to provide additional noise coverage to serve as a distraction from any sounds that may be made by us.

"You know what the ironic thing is, Sergio," Lex sardonically starts, her voice bounding and reverberating off the tiled walls, down the curve of the old tunnels, "I don't have feelings, so I don't care about them. I don't care about family or loyalty. It's never been about that for me. I've just wanted a chance to get to you. It's been a long time, Sergio. What's it been, twelve, thirteen years? I knew that you'd personally be here, so I sent them to scout the location. It wasn't a trap for them. It was a trap for you. And by the look on their faces, they have all seemed to figure out that they're causalities in a fight that's bigger than them, too."

For the first time, Lex tosses a look over to her brothers and Steve. She smirks at the red dots, not seeming to care about the implied threat, nor the other men El Diablo has lurking no doubt in the shadows. To their credit, Dave, Steve, Luke and Will each act hurt and betrayed, even to the point where I wonder if they're faking their reactions or if they're actually feeling those emotions and they're worried that what Lex is saying to taunt Moreno is true.

With a sneer, Lex continues, "If I did my math right, and when it comes to money, you know I always do, I calculated the combined contracts on your head, all twenty-seven of them. I believe the aggregated total amounts

336

to what, two hundred and seven million dollars? I could do some major damage with that on Fifth Avenue."

Once Lex mentions the outstanding contracts, El Diablo, or Sergio Moreno, looking visibly annoyed, finally comes out of the shadows and steps into the faint, evening light. Now we get a chance to finally get a good look at the man who has wreaked havoc on our lives over the past few days.

Sergio Moreno is a little over six feet tall with thick grey and black hair and shifting jet black eyes. Tall, dark and handsome. Even I can feel his magnetism and dangerous charisma from where I stand in the shadows. Sergio has a lean build with tattoos all up and down his arms and tendrils of ink creep up past his shirt's neckline, lining his neck at odd angles. His scars intermingle amongst the black ink, with what looks like an old knife scar cutting horizontally across his right cheek. Sergio Moreno's expression is contorted with pure anger. Lex struck a chord with this guy, just by taunting and challenging him. Good, she's knocking him off-kilter and off his game.

When I subtly look around for Kev and Sean, out of the corner of my eye, I see just the slightest flash of movement and outline of the youngest West where the rest of the Wests and Steve are being stationarily held. It's a completely open floor plan, but there are a lot of shadows our side can take advantage of, it would seem like the Wests have done just that. Sergio aggressively steps toward Lex, facing her head on, his shadow drawn out behind him.

"Alex West, you have always lived up to the hype. But I will admit, I was expecting a large male, not some little girl who looks like she just graduated from high school," Sergio states with derision.

With disdain lacing his voice, Sergio continues to provoke Lex, "I remember that time you just brought up, twelve and a half years ago as you so aptly guessed. Columbia. You were there for a top government official. I thought about taking that contract, but ultimately decided to turn it down. Not enough money. And not a big enough challenge for me. Apparently, you struggled with that contract. It ended up being a little messy, no? Some mistakes, no?"

337

"You know what else is funny?" Lex casually asks, ignoring the taunts and not taking Sergio's attempt at the bait.

Without waiting for an answer, she sarcastically continues on, "Your assumption about my gender is the very belief everyone has when I meet them face-to-face. What's even more amusing is that every person I've encountered with your same assumption is dead. Not to blatantly yell foreshadowing in your face, but the odds are not in your favor, mi amigo. I don't like statistical anomalies, and I definitely am not interested in messing up my perfect win rate with the likes of you."

After speaking, Lex shrugs her slim shoulders and stands directly in front of the red dot targeting her twin. Dave seems to instinctively know what she's planning to do, probably due to their Twin Power. While Lex was moving around in her subtle circling pattern as she was speaking, she has drawn out an additional eight men from the blackened corners, all of these men willing to protect Sergio with their lives. But with her movements, Lex is forcing them to also step into the room's pale light, exposing their locations from the safe cloak of darkness.

I try to see through the shadows to ascertain if there are any additional threats still lurking out of our range of visibility. Sensing my agitation, one of the agents behind me quietly informs me that our other teams have already taken care of those threats. I need to trust that the West agents know what they're doing and that they'll provide the coverage Lex needs. I just need to focus on doing what the Wests have asked of me. They all have been doing this job for a lot longer than I have. I just need to keep that in mind and in perspective.

Turning my focus and attention back to the scene unfolding in front of me, I watch Lex's movements and look up towards where our additional team in the rafters should be positioned. In a calm and calculated measure, Lex takes a half step toward Sergio, instantly causing all the red dots of the sniper rifles to frantically turn to her, knowing that she's the immediate and imminent threat.

Once all the attention is directed onto her, I realize that with her movement, that she's giving Will, Steve, Luke and Dave a chance to get into position, as well as the rest of us to prepare. She knows the four captives would have already freed themselves as they waited for her, doing all that they could to prepare for her, their brothers and the rest of the West agents' arrival. I also know that Dave, Will, Steve and Luke wouldn't want to not be a part of this fight. I'm sure they are harboring bitterness that Moreno got the jump on them earlier today.

In the next couple of moments, everything seems to accelerate at warp speed. In what I can only describe as a flash, Lex is directly right in front of Sergio Moreno, closing the gap that was just a couple of feet that previously stretched between them, seemingly like a chasm. Lex didn't show any signs of rushing her opponent, not even a flinch, which is one of the reasons why it was so unexpected. From where I'm positioned, I can see Sergio's face, as well as the eight men around him, all in various states of shock. No one was expecting Lex's swift advancement either, as they all try to figure out, on they fly, how she moved so fast and evaded the multitude of fatal sniper red dots.

Lex had drawn a knife while she moved forward. With disgusted venom in her eyes, Lex sinks the blade into Sergio's liver, maintaining eye contact, with cold eyes and undivided focus. The knife is driven in so deep, I'm sure the hilt has made its impression on Sergio Moreno's skin. A small, malevolent smile curls the edges of her lips as Lex sees Sergio's eye widen and flash with pain. She quickly spins him around, manipulating and controlling him by the knife buried in his side, forcing to be her human shield. In response, eight weapons turn toward Sergio and Lex. She confidently looks at her eight adversaries who are all yelling at her and threatening her life and the lives of her family in a mix of Spanish and English. She's not even the slightest bit fazed, her shoulders are relaxed.

Sergio gasps out with a hideous smile plastered on his face, "You're trapped, Alex West. What exactly are you going to do now?"

She emits a humorless laugh, the haunting sound echoing down the tunnels and up to the ceilings, "I'm not worried because I have something stronger than you. A weapon that can't be bought with any amount of money or threats. I have my family."

As Lex finishes speaking, she twists the knife deeper in Sergio's side, eliciting a scream of agony from El Diablo. She pushes his compliant body aside and rushes right into the line of fire, eyeing one of the largest men in her advancing attack. As she makes impact, the man's gun goes off, bullets spraying into the ceiling. The seven remaining armed men quickly spin around to turn their focus and the muzzles of their weapons onto Lex.

Before another shot can be fired, the three West brothers and Steve crash into the back of the seven men, taking them by surprise and throwing them off their footing. Seven automatic rifles go off in tandem as all of the men crash forward. By Sergio and Lex's body language, one or both of them were accidentally hit in the process of disarming the eight men.

And then suddenly, my ears go deaf. The West Enterprises agents around me begin firing their own weapons, neutralizing the other men who have started coming out of the shadows to provide additional backup to Moreno and his now disarmed eight men. I notice Dave, Luke, Will and Steve are moving a little slower than usual. Lex already had noticed this too as she kicks in Sergio's head and focuses her attention on Dave's assailant. Without saying or signally anything, she tackles Dave's man, forcing her adversary to the ground as Dave stomps the guy's head in with his combat boots, neutralizing him in a mere matter of seconds. Then the twins each go to Will and Luke to provide additional back up and assistance. Kev and Sean cover their family members along with their teams in the catwalks by continuing to take out men from above, picking them off quickly, one by one, rapid fire. The tide begins to quickly sway; the battle is being won by West Enterprises. Sergio Moreno's men have stopped coming out of the shadows. There are only a handful of men who are left standing, and the Wests and Steve are quickly and efficiently neutralizing them.

It's truly incredible to watch all of the Wests work together. I had always thought of Sean as being the pacifist of the Wests. But when his family is being threatened, the youngest West turns into a vicious weapon, not all unlike his sister. Kev is showing off his elite martial arts fighting skills while Steve and Luke use their larger sizes to their advantage by beating down their adversaries with brute force and strength. Will is

340

standing over his opponent, out of breath, the eldest West being more of a street fighter.

I look over to the twins and of course, I am impressed. Dave is in front of the twins' opponent, attacking the guy's abdomen while Lex has jumped up on the guy's back, punching him in the neck and head while her legs are gripping the enemy's shoulders and pining their assailant's arms awkwardly to his side. The twins are ruthless but efficient. When their man's knees buckle, Dave extends a hand to Lex who effortlessly takes it as she flips over their opponent, landing next to Dave's side. This whole exchange took only a few minutes, but it seemed like time stood still as I continued to watch the action unfold.

Once every opponent is down, either by force or by their own surrendering volition, the West family and Steve are all looking at each other with various emotions crossing over their faces. My team and I have come into the subdued light and gather with the rest of our West Enterprises agents on the former subway platform level. The catwalk teams have moved the surviving sniper prisoners down to our level and they are currently triaging what to do with the bodies upstairs. One agent mentions disposal teams coming in to do clean up once the area is fully cleared. I never thought about it before, but it makes sense that West Enterprises has a dedicated team for that.

Looking over at the West family and Steve, I take stock of everyone's injuries. Will has a bruise rapidly forming under his left eye, the deep purples and blues already discoloring his skin. Kev's hands and knuckles are a bloody, open and raw mess. Will rips off strips of his shirt and helps Kev bandage his hands like Kev's a boxer and Will's his coach. Sean has a head wound with blood trickling down the side of his face, but he waves off medical assistance from one of the men on my team. Luke is on the ground with a split lip while he holds his side, muttering something about broken or fractured ribs. Steve, bent over Luke, has a gash above his right eye and his left arm is limply hanging at his side. Dave has a cut on his cheek and bruising on his jaw. Lex is bleeding from a cut above her left eye while showing the beginning stages of bruising on her neck.

341

When I look closer, I can see the bruise is in the shape of a handprint. Concerned, I begin to ask her who did that to her, to avenge her injury. "I'm fine," she reassures, knowing and interrupting my question and nodding with a patient but tired smile.

Dave adds in an eerily cheery mood, "Yeah, we've all looked a lot worse, man. We'll be good in a week or two."

As Lex gives her twin a rueful look, I see a flash of movement just out of the corner of my eye. Lex sees it too and immediately goes on the defensive. Her entire frame leans forward, anticipating another wave of attacks. As if time stands still again, I see one of the men who was previously neutralized and who has just regained consciousness lift up a gun near his hand and aim it at Will, the closest West family member. The oldest West is unsuspecting, not realizing that he is still being threatened and is in imminent danger.

Lex immediately dashes over in front of Will and pushes him out of the way just as I hear the shot go off. She cries out in pain as the bullet hits her left side. If she wasn't there, it would have instantly killed Will. The bullet was aimed upward, directly targeting his heart.

As she crashes into the ground, her brothers all immediately turn their weapons on the man who shot their sister and who attempted to execute the head of West Enterprises in cold blood. In a display of grotesque choreography and gruesome vengeance, the adversary looks like he's dancing as Will, Dave, Kev, Sean and Luke fire multiple rounds from guns obtained from our support agents into the rogue enemy. The target is unquestionably down, the din of gunfire subsiding into an eerie and unsettling silence.

After the smoke has cleared, I see that Will is helping Lex stand while Dave and Luke are standing by her side. Kev has checked the body while Sean checks to make sure everyone else is dead by methodically and emotionlessly putting a bullet in their heads. Sean will no longer be a pacifist in my eyes. He's cunning, just like his siblings, not the anomaly I originally had thought that he was. He's just more inconspicuous about it than his siblings.

"Lex," Will says frantically, gasping out his words, "are you okay? What were you thinking? Were you trying to get yourself killed?"

"No," Lex rasps out as she holds her side with one hand and smacks Will with her other with what I can assume is sibling love, "I was trying to keep you from getting killed, you idiot."

Kev affectionately looks at his sister as he says, "That's where you're mistaken, little sister. It's our job to protect you."

"Chauvinistic old men," she wheezes out in a teasing voice while rolling her eyes good-naturedly.

I can hear the pain in her voice, but she is still standing and holding her head up with pride. My heart bursts with joy and admiration for the woman I love.

With a cold voice that I have never heard used before, Sean throws a question to the group, "What do you want to do about him?"

We look to where Sean is staring at and see Sergio Moreno, aka El Diablo, grinning on the ground, holding his arm. His injuries are blatantly on display where his skin is exposed, blood and dirt mixing that if he had the time, he'd have to worry about infection. But even so close to death, Moreno can't seem to stop taunting the West family.

"I've got this," Lex says as she pushes away from her brothers' hold.

She limps to stand over Sergio and she starts to humorlessly laugh, the maniacal sound filling everyone's ears. After a few seconds, her frenzied howling is unsettling. So much so that even my teeth are on edge as I notice her brothers clenching their jaws.

"You didn't win, Moreno. You taunted me, you took what I value most in this world. But I got them back. And I'm still standing. Now, I'm going to take what you value, the only thing that you care about in this whole world besides money," she says in the coldest voice I've ever heard, my body reacting with an uncontrollable shiver.

Now I understand why people said Alex West was evil. How other West agents whispered how she could be heartless, cold and unrelenting. Lex's

343

voice alone is sending chills all over my body and my chest is filled with dread and anxiety. Even with me being on her side, I know that she's also exercising a modicum of restraint.

Lex lifts her head to look at all of her brothers for confirmation before she directs her gaze back to her prey. "Hmm... how much is your life worth to you, then?" she asks with an evil smile on her face.

Moreno's eyes widen as he begins to understand that Lex is going to kill him, right here and now. There won't be any legal proceedings, he won't be detained or taken into West Enterprises' custody. Upon this realization, he tries to back away from her, but she predatorily advances in, strategically boxing him against a wall. Her brothers follow in her footsteps to form an impenetrable wall behind her, securing Moreno in a death half circle.

With nowhere else to go, Moreno anxiously looks around, desperately looking for an escape. "I have money. I have information. I know how your father died," Moreno desperately offers up, trying to bargain for his life, "I know that we could be quite a pair, you and me, Alex West. An invincible, powerhouse pair, harbingers of death, my dear. With my money and your skill, together, we'd be unstoppable."

For a brief second, I see the surprise register on Lex's face at Moreno's joint venture proposal. She definitely wasn't expecting that proposition again. But she's already made up her mind and is absolute in her resolution.

"You see," Lex continues, brushing off and ignoring the appeal to her emotions by using information about her father and his offer of a partnership, "you can come after me every day of the week and I really don't, or won't, care. You'd have to take a number and stand in line to join the ranks of people who want me dead. However, your fatal mistake was to take my family. That offense, *mi amor,* is unforgiveable. And you of all people know that money doesn't matter to someone like me. My father is already dead. And I would never associate with you, not for an entire lifetime of profits. So, you're out of plays, mi amigo, I'm not interested in the cards you're trying to play. I will ask you again, how much do you value your life?"

Lex's voice is dripping with sarcasm and venom, her hatred palpable, her anger crackling like a live wire, her electricity resounding in the air. I hazard a swift glance around at the other West agents and she has everyone's rapt attention, even the prisoners sitting in handcuffs and chains. All of us are completely chilled and unsettled to our core, watching Alex West live and in person.

Moreno, finally understanding the severity and futility of his situation, begins to frantically nod and beg for his life just as Lex rips out the knife in his side. Moreno's screams echo throughout the tiled building, enhanced by the resounding damn acoustics. El Diablo's hands immediately go to his side, trying to cover the wound as blood seeps and pours through his fingers. I look to Lex's brothers, then to Steve who is just behind the Wests. They're watching her with intent and curtailed expressions. I can feel their anger toward Sergio Moreno coming off them in currents as well.

Sean catches me looking at them and simply says, "It has to be done. He knows too much about her, about the family."

I nod, swallow and turn my head toward the pathetic excuse of a man Lex has turned Sergio Moreno into. I think about the games he played with us, the frustrations we had over changing our operation's course and all of the worry and fear he caused about the safety of Lex's family that we've experienced over the past twenty-four hours. I know deep down in my gut that Sean is right. If the Wests let him live, Moreno would be a lifelong threat, probably selling West family information and secrets on the black market to the highest bidder.

I turn my attention fully back at Lex with a hardened expression as I hear Moreno rasp out a final, "Go to hell!"

With a chuckle and a smile, she takes her nine and points it at the dead center of his head, straight at his kill zone. "Save me a seat," she taunts her final insult to her prey before she pulls the trigger, a loud echoing bang, then a deathly silence fills the air.

Sergio Moreno's body collapses into a heap as Lex turns back to face us. In this moment, I see her face and the mask she wore when she was a former assassin. Her residual anger and determination from the shocking scene before her are still reflected on her face. Her eyes are glowering, her stance is ready for another attack and her fists are loosely clenched, still holding the knife dripping with blood in one hand and her nine-millimeter handgun in the other. Deadly, formidable and badass: Alex West.

Slowly, I see the assassin mask recede and start to fade as Lex steadily blinks her eyes to gather herself. Her face softens and her body posture begins to relax as she looks over and assesses her brothers, Steve and me.

When her eyes meet mine and she's staring right at me, Lex directs her question right at me, "You good?"

I nod, frozen, unable to go to her and unable to speak, still slightly reeling from seeing the true Alex West up close and personal. She tilts her head ever so slightly, noting my reluctance. There's a slight flash of sadness that passes in her eyes, but she wisely gives me the space that I seem to be emitting that I need. Even though I would never want to hurt the woman that I'm in love with, I can't seem to get my feet to move toward her, fear locking my legs into place.

My eyes re-focus on the blood freely running down Lex's clothes from the gunshot wound to her side, the dark red creating camouflaged and glossy trails on the black fabric of her shirt. She doesn't seem to feel it, the adrenaline is probably still disguising the pain for now. But she's losing blood in a short amount of time. I notice small pools of blood in the areas in the spots where she was previously standing. I'm immediately concerned with the current blood loss and its impact to her West Enterprises attack recovery.

Noticing the same biological puddles, Dave limps over to his twin as he grabs her hand, worry evident in his voice, "Lexi, you okay?"

Lex looks at Dave, her eyes suddenly becoming unfocused. Lex looks like she's starting to sway, just ever so slightly.

"Shit, she's gonna to crash," Luke yells and he runs over to his sister. Will is by her side in a matter of seconds. Will and Dave sling her arms around their shoulders before she falls to the ground and they help support Lex as we all begin to swiftly leave the area.

"We'll go get the cars," Sean offers as Kev, Steve and the West agents rush off quickly to get back above ground. Luke and I move in to assist Will and Dave, helping them to lift her over rubble or debris and climb the various sets of stairs.

Luke keeps repeating the same mantra with anxiety and clear panic lacing his tone, "C'mon, Sissy, stay with us."

"She's fading. Come on, Lex, you've been through worse. Stay with us," Will says, the trepidation apparent in his voice.

"She won't make it to a hospital at this pace. With her previous injuries complicating and compounding on what she got tonight, we need to hurry!" Dave exclaims with urgency dominating his tone.

Taking action, I shrug off my Kevlar vest and pull off my tee shirt. I toss the shirt to Luke as I go around to her right side and pick her up, making sure that her wound is toward them. Her hands automatically circle around my neck, Lex holding on to me for balance, for strength, for life. Luke, understanding my intent, takes my shirt and presses it firmly into Lex's side. She groans softly as Dave and Will position themselves next to me, taking on some of her weight as much as possible, given that all of the West brothers are injured in some sort of way.

We swiftly walk in silence toward the stairs and the awaiting SUVs, all four of us supporting her, carrying her as one unit. When we get close to the vehicles, Kev jumps out and opens the door to the backseat. I notice his SUV only has Sean in it. The other men must be packed into the remaining two SUVs or are inconspicuously waiting for the next wave of vehicles to take them back to West Enterprises for mission debriefs. I remember that there are bodies that need to be taken care of, logistics that need to be coordinated. None of that matters right now to me, though. All that matters is this, getting Lex and her brothers quick medical assistance.

We gently load Lex into the back where Sean has his hands out to help gently pull and position her inside. After Lex is secured in the car with an artistic arrangement of seatbelts, Will jumps in the passenger seat, Kev takes the wheel and Luke, Dave and I hurriedly pile in the third row, carefully climbing over Lex and the injured Sean.

"Steve will meet us back at West Enterprises. He will be the one responsible for debriefing the men there, finalizing our plan's details and then he'll wait for our call," Kev informs us before putting the vehicle into gear.

We all sit with our own thoughts as we speed towards New York Presbyterian Lower Manhattan Hospital.

PART IV

Cole Harris

We have been at the hospital for about two hours now. Will has been sitting with me in the waiting room. The doctors took the rest of the Wests back for medical treatment. Kev needed to have his hands wrapped up, since his knuckles were split open. Dave had to have a few butterfly stitches sewn into his cheek and Luke needed his torso taped up since he had a couple of ribs fractured. Sean and Lex were thankfully the only two who needed serious medical attention.

When we first entered the emergency room, the nurses recognized the West family immediately. Will later explained that since West Enterprises frequently fulfills government contracts, they are used to seeing the West family members in various states of distress or injury. No questions are ever asked, especially when bullet holes are blatantly obvious during preliminary exams. For that discretion and protection of their privacy, the West family are loyal to this hospital. Apparently, the Wests are anonymous donors too, which seems to expedite each West's intake and admittance process.

Each of the brothers and I have had customary MRIs and EKGs, checking for internal damage and bleeding. I protested, saying that it was unnecessary for me to get checked out as I wasn't ever in harm's way. But Kev was in no mood to argue, so I was quick to relent. I didn't want to add onto the family's stress with everything else that was going on. Sean was immediately taken to the back for head trauma and a concussion while Lex was taken in to look at the bullet wound in her side. We later learned that the bullet wound was a deep graze. Will breathed a big sigh of relief when the doctors came out to give us that particular update.

Kev, Dave and Luke trickle into the waiting area with various bandages, wraps and their hospital discharge papers in hand. Sean eventually is brought out in a wheelchair with a large bandage and gauze wrapped around his head.

"Nine stitches," the youngest West indignantly grumbles out, "that bastard caused me to have nine stitches. In my head! They shaved some of my hair off too, I look like I just got home from World War II. Man, if Lex hadn't killed him, I would have hunted him down and eviscerated him myself."

"At least it wasn't a bullet and you don't have a concussion," Will minces out.

The eldest West has been on edge ever since we arrived, presumably overwhelmed with guilt and responsibility. Kev puts a freshly bandaged hand on Will's shoulder, trying to diffuse the situation.

"She knew what she was doing," I quietly voice in her defense.

"Yeah, yeah. But we need to talk to her about always getting shot. This nonsense needs to end, for my sake at the very least. I mean, she's always the one dodging the bullets and in the hospital while we all sit and wait for updates. If she'll be okay. What short or long-term damage there will be, if any, that she sustained. I'm not sure how much more of this I'll be able to take," Will begrudgingly admits.

All of the West brothers nod their heads in tired agreement as an anxious silence and sense of anticipation falls over us.

After another elongated thirty minutes, a doctor comes out into the private waiting area that we were escorted into upon our arrival. "Elyse West?" she asks the room, searching for family members.

I turn my head with a start, remembering that Lex goes by Elyse instead of Alexandra or Alex in public, that is, outside of her family and West Enterprises. I join the rest of the West family as they crowd around the doctor, waiting for her to provide an update.

To her credit, the doctor holds her own while five brothers expect positive results for their sister, subconsciously using their size to intimidate the doctor, so she gives them the good news that they're looking for.

"I'm expecting Ms. West to make a full recovery," she begins as all five of the brothers' shoulders collectively relax, sighs escaping their lips.

"However, we have run into a somewhat minor issue..." the doctor continues with a tinge of nervousness in her tone.

"What issue?" Kev uncharacteristically but hurriedly interrupts, his posture becoming tense and apprehensive again.

"What do you mean?" Luke counters, speaking over Kev while he pulls his shoulders back, standing at his full height.

Taking a small step forward, I hear the shortly fired questions from Will as he spits out, "How is she? What's going on?"

"When can we see her?" Dave succinctly finishes all of the West brothers' thoughts, as well as mine.

"Gentlemen," the doctor tries to lower the tension in the room and take back control of the situation and conversation, "she is fine. She's in recovery, awake and doing well. But... she's already dressed and ready to go. She's demanding that she be allowed to leave immediately and is insisting on her discharge papers being expedited for her immediate release."

Smiling, I instantly know that Lex is going to be fine. "Is there any reason why she can't be discharged?" Will politely asks, the restraint clear in his voice as he awaits the doctor's response.

The doctor tentatively answers, slightly taken aback by the question, "Well, no. But I would strongly advise that we keep her overnight to observe her, to make sure there's no head trauma."

Luke shakes his head as Dave firmly and dismissively says, "We can do that back at West Enterprises headquarters."

"Yes, please release her. Immediately. Trust us, you do not want her here overnight if she is already strongly resisting your suggestions to stay," Sean diplomatically finishes.

The doctor, without a word, looks at all five brothers, whose eyes are deadly serious. "Okay," she slowly says as she shakes her head before she turns to go back into the restricted staff area.

Within fifteen minutes, Lex is wheeling herself out to the waiting room in her designated hospital wheelchair. "Damn, I thought they were never going to let me go," she jokes and she gingerly gets to her feet.

Lex has about five butterfly stitches above her left eye and her side has a noticeable bulkier size, the clear sign of bandages, gauze and padding.

"Can we go home now or are you all going to gawk at me some more? We need to go now before they demand that I be wheeled out to the door, as if I can't walk on my own and am in dire need of a wheelchair," Lex pleads. Not one of us says a word or moves.

Lex impatiently starts to walk towards the main waiting room, the rest of us slowly following her, unsure of if she's actually been released.

"C'mon! I'm not dead yet," Lex adamantly says while the people in the waiting room look on with a mix of shock and amusement.

Will is the first to pick up his pace and he reaches for her. Lex leans into her older brother, not so gently nudging the offensive wheelchair out of her way.

I can barely hear Will as he whispers "thank you" in Lex's ear, the emotion just below the surface.

She turns and kisses him lightly on his cheek before teasingly saying, "Of course. That's what sisters are for, right?"

Her brothers take turns hugging her and then she's staring at me while she leans on Dave. "Hey, Cole," she says casually. I can tell that she's still unsure of how I'll react to her based upon how I didn't go to her while we were underneath the city's streets.

I take the couple of remaining strides toward her and tenderly pull Lex into my arms, wrapping my arms around her good side, kissing her forehead. I try to apologize to her in my embrace, silently telling her that I'm ashamed for not coming to her in the subway station. Lex seems to understand all that I can't find the words to say. She wraps her arms around my waist as I support her body before we all head out into the night, going home together.

***

After parking in the West Enterprises' garage, we all trudge into the kitchen, worn from battle, exhausted and beyond drained. The house welcomes us with a comfortable and familiar silence. Steve had texted Luke about an hour ago saying that he went to the hospital for his own medical evaluation after debriefing all of the agents. He let us know that he'd catch up with everyone later this week once things settle. Steve also asked how everyone was doing and sent well wishes for the West family's speedy recovery.

Dave immediately heads to the fridge and grabs a case of beer.

Sean goes over to the wine rack and casually informs us, "I'm going to open this bottle of red and let it breathe. We can have it when we all come back up, something to look forward to when we return."

With a smile, Sean pulls the corkscrew from the kitchen drawer, expertly pops the cork and sets the wine bottle on the counter. Luke and Sean quickly grab the beach blankets while Kev grabs some snacks from the pantry and shoves them in a beach bag.

Will and I immediately lead Lex down to the beach, the stairs proving to be slightly precarious given Will and Lex's injuries. Once we're at our informally designated group spot, we help Lex settle in and sit on the blankets Luke has draped across the sand. *Just like old times,* I think to myself with a feeling of peace and normalcy settling over my conscience. We can always tell that Lex is happy when we're together on the beach at night, her family surrounding her under the canopy of galaxies and blinking stars.

We drink and talk about random, light topics as we munch away on our snacks, consciously aware of how we all have missed a couple of meals today. The West family shares stories of when they were younger and how Lex and Dave would always be up to something, usually getting into trouble. The West siblings regaled the group with the creative methods the twins employed when they were trying to get themselves out of said trouble. The conversations are all casual, with no mentions of work or the ordeal we all just went through together. Just a family enjoying the beach in the evening.

After about another hour, delirium finally begins to set in and we're all laughing until we're gasping for air, clutching our sides, our faces are red with joy.

"Don't make me laugh, my ribs are killing me!" Luke exclaims, as he tries to contain his laughter.

"I can't laugh any more. Will, stop telling stories," Lex jovially interjects as she tries to rein in her giggling.

Will chuckles at his siblings' plight, considering he just shared a story of when Kev and Will were on a job and Kev accidently slipped into a pool during a reconnaissance mission.

We continue to laugh, joke, tease and share stories as the night slowly fades into morning, the early tendrils of dawn beginning to claw their way across the summer sky. The West family is in repose, all of them reclining on the blanket, a reassuring sight to see. Lex is resting her head in my lap as the rest of the brothers have started to doze off a little, the previous few days' excitement and energy beginning to take its unrelenting toll on all of us.

We all get to a point where we collectively decide that it's best to go back up to the house, noting the adrenaline is quickly wearing off and some of the pain medications are also starting to slow down. We all decide that the best thing for all of us to heal and reclaim our bearings is to get some proper sleep and rest in our designated bedrooms. Kev and Sean shake out and fold the beach blankets while I help Will clean up the trash we made.

Luke and Lex are gingerly packing up the leftover food and drinks we hadn't touched while Dave closely supervises as he repacks the beach bag.

"Oh shoot, I forgot we have a bottle of red. I'll re-cork it and we can have it tomorrow with a nice steak dinner," Will says, already planning tomorrow's dinner. Well, I guess it's technically today, but I'm not worrying about semantics with this little sleep.

Our group has just climbed upstairs to the deck off the main living area of the house, still laughing and joking, all of us still in a state of exhaustion. The conversation easily continues as we start to trek through the house's French doors. Lex opens the one door and instantly shushes us, immediately cautious with an aggressively defensive stance.

"Guys. There's a wine glass on the counter that wasn't there when we left," Lex whispers to the six of us.

Immediately, the West brothers are wide-awake and have their hidden weapons drawn as they stand around Lex and me, creating a human barrier. I hold onto Lex's shoulders, trying to also shield her as we all slowly enter the room as one unit. I can see the outline and silhouette of someone sitting in one of the living room chairs, their back to us as they face the black screen of the television.

Luke addresses the intruder roughly, telling them to immediately stand up and put their hands on their head. The figure doesn't stand, nor do they not turn around. The brothers are all shouting at the figure in various languages, weapons pointed and at the ready, commanding the intruder to surrender, until Lex yells out, "Wait!" Lex's voice rings over the commotion, cutting through the harsh commands of her brothers, compelling everyone into silence.

Lex deftly slips through the male Wests and their hastily formed defensive line and approaches the figure cautiously, with a butcher knife she inconspicuously grabbed from the kitchen in her hand, the blade expertly tilted down and away from her body.

"Lex," Kev hisses, and in that word, there's no mistaking the protective big brother warning obviously evident in his tone.

"There's something familiar about…" Lex mutters to herself as she tilts her head, trying to figure out the conundrum in front of her.

The seated figure slowly stands with their arms up in the air and turns around to face our group. The West family goes from an aggressive unit to a cluster of shocked faces and shaking hands. The dead quiet a complete antithesis to the racket of the yelling and authoritative orders that resounded just moments ago.

The figure finally comes out of the shadows, into the early morning light of dawn, as they take a step towards us. Now that I can fully see the trespasser, I identify them as an older male. I study his face, but I don't recognize this man from all of the files that I've reviewed. As I look at the West family, I see that they immediately recognized him the exact moment that he stood up, when he just was an enshrouded figure in darkness, when he was still just a faceless silhouette.

The world seems to stop spinning when I hear Lex's gasp, shattering the hush as she tentatively asks the silent figure, "Dad?"

About the Author

An avid bibliophile and book club lover, *West, Alex* is Olivia's debut novel. A first-generation Asian immigrant, she has always loved the greatest city in the world—New York City. Olivia lives in the United States, and her natural curiosity leads her on adventures and traveling around the world. Her favorite type of day involves curling up with her pets and, of course, a good book.

Acknowledgments

To the Pegasus team, who guided and advised me. Specifically, Elaine—for your responsiveness. Lesley—for your continued diligence. Lauren—for your creativity.

ED—Thank you for your tactical support and insight. B. Tyler—for composing a musical piece that inspired an entire universe.

PS-G—Thank you for being my cheerleader from the beginning. To my book club ladies, thank you for being unabashedly supportive of this adventure.

JO, JR, CB, and P (and M)—Your unconditional love and patience. EW—for our lifelong friendship, editorial support and championing compassion. JR—I'm forever grateful for your undying belief, endless patience and relentless support.

Finally, thank you for the lasting impact of all the heroes and villains in this book and in my story.